Do
TRO

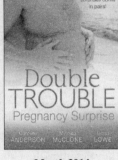

February 2014

March 2014

Double TROUBLE
Pregnancy Surprise

Caroline
ANDERSON

Melissa
McCLONE

Fiona
LOWE

MILLS & BOON

Published in Great Britain 2014
by Mills & Boon, an imprint of Harlequin (UK) Limited,
Eton House, 18-24 Paradise Road, Richmond, Surrey, TW9 1SR

DOUBLE TROUBLE: PREGNANCY SURPRISE
© 2014 Harlequin Books S.A.

Two Little Miracles © 2008 Caroline Anderson
Expecting Royal Twins! © 2011 Melissa Martinez McClone
Miracle: Twin Babies © 2009 Fiona Lowe

ISBN: 978 0 263 24586 8

011-0314

Harlequin (UK) Limited's policy is to use papers that are natural, renewable and recyclable products and made from wood grown in sustainable forests The logging and manufacturing processes conform to the legalenvironmental regulations of the country of origin.

Printed and bound in Spain
by Blackprint CPI, Barcelona

Two Little
MIRACLES

CAROLINE ANDERSON

Caroline Anderson has the mind of a butterfly. She's been a nurse, a secretary, a teacher, run her own soft furnishing business and now she's settled on writing. She says, 'I was looking for that elusive something. I finally realised it was variety and now I have it in abundance. Every book brings new horizons and new friends and in between books I have learned to be a juggler. My teacher husband John and I have two beautiful and talented daughters, Sarah and Hannah, umpteen pets and several acres of Suffolk that nature tries to reclaim every time we turn our backs!' Caroline also writes for the Mills & Boon® Medical Romance™ series.

PROLOGUE

'I'M NOT going with you.'

Her voice was unexpectedly loud in the quiet bedroom, and Max straightened up and stared at her.

'What? What do you mean, you're not coming with me? You've been working on this for weeks—what the hell can you possibly have found that needs doing before you can leave? And how long are you talking about? To-morrow? Wednesday? I need you there now, Jules, we've got a lot to do.'

Julia shook her head. 'No. I mean, I'm not coming. Not going to Japan. Not today, not next week—not ever. Or anywhere else.'

She couldn't go.

Couldn't pack up her things and head off into the sunset—well, sunrise, to be tediously accurate, as they were flying to Japan.

Correction: *Max* was flying to Japan. She wasn't. She wasn't going anywhere. Not again, not for the umpteenth time in their hectic, tempestuous, whirlwind life together. Been there, done that, et cetera. And she just couldn't do it any more.

He dropped the carefully folded shirt into his case and turned towards her, his expression incredulous. 'Are you serious? Have you gone crazy?'

'No. I've never been more serious about anything. I'm sick of it,' she told him quietly. 'I don't want to do it any more. I'm sick of you saying jump, and all I do is say, "How high?"'

'I never tell you to jump!'

'No. No, you're right. You tell me *you* need to jump, and I ask how high, and then I make it happen for you—in any language, in any country, wherever you've decided the next challenge lies.'

'You're my PA—that's your job!'

'No, Max. I'm your *wife*, and I'm sick of being treated like any other employee. And I'm not going to let you do it to me any more.'

He stared at her for another endless moment, then rammed his hands through his hair and glanced at his watch before reaching for another shirt. 'You've picked a hell of a time for a marital,' he growled, and, not for the first time, she wanted to scream.

'It's not a marital,' she said as calmly as she could manage. 'It's a fact. I'm not coming—and I don't know if I'll be here when you get back. I can't do it any more—any of it—and I need time to work out what I do want.'

His fists balled in the shirt, crushing it to oblivion, but she didn't care. It wasn't as if she'd been the one who'd ironed it. The laundry service took care of that. She didn't have time. She was too busy making sure the cogs were all set in motion in the correct sequence.

'Hell, Jules, your timing sucks.'

He threw the shirt into the case and stalked to the window, ramming his hand against the glass and staring out over the London skyline, his tall, muscled frame vibrating with tension. 'You know what this means to me—how important this deal is. Why today?'

'I don't know,' she said honestly. 'I just—I've hit a brick wall. I'm so sick of not having a life.'

'We have a life!' he roared, twisting away from the window and striding across to tower over her, his fists opening and closing in frustration. 'We have a damn good life.'

'No, we go to work.'

'And we're *stunningly* successful!'

'Business-wise, I agree—but it's not a life.' She met his furious eyes head-on, refusing to let him intimidate her. She was used to Max in a temper, and he'd never once frightened her. 'Our home life isn't a success, because we don't *have* a home life, Max. We didn't see your family over Christmas, we've worked over New Year—for God's sake, we watched the fireworks out of the office window! And did you know today's the last day for taking down the decorations? We didn't even *have* any, Max. We didn't *do* Christmas. It just happened all around us while we carried on. And I want more than that. I want—I don't know—a house, a garden, time to potter amongst the plants, to stick my fingers in the soil and smell the roses.' Her voice softened. 'We never stop and smell the roses, Max. Never.'

He frowned, let his breath out on a harsh sigh, and stared at his watch. His voice when he spoke was gruff.

'We have to go. We're going to miss our flight. Take some time out, if that's what you need, but come with me,

Jules. Get a massage or something, go and see a Zen garden, but for God's sake stop this nonsense—'

'Nonsense?' Her voice was cracking, and she firmed it, but she couldn't get rid of the little shake in it. 'I don't believe you, Max. You haven't heard a damn thing I've said. I don't want to go to a Zen garden. I don't want a massage. I'm not coming. I need time—time to think, time to work out what I want from life—and I can't do that with you pacing around the hotel bedroom at four o'clock in the morning and infecting me with your relentless enthusiasm and hunger for power. I just can't do it, and I won't.'

He dashed his hand through his hair again, rumpling the dark strands and leaving them on end, and then threw his washbag in on top of the crumpled shirt, tossed in the shoes that were lying on the bed beside the case and slammed it shut.

'You're crazy. I don't know what's got into you—PMT or something. And anyway, you can't just walk out, you've got a contract.'

'A con—?' She laughed, a strange, high-pitched sound that fractured in the middle. 'So sue me,' she said bitterly, and, turning away, she walked out of their bedroom and into the huge open-plan living space with its spectacular view of the river before she did something she'd regret.

It was still dark, the lights twinkling on the water, and she stared at them until they blurred. Then she shut her eyes.

She heard the zip on his case as he closed it, the trundle of the wheels, the sharp click of his leather soles against the beautiful wooden floor.

'I'm going now. Are you coming?'

'No.'

'Are you sure? Because, if you don't, that's it. Don't expect me to run around after you begging.'

She nearly laughed at the thought, but her heart was too busy breaking. 'I don't.'

'Good. So long as we understand one another. Where's my passport?'

'On the table, with the tickets,' she said without turning round, and waited, her breath held.

Waited for what—some slight concession? An apology? No, never that. *I love you?* But she couldn't remember when he'd last said those words, and he didn't say them now. She heard his footsteps, the wheels of his case on the floor, the rattle of his keys, the rustle of paper as he picked up the flight details, his passport and tickets, then the click of the latch.

'Last call.'

'I'm not coming.'

'Fine. Suit yourself. You know where to find me when you change your mind.' Then there was a pause, and again she waited, but after an age he gave a harsh sigh and the door clicked shut.

Still she waited, till she heard the ping of the lift, the soft hiss of the door closing, the quiet hum as it sank down towards the ground floor.

Then she sat down abruptly on the edge of the sofa and jerked in a breath.

He'd gone. He'd gone, and he hadn't said a word to change her mind, not one reason why she should stay. Except that she'd be breaking her contract.

Her contract, of all things! All she wanted was some time to think about their lives, and, because she wouldn't go with him, he was throwing away their marriage and talking about a blasted *contract*!

'Damn you, Max!' she yelled, but her voice cracked and she started to cry, great, racking sobs that tore through her and brought bile to her throat.

She ran to the bathroom and was horribly, violently sick, then slumped trembling to the floor, her back propped against the wall, her legs huddled under her on the hard marble.

'I love you, Max,' she whispered. 'Why couldn't you listen to me? Why couldn't you give us a chance?'

Would she have gone with him if he'd stopped, changed his flight and told her he loved her—taken her in his arms and hugged her and said he was sorry?

No. And, anyway, that wasn't Max's style.

She could easily have cried again, but she wouldn't give him the satisfaction, so she pulled herself together, washed her face, cleaned her teeth and repaired her make-up. Then she went back out to the living room and picked up the phone.

'Jane?'

'Julia, hi, darling! How are you?'

'Awful. I've just left Max.'

'What! Where?'

'No—I've *left* him. Well, he's left me, really…'

There was a shocked silence, then Jane said something very rude under her breath. 'OK, where are you?'

'At the apartment. Janey, I don't know what to do—'

'Where's Max now?'

'On his way to Japan. I was supposed to be going, but I just couldn't.'

'Right. Stay there. I'm coming. Pack a case. You're coming to stay with me.'

'I'm packed,' she said.

'Not jeans and jumpers and boots, I'll bet. You've got an hour and a half. Sort yourself out and I'll be there. And find something warm; it's freezing up here.'

The phone went dead, and she went back into the bedroom and stared at her case lying there on the bed. She didn't even *own* any jeans these days. Or the sort of boots Jane was talking about.

Or did she?

She rummaged in the back of a wardrobe and found her old jeans, and a pair of walking boots so old she'd forgotten she still had them, and, pitching the sharp suits and the four-inch heels out of the case, she packed the jeans and boots, flung in her favourite jumpers and shut the lid.

Their wedding photo was on the dressing table, and she stared at it, remembering that even then they hadn't taken time for a honeymoon. Just a brief civil ceremony, and then their wedding night, when he'd pulled out all the stops and made love to her until neither of them could move.

She'd fallen asleep in his arms, as usual, but unusually she'd woken in them, too, because for once he hadn't left the bed to start working on his laptop, driven by a restless energy that never seemed to wane.

How long ago it seemed.

She swallowed and turned away from the photo, dragged her case to the door and looked round. She didn't want anything else—any reminders of him, of their home, of their life.

She took her passport, though, not because she wanted to go anywhere but just because she didn't want Max to have it. It was a symbol of freedom, in some strange way, and besides she might need it for all sorts of things.

She couldn't imagine what, but it didn't matter. She tucked it into her handbag and put it with her case by the door, then she emptied the fridge into the bin and put it all down the rubbish chute and sat down to wait. But her mind kept churning, and so she turned on the television to distract her.

Not a good idea. Apparently, according to the reporter, today—the first Monday after New Year—was known as 'Divorce Monday', the day when, things having come to a head over Christmas and the New Year, thousands of women would contact a lawyer and start divorce proceedings.

Including her?

Two hours later she was sitting at Jane's kitchen table in Suffolk. She'd been fetched, tutted and clucked over, and driven straight here, and now Jane was making coffee.

And the smell was revolting.

'Sorry—I can't.'

And she ran for the loo and threw up again. When she straightened up, Jane was standing behind her, staring at her thoughtfully in the mirror. 'Are you OK?'

'I'll live. It's just emotion. I love him, Janey, and I've blown it, and he's gone, and I just hate it.'

Jane humphed, opened the cabinet above the basin and handed her a long box. 'Here.'

She stared at it and gave a slightly hysterical little laugh. 'A pregnancy test? Don't be crazy. You know I can't have children. I've got all that scarring from my burst appendix. I've had tests; there's no way. I can't conceive—'

'No such word as can't—I'm living proof. Just humour me.'

She walked out and shut the door, and with a shrug Julia read the instructions. Pointless. Stupid. She couldn't be pregnant.

'What on earth am I going to do?'

'Do you want to stay with him?'

She didn't even have to think about it. Even as shocked and stunned as she was by the result, she knew the answer, and she shook her head. 'No. Max has always been really emphatic about how he didn't want children, and anyway, he'd have to change beyond recognition before I'd inflict him on a child. You know he told me I couldn't leave because I had a contract?'

Jane tsked softly. 'Maybe he was clutching at straws.'

'Max? Don't be ridiculous. He doesn't clutch at anything. Anyway, it's probably not an option. He told me, if I didn't go with him, that was it. But I have to live somewhere; I can't stay with you and Pete, especially as you're pregnant again, too. I think one baby's probably enough.' She gave a shaky laugh. 'I just can't *believe* I'm pregnant, after all these years.'

Jane laughed a little self-consciously. 'Well, it happens to the best of us. You're lucky I had the spare test. I nearly did another one because I didn't believe it the first time, but we've just about come to terms with it—and I'm even getting excited now about having another one, and the kids are thrilled. So,' she said, getting back to the point, 'Where do you want to live? Town or country?'

Julia tried to smile. 'Country?' she said tentatively. 'I

really don't want to go back to London, and I know it's silly, and I've probably got incredibly brown thumbs, but I really want a garden.'

'A garden?' Jane tipped her head on one side, then grinned. 'Give me a minute.'

It took her five, during which time Julia heard her talking on the phone in the study next door, then she came back with a self-satisfied smile.

'Sorted. Pete's got a friend, John Blake, who's going to be working in Chicago for a year. He'd found someone to act as a caretaker for the house, but it's fallen through, and he's been desperately looking for someone else.'

'Why doesn't he just let it?'

'Because he'll be coming and going, so he can't really. But it's a super house, all your running and living expenses will be paid, all you have to do is live in it, not have any wild parties, and call the plumber if necessary. Oh, and feed and walk the dog. Are you OK with dogs?'

She nodded. 'I love dogs. I've always wanted one.'

'Brilliant. And Murph's a sweetie. You'll love him, and the house. It's called Rose Cottage, it's got an absolutely gorgeous garden, and the best thing is it's only three miles from here, so we can see lots of each other. It'll be fun.'

'But what about the baby? Won't he mind?'

'John? Nah. He loves babies. Anyway, he's hardly ever home. Come on, we're going to see him now.'

CHAPTER ONE

'I've found her.'

Max froze.

It was what he'd been waiting for since June, but now—now he was almost afraid to voice the question. His heart stalling, he leaned slowly back in his chair and scoured the investigator's face for clues. 'Where?' he asked, and his voice sounded rough and unused, like a rusty hinge.

'In Suffolk. She's living in a cottage.'

Living. His heart crashed back to life, and he sucked in a long, slow breath. All these months he'd feared...

'Is she well?'

'Yes, she's well.'

He had to force himself to ask the next question. 'Alone?'

The man paused. 'No. The cottage belongs to a man called John Blake. He's working away at the moment, but he comes and goes.'

God. He felt sick. So sick he hardly registered the next few words, but then gradually they sank in. 'She's got *what*?'

'Babies. Twin girls. They're eight months old.'

'Eight—?' he echoed under his breath. 'So he's got children?'

He was thinking out loud, but the PI heard and corrected him.

'Apparently not. I gather they're hers. She's been there since mid-January last year, and they were born during the summer—June, the woman in the post office thought. She was more than helpful. I think there's been a certain amount of speculation about their relationship.'

He'd just bet there had. God, he was going to kill her. Or Blake. Maybe both of them.

'Of course, looking at the dates, she was presumably pregnant when she left you, so they could be yours—or she could have been having an affair with this Blake character before.'

He glared at the unfortunate PI. 'Just stick to your job. I can do the maths,' he snapped, swallowing the unpalatable possibility that she'd been unfaithful to him before she'd left. 'Where is she? I want the address.'

'It's all in here,' the man said, sliding a large envelope across the desk to him. 'With my invoice.'

'I'll get it seen to. Thank you.'

'If there's anything else you need, Mr Gallagher, any further information—'

'I'll be in touch.'

'The woman in the post office told me Blake was away at the moment, if that helps,' he added quietly, and opened the door.

Max stared down at the envelope, hardly daring to open it. But, when the door clicked softly shut behind the PI, he eased up the flap, tipped it and felt his breath jam in his throat as the photos spilled out over the desk.

Oh lord, she looked gorgeous. Different, though. It took

him a moment to recognise her, because she'd grown her hair and it was tied back in a ponytail, making her look younger and somehow freer. The blonde highlights were gone, and it was back to its natural soft golden-brown, with a little curl in the end of the ponytail that he wanted to thread his finger through and tug, just gently, to draw her back to him.

Crazy. She'd put on a little weight, but it suited her. She looked well and happy and beautiful, but oddly, considering how desperate he'd been for news of her for the last year—one year, three weeks and two days, to be exact—it wasn't Julia who held his attention after the initial shock. It was the babies sitting side by side in a supermarket trolley. Two identical and absolutely beautiful little girls.

His? It was a distinct possibility. He only had to look at the dark, spiky hair on their little heads, so like his own at that age. He could have been looking at a photo of himself.

Max stared down at it until the images swam in front of his eyes. He pressed the heels of his hands against them, struggling for breath, then lowered his hands and stared again.

She was alive—alive and well—and she had two beautiful children.

Children that common sense would dictate were his.

Children he'd never seen, children he'd not been told about, and suddenly he found he couldn't breathe. Why hadn't she told him? Would he ever have been told about them? Damn it, how *dared* she keep them a secret from him? Unless they weren't his…

He felt anger building inside him, a terrible rage that filled his heart and made him want to destroy something the way she'd destroyed him.

The paperweight hit the window and shattered, the pieces bouncing off the glass and falling harmlessly to the floor, and he bowed his head and counted to ten.

'Max?'

'He's found her—in Suffolk. I have to go.'

'Of course you do,' his PA said soothingly. 'But take a minute, calm down, I'll make you a cup of tea and get someone to pack for you.'

'I've got a bag in the car. You'll have to cancel New York. In fact, cancel everything for the next two days. I'm sorry, Andrea, I don't want tea. I just want to see my—my wife.'

And the babies. His babies.

She blocked his path. 'It's been over a year, Max. Another ten minutes won't make any difference. You can't go tearing in there like this, you'll frighten the life out of her. You have to take it slowly, work out what you want to say. Now sit down. That's it. Did you have lunch?'

He sat obediently and stared at her, wondering what the hell she was talking about. 'Lunch?'

'I thought so. Tea and a sandwich—and then you can go.'

He stared after her—motherly, efficient, bossy, organising—and deeply, endlessly kind, he realised now—and felt his eyes prickle again.

He couldn't just sit there. He crunched over the paperweight and placed his hands flat on the window, his forehead pressed to the cool, soothing glass. Why hadn't he known? How could she have kept something so significant from him for so long?

He heard the door open and Andrea return.

'Is this her?'

'Yes.'

'And the babies?'

He stared out of the window. 'Yes. Interesting, isn't it? It seems I'm a father, and she didn't even see fit to tell me. Either that or she's had an affair with my doppelganger, because they look just like I did.'

She put the tray down, tutted softly and then, utterly out of the blue, his elegant, calm, practical PA hugged him.

He didn't know what to do for a second. It was so long since anyone had held him that he was shocked at the contact. But then slowly he lifted his arms and hugged her back, and the warmth and comfort of it nearly unravelled him. Resisting the urge to hang on, he stepped back out of her arms and turned away, dragging in air and struggling for control of the situation.

'Goodness, aren't they like you?'

She was staring down at the photos on the desk, a smile on her face, and he nodded. 'Yes. Yes, they are. I've seen pictures of me—'

Was that his voice? He cleared his throat and tried again. 'I must have been that sort of age. My mother's got an album—' And then it hit him. She was a grandmother. He'd have to tell her. She'd be overjoyed.

Oh, hell. His eyes were at it again.

'Here, drink your tea and eat the sandwiches, and I'll get David to bring the car round.'

The car. A two-seater, low, sexy, gorgeous open-top sports car with a throaty growl and absolutely nowhere to put baby seats, he thought as he got into it a few minutes later. Never mind. He could change it. He tapped the address into the satnav and headed out of town, the hood down and the icy February wind in his hair, trying to blow away the cobwebs and help him think—because he still had no idea what on earth he was going to say to her.

He still had no idea nearly two hours later, when the satnav had guided him to the centre of the village, and he pulled up in the dusk and looked at the map the PI had given him.

There was the bridge over the river, just ahead of him, so it should be here on the right, down this drive.

He dragged in a deep breath, shut the hood because he suddenly realised he was freezing and it was starting to mist with rain, and bumped slowly down the drive, coming out into an open area in front of the house.

He saw a pretty, thatched, chocolate-box cottage in the sweep of his headlights, and then he saw her walking towards the window in a room to the right of the front door, a baby in her arms, and his heart jammed in his throat.

'Shush, Ava, there's a good girl. Don't cry, darling— Oh, look, there's somebody coming! Shall we see who it is? It might be Auntie Jane!'

She went to the window and looked out as the headlights sliced across the gloom and the car came to rest, and felt the blood drain from her face.

Max! How—?

She sat down abruptly on the old sofa in the bay window, ignoring the baby chewing her fist and grizzling on her shoulder, and her sister joining in from the playpen. Because all she could do was stare at Max getting out of the car, unfurling his long body, slamming the door, walking slowly and purposefully towards the porch.

The outside lights had come on, but he must be able to see her in the kitchen with the lights on, surely? Any second now.

He clanged the big bell and turned away, his shoulders rigid with tension, hands jammed into the pockets of his trousers, pushing the jacket out of the way and ruining the beautiful cut.

He was thinner, she realised—because of course without her there to nag and organise he wouldn't be looking after himself—and she felt a flicker of guilt and promptly buried it.

This was all his fault. If he'd listened to her, paid more attention last year when she'd said she wasn't happy, actually stopped and discussed it— But no.

Don't expect me to run around after you begging. You know where to find me when you change your mind.

But she hadn't, and of course he hadn't contacted her. She'd known he wouldn't—Max didn't beg—and she'd just let it drift, not knowing what to do once she'd realised she was pregnant, just knowing she couldn't go back to that same situation, to that same man.

Even if she still cried herself to sleep at night because she missed him. Even if, every time she looked at his children, she felt a huge well of sadness that they didn't know the man who was their father. But how to tell him, when he'd always said so emphatically that it was the last thing he wanted?

Then Murphy whined, ran back to the door and barked, and Ava gave up grizzling and let out a full-blown yell, and he turned towards the window and met her eyes.

She was so close.

Just there, on the other side of the glass, one of the

babies in her arms, and there was a dog barking, and he didn't know what to do.

You can't go tearing in there like this, you'll frighten the life out of her. You have to take it slowly, work out what you want to say. Oh Andrea, so sage, so sensible. Jules would approve of you.

But he still didn't know what on earth he was going to say to her.

He ought to smile, he thought, but his mouth wasn't working, and he couldn't drag his eyes from her face. She looked—hell, she looked exhausted, really, but he'd never seen anything more beautiful or welcome in his life. Then she turned away, and he felt his hand reach out to the glass as if to stop her.

But she was only coming to the door, he realised a second later, and he sagged against the wall with a surge of relief. A key rattled, and the big oak door swung in, and there she was, looking tired and pale, but more beautiful than he'd ever seen her, with the baby on her hip and a big black Labrador at her side.

'Hello, Max.'

That was it? A year, two children, a secret relationship and all she could say was *'Hello, Max'*?

He didn't know what he'd expected, but it wasn't that. He felt bile rise in his throat, driven by a rage so all-consuming it was threatening to destroy him from the inside out—a year of grief and fear and anger all coming to a head in that moment—but he remembered Andrea's words and tamped it down hard. He could do this, he told himself, so he gritted his teeth and met her eyes.

'Hello, Julia.'

* * *

He was propped against the wall, one arm up at shoulder height, his hair tousled and windswept, his eyes dark and unreadable. Only the jumping muscle in his jaw gave him away, and she realised he knew.

'Hello, Julia.'

Julia, not Jules. That was a change. She wondered what else had changed. Not enough, probably. Inevitably. She gathered her composure and straightened up, taking control of the situation if not her trembling body.

'You'd better come in,' she said. After all, what else could she do? She had a feeling he was coming in if he had to break the door down, so she might as well do this the easy way.

He followed her back to the kitchen, his footsteps loud on the tiles, and she could hear Murphy fussing around him and thrashing his tail into all the furniture and doors. She thought of Max's suit and how it would look decorated in dog hair, and stifled a smile. He'd hate that. He was always so particular.

'Shut the door, keep the heat in,' she instructed, and he shut it and turned towards her, that muscle jumping in his jaw again.

'Is that all you've got to say? A whole year without a word, and all you've got to say is "Shut the door"?'

'I'm trying to keep the babies warm,' she said, and his eyes tracked immediately to the baby in her arms, his expression unreadable. Supremely conscious of the monumental nature of the moment, she locked her legs to stop them shaking and said, 'This is Ava,' and, gesturing with her free hand towards the lobster-pot playpen near the Aga, added, 'and this is Libby.'

And, hearing her name, Libby looked up, took the

bubbly, spitty teething ring out of her mouth and grinned. 'Mum-mum,' she said, and, holding up her arms, she opened and closed her hands, begging to be picked up.

Julia went to move towards her, then stopped and looked at Max, her heart pounding. 'Well, go on, then. Pick up your daughter. I take it that's why you're here?'

He was transfixed.

Your daughter.

Oh lord. It was ages since he'd held a baby. He wasn't even sure he'd ever held one this age. Older, yes, and probably walking, but not small, dribbly and gummy and quite so damned appealing, and he was suddenly terrified he'd drop her.

He shrugged off his jacket and hung it over a chair, then reached into the playpen, put his hands under her armpits and lifted her out.

'She's light! I thought she'd be heavier.'

'She's only a baby, Max, and twins are often small, but don't be scared of her. They're remarkably robust. Say hello to Daddy, Libby.'

Daddy?

'Mum-mum,' she said, and, reaching up, she grabbed his nose and pulled it hard.

'Ouch.'

'Libby, gently,' Julia said, easing her fingers away, and told him to put her on his hip, then handed him Ava, settling her in the curve of his other arm. 'There you go. Your children.'

He stared down at them. They were like peas in a pod, he thought, wondering how on earth she told them apart, and they smelt extraordinary. Like nothing he'd ever smelt before. Sweet and clean, and somehow…

Then Ava reached out to Libby, and they beamed at each other and turned and stared up at him with brilliant blue eyes exactly the colour of his own, and they smiled at him in unison, and, without warning, Max fell headlong in love.

'Here, you'd better sit down,' Julia said with a lump in her throat, and pulled a chair out from the table and steered him towards it before his legs gave way. He had a thunderstruck look on his face, and the girls were clearly as fascinated as he was. They were pawing his face, pulling his ears, grabbing his nose and twisting it, and he just sat there looking amazed and let them do it.

Then he looked up at her, and she saw that behind the burgeoning love in his eyes was a simmering anger fiercer than any she'd ever seen before, and she fell back a step.

He hated her.

She could see it in his eyes, in the black, bitter rage that filled them, and she turned away, tears welling. 'I'll put the kettle on,' she said, more to give her something to do than anything. But then Ava started to cry again, and Libby whimpered, and she plonked the kettle down on the hob and turned back and took Ava from him.

'Come on, sweetheart,' she murmured, her voice sounding fractured and uncertain, and Ava picked up on it and threw herself backwards. She caught her easily, snuggling her close, and the baby started to tug at her jumper.

Oh, hell. Her breasts were prickling, the babies needed feeding, and Max—Max, who knew her body better than she knew it herself—was sitting there watching her with black, brooding eyes.

'I need to feed her,' she said, and then Libby joined in and started to yell. 'Both of them.'

'I'll help you.'

'I don't think you can. You don't have the equipment,' she said with an attempt at levity, and as the penny dropped a dull flush of colour ran over his cheekbones.

'Um—here,' he said, handing Libby to her. 'I'll—um—'

'Oh, sit down, Max,' she said, giving up and heading for the sofa in the bay window. There was no point in procrastinating. And, anyway, he wasn't going to see anything he hadn't seen before. She sat down, pulled the cushions round to rest the babies on, one each side, undid her bra, pushed it out of the way and plugged them in.

He didn't know where to look.

He knew where he wanted to look. Couldn't drag his eyes away, in fact, but he didn't think it was exactly polite to stare.

He stifled a cough of laughter. Polite? This situation was so far from being *polite* that it was positively off the chart, but he still couldn't sit there and stare.

'Kettle's boiling. I'd love a cup of tea,' she said, and he realised she was looking at him.

'Ah—sure.'

He got up, went over to the Aga and lifted the kettle off, then didn't know where to put it. On the lid? Maybe. He put the lid down, then realised there was room beside it. What a ridiculous system. What on earth was wrong with an electric kettle or the tap for boiling water they had in their apartment?

Their apartment?

Still? A year later?

'Where are the mugs?'

'Over the sink. The tea's in the caddy there by the Aga, and the milk's in the fridge in the utility room. Put some cold water in mine, please.'

He put the teabags in the mugs, stepped over the dog, fetched the milk and sloshed it in the tea, then put the milk away, stepping over the dog again, and took Julia her mug.

'Thanks. Just put it there on the end of the table,' she said, and he set it down and hesitated.

He could see the babies' mouths working on Julia's nipples, a bluish film of milk around their lips, fat little hands splayed out over the swollen white orbs of her breasts. They were so much bigger than normal, the skin on them laced faintly with blue veins, and he was fascinated. There was just something basic and fundamental and absolutely *right* about it.

And he felt excluded.

Isolated and cut off, kept out of this precious and amazing event which had taken place without him.

Cheated.

He turned away, taking his tea and propping himself morosely against the front of the Aga, huddling against its warmth. He felt cold right to his bones, chilled by his exclusion. And angry.

So furiously bloody angry that he was ready to hit something. A door? A wall? Not Jules. Never Jules, no matter how much she might infuriate him. It was only his surroundings that bore the brunt of his recent ill-temper, and right then he was ready to tear the house apart.

'Max?'

He glanced across at her.

'Could you take Ava for me? She's finished, she just needs to burp. Could you walk round with her? Oh, and you'd better have this; she might bring up some milk on you.'

She handed him a soft white cloth—a muslin nappy; how did he know that?—and then his daughter. His precious, precious daughter. God, that was going to take some getting used to. She was sunny now, all smiles again, but then she burped and giggled, and he wiped her mouth with the corner of the cloth and smiled at her.

'Lager lout,' he said with an unaccustomed wave of affection, and she giggled again and grabbed his nose. 'Hey, gently,' he murmured, removing her hand, and, lifting his tea to his mouth, he was about to take a sip when her hand flew up and caught the mug and sent it all over him.

Without thinking he swung her out of the way, but there was nothing he could do to save himself from it and it was hot—hot enough to make him yelp with shock—and Ava screwed up her face and screamed. Oh, lord. Water. Cold water. He carried her to the tap and sloshed cold water over her, holding her hand under the dribbling tap just in case, while Julia put Libby down and ran over.

'Give her to me,' she said, and quickly laid her on the table and stripped off her clothes. The muslin nappy had caught most of it, and there wasn't a mark on her, but it could so easily have been a disaster, and he felt sick. Sick and stupid and irresponsible.

'What the hell did you think you were doing? You don't hold a cup of boiling tea over a child!' Julia raged, and he stepped back, devastated that he might so easily have caused his tiny daughter harm.

'I'm sorry. I didn't think— Is she all right? Does she need to go to hospital?'

'No, you must have missed her, she's fine—no thanks to you.'

'You gave her to me.'

'I didn't expect you to pour tea over her!'

'It missed her.'

'Only by the grace of God! It could have gone all over her! Of all the stupid, stupid—'

'You were holding your tea over them!'

'It had cold water in it! What do you think that was for? Shush, sweetheart, it's OK.' But the babies were both screaming now, upset by the shouting and the whining of the dog, and he stepped back again, shaking his head.

'I'm sorry,' he said roughly. 'Jules, I'm so sorry—'

He scrubbed his hand through his hair and turned away, furious with himself for his stupidity, but he wasn't to be allowed to wallow.

'Here, hold her. I need to change her. I'll get her some clean, dry clothes.' And then she paused and looked up at him, her lashes spiked with tears, and her voice softened. 'She's all right, Max. It was just the shock. I'm sorry I yelled at you.'

'She could have been—' He broke off, and Julia's face contorted.

'Don't. It was an accident. Just hold her. I'll only be a moment.'

He didn't move a muscle. Just stood there, motionless, until she came back into the room armed with nappies and tiny clothes, and took the screaming baby out of his arms. Then he sat down, buried his face in his hands and sucked in a breath.

'Can you cuddle Libby, please?'

He pulled himself together and sat up. 'Do you trust me?' he asked tersely, and she gave him a grim smile.

'I have to, don't I? You're their father.'

'Am I?'

'Max, of course you are! Who else?'

'I don't know, but perhaps we should get a DNA test.'

Her face went white. 'Whatever for? I wouldn't lie to you about that. And I'm not about to start asking you for money to support us, either.'

'I wasn't thinking about money, I was thinking about paternity. And I wouldn't have thought you would lie about it, but then I wouldn't have thought you'd leave me without warning, shack up with another man and have two children without bothering to share the information with me. So clearly I don't know you nearly as well as I thought I did and, yes, I want a DNA test,' he said, his anger rising to the surface again. 'Because, apart from anything else, it might be handy in court.'

'Court?' She looked aghast. 'Why court? I'm not going to do anything to obstruct your access.'

'I don't know that. You might move again—go into hiding somewhere else. I know you've got your passport with you. But on the other hand, if you decide to go for maintenance, I want to be damn sure it's *my* kids I'm paying for.'

She gasped, her eyes wounded, and he felt a total heel.

'Don't bother to turn the tears on,' he growled, hating it—because he thought she was going to cry and Jules never, ever cried—but his words rallied her and she straightened up and glared at him.

'I'd forgotten what a bastard you are, Max. You don't need a test to prove you're the father! You were with me every minute of the day and night when they were conceived. Who else could it possibly have been?'

He shrugged. 'John Blake?'

She stared at him, then started to laugh. 'John? No. No, John's not a threat to you. Trust me. Apart from the fact that he's in his late fifties and definitely not my type, he's gay.'

The surge of relief was so great it took his breath away. She hadn't had an affair—and the babies were his. Definitely.

And one of them was still screaming for attention.

He picked Libby up, moving almost on auto-pilot, and went over to where Julia was dressing Ava. She ran her eyes over his chest. 'Your shirt's soaked. Are you all right?' she asked, without a flicker of compassion, and he told himself he didn't deserve it anyway.

'I'm sure I'll live,' he replied tersely. 'Is she really OK?'

'She's fine, Max,' Julia said, her voice grudging but fair as ever. 'It was an accident. Don't worry about it.'

Easy to say, not so easy to do. Especially when, some time later, after they'd been fed little pots of disgusting-smelling goo—how lamb and vegetables could possibly smell so vile he had no idea—Julia put the babies down in their cots for a sleep and made him take off his shirt, and he saw the reddened skin over his chest and shoulder. If that had been Ava...

He nearly retched with the thought, but Julia's soft sound of dismay stopped him in his tracks.

'Idiot. You told me you were all right!' she scolded softly, guilt in her eyes, and then spread something green and cool over his skin with infinite gentleness.

'What's that?' he asked, his voice a little hoarse, because it was so long since she'd touched him that the feel of her fingers on his skin was enough to take the legs out from under him.

'It's aloe vera gel,' she murmured. 'It's good for burns.'

And then she looked up and met his eyes, and time stopped. He couldn't breathe, his heart was lodged in his throat, and for the life of him he couldn't look away.

He wanted her.

He was still furious with her for keeping the babies from him, for leaving him without warning and dropping off the face of the earth, but he'd never stopped loving her, and he loved her now.

'Jules—'

She stepped back, the spell broken by the whispered word, and screwed the lid back on the gel, but her fingers were trembling, and for some crazy reason that gave him hope.

'You need a clean shirt. Have you got anything with you?'

'Yes, in the car. I've got a case with me.'

She looked back at him, her eyes widening. 'You're planning on staying?' she said in a breathless whisper, and he gave a short huff of laughter.

'Oh yes. Yes, Jules, I'm staying, because, now I've found you, I'm not losing sight of you or my children again.'

CHAPTER TWO

HE WENT out to his car to get a dry shirt, and she watched him through the window, her hand over her mouth.

He was staying?

Oh, lord. Staying *here*? No! No, he couldn't stay here, not with her! She couldn't let him get that close, because she knew him, knew that look in his eyes, knew just how vulnerable she was to his potent sexual charm. He'd only have to touch her and she'd crumple like a wet tissue.

She was shocked at the change in him, though.

He'd lost weight; she'd been right. He was thinner, the taut muscles right there under her fingers as she'd smoothed the gel on his reddened skin. His hair was touched with grey at the temples, and he looked every one of his thirty-eight years. He'd aged in the last year more than he'd aged in all the years she'd known him, and she felt another stab of guilt.

She told herself it wasn't her fault he didn't look after himself, but she hadn't expected him to look so—so *ravaged*. His ribs had been clearly visible in the kitchen light, but so, too, had every muscle and sinew, and she realised that, although he was thinner and looked driven, he was fit.

Fit and lean and hard, and she felt her mouth dry as he got his case out of the boot, plipped the remote control and headed back towards the door, showing her the firm definition of those muscles and ribs in the harsh security lighting. He'd been working out, she thought. Or running. Or both. He often did, usually when things were tricky and he needed to think.

Or to stop himself thinking.

Was that her fault? Possibly. Probably. Oh hell, it was such a mess, and just to make things worse he'd scalded himself when Ava had lunged at him. He must be freezing, she thought, with that wet gel over his burn. It wasn't bad really, but he'd looked so stricken when he'd seen the pink mark across his skin, as if he'd been thinking that it could have been Ava, and she felt dreadful for shouting at him.

She'd just been so tense, and it had been the last straw.

'Is there a pub or somewhere I can stay?' he asked, coming back into the kitchen and crouching down to open his case, pulling out a soft sweater and dragging it over his head in place of the shirt.

She opened her mouth to say yes, but some demon in his pay had control of it, because all that came out was, 'Don't be silly, you can stay here. There are plenty of rooms.'

'Really?' he asked, studying her with concern, and something else that might have been mockery in his eyes. 'Aren't you worried that I'll compromise your position in the village?'

She laughed at that. 'It's a bit late to worry about compromising me, Max,' she said softly. 'You did that when you got me pregnant. And frankly the village can take a running jump.'

He frowned, and turned his attention back to his case, zipping it shut and standing it in the corner. 'What about Blake?' he asked, his mouth taut.

'What about him? I'm caretaking. I'm allowed visitors, it's in my agreement.'

'You have an agreement?'

'Well, of course I have an agreement!' she said. 'What did you think, I was just shacked up with some random man? He's a friend of Jane and Peter's, and he was looking for someone to house-sit. Don't worry, it's all above board.'

'The woman in the post office seemed to think otherwise.'

'The woman in the post office needs to get a life,' she said briskly. 'Anyway, as I've already told you, he's gay. Are you hungry?'

He frowned. 'Hungry?'

'Max, you need to eat,' she said, feeling another stab of guilt over who if anyone fed him these days, who told him when he'd worked late enough and that it was too early to get up, who stopped him burning the candle at both ends and in the middle.

Nobody, she realised in dismay, looking at him really closely. Nobody at all, and least of all himself. He was exhausted, dark hollows round his eyes, his mouth drawn, that lovely ready smile gone without trace.

She felt tears filling her eyes, and turned away.

'There's some chicken in the fridge, or I've got all sorts of things in the freezer.'

'Can't we go out?'

'Where, with the twins?'

His face was a picture, and she shook her head and

stifled a laugh. 'I can't just go out, Max. It's a military operation, and I don't have instant access to a babysitter.'

'Does the pub do food?'

'Yes. It's good, too. You could go over there.'

'Would they deliver?'

'I doubt it.'

'I could offer them an incentive.'

'I'm sure you could,' she said drily. 'Why don't you go down there and sweet-talk them? It's only just the other side of the river. It'll take you two minutes to walk it. Or you could just eat there if you're worried I'll poison you.'

He ignored that. 'Do they have a menu?'

'They do. They're very good. It's a sort of gastro-pub. You could choose something and have a drink while they cook it. It'll take about twenty minutes, probably.'

And she could have a shower and change into something that didn't smell of baby sick and nappy cream, and brush her hair and put on some make-up— No, no make-up, she didn't want to look too desperate, but she could call Jane.

'It's a bit early. I could go later.'

'Except the babies may wake later, and it's easier to eat when they're asleep. Besides, they only serve until nine, and anyway I'm starving. I forgot about lunch.'

Still he hesitated, but then he gave a curt nod, shrugged on his jacket and headed for the door. 'What do you fancy?'

'Anything. You know what I like.'

He sipped his beer morosely and stared at the menu.

Did he know what she liked? He used to think so. Skinny sugar-free vanilla lattes, bacon rolls, almond croissants, really bitter dark chocolate, steamed vegetables, pan-fried sea bass, a well-chilled Chablis, sticky-toffee pudding with thick double cream—and waking up on Sunday morning at home in their apartment and making love until lunchtime.

He'd known how to wring every last sigh and whimper out of her, how to make her beg and plead for more, for that one last touch, the final stroke that would drive her screaming over the edge.

'Are you ready to order, sir?'

He closed his eyes briefly and then looked up at the pretty young waitress with what he hoped was something resembling a normal smile. 'Um—yes. I'll have the rib-eye steak, please—rare—and the—' He hesitated. The pan-fried salmon, or the chicken breast stuffed with brie and pesto?

Then he remembered her saying she had chicken in the fridge. 'I'll have the salmon, please. And I'd like to take them away, if you can do that for me? I know you don't usually, but we don't have a babysitter and, well, it's the closest we can get to going out for dinner. I'll drop the plates back tomorrow.' This time the smile was better, less jerky and awkward, and she coloured slightly and smiled back.

'I'm sure we can do that for you, sir,' she said a little breathlessly, and he hated himself for the little kick of pride that he could still make the girls go silly with a simple smile.

'Oh, and could I have a look at the wine list? I'd like to take a couple of bottles home, if I may?'

'Of course, sir. I'll take this to the kitchen and bring the wine list back to you.'

She was back with it in moments, and he chose a red and a white, paid the bill and settled back to wait.

Funny. This time yesterday he would have been too busy to wait for his food. He would have had it delivered. Even if they didn't deliver, he would have had it delivered, because everything had a price. You just had to pay enough.

But tonight, after he'd made a couple of phone calls and checked his email on his BlackBerry® Smartphone, he was glad just to sit there in the busy pub, which was more of a restaurant than a watering hole, and take time out from what had been probably the most momentous day of his life. Unless…

But he didn't want to think about that other day, so he buried the thought and tapped his fingers and waited…

'That was lovely. Thank you, Max. It was a really nice idea.'

'Was it all right? My steak was good, but I knew you wouldn't want that, and I thought the fish was safe, but I didn't know if you'd want a pudding.' He frowned. 'I realised I didn't know what you would want.'

She felt the smile coming and couldn't stop it. 'You aren't alone. I often don't know what I want.'

One brow flew up in frank disbelief. 'Are you telling me you've become indecisive?'

She laughed at that. 'I've always been indecisive if it affects me personally. I've just trained myself to remember that I'm going to eat it, not marry it, so it really doesn't matter that much. Well, not with food, anyway. Other things—well, they're harder,' she admitted slowly.

His eyes turned brooding as he studied her. 'Is that why you didn't contact me? Because you couldn't decide if it was the right thing to do?'

She looked down, guilt and remorse flooding her. 'Probably. But you just wouldn't listen, so there didn't seem to be any point in trying to talk to you—and you hadn't tried to talk to me, either.'

He sighed shortly. 'Because I told you to get in touch when you wanted me.' He paused, then added, 'The fact that you didn't…'

She nearly let that go, but in the end she couldn't. There was just something in his eyes she couldn't ignore. 'I nearly did. So many times. But I told myself that if you were prepared to listen, to talk about it, you'd ring me. And you didn't.'

'I tried. I couldn't get you. Your number was blocked and I had no idea why.'

'My phone was stolen. But that wasn't till June! So you didn't try for nearly six months, at least.'

He looked away, his jaw working, so she knew before he spoke that she was right. 'I was waiting for you to call me. I thought, if I gave you space—and when you didn't call a bit of me thought, to hell with you, really. But then I couldn't stand it any longer—the uncertainty. Not knowing where you were, what you were doing. It was killing me. So I called, and then I couldn't get you. And you weren't spending any money, you weren't using your account.'

'John pays my living expenses and runs the car.'

'Very generous,' he growled.

'He is. He's a nice man.'

His jaw clenched at that—at the thought of another man supporting her. Well, tough. He'd get over it. It was only a job.

'He's been marvellous,' she went on, turning the screw a little further. 'He was really understanding when the babies were born, and he got a friend to stay until I was able to come home.'

'Home?'

She smiled at him wryly. 'Yes, home. This is home for us—for now, anyway.' She didn't tell him that John was returning soon and she'd have to find somewhere else. Let him think everything was all right and there was no pressure on her, or he'd use it to push her into some kind of reconciliation, and she wasn't buying that until she was sure he was ready for it. If ever.

'That's when my phone was stolen, in the hospital, and I reported it and had the card blocked. But Jane gave me her old pay-as-you-go to use for emergencies, so I cancelled the contract. There didn't seem to be any point in paying an expensive tariff when most of the time I'm at home with the babies and I've got the landline.'

'And you didn't think to give me either of those numbers?'

She laughed a little bitterly. 'What, because you'd phoned me so regularly over the previous six months?'

His jaw clenched. 'It wasn't that. I told myself you'd contact me if you wanted me. I made myself give you space, give you time to sort out what you wanted. You said you needed time to think, but then I wondered how much time it could possibly take. If you needed that much, then we probably didn't have anything worth saving in your eyes, and I was damned if I was going to weaken and call you. But then when I couldn't get hold of you I got a PI on the job—'

'A PI!' she exclaimed, her guilt and sympathy brushed aside in an instant as her anger resurrected itself. 'You've had someone spying on me?'

'Because I was worried sick about you! And, anyway, how the hell do you think I found you? Not by accident, all the way out here.'

'Well, not by trawling round yourself, that's for sure,' she said drily, ignoring yet another twinge of guilt. 'You'd be too busy to do that kind of thing yourself. I'm surprised you're here now, actually. Shouldn't you be somewhere more important?'

He gave her a sharp look. 'If it was more important, I'd *be* in New York now,' he growled, and she shook her head, the guilt retreating.

'I might have known. So when did you find out I was here?'

'Today. This afternoon—two-thirty or so.'

'Today?' she said, astonished. She'd thought, when he said about the PI, that he'd known where she was for ages. 'So you came straight here?'

He shrugged. 'What was I supposed to do? Wait for you to disappear again? Of course I came straight here—because I wanted answers.'

'You haven't asked me any questions yet—apart from why didn't I contact you, which I've told you.'

'And who's the father.'

She sat up straighter and glared at him. 'You *knew* they were yours! You weren't the slightest bit surprised. I expect your private eye took photos!'

He held her furious glare, but there was a flicker of something that might—just might—have been guilt. She ignored it and ploughed on.

'Anyway, why would you care? You told me so many times you didn't want children. So what's changed, Max? What's brought you all the way up to sleepy old Suffolk in the depths of winter to ask me that?'

He was still looking her straight in the eye, but for the

first time she felt she could really see past the mask, and her traitorous heart softened at the pain she saw there. 'You have,' he said gruffly. 'I've missed you, Jules. Come back to me.'

Oh no, Jane had been right, he was going to do the sweet-talking thing, but she'd been warned, and she wasn't falling for it. 'It's not that easy.'

'Oh, you're going to start the lifestyle thing again, aren't you?' he said, rolling his eyes and letting out his breath on a huff.

'Well—yes. You obviously haven't changed; you look dreadful, Max. How much sleep did you have last night?'

'Four hours,' he admitted grudgingly, looking a little uncomfortable.

'Four hours of sleep, or four hours in the apartment?'

'Sleep,' he said, but he looked uncomfortable again, and she had a feeling he was hiding something, and she had a feeling she knew what.

'Max, how many hours are you working at the moment, on average? Fifteen? Eighteen? Twenty?' she added, watching him carefully, and she saw the slight movement when she hit the nail on the head. 'Max, you idiot, you can't do that! You need more than four hours' sleep! And where *are* you sleeping? The apartment, or in the office?'

'Why do you care?' he asked, his voice suddenly bitter, and he lifted his head and seared her with his eyes. 'What the hell is it to you if I burn myself out trying to—?'

'Trying to?' she coaxed, but then wished she hadn't because, his voice raw, he answered her with an honesty that flayed her heart.

'Trying to forget you. Trying to stay awake long enough

that I fall asleep through sheer exhaustion and don't just lie there wondering if you're alive or dead.'

She sucked in her breath. 'Max—why would you think I was dead?'

'Because I heard nothing from you!' he grated, thrusting himself up out of the chair and prowling round the kitchen, the suppressed emotion making his body vibrate almost visibly. 'What was I supposed to think, Julia? That you were OK and everything was fine in La-La Land? Don't be so bloody naïve. You weren't spending anything, your phone wasn't working—you could have been lying in a ditch! I've spent the days searching for you, phoning everyone I could think of, nagging the backside off the PI, getting through PAs like a hot knife through butter, working myself to a standstill so I could fall over at the end of the day so tired I didn't have the energy or emotion left to—'

He broke off and turned away, spinning on his heel and slamming his hand against the wall while she stared at him, aghast at the pain in his words—pain that she'd caused.

Didn't have the energy or emotion left to—what? Cry himself to sleep, as she did?

No. Not Max.

Surely not?

She got up and crossed over to him, her socks silent on the stone-flagged floor, and laid a hand on his shoulder. 'Max, I'm so sorry,' she whispered, and he turned and dropped his shoulders against the wall and stared down at her.

'Why, Jules?' he asked, his voice like gravel. 'Why? What did I ever do to you that was so bad that you could treat me like that? How could you not have told me that I was going to be a father?'

'I wanted to, but you were always so anti-children—'

'Because you couldn't have any, and because—'

'Because?'

He shook his head. 'It doesn't matter. It's irrelevant now, but we were talking theory, there, not practice. When you found out you were pregnant— When did you find out, by the way?'

She swallowed. 'While you were on your way to Tokyo. Jane took one look at me and gave me her spare pregnancy test.'

His eyes widened. 'All that time? Right from the very first minute you knew, and you kept it from me? Jules— how? Why?'

'I didn't think you'd want to know. I wanted to tell you— I wanted so much for you to be there with me, to share it.'

'I would have been,' he said gruffly, his eyes tormented. 'I would have been with you every step of the way if you'd given me the chance.'

'But only when you weren't too busy.'

He looked away. 'I wouldn't have been too busy for that.'

'Of course you would.'

'No. Not for something like that. You should have given me the choice, Julia, not taken that decision away from me. You had no right to do that.'

He was right, of course. So right, and his anger and grief at the lost time cut right through her. She wanted to hold him, to put her arms round him, but she had no right to do that any more. How could she comfort him for the hurt she'd caused? And anyway there was no guarantee he wouldn't reject her, and she couldn't stand that.

And then he looked up and met her eyes, and she

realised he wouldn't reject her at all. She was locked in the blue fire of his gaze, unable to breath for the emotion flooding through her.

He reached out his hand and cupped her cheek tenderly, and she realised his fingers were trembling. 'I need you,' he said under his breath. 'I hate you for what you've done to me, but, God damn you, I still need you. Come back to me. Please—come back to me; let's make a life together. We can start again.'

She stepped back, her legs like jelly. It would be so easy…

'I can't. Not to that life.'

'To what, then?'

She shrugged. 'I don't know. Just not that. Not the endless jetting round the world, the profit-chasing and the thrill of the stock market, the crazy takeovers, the race to the top of the rich list—I don't want to know any more, Max, and I can't do it, especially not with the babies. That's why I left you, and nothing's changed, has it? You should be in New York now, and, OK, you're here—but I bet you've been on the phone while you were in the pub or on the way over, or on the drive up here, or later after I go to bed you'll find calls you have to make. Am I right?' she pushed, and he sighed and nodded.

'Yes, damn it, you're right, of course you're right, but I have a business to run.'

'And staff. Good staff. Some excellent people, who are more than capable of keeping things going. So let them, Max. Give them a chance to prove themselves, and take time out to get to know your children.'

'Time?' he asked cautiously, as if it was a foreign concept, and she would have smiled if her life hadn't depended on it. As it was she was on the verge of tears, and she tilted her chin and put a little backbone into her voice.

'Two weeks. Two weeks here, with me, with no phones, no news, no papers, no laptop or email or post—just us. A holiday—you know, one of those things we've never had? You, me and the babies, to see if there's any way we can make a family.'

He was shaking his head. 'I can't take two weeks—not just like that. Not without any contact.'

'You can contact them and tell them,' she said. 'I know you'll need to do that. Look, I can't talk about this any more. It's been a hell of a day, and I'm shattered. I'm going to bed, and I suggest you do, too. You can have the room beyond the babies, it's all ready. And think about what I said. If you're really serious about us getting back together, then I want that two weeks. No compromises, no cheating, no bending the rules. Just you, me and the babies. Phone your PA and fix it first thing in the morning.'

One of those elegant, autocratic brows gave an ironic quirk. 'That sounds very much like an order.'

'Just laying down the ground rules. Either you're going to engage with this or you're not.'

'Just give me one good reason why I should.'

She laughed softly. 'I can give you two—and if you want to be part of their lives you'll do this. Because I'm not subjecting them to an absentee father who can't keep his family commitments and doesn't know the difference between work and home.'

He stared at her searchingly for the longest moment, then, just when she thought he'd refuse, he nodded.

'OK. I'll call Andrea in the morning and set it up. And

you can have your two weeks. But make no mistake, I'm doing this for the children, because you're right—they deserve more than an absentee father. But it's going to take a long while before I can forgive you for cheating me of their first months, and for keeping something so monumentally important from me. So don't expect me to be all sweetness and light, because I'm still so angry with you I can't even find the words for it.'

Her eyes filled, and she swallowed the tears. 'I know. And I'm sorry. I didn't mean to hurt you, but, for what it's worth, I still love you.'

'You still love me? You can stand there and say that, and yet you walked out and didn't come back?' he said incredulously.

'Because it was killing me,' she told him unevenly. 'And I couldn't remember who we were. But I do still love you. That's never been in doubt.'

'Then come back to me.'

'No. Not just like that. It's not enough, not on its own. There has to be more. And I want to know if we've got anything left, when our old life's stripped away and all we've got to fall back on is each other. I think we could both be in for a shock.'

CHAPTER THREE

'ANDREA, it's—'

'Max! Are you all right?'

He blinked, a little startled by her concern. 'Fine,' he lied. 'I'm fine. Look, I need you to do something for me.'

'Of course,' she agreed, but then, before she let him move on, she added, 'Max, how are things?'

Bizarre. Confusing. 'I'm not sure,' he said honestly. 'I need time to find out. Can you clear my diary for the next two weeks?'

'I've done it,' she said, surprising him yet again. 'Well, I've shuffled what I can, and cleared most of it. I'm still waiting for Yashimoto to come back to me.'

Damn. He'd forgotten about Yashimoto. He was supposed to have been going on to Tokyo from New York to firm up the new contract.

'Maybe—'

'Max, I'll get him. It's not a problem. He can deal with Stephen—'

'No. Stephen doesn't know all the ins and outs. Get them both to call me—'

'Ma-ax?'

The warning voice from behind him made him turn, to find Jules propped up against the door frame cradling a cup of tea in her hands, one foot rested on the other, her bare toes looking curiously vulnerable. Not so her face. She was staring at him unflinchingly, and her expression was uncompromising. 'No phone calls,' she reminded him, a thread of steel that he'd forgotten about in her voice, and he gave a low groan of frustration and turned his back on her.

'OK. Scratch that, deal with him yourself, let Stephen handle it. I need to— Well, there are...'

'Rules?' Andrea said softly, and he sighed.

'Two weeks, no business, no distractions.'

'Well, hallelujah! I think I'm going to like your wife. I just hope I get the chance to meet her. Don't blow it, Max.'

Lord, what had happened to her? She was supposed to be on his side! 'I'll do my best,' he muttered. 'Look, I know it's against the rules, but if there really *is* a problem...'

'If there really is a problem I will, of course, ring you. Give me your wife's number.'

'What?'

'You heard. I'll call her.'

'You don't need to trouble her.'

'No, I don't suppose I do, but I'll give her the veto.'

He said something rude, then apologised and handed the phone to Julia. 'She wants your number—for emergencies.'

'Right,' she said, and took the phone out of his hand and walked off with it, shutting the door behind her with her foot.

He swore again, scrubbed his hand through his hair and then heard a cry from the babies' room.

His daughters. That was what this was all about, he

reminded himself, and, padding across the landing in bare feet, he went in there and lifted the one who was awake out of her cot and smiled at her.

Ava? He wasn't sure, so he said, 'Are you Ava?' out loud, and she turned her head and looked at the other cot. 'Libby?'

She turned back and beamed, reaching up and pulling his ear. Oh, well, it gave his nose a break. He shifted her slightly so she couldn't reach, and then sniffed. Hmm. She had a problem that was mercifully outside his experience, but that was fine. Jules wouldn't be long.

Would she?

'Max?'

'I'm in here,' he said, coming out of the babies' room with Libby in his arms. 'Are you happy now?'

'Mmm. She sounds nice. I've given her my number and my other contact details, just in case.'

'In case what? The office catches fire?'

'That would be pointless. What are you going to do, spit on it? Did you wake Libby?'

'No, she was awake. She—um—needs you.'

She chuckled and took the baby, kissing her and nuzzling her nose against her neck. 'Hello, monster. Is Daddy chicken?'

She started to cluck and squawk, and Libby thought it was hilarious and got the giggles, and she looked at Max over her head and saw his glower crumble and fade under the influence of Libby's delicious chuckles.

'Of course, part of the bonding process is learning about nappies,' she told him deadpan, and she could have sworn his colour drained a fraction. 'It's OK, I'll let you practise on a harmless one,' she said with a grin, and nearly laughed out loud when his shoulders dropped in relief.

He propped himself up in the doorway and watched her from a safe distance as she dealt with Libby, then she put the little girl back in his arms and washed her hands. Then she lifted Ava out and cuddled her while she found a clean nappy and got it ready, then changed her, too, and dropped the nappy in the bucket.

'Are those cloth nappies?' he asked, peering a little closer now it was safe.

She turned her head and raised an eyebrow at him. 'Don't look so shocked.'

'I—I'm not. I'm just surprised. I would have thought— I don't know; all that washing. You could just chuck disposables.'

'Mmm. Eight million a day, going into landfill.'

'*Eight million?* Good grief!'

'Mmm. Just in this country. And they don't biodegrade, either, so they're there for hundreds of years. Or I can wash these and dry them on the Aga. It's easier, cheaper and better, and they're not even made of cotton, they're made of bamboo. And they're lovely and soft. Right, Ava, that's you done!'

'How on earth do you manage both of them at once on your own?' he asked, looking utterly out of his depth, and she summoned a grin and shrugged.

'You learn coping strategies,' she said honestly. 'You deal with the urgent one first, and the other one gets to wait. It's normally Libby who waits, because Ava's got a shorter fuse.'

'So she's learned to manipulate you already?' he said,

sounding astonished for the second time in as many minutes, which made her laugh out loud.

'Of course.' She gave him a dry look. 'She takes after you.'

His head jerked back and he eyed her doubtfully. 'I'm not sure that's a compliment.'

She chuckled. 'It's not. But babies are amazing. They're such good little survivors, and it doesn't take them long to sort out a pecking order. They'll have you sussed in no time flat, you wait and see. Right, girls, time for breakfast.'

'Not more of that disgusting goo,' he pleaded, looking appalled.

'No. They have instant multi-grain porridge for breakfast, and fruit. That's good and messy. I'll let you clean them up.'

He looked horrified, and she nearly laughed again. But then she remembered that any normal father of eight-month-old babies would *know* what their children had for breakfast, and how to change a nappy, and that they were manipulative and very good at engineering the adults around them.

Except, of course, that Max hadn't had the chance, and that was her fault.

Turning away so he didn't see the thoughtful frown on her face, she headed downstairs with Ava, leaving him to follow with Libby. And, if she was really lucky, she'd be able to get through breakfast without drooling over the sight of him in that robe which showed altogether too much of those toned, muscular legs. Not to mention the fact that she knew only too well just how little he'd have on underneath it.

And it was absolutely nothing to do with her. Not now, and not ever again, unless they could turn this situation around and find a way to get the two of them back together. Still, at least he'd phoned his PA, as instructed.

She sounded sensible. Nice. Decent, and utterly on her side. She was looking forward to meeting her—but not yet. There was a lot of ground to cover before they reached that point, and she was going to make damn sure they walked over every single inch of it.

'Right, girls, want some breakfast?'

He had to learn the hard way, of course, not to put the bowl close enough for Libby to slap her little hand in.

And then there was catching it before she had time to rub it in her hair. And on his face when he leant in to clean her up. Oh, boy, he'd need a shower by the time they were finished.

'Here.'

He looked up and took a warm, damp cloth from Jules, smiled his thanks and wondered where to start.

'Move the bowl,' she offered, and he pulled it out of reach and swiped most of the gloop off Libby's hand before she could stick it anywhere else, conscious of Jules hovering in range just in case he couldn't manage.

'Right, monster, let's try again,' he said, putting the cloth out of reach on the edge of the sink and settling down with the bowl and spoon. 'Open wide.'

He got most of it into her before she decided she'd had enough and spat it out at him with a cheerful grin, and he closed his eyes and laughed in exasperation before getting up, rinsing out the cloth and tackling her mucky little face.

Which she hated, apparently, because she screamed the place down until he stopped, then beamed again.

'You're a madam,' he told her, grabbing her sticky hands

and sorting them out one by one, and she giggled and tried to squirm out of the chair.

'What now?' he asked Jules.

'Bath time.'

'Bath—?' He rolled his eyes and sighed. 'Sounds messy.'

'It is. I'll let you do it.'

'Bathe them?' he asked, feeling a little flicker of panic.

'You'll cope,' she assured him drily, but he wasn't sure. He had a horrible feeling it was just another opportunity for him to make an idiot of himself or do something else wrong.

'I'll get dressed,' he said, and she laughed.

'I shouldn't bother. You'll probably get soaked.'

And her mouth twitched, and he realised she was enjoying this. Hugely.

He clamped his teeth together to hold back the retort, carried Libby upstairs and stopped by the bathroom door. 'So now what?'

'Put her on the floor on her tummy so she can practise crawling, and run the bath. Here, you can have Ava, too. I'll go and find some clothes for them. Don't undress them yet, though. They'll get cold waiting for you.'

Cold? How could they possibly get cold? The bathroom was steaming. But they were just little people. What did he know? He'd nearly scalded Ava last night. He wasn't going to argue.

Run the bath, he thought, and remembered something from his mother's wisdom: run the cold first, so the bath never has just hot in it.

Wise woman.

He ran the cold, then turned the hot tap on and swished

it about until he thought it was hot enough. Was it? Hell, he wasn't going to risk another scald. He turned the hot off. Hmm. Maybe.

'Ava? What are you doing?'

He rescued the loo brush from her before she stuck it in her mouth and pointed her in the other direction, then yelled, 'I've run the bath.'

'Is it hot?'

'No!' he retorted with only a trace of sarcasm, and he heard her chuckle.

'Undress them, then. I'll be in in a second.'

So he undressed Ava, as she was heading for the brush again, and then Libby, and then he put her back down on the bath mat, rescued Ava yet again from the corner by the loo, and lowered her carefully into the water.

And yanked her out again instantly when she let out a piercing yell.

'What *now*?' Jules had flown into the room and snatched her from him, shielding her in her arms and glaring at him like a lioness defending her cub. 'I thought you said it wasn't hot!'

'It isn't!'

She bent over and touched the water, then shook her head and laughed weakly, sitting down on the side of the bath and shaking her head. 'No. You're right; poor little mite. It's freezing.'

'Freezing?'

'Mmm.'

Freezing. He sighed. 'I didn't want—'

'To burn them?' Her smile faded. 'OK. I'm sorry. I just thought it was common sense.'

'Well, clearly I haven't got any,' he retorted, sick of the whole business and wondering what he was going to do wrong next, but she took pity on him.

'Max, you're doing fine. Here, look, use the inside of your wrist. It should feel comfortable—not hot or cold. That's the best test.'

Hell. He was never going to survive this fortnight.

Never mind the rest of his life.

'How can it be so hard?' he grumbled gently, retrieving Libby this time from the loo brush and plopping her in the bath beside her sister. 'Fourteen-year-old girls manage it.'

'No, they don't. They manage to get pregnant, but they don't manage to look after babies without support and coaching and lots of encouragement. Having ovaries doesn't make you a good mother, and not knowing how to run a bath doesn't make you a bad father. You'll get there, Max,' she added softly.

And he swallowed hard and looked away, because they were kneeling side by side, their shoulders brushing, and every now and then she swayed against him and her hip bumped his, and all he could think about was dragging her up against him and kissing her soft, full lips…

'Ow!'

Jules laughed and detached Libby's fingers from his hair, and the scent of her skin drifted across his face and nearly pushed him over the brink.

'Right, what next?' he asked, and forced himself to concentrate on the next instalment of his parentcraft class.

Eventually they were washed, dried and dressed in little denim dungarees and snugly warm jumpers, and Jules declared that as soon as he was dressed himself they were going out for a walk as it was a lovely day.

'Can they walk?' he asked, and she rolled her eyes.

'Of course not. We'll take the buggy.'

Obviously. Of course they couldn't walk. They could barely crawl. Except towards the loo brush. He put it on the window sill out of reach while he thought about it, and had a quick shower to get the baby breakfast out of his hair. And eyes. And nose.

Then he threw on his clothes and went down to the kitchen to join them. 'Right, are we all set?'

She eyed him thoughtfully. 'Jeans?'

'You know I don't own jeans,' he said, and then gave a short sigh when she rolled her eyes. 'What? What, for God's sake? Is it a character flaw that I don't own jeans?'

'No,' she said softly. 'It's a character flaw that you don't *need* to own jeans.'

He worked out the difference eventually, and scowled at her. 'Well, I don't—either own them, or need them.'

'Oh, you need them, of course you do. How are you going to crawl around the floor with the girls and the dog in your hand-tailored Italian suit-trousers?'

He stared down at his legs. Were they? He supposed they were, and, when she put it like that, it did sound ridiculous. 'We could go and buy some,' he suggested.

'Good idea.'

'And while we're in town we can go to the Mercedes garage and talk about changing the car for something a little more baby-friendly.'

'There's nothing wrong with my car, and, anyway, it's John's!'

'Not yours,' he explained patiently. 'Mine.'

She swivelled her head and stared out of the window at his car. 'But Max—you love it,' she said softly.

He shrugged. 'So? I need a baby-carrier, Jules. No matter what happens with us, I need a baby-carrier. So I might as well do something about it now. And there's no room at the apartment for more than one car, so it'll have to go.'

'You could leave it here. Take mine when you have the girls.'

'I thought it was Blake's car?'

She frowned. 'Oh. Um—yes, it is,' she agreed. 'So I can't really let you have it.'

'So it's back to plan A.'

She looked at his car and chewed her lip doubtfully. She'd never driven it—never driven any of his sports cars. She'd had a little city car when he'd met her, and she'd hardly used it, so she'd sold it when they'd moved in together and she hadn't bought another one.

But she knew how much he loved it. It would be such a shame if he had to get rid of it. 'Or plan C,' she suggested. 'You buy another one, and leave it here for when you come up.'

He stared at her, then looked away to conceal his expression, because he'd suddenly realised they were talking as if she was going to be staying here, and he was going back to London without them.

And he didn't like it one bit.

They bought the jeans and some casual shoes and a couple of jumpers in one of the high-street department stores, and he emerged from the changing room looking stiff and uncomfortable and utterly gorgeous. 'Better?' he asked, a touch grumpily, and she smiled.

'Much. Right, let's go and sort the car out.'

They did. It was easy, because they had an ex-demonstration model which he could have instantly, and he held his hand out. 'Phone?'

'It's at home. But I've got Andrea's number in mine, if you want to call her to get the car on cover.'

He rolled his eyes and took her phone, made the call and handed it back in disgust. The negotiations complete, the salesman handed him the keys, and they headed back to the house in convoy, her with the babies, him alone in his new and very alien acquisition.

He followed her into the house and held out his hand again.

'So—my phone?'

She smiled a little guiltily. 'It's fine. You don't need it.'

'I might.'

'What for?'

'Apart from calling Andrea just now to get the car on cover—emergencies?'

'What—like contacting one of your business associates to set up a new deal, or checking that one of your overpaid and undervalued team is doing his or her job?'

'They aren't undervalued!' he protested, but she just arched a brow and stared straight back at him until he backed down. 'OK,' he sighed. 'So I have delegation issues.'

'Hallelujah!' she said, sounding so like Andrea that it made him want to strangle them both—or do something to ensure that they never spoke to each other again! 'So, anyway, you don't need your phone.'

'But what if there *is* an emergency?'

'Like what?'

He shrugged. 'I don't know. Like I set fire to the house or fall over on you all and squash you or drop one of the babies down the stairs—'

She went pale. 'Use the house phone.'

'What if we're out like we were this morning?' he pushed, the empty pocket in his jeans making him feel nervous and a little panicky.

'I'll have my mobile. You can use that. It's always in my bag.'

His eyes slid to the bag, just there on the side in the kitchen. It hadn't moved since he'd arrived last night, apart from to go to town with them, and, now he knew her phone was in it, the temptation to borrow it and sneak down the garden and make a couple of calls was overwhelming. Except, of course, he didn't have the contact numbers.

'Max, get over it,' she said firmly, and he realised there was no way he was going to talk her round. He swallowed hard and told himself Andrea would ring when she needed him. Except that he'd forgotten to tell her…

'Max, let it go. Andrea said she'd ring if it was urgent.' And then she added curiously, 'What's she like? She sounded nice.'

He smiled at that, a little wryly. 'I don't know if I'd call her "nice". She's fifty-three, slim and elegant, and frighteningly efficient; she rules me with a rod of iron. You'll probably love her, but it's not like having you there, Jules. It was great working with you. You just knew what I wanted all the time and it was there, ready. I hardly had to think the thought, and sometimes I didn't even need to do that. I miss you.'

'I'm not coming back just because your new PA isn't as good as me,' she retorted, but his mouth quirked and he shook his head.

'Oh, she's good, but at the end of the day, when we've finished work, she doesn't look at me like you did,' he said, his voice lower. 'As if she wants to rip my clothes off. And I don't undress her in the shower and make love to her up against the tiles until the security staff wonder who the hell's being murdered because of all the screaming.'

She felt a tide of colour sweep over her at that, and shook her head. 'Max, stop it. It was only once.'

'And it was amazing,' he said softly, and, reaching out his hand, he cupped her flushed cheek and lifted her chin, as his mouth came down and found hers in a gentle, tender kiss that could so easily lead to…

She stepped back, her legs like jelly. 'Max, no! Stop it.'

He straightened up, his eyes burning, and gave a crooked smile. 'Sorry,' he murmured, but he didn't look in the least bit sorry. He looked like the cat that got the cream, and she could have screamed with frustration.

'So—how about that walk we were going to have?' he said, which just showed what he knew about babies and their timetabling.

'The girls need lunch and a nap, and so do I. We can go for a walk later if it's still nice.'

'What am I supposed to do, then?' he asked. She realised he was utterly at a loss with so much unstructured time on his hands, and she gave a wicked little smile.

'You could wash the nappies.'

* * *

He'd never gone in her handbag.

It was one of those unwritten rules, like swearing in front of ladies and leaving the seat up, that his mother had drummed into him as a child.

But, with the house quiet and all of them asleep, he stood, arms folded, and stared at her bag. It was only the phone. Just one call. He could sneak down the garden, or out to the car, and she'd never know.

He could even see the corner of it, sticking up out of the pile of junk that she seemed to have in it. And that was a change. Her bag had always been immaculately well organised before, and now it was a walking skip.

With a phone in it.

He caught the corner of it gingerly between finger and thumb and lifted it out of the bag as if it would bite him. It was a very ordinary phone, and he knew how to use it because he'd made a call on it this afternoon. And he knew Andrea's number was in there. He had to talk to her, he told himself, trying to justify it.

He had to.

He went into the address book and then, on impulse, he scrolled down to M, and there he was: Max, and his mobile number. And the apartment. And work. He looked under ICE—in case of emergency—and found his numbers all repeated.

In her new phone.

Because of the girls, he reminded himself, squashing the leap of hope, and then had a thought. If he rang his mobile number, it would ring, and he'd be able to find it...

What on earth?

She lifted her head, stared at the pillow and pulled it aside.

Max's phone was ringing—on silent, because she'd silenced it, but the vibration had alerted her. And the number that had come up was her mobile.

Which was in her handbag.

'You're cheating,' she said into it, and there was a muttered curse and he cut the connection. Suppressing a smile, she threw back the covers and slipped out of bed, pulled on her jeans and jumper, ran her fingers through her hair and went downstairs.

He was standing by the bag, her phone in hand, looking defiant and guilty all at once, and she felt suddenly sorry for him, plunged head-first into this bizarre situation that was totally outside his experience, dislocated from everything that was familiar.

Except her, and even she'd changed beyond recognition, she realised.

She smiled. 'It's OK, Max, I'm not going to bite.'

'Just nag me.'

'No. Not even nag you. I'm going to ask you, one more time, to take this seriously. To give it your best shot, to see if we can make a go of it. If not for us, then for the girls.'

He swallowed hard, and looked away. 'I need to make a call, Jules. There's something important I forgot to tell Andrea.'

'Is anyone going to die?'

He looked startled. 'Of course not.'

'Or be hurt?'

'No.'

'So it doesn't really matter.'

'It'll just hold things up a few days until they realise.'

'Realise?'

'There's a document I was going to get faxed to Yashimoto.'

'And he won't ask Stephen or Andrea for it?'

He shrugged. 'I don't know.'

'So what's the worst that will happen? You'll lose a few thousand?'

'Maybe more.'

'Does it matter? I mean, it's not as if you're strapped, Max. You don't ever have to work again if you don't want to. A few pounds, a few days out of a lifetime, isn't so much to ask, is it?'

He turned slowly back to her, his eyes bleak. 'I thought we had it all. I thought we were happy.'

'We were—but it all just got too much, Max. And I'm not going back to it, so if you can't do this, can't learn to delegate and take time out to enjoy your family, then we don't have a future. And, to have a future, we have to be able to trust each other.'

He didn't move for a moment, but then he sighed softly, threw her phone back into her bag and straightened up.

'You'd better show me how to work the washing machine, then, hadn't you?' he said with a little twisted smile, and she felt the breath ease out of her lungs.

'It'll be a pleasure,' she said, almost giddy with relief, and, leading him into the utility room, she introduced him to the concept of home laundry.

CHAPTER FOUR

THE babies were cute.

Sweet, messy, temperamental and cute. And *boring*.

Not when they were awake, but when they were asleep, and Jules was asleep, and the house was so quiet he wanted to scream.

And it struck him he was the one doing all the adjusting.

How fair was that? Not fair at all, he thought, simmering, and it hadn't been his idea that he'd been cut out of their lives.

So far—thirty-odd hours in—he'd learned to run a bath the right temperature, how to put the washing machine on, how to aim food at a baby's face, not always successfully, and how not to drink tea. That had been lesson one, and one he was unlikely ever to forget.

But now, at eleven o'clock at night, when he would usually be working on for at least another three hours, Julia had gone to bed, the babies were settled till the morning and there was nothing to do.

Nothing on the television, no way of keeping in touch with Yashimoto—who would by then have been back in the office, because he started early—and no way of contacting anyone in New York, where they'd all still be at work.

He paced around the kitchen, made tea, threw it down the sink, because he'd drunk gallons of the stuff during the day, and contemplated the wine he'd brought back the night before from the pub. He'd only had a couple of glasses, so there was nearly two bottles, but he didn't drink alone. Dangerous.

Then he thought of the pub.

He stepped out of the back door to let Murphy out into the garden, and coincidentally see if the pub lights were on, and realised it was in darkness. Of course it was, he thought in disgust. It was a gastro-pub in the country—a restaurant, really, more than a pub—and they stopped serving at something ridiculous like nine, so he couldn't even go there and drown his sorrows. And it was so damned *quiet*!

Except for that screaming he could hear in the background. He'd heard it a moment ago, and now he was standing outside the French doors he could hear it clearly, a truly blood-curdling noise, and it chilled him to the bone. Murphy's hackles were up and he was growling softly, so Max called him back inside and shut the door, then went upstairs and knocked on Julia's bedroom door. She opened it a moment later, wearing pyjamas with cats all over them and rumpled with sleep, and he had to force himself to stick to the point.

'There's a noise,' he said without preamble, not letting himself look at the little cats running about all over her body. 'Screaming. I think someone's being attacked.'

She cocked her head on one side, listened, and then smiled. 'It's a badger,' she said. 'Or a fox. They both scream at night. I'm not sure which is which, but at this time of year I think it's probably a badger. The foxes make more noise in the spring. Did it wake you?'

And then she looked at him and sighed. 'Oh, Max—you haven't been to bed yet, have you? You ought to sleep. You're exhausted.'

'I'm not exhausted. I'm never asleep at this time of night.'

'Well, you should be,' she scolded softly, then went back into her bedroom and emerged again, stuffing her arms into a fluffy robe that hid the cats, to his disappointment. 'Tea?'

He didn't want tea. The last thing he wanted was tea, but he would have drunk neat acid just then to have her company.

'Tea sounds great,' he said gruffly, and followed her downstairs.

It couldn't be easy for him, to be lobbed in at the deep end, and it didn't get much deeper than twins. He'd never been someone who needed much sleep, and, with nothing to do in the night but think, he must be turning this whole situation over and over in his mind.

Good, she told herself. Maybe he'd see the error of his ways.

Or maybe she'd just drive him away.

'Is there any wood on the fire?' she asked, and he shrugged.

'I don't know. There was. I put the guard up—does it stay alight all night?'

'I don't normally light it,' she confessed. 'The girls and I spend most of our time in the kitchen.'

'So why did you ask?'

'Because I thought—I've got DVDs of the girls, right from when they were born. Actually, from before. I've got a 4D-DVD of the scan. It's amazing.'

'4D?'

'Mmm—3D and real time. They call it 4D. You can see them moving, and it's amazingly real. And I've got lots of stuff of them when they were in special care, and all the things they do for you, like hand- and footprints and their tiny little name-bands and weight charts and stuff like that. I thought, if it was warm in there, we could watch them, but you'll probably think it's all really boring—'

'No! No, I won't. I—I'd like to see,' he said gruffly, sounding curiously unlike Max, uncertain and hesitant. He was never hesitant, and she looked at him searchingly.

'Good,' she said softly. 'Go and see if you can revive the fire, and I'll bring us tea.'

And biscuits, some rather gorgeous chocolate biscuits that were more chocolate than biscuit, and some cheese and crackers, because she knew he'd be hungry and he frankly needed fattening up.

He was crouching by the fire when she went in, blowing on the embers and trying to breathe life into the glowing remains, and as she put the tray down the logs flickered to life and a lovely orange glow lit the hearth.

'Oh, that's super. Well done. Here, have some cheese and biscuits,' she instructed, and rummaged in the cupboard next to the television for the DVDs.

'Scan first?' she suggested, and his brows pulled down slightly, as if he was troubled.

He nodded, and she slipped it into the slot and sat back against the front of the sofa by his legs, cradling her tea in her hands while the images of the unborn babies unrolled in front of them.

'How pregnant were you when this was taken?' he asked

softly, a little edge in his voice that she'd never heard before, and she swivelled round and looked up at him, puzzled.

'Twenty-six weeks.'

A shadow went over his face, and he pressed his lips together and stared at the screen as if his life depended on it. She turned back and watched it with him, but she was deeply conscious of a tension in him that she'd never felt before. When the DVD was finished and she took it out, she felt the tension leave him, and, as he leant back against the sofa to drink his tea, his hand shook a little.

Odd. Max's hands never shook. Ever. Under any circumstances. And yet he'd always been so adamant that he didn't want children, that their lives were complete without them. So why had the images of his children before they were born been so moving to him?

The fire was roaring away now, and Murphy heaved himself up from his position in front of it and came over, flopping down against Max's legs. Max leant down and scratched the dog's neck and pulled his ears, an absent expression on his face, and Murphy lifted his head and gazed adoringly at Max as if he'd just found his soulmate.

'I think you've got a new friend,' she said, and Max gave a crooked little grin and smoothed Murph's head with a gentle hand.

'Apparently so. I expect he misses John.'

'I expect he wants the crackers on your plate,' she said pragmatically, and Max chuckled and the mood lifted a fraction, and she breathed a little easier.

'So—what's next?' he asked, and she put on the first film of the girls after they'd been born.

'Here they are—they're two days old. They were born at thirty-three weeks, because my uterus was having trouble expanding because of the scarring and they'd stopped growing. Jane and Peter came in and filmed it for me. They were amazing—so supportive.'

'I would have been supportive,' he said, his voice rough, and she felt another stab of guilt.

'I didn't know that, Max. You'd always been so against the idea of children. If I even so much as mentioned IVF you flew off the handle. How was I to know you wanted to be involved?'

'You could have asked me. You could have given me the choice.'

She could have. She could have, but she hadn't, and it was too late now to change it. But she could apologise, she realised, and she turned towards him and took his hand.

'I'm really sorry,' she said, making herself meet his eyes and steeling herself for the anger that she knew she'd see in them. But instead of anger there was pain. 'Max?' she whispered, and he pulled his hand away and stood up.

'Maybe we'll do this another time,' he said, and without a word he headed for the door. She heard him go upstairs; heard the bathroom door close and water running. With a sigh she turned off the DVD player and the television, put the fire-guard up and cleared away their cups and plates, then put Murphy out one last time before shutting him in the kitchen and going upstairs.

She heard the shower turn off as she went into her own bedroom and closed the door, then a few minutes later she heard him come out of the bathroom and go down the landing to his bedroom, closing the door with a soft click.

She didn't sleep for hours, and, when she woke, it was to hear the back door open and Max calling the dog. The sky was just light, the day barely started, and, as she lifted herself up on one elbow, she saw Max heading down the drive with Murphy trotting beside him. He was wearing jogging bottoms and trainers with a T-shirt, and she watched him turn out onto the hill, cross the river and run away up through the village out of sight, the dog at his heels.

She didn't know what was wrong, but she had a feeling it wasn't the obvious. There just seemed to be something else going on, something she didn't know about, and she didn't know if she could ask.

Probably not. He'd been pretty unapproachable last night. Maybe he'd tell her in his own good time, but one thing was absolutely certain.

Max was right out of his comfort zone, and living with him for the next two weeks was going to be interesting, to say the least.

Not to mention frustrating and heartbreaking and undoubtedly painful.

She just hoped it would prove to be worth it…

He ran along the lane out of the village, turned left along another tiny, winding lane, cut down across a field and over the river on a flat iron bridge—used by tractors, he supposed—and then up to a bridlepath that cut through to the village again just opposite the drive to Rose Cottage.

It had taken twenty minutes, so he supposed it was about three miles. Not far enough to numb him, but enough to take the edge off it and distract him from the endless turmoil in his mind.

The light was on in the kitchen as he jogged across the drive, and Jules was watching him, her face unreadable at that distance through the old leaded lights. But she had her arms full of washing or something, and she was in that fluffy dressing-gown again, presumably with the little cats underneath.

He suppressed a groan and walked the last few steps to the back door and let himself in, a wet and muddy Murphy by his side.

'Bed!' she ordered, and the dog turned and went into his bed in the space under the stairs.

'Is that just him, or do I have to go in there, too?' Max asked, and she smiled a little uncertainly and searched his face with troubled eyes.

'Are you all right?'

'Fine. We've had a good run—'

She stopped him with her hand on his arm and looked up into his eyes with that way of hers that made him feel uncomfortable and vulnerable. 'Are you really all right?'

'I'm fine,' he said, a little more sincerely, because he was, really. It was just that DVD which had stirred things up, made him sad and emotional all over again, and he hated it. Hated being out of control of his feelings—hated his feelings, full stop.

'I've made tea,' she said, and he opened his mouth to tell her he didn't want any damn tea, then shut it, smiled and nodded.

'Thanks. Are the babies awake yet?'

She shook her head. 'No. They will be soon. Why?'

'Oh, just wondered. I need a shower, but I don't want to disturb them. I'll have my tea and wait a bit, if you can stand me all sweaty and mud-splattered.'

She ran her eyes over him and gave a tiny huff of laughter, but, as she turned away, he noticed a soft brush of colour in her cheeks. Really? He could still do that to her?

'I'm sure I can stand you for long enough to drink your tea,' she said lightly, but her voice was a little strange, not quite itself, and she was folding and smoothing nappies on top of the Aga as if her life depended on it.

He thought of their kiss, just the lightest touch of his lips to hers, and heat seared through him. Because he wanted to do it again, wanted to haul her up against him and tunnel his fingers through that tousled, rumpled hair, and plunder her mouth with his until she was whimpering with need and clawing at him for more...

'On second thoughts, maybe I'll go and have a look through my clothes and find something to wear after my shower,' he said, and retreated to the door before he embarrassed himself.

'What's wrong with yesterday's new clothes?' she asked, and he hesitated in the doorway, one foot on the bottom of the stairs just outside in the hall, and looked at her over his shoulder.

'Nothing. I just wasn't sure if I they'd be right for what we're doing today.'

'So what are we doing?' she asked, looking puzzled.

Good question. 'Taking the girls to the seaside,' he told her, thinking on his feet. 'It's a gorgeous day, and the forecast is mild and sunny all day.'

'In which case your jeans and jumper will be perfect.

Come back and sit down and drink your tea. If you start banging about in the room next to them, they *will* wake up, at this time of day, and frankly the peace is short-lived enough.'

He swallowed, crushed the lust that was threatening to give him away. But he needn't have worried because she scooped up the washing and carried it out to the utility room, and he took his tea over to the sofa in the bay window and sat down with one foot hitched up on the other knee, and by the time she came back in he had himself back under control.

Just.

He was right, it was a gorgeous day.

They took the babies to Felixstowe, parked the car at one end of the prom and walked all the way along to the other end. The wind was from the north-west, so they were totally sheltered by the low cliffs at the north end. But, when they turned back into the wind, it was a little cooler so Max turned the buggy round and towed it, while she walked beside him and enjoyed the freedom of being able to swing her arms as she walked.

'Do you know,' she pointed out, 'that, apart from corporate trips when we've been abroad, this is the first time in six years that we've been to the beach?'

He glanced sideways at her and pulled a face. 'I suppose you're right. It's not something I've ever thought of doing—not in England, anyway. And I've never been a beach-holiday person.'

'I'm not talking about beach holidays,' she said. 'I'm talking about walking by the sea, with a good, stiff breeze tugging my hair and the taste of salt on my skin. It's gorgeous—bracing and healthy and—oh, wonderful!'

And then she looked at him, and saw him watching her with something very familiar and deeply disturbing in his eyes, and she coloured and turned away quickly. 'Oh look—there's a ship coming in,' she said, which was ridiculous because there had been lots, but she caught his smile out of the corner of her eye and the breath stuck in her throat.

He had no right doing that to her—bringing back so many memories with just one slow, lazy smile. They might not have walked on the beach, but they'd made love many, many times on their roof terrace overlooking the Thames, with the smell of the river drifting up to them and the salty tang in the air. And she could tell, just from that one glance, that he was remembering it as well.

'I'll just make sure the babies are all right,' she said hastily, and, going round to the other side of the buggy, she tucked them up and then followed behind, staring at his shoulders as he towed the babies and strolled along with the air of a man who did it every day of the week.

Just like a real father, with a wife and two beautiful children, not a pressed man who'd been forced to submit to some bonding time with his newly discovered infants.

Oh, what a mess.

Would they ever get out of it?

'Jules?'

She realised she'd stopped, and he'd stopped, too, and had turned to look at her, his eyes troubled.

He let go of the buggy and came round to her side. 'What's wrong?'

She shrugged, unable to speak, and with a little sigh he put his arms round her and eased her against his chest.

'Hey, it'll be all right,' he murmured, but she wasn't so sure. It was less than two days, and he'd already broken the rules by stealing her phone and trying to find his. Goodness knows what else he'd do while her back was turned. He was up half the night—could he be using her phone?

Did she care? So long as he was there in the day and trying, did it matter if he cheated?

Yes!

Or—no, not really, so long as he learned the work-life balance lesson?

'Come on, let's go and get a coffee. There's a little café I noticed near the car. I've brought drinks for the girls, and maybe they can warm up their jars.'

'Gloop?' he said, looking wary, and she thought of his new jumper and smiled.

'It's OK, I'll feed them, if you like,' she promised. 'I'll just let you pay.'

'It'll be a pleasure,' he said with a sigh of relief, and, going back to the other side of the buggy, he towed it the rest of the way to the car without a murmur.

The babies were ready for bed early that night.

'It must be the sea air,' Jules said as she heated their supper—pots of home-made food this time, he noticed, and wondered if it was better for them.

'Does that have all the right nutrients in it?' he asked, and she stared at him as if he was mad.

'It's food—not a chemical formula. Roast chicken,

broccoli, carrots, roast potatoes, gravy made with stock—of course it's got all the right nutrients.'

'And you cooked it?'

'Well, of course I cooked it!' she said with an exasperated sigh. 'Who else?'

He shrugged. 'Sorry. It's just—I hardly ever saw you cook, and I don't think you ever did a roast.'

'No, of course not. We never had that long to do something so unimportant—'

'Jules, stop it! I was just—'

'What? Criticising the way I'm looking after my children?'

'They're my children, too!'

'So learn how to cook for them,' she said crossly, and threw a cookery book at him. 'Here you go. There's chicken breast, mince, salmon steaks, prawns and pork chops in the freezer. Take your pick. You can do supper for us while I get the girls in bed.'

And, stalking off with one of them in each arm, she left him sitting there staring blankly at the book.

Jeez. He could make coffee and toast and scrambled eggs, at a push. And he could unwrap stuff and shove it in the microwave, or pick up the phone and order.

But—cook? Real ingredients? Hell's teeth, he hadn't done that for years. Fifteen years? Not since…

He opened the book and flicked through the pages. What was it they'd had in the pub? Chicken breast stuffed with brie and wrapped in bacon, or something like that. She'd given him cheese last night—not brie, but cheddar. Would that do? Maybe. And how about bacon?

He stepped over the dog and investigated the fridge.

No bacon. No brie, either, come to that, and very little cheddar.

But there was pesto, and he thought he'd seen some pasta in the store cupboard in the kitchen when she'd been rummaging for biscuits.

So—pasta with chicken and pesto? A few toasted pine-nuts and a bag of salad…

No salad. Probably no pine nuts.

Peppers?

He hauled out a few things he'd seen served with similar dishes, set them all on the kitchen table and settled down with them to try and find a recipe that tied at least some of them in. Then, having found one, he had to work out how to use the microwave and, worse, how to use the Aga. Or even find the tools to reach that point.

Starting with a sharp knife, and a chopping board, and a deep, heavy pan. That was what the instructions said.

He found them, thawed and sliced the chicken, fried it in the pan with olive oil, onion and peppers, opened the pesto—and discovered mould.

Damn!

But there was rice, too, and prawns, so—how about paella? How the hell did you make paella?

He turned back to the book, wondering how long, exactly, Jules could remove herself from the kitchen. Long enough for him to ruin every single ingredient!

Simple. He'd order something in. Even she couldn't object to him doing that on the house phone.

Except he was supposed to be doing this himself, and rising to a challenge wasn't something that normally held him back. So—paella. How hard could it be?

* * *

'Oh! Risotto?' she said hesitantly, poking it and sniffing.

'Paella,' he corrected. 'The pesto was off.'

'Oh, it would be. There's a new one in the cupboard.'

He rolled his eyes and sighed. 'Right. Well, I was adaptable,' he said, sounding pleased with himself, and she sniffed again.

'How much garlic did you use?'

'I don't know. It said two cloves. It seemed a lot, so I only used one.'

'Clove, or bulb?'

He frowned in confusion. 'What's the difference?'

'Um—the bulb is the whole thing, a silvery-white papery thing with bumps and a stalk in the middle. A clove is one of the little bits inside.'

He scowled and turned away. 'Well, you should have been here if you're going to complain.'

'Hey, I haven't complained.'

'You haven't tasted it yet.'

'Well, so it might be a bit garlicky. So what? I'm not going to kiss anyone, am I?' she said, and then wished furiously that she could repossess her words, because he turned slowly and studied her.

'It could be arranged,' he murmured, his eyes dragging slowly over her as if he was trying to peel away her clothes.

'In your dreams,' she muttered, and took out two bowls. 'Here—dish up. I'll get us a drink. Do you want some of that wine?'

'I wouldn't mind the white. The red could be a bit heavy.'

'Oh, I don't know,' she said wickedly. 'It might balance the garlic.'

Foolish girl. He threw the spoon back into the pan and

stalked off into the hall, disappearing out of the front door and slamming it behind him, shrugging on his jacket as he went.

Oops. That had been mean of her to tease him. She knew he couldn't cook, and he'd done his best. And, apart from the garlic and the fact that it was a bit over-cooked, it looked fine.

His car—the sports car, the silly, fast, dangerous one— shot off the drive in a spray of gravel, and she sighed and covered the pan, pulled it to the side and sat down to wait. Either he'd come back, she thought, in which case she'd apologise, or he wouldn't, in which case—

What? She'd lost the girls their father, and herself the only man she'd ever loved, just for the sake of keeping her sassy mouth shut?

Oh, damn. And she couldn't even phone him to apologise.

CHAPTER FIVE

HE HIT the M25 before he saw sense, and he came off at the first junction, pulled up in the tatty, run-down service area, cut the engine and slammed his hands down on the steering wheel.

What the hell was he doing? She'd been *teasing* him! That was all. Nothing drastic. She'd always teased him, but he'd forgotten. Forgotten all sorts of things. What it felt like to hold her, what it felt like to touch her, to bury himself inside her—

He swallowed hard. No. He couldn't let himself think about that. It was too soon; he was way off being allowed that close to her. But he wanted her, wanted to touch her, to hold her, to feel her warmth.

God, he was *lonely*. So damned lonely without her.

So he couldn't do this, couldn't throw in the towel, give up on his beautiful little girls and run away, because she'd teased him about the bloody garlic!

With a shaky sigh, he started the engine, pulled out of the car park, shot back down the slip road onto the A12 and went back to his wife.

* * *

He wasn't coming back.

She'd sat in the window, huddled by the glass with a fleece wrapped round her shoulders and waited until the pub was shut, but there was still no sign of him.

What if he'd broken down? What if he'd gone off the road in a fit of temper? He seemed so angry these days, angrier than she'd ever seen him. Was that her fault? It must be. What else could it be?

And now he was who knew where, maybe lying upside down in a ditch full of water.

Lights sliced across the garden, blinding her with the glare of his headlamps as he turned in and cut the engine. The security lights came on as he got out of the car, and then she heard the car door slam and his feet crunch across the gravel as he approached the front door.

He paused and looked at her through the window, his face sombre, and then, with a slight shake of his head, he walked to the door, and she heard it open and close. Then he was there, filling the hall doorway with his brooding, silent presence.

'I'm sorry,' he said.

'No, I'm sorry,' she said, getting up and walking towards him, her foot a little stiff from sitting with it tucked under her for so long while she watched for him. 'I shouldn't have been so mean to you.'

'It's OK. It's not your fault,' he said gruffly. 'I overreacted.'

'No, you didn't. You were doing your best. I know you can't cook, and I should have given you more help, not just flung you in at the deep end and expected you to cope because you criticised me.'

'I didn't. Or, at least, I didn't mean to. I was just asking. I'm sorry if it came over as criticism.'

So many sorries. From Max? She shook her head slowly and went over to the Aga. 'Forget it. Have you eaten?'

'No. I was going home. I'd got to the M25 before I came to my senses.'

She frowned. 'That's fifty miles!'

'I know. I was— Well, let's just say it took a while for me to calm down. Which is ridiculous. So, in answer to your question, no, I haven't eaten, and yes, please, if it isn't ruined. Not that I think you could ruin it. I'd already done a fair job.'

'It'll be fine,' she told him, determined to eat it if it choked her. 'So, I believe I was going to pour you a glass of wine?'

He gave a choked laugh. 'That sounds good.'

'Red or white?'

He smiled. 'I'll finish the red. It'll balance the garlic,' he said with irony, and she smiled back and handed him the bottle and a glass. She turned back to the paella, taking the lid off and blinking at the smell, but she dished up without a word, and they sat down at the table and ate it in a slightly strained and civilised silence, until finally Max pushed it away and met her eyes.

'Bit heavy on the seasoning for me,' he said wryly, and she put her fork down and smiled with him.

'I'm not really hungry,' she lied. 'Shall I make some tea?'

'No. I'm fine with the wine, but I could do with some toast or something.'

'Cheese and biscuits? Or I might be able to find an apple pie in the freezer I could put in the oven?'

'Sounds nice. We can have it later, after the cheese and biscuits.'

She chuckled and cleared away the table, put the cheese and biscuits out and the apple pie in the oven, then got herself a glass and poured a little wine into it.

'Sorry, I didn't realise you wanted some.'

'It's OK. I don't usually, because I'm still feeding them, but tonight—well, I just thought I'd join you.'

'Feel free.'

She swirled it round in the glass, then met his eyes over the top of it. 'So—why were you so angry?' she asked tentatively. 'It wasn't just the garlic thing.'

He sighed sharply and ran his hand through his hair, then met her eyes again. 'I don't know, it's— Well, it's this place, really.'

'The cottage? It's lovely!'

'Oh, I'm sure, but I just hate the idea of it. You're my wife, Jules. I don't want you living in another man's house.'

She pulled back and leant against the chair, eyeing him over the table and wondering if she'd been a bit too quick to forgive. 'Isn't it fortunate, then, that it's nothing to do with you? Because we're happy here.'

'And you couldn't be happy in your own house?'

'You mean your own house?'

He sighed. 'No, yours. I'd buy you one—in your own name. God knows I owe you that, at the very least, if you won't come back to me. We're talking about housing my children, for heaven's sake.'

'I can house your children.'

'Yes, in someone else's house, living off his generosity! I don't like it, Jules. I don't like it at all. I don't like staying here, I don't like the idea that he could come back at any time and have the right to be here. I want privacy while we sort this out, and all the time I feel as if I'm waiting for the other shoe to drop.'

She studied him thoughtfully for a moment, then gave a gentle sigh. 'Well, then, perhaps it's just as well that you want to buy me a house, because he's coming back in a month and I'm going to be homeless.'

His eyes narrowed. 'You could always come back to me.'

'What, to the apartment? I hardly think so.'

'We could buy a house in London. Hampstead, or somewhere like that, or Barnes or Richmond—'

'Or I could stay here in Suffolk, near my friends.'

'You've got friends here?'

He sounded so shocked and surprised she nearly laughed. 'Well, of course I have. Jane and Peter, and I've made other friends, lots of them, through the hospital and the twins' support group, and the Real Nappy network—'

'The *what*?'

'The Real Nappy network. And there's a coffee group for young mums in the village which I go to.'

He stared at her as if she'd sprouted horns.

'So—you want to stay out here?'

'Yes. At least—until we know how it's going to go with us. I don't have any infrastructure in London, Max. I'd be so lonely there, and I know if we're in London you'll just be off all the time, popping into the office for a minute or whatever, and before I know what's what you'll be in New York or Tokyo or Sydney.'

'OK. So you want a house here. Are there any for sale?'

She did laugh at that. 'I have no idea, Max. I haven't been looking.'

'So what were you going to do?'

She looked down, her laughter dying. 'I'm not sure.' Go back to him? No. But tell him? Contact him? Almost certainly, because not to do so was too unfair.

'How's the pie?'

'Oh. I don't know.'

She opened the oven and pulled it out; it was crisp and golden and full of the fragrance of apples. 'It's done.'

'So let's eat it, and worry about the house later.'

Hell. She wanted to stay out here, in the middle of Suffolk?

With her friends—friends he'd never met—friends he'd only heard about, because she'd hardly ever seen them, so he hadn't been able to track her down through them because he'd had no idea how to go about finding them.

She'd met up with Jane in town a few times, spent a weekend or two with her when they'd lived in Berkshire. He dimly remembered her saying they were moving, but not where to, just that it would be further. And, since he'd had no idea what Jane's surname was, that hadn't been a lot of help.

And they were more important to her than him?

No. Stop it. She hadn't said that. She'd simply said that, until they knew what was happening with them, she wanted to stay near her infrastructure.

Well, he could understand that. He felt pretty damn lost without his.

'Is it OK?'

He frowned. What?

'The pie—is it OK?'

The pie. He stared at his plate, almost empty, and realised he'd hardly tasted it. He blinked in surprise.

'Yes, it's fine. It's lovely. Thanks.'

'You were miles away.'

He gave her a crooked smile. 'Actually, no, I was right here, wondering what happens next,' he confessed.

'Next?'

'About the house, I mean.'

She stared at him for a second, then looked hastily away, soft colour invading her cheeks. 'Oh. Um—right. Well, I suppose I have to start looking.'

What on earth had she thought he was talking about? Unless…

No. She wasn't interested; she'd made that clear. She'd been giving out hands-off signals since he'd arrived, pretty much. Apart from that one stolen kiss that she'd stopped in its tracks, she hadn't so much as brushed against him except by accident.

So why was she blushing?

'We could look on the Internet,' she said, and he felt his radar leap to life.

'Internet?'

'Mmm—in the study. It's John's, but he's happy for me to use it. He emails me regularly, and I reply, telling him how things are and sending him photos of Murphy and the babies.'

The babies? She sent John Blake photos of his babies? And then he stopped thinking about John Blake and paid attention to the core business.

There was a computer in the house. A computer with Internet access. Which meant he could check his email, keep in touch with his colleagues and employees, and keep an eye on what was going on in the financial markets. Before he went completely insane from the lack of information.

'Good idea,' he said. 'Let's load the dishwasher and go and have a look.'

'Sure.'

She went over to the sink and scraped the remains of their meal down the sink into the waste-disposal unit, then turned back to get the rest of the things just as he arrived at her elbow with another plate and a pan.

'Whoops,' he said with a grin, shifting the pan out of the way before she collided with it, and instead she collided with his chest, her soft, full breasts squashing against him and her eyes flying up to meet his, wide and startled.

'Steady,' he murmured, putting the pan down on the side and setting the plate back onto the table, and then, suddenly reluctant to lose that soft, warm contact, he let his arms drift round her and drew her closer.

'Max?' she whispered, her voice little more than a breath. But it was enough—just that soft word telling him all he needed to know about how much she wanted him, and, without waiting for any further invitation, he lowered his head, closed his eyes and touched his mouth to hers.

She couldn't let him do this.

She couldn't...

She must taste of garlic. How he could tell after the paella, she didn't know, but she thought back to their row, to her comment that it didn't matter because nobody was going to kiss her.

But Max was kissing her as if his life depended on it—

and suddenly she didn't care about the garlic, only about kissing him back, feeling the strength of his arms around her, the powerful thighs bracketing hers, the harsh sound of his breathing muffled against her face as he plundered her mouth with his, his lips and tongue urgent, his body hard against hers, trapping her between him and the sink so she was under no illusions about his reaction.

One hand slid round under her jumper and cradled her breast, and she whimpered softly. The sound caught in his mouth and echoed back to her in a deep, primitive groan that was dragged up from his boots.

'Jules, I need you,' he whispered harshly, his mouth tracking over her jaw, his teeth nipping her, not enough to hurt but just enough to drive her further over the edge. And then his tongue stroked over the tiny insult, soothing, tasting, his lips dragging softly over her skin and leaving fire in their wake.

He was driving her crazy, and he knew it, but she couldn't stop him. There was no way she could stop him, because she needed this every bit as much as he did.

Or so she thought, until the little voice clamouring at the back of her subconscious fought its way up to the surface and she realised that one of the babies was crying. Suddenly Max was shunted off the top of her list, and she felt the passion die away, replaced by the fundamental fact of her motherhood.

'Max,' she said, turning her head away, and he groaned and dropped his head onto her shoulder.

'No, Jules. Don't stop me, for God's sake, please.'

'The babies,' she said, and he went still for a second, then sighed heavily and eased away, slashes of colour on his cheekbones, his eyes dark with arousal as he stared down at her. His chest was heaving, and, after the longest moment, he closed his eyes and turned away.

'Go and sort them out,' he said. 'I'll wait for you.'

But she knew that would be the stupidest thing she could do.

'No, Max. I don't think that's a good idea. I'm going to go to bed.'

'No!'

'Yes. I'm sorry. It's not— We aren't ready yet.'

He gave a rude snort, and, without waiting for him to say another thing, she fled for the stairs.

'She's not ready, Murphy. What do you think of that?'

Murphy thumped his tail and gazed up at Max with adoring eyes, and he sighed and rubbed the dog's ears gently. 'Yeah, I quite agree. Rubbish, isn't it? What am I going to do if she's never ready, Murphs? This is driving me crazy. The whole damn situation's driving me crazy.'

He poured the last glass of wine out of the bottle and stared morosely at it. If only there was something to *do*!

Something more gripping than taking his wife to bed and making love to her until she was so desperate for him that she couldn't speak, couldn't breathe, couldn't do anything except scream and sob with need.

He swore, short and to the point, and, picking up the TV remote, he turned the set on and channel-hopped. Nothing. Even the news was dull, nothing to hold his interest, and he was on the point of hurling the handset through the window when Jules appeared in the doorway, dressed in her little cat-pyjamas and that fluffy dressing gown, her bare feet sticking out of the bottom and looking vulnerable and appealing.

He wanted to kiss them, take each toe in his mouth and suck it slowly.

'Is it safe to come in?'

He gave a rough sigh. 'Yes, it's safe. I'm sorry. It's just—it's been a hell of a long time.'

She nodded and came in, perching on the edge of the chair opposite him and eyeing him warily. 'I'm not really being fair to you, am I? You're not used to this, and you must be bored to death.'

'I am. There's just nothing for me to do except think about you and wonder what the hell I did that was so wrong.'

'Nothing. You did nothing. That was the trouble, Max. You just carried on as you always had, and took me with you. And it wasn't enough.'

'It was enough for me. I loved working with you—watching your incredible ability to organise and sort stuff. Things just happened when you were around, and it was amazing. I didn't realise what I'd got until I lost you.'

She sighed softly, and huddled further down in her dressing gown. 'Max, if this is going to work, you're going to have to cut back on your time in the office, you know that, don't you? Your time away, particularly. It's just not conducive to family life.'

'My family managed. My father worked the same sort of hours.'

'And he died of a heart attack at forty-nine! That's only eleven years away for you, Max. Your daughters will be just starting secondary school. And I'll be a widow at forty-four. That's not something to look forward to.'

God. Eleven years? Was that all? No wonder his mother had found another man to share her life. She was only sixty-two now, fit and active and full of life. And her husband had died far too young; he could see that now.

Was that in store for him? Would he go to work one day and find not his PA but the Grim Reaper waiting for him, as his father had?

'I'm doing it for us,' he said, but his words had a hollow ring to them, and she shook her head.

'No. You're doing it for you, because you can, because you're driven by the need to succeed, but there are other ways to succeed, Max—other things you can do.'

'Such as?'

She shrugged. 'Be a good father to your children? Enjoy your life? Take up a hobby—sport of some kind. Not running. That's just a solitary thing you do to stop you thinking.'

Hell. Was there anything this woman missed?

'Fancy a game of chess?' she asked out of the blue, and he stared at her and then gave a soft chuckle.

'Yeah, why not? Although I'll probably beat you.'

'I doubt it. I've been practising. I play with John when he's here.'

Him again.

'Does he beat you?'

'Not often.'

Well, there was a challenge. He leant back and smiled. 'Bring it on,' he said softly.

Oh, dear. She recognised that look.

Oh, well, at least it wouldn't be boring. She got the chess pieces out, opened the coffee-table to reveal a chess board, then took a black and white pawn, shuffled them behind her back and held her closed fists out.

'Right,' he said, and she opened her right hand and sighed at his smug grin.

'OK, you start,' she said, and handed him the white pieces.

It was all downhill from there, really, because she was finding it really hard to concentrate.

'Check.'

She stared at the board in disbelief. What on earth had happened to her? She'd completely lost her focus.

She moved her queen, he tutted and took her bishop, and said, 'Check.'

Again? She stared at the board for ages, conscious of Max's hands dangling loosely between his knees, his shoulders hunched over, broad and square and powerful, his head so close she could see the individual hairs, soft and glossy and so enticing.

'Are you sure you want to do that?'

She looked down at the board, muttered under her breath and changed her mind, then sat back. 'OK.'

'Oh, dear.' He moved his final piece, gave her a wicked smile and murmured, 'I believe you'll find that's checkmate.'

What? 'Oh, rats,' she said, slumping back against the chair. 'I'd forgotten how good you are.'

'I'll take that as a compliment,' he said with a smile, and set the pieces up again.

'Oh, no,' she said, laughing and holding up her hands. 'Not tonight. I'm tired and I'm just not focusing. We'll have another go tomorrow.'

By which time she'd have pulled herself together and repossessed her mind.

'Right, it really is time for bed,' she said, and met his eyes. 'Max, why don't you have an early night?'

'What, and lie just feet away from you and think about you? I don't think so. It's been over a year, Jules. That's a long time.'

And then it occurred to her that, in that year, there might have been another woman. Several, in fact. Did she want to know?

Yes.

'Have you—have there…?' She trailed off, unable to say the words, but he understood and let his breath out on a huff of disbelief.

'You really think that of me? Julia, we're married. I may not have been the best husband, but I meant my vows. I haven't looked at, or touched, or thought about another woman since I met you. And, since you left me, I've thought about very little else. So, forgive me if I don't want to go upstairs and lie down politely within spitting distance of you and go quietly to sleep!'

She felt hot colour scorch her cheeks, and stood up hastily and headed for the door. 'I'm sorry. I didn't mean to be so insensitive. For what it's worth, I've missed you, too.'

'Jules! Julia, wait!'

She stopped, her hand on the latch, and he came up behind her and turned her gently into his arms.

'I'm sorry. I'm just ratty because I need you. I'm feeling like a caged lion at the moment, and I'm lashing out at anything in range. And it just happens to be you, every time. And it's rubbish, because all I want to do is hold you—'

And, without another word, he folded her carefully against his chest and rested his head against hers. She could feel his heart beating, feel the tension radiating off him, but she knew it would go no further, that he wouldn't kiss her or touch her or do anything she didn't invite directly, because for all his faults he loved her.

'Oh, Max,' she sighed, and, sliding her arms around him, she held him close. 'I'm sorry it's so difficult.'

'It doesn't need to be. You could come back to me.'

'We've been through that,' she reminded him, and eased out of his arms. 'I'm not coming back—not until I have concrete proof that you're changing for good. And, so far, there's no evidence of that at all.'

He stared down at her sombrely, then nodded. 'OK. So tomorrow, let's go to London, and we'll go to the office and I'll make some calls and see what I can do. And I'd like to go and see my mother.'

His mother! Of course! She'd missed her. Linda Gallagher was the closest thing she had to a mother now, and she knew the woman would be more than supportive of her in trying to get Max to cut back on his hours. After all, she'd lost her own husband far too young, and she wouldn't want the same thing to happen to her son. And she'd adore the babies.

'Have you told her yet?'

He shook his head. 'No. How can I? I don't have a phone,' he said with irony, and she sighed.

'You could have used the house phone for that.'

'Only I don't have the number.'

'You should know your mother's number,' she chided, and he shrugged.

'Why? It's in my phone—only, silly me, I don't have my phone any more, it seems, because it's been confiscated.'

'I'd give it back to you if I felt I could trust you,' she said frankly, and his mouth twitched.

'Better keep it, then,' he said softly, and, bending his

head, he brushed his lips over hers. 'Go to bed, Jules. I'll see you in the morning—and we'll go and sort everything out.'

If only she could believe it.

CHAPTER SIX

'I'D BETTER make some calls,' he said as they sat over breakfast the next morning. 'Prime Andrea.'

'What about your mother?'

He pulled a face. 'Yeah. Her, too. But mostly business.'

'I'll get your phone,' she said, and ran upstairs to retrieve it from the safety of her bedroom. She went back down and handed it to him. 'You seem to have a few missed calls that have got under Andrea's radar,' she said wryly, and he glanced at the screen and gave a frustrated sigh.

'I have to deal with some of these.'

'I don't doubt it. You've got an hour,' she told him, and, scooping up the babies, she took them upstairs and bathed and dressed them.

'You're going to meet your grandmother today,' she told them with a smile. 'She's going to love you.' But she might not be so warm with her daughter-in-law, Julia realised sadly, her smile fading. A whole year—more—of being out of contact while Max had searched for her might not have done anything to endear her to the woman, and she re-gretted that.

But how could she have stayed in touch and yet not have

kept Max informed? She couldn't, but she felt another stab of guilt. Max might not have been the most reasonable of husbands, but he'd never kept anything from her, and she was beginning to realise just how much she'd done him wrong by not telling him she was pregnant.

'Oh, Ava, no!' she cried, reaching out and catching the baby before she toppled over backwards. 'When did you learn to stand up? You're going to be such a pixie, aren't you?'

Ava grinned and giggled, and, grabbing hold of the edge of the quilt in her fat little fists, she pulled herself up again.

'You're trouble,' she said, and then realised Libby was crawling out of the door and heading for the top of the stairs. 'Libby!' she called, and ran after her, to find Max sitting on the top step with his daughter in his arms, rubbing noses and laughing.

'I think you need a stairgate,' he said, and she nodded.

'I do. I bought one, but I can't fit it. It's not wide enough. I've been meaning to find another one.'

'I'll sort it,' he said, and, getting to his feet, he hoisted Libby up in the air and blew a raspberry on her tummy.

Heavens. Max, blowing raspberries? Maybe there was hope after all…

Andrea was amazing.

Crisp, efficient, much too old for Max—in case she'd been worried—and about as approachable as a pet piranha, but she took one look at them both that morning and smiled. 'Good,' she said to Max. 'You're looking like a human being at last. You needed a break.'

'I'm going crazy,' he said bluntly, but Andrea just smiled at him and then switched her attention to Julia.

'So—is he behaving?'

Julia rolled her eyes. 'Sort of. He keeps trying to steal his phone from me.'

'Well, he will. He plays hardball, you should know that.'

'But it's not a game.'

'No. I think he realises. If he didn't, he wouldn't be there with you. Now, if I might borrow him for a little while, there are several urgent things he needs to deal with and then you can have him back.'

'You can come,' he said to her. 'See what we're up to.'

And be sucked in? 'We'll be fine,' she said, deciding to trust him, and she settled on a chair in her old office with the babies at her feet and looked around.

Odd, how alien it seemed, and yet how familiar. Nothing had really changed, only her—and she'd changed beyond recognition, apparently, if the blank look on the face of the man who stuck his head round the door was anything to go by.

'Oh—sorry. I was looking for Andrea,' he said.

She smiled at the familiar face. 'Hello, Stephen,' she said, and he did a mild double-take and stared at her.

'Julia?'

'That's me,' she said lightly, wondering whether to be flattered or not, and Stephen gave a startled laugh.

'Well—how are you? I thought—' He broke off, clearly unsure quite what to say, and for the first time she wondered about the public rather than private impact that her disappearance had had on Max.

'I've been busy,' she said wryly, and he stared at the girls and gave a tiny, choked laugh.

'I can see. Amazing. I had no idea.'

Nor had Max, but she wasn't going to discuss their

private life with one of his employees, even if he had once been a friend of hers, and one of Max's most reliable right-hand men.

The most reliable. 'So how's Yashimoto?'

'Stunned. You know Max is selling the company back to him?'

It was her turn to stare. 'He is?'

'Yes, apparently. I couldn't believe it. He's fought so hard to turn it round, and now he's just giving it away. Still, it's in much better shape, and Yashimoto will make a better job of it now with the benefit of Max's advice, so he's happy. But it's Max I can't fathom. I thought you would have known all about it, since you were so involved with setting up the deal in the first place.'

She shook her head. 'Max and I don't talk about business now.'

'No. Good idea, not taking work home. Doesn't sound like Max, but babies change you. Did you know we've had a little boy?'

She smiled. 'No, I didn't. Congratulations—and make sure you see plenty of him.'

'I will. In the meantime, I'd better go and join this meeting.'

'I think they're in Max's office.'

'Cheers. And it's lovely to see you again.'

He shut the door and left her there to contemplate the bombshell he'd dropped.

When had Max decided to sell Yashimoto's company back to him? Yesterday? Today? Or much earlier, and she just hadn't known because they hadn't discussed business at all, as she'd told Stephen?

She had no idea, but she was puzzled, whatever. Did it mean he was taking her seriously and cutting back on his business interests? Or had it already been in the pipeline? She needed to know, because the difference was crucial. She didn't want to go thinking that he was making sweeping changes when all the time he'd been following one of his incredible hunches.

Oh, well. She'd find out later. In the meantime, she had bigger things to worry about, because shortly she was going to see her mother-in-law again, and she was feeling curiously apprehensive.

She needn't have worried.

Linda Gallagher took one look at her with the girls, clapped a hand over her mouth and burst into tears.

'Oh, Julia, my dear girl—oh, my dear, dear, girl!' And, without another word, she threw her arms around her and hugged her hard.

Julia blinked away her own tears and hugged her back, and then she was released, and Linda was exclaiming over the babies and crying on Max and hugging him until she thought his ribs would break.

'Come in—come on in, all of you. Richard? Look, it's Max, and he's brought Julia and—'

And she started to cry again.

'Julia?'

Richard, Linda's partner, studied her for a moment and then gave a fleeting smile and kissed her cheek. 'It's good to see you again. And you've been busy.'

'A little,' she said wryly. 'I'm sorry to drop such a bomb-shell on you. It seems to be a day for them.'

Because Max *had* only decided to sell back to Yashimoto this morning, she'd found out. So he was taking her seriously, and going to huge lengths to change things.

Max took charge of the babies, tucking one under each arm and heading into the house with his mother fussing, clucking and mopping up her tears, and Richard helped her take the seats out of the car and into the house so the girls could sit in them to have their lunch.

'I'm so glad you're here,' he said quietly as he closed the front door. 'Linda's really missed you, and Max has been—well—difficult doesn't even scratch the surface.'

She shook her head. 'I'm sorry.'

'No. Don't worry about me. But Linda probably deserves an explanation, when you can give her one, and— it's between you and Max, really, I guess. But it's great to see you again, and to see him smiling. And a father. That's not something we thought we'd ever see.'

'No. None of us thought that.'

Well, not as long as he was with her, at least, what with her medical problems. But apparently miracles did happen, and she had two of them.

Three, if Max turning his life around was to be believed. She still wasn't sure he was, but time would tell.

In the meantime, she followed Richard into the sitting room and found Linda on the floor with her back to the sofa, and Libby crawling busily over her while Ava headed for the plant stand in the corner.

'I don't think so,' she said, disengaging her fingers from the fine mahogany legs of the stand before she pulled it over on herself. 'You need to be put in the stocks, young lady. Come and say hello to your grandmother.'

And, turning her round, she dangled her across the room by her fingers, while her little legs tried valiantly to keep up.

'She's going to walk early,' Linda said, shaking her head. 'Just like Max. He was a nightmare. And she won't be far behind,' she added, grabbing Libby, who was climbing up her front and trying to get on the sofa. 'How on earth do you keep up with them?'

She gave a tired laugh. 'Oh, I have no idea. It's getting worse by the day. I thought when they were in ITU and I'd just had my C-section that it couldn't get any worse—'

'You had a C-section?'

Max's face was shocked, and she realised she hadn't actually told him anything about their birth.

'Yes,' she said softly. 'I had to. The adhesions were too bad, they wouldn't contemplate letting me deliver, especially not at thirty-three weeks.'

His face was ashen. She had no idea why the idea had shocked him so much, but obviously it had, and she realised she'd done yet another thing wrong. *Oh, Max.*

'Hey, it's OK, we're all fine,' she assured him, but he still looked pale.

'You should have called me,' Linda said gently. 'I would have come and helped you.'

'And told Max?'

Her face contorted, and she swallowed hard and bit her lip. 'I'm sorry; it's none of my business.'

'It's not you,' she said hurriedly. 'We were just having problems—'

'*You* were having problems. I was too wrapped up in my life to realise,' he said, his fairness and honesty amazing her yet again. 'Julia pointed out to me yesterday that I'm only eleven years younger than Dad was when he died. And I don't want to go the same way.'

'Good,' Linda said, her eyes filling. 'He was a good man, your father, but he didn't know when to stop, and I've been so worried about you. Maybe this was exactly what you needed to bring you to your senses.'

'Well, let's hope so,' Julia said quietly. 'Linda, I could do with heating some food for them. They're going to start to yell in a minute; they've had a long morning.'

'Of course. Come on through to the kitchen; the men can look after them for a minute.'

And, Julia thought realistically, it would give Linda a chance to grill her about her motives.

Except she didn't, not at first; she just put the kettle on, put the baby food in the microwave and then turned and gave Julia a hug.

'Oh, I've missed you,' she said, letting her go. 'I realise you couldn't contact me if you felt you couldn't talk to Max, but I have missed you.'

'I've missed you, too,' she said with a lump in her throat. 'I could have done with a mum while they were in hospital. I had Jane, but she'd just had her own baby, and it was difficult for her.'

Linda's face was troubled, and after a moment she said, 'Do you mind if I ask you something? Why didn't you tell him you were pregnant? Was it because of Debbie?'

'Debbie?' she asked, a feeling of foreboding washing over her. 'Who's Debbie?'

Linda's face was a mass of conflicting emotions. 'He hasn't told you?' she said in the end, and Julia shook her head.

'I know nothing about anyone called Debbie. Who is she? Don't tell me he's having an affair—'

'No! Oh, good grief, no, nothing like that. Oh, my goodness—' She covered her mouth with her hand and stared at Julia, then shook her head and flapped her hand as if she was seeking a way out. 'Um—I'm sorry, I shouldn't have said anything. It's not my story to tell. You'll have to ask Max. Oh, dear God, I can't believe he hasn't told you.'

'Is it something to do with why he doesn't want children?' she asked, watching Linda carefully, but Linda obviously felt she'd said more than enough, and she shook her head and held up her hand.

'No. I'm sorry, darling, I can't tell you. You'll have to talk to Max, but—tread carefully. At the time— No, you'll have to ask him yourself, I can't say any more.' She straightened up, the pots of food in her hand, and found a smile. 'Come on, let's go and feed the babies. I never thought I'd ever be a grandmother, and I don't intend to waste a minute of it.'

They had a lovely afternoon.

After lunch—which his mother had thrown together after a hasty trip to the supermarket deli-counter earlier when he'd phoned to warn her they were coming—they took the babies out for a walk on Hampstead Heath.

'We should have brought Murphy,' he said, but Julia just laughed.

'I don't think so. He's better off at home. He'd be a nightmare in the mud, and your mother's house isn't exactly designed for dogs, with all that pale carpet.'

'OK,' he said with a wry grin. 'Maybe you're right.'

'Of course I'm right. I'm—' She broke off, and he eyed her thoughtfully.

'Always right?' he offered, and she shook her head, tears she'd scarcely shed before this week filling her eyes for the hundredth time.

'I'm sorry.'

'Hey, not now. We're having a happy day.'

He held out his hand, and after a moment she slipped her fingers into his and squeezed, but there was a bit of her that wondered if he was putting on a show for his mother's benefit.

But he didn't hold her hand for long, because the buggy got stuck and he had to go and help Richard lift it up some steps, and then his mother put her arm through his and started to talk to him, and Julia was left with Richard and the babies.

'He's looking better.'

'He needed to. He was haggard when he arrived on Monday. I was shocked. I'd managed to convince myself that he didn't care—'

'Didn't care?' Richard gave a short cough of laughter. 'Oh, no. He cared. I've never seen a man so tortured. He was devastated when he couldn't find you. I really think he imagined you were dead.'

Oh, lord. She closed her eyes for a second and stumbled, but Richard caught her arm and gave it a reassuring squeeze.

'You'll sort it out between you,' he said comfortingly. 'Just give it time.'

She'd given it two weeks, and nearly a third of that was gone. It was Thursday now, and he'd been there since Monday. So that was another ten days. Would it be enough to convince her that he'd changed? Or enough for him to know just what he was taking on?

She didn't know. But Yashimoto was going to be out of the picture soon, and that meant no more trips to Tokyo. If he could do the same with the New York operation, so he only had his UK businesses to worry about, then maybe, just maybe, they'd be all right.

But, in the meantime, she had to find a way of asking him about Debbie, and, until she knew exactly who she was and what she meant to him, she had no idea what the future might hold. She just knew that, if Linda was to be believed, Debbie was hugely significant.

If only she knew what it was she was asking him...

'Poor old Murphs. Did we abandon you, mate?'

Max ruffled his ears and stroked his side, and Murphy leant against him and thumped his tail enthusiastically.

'I think that means "feed me",' Jules said drily, and he laughed and picked up his bowl.

'Hungry, are you?' he said, and the tail went faster. 'Shall I feed him?'

'Mmm—but, if you could take him out for a run first, that would be great. I'll bath the girls.'

'Are you sure you can manage?'

'I'm fine. Go on, off you go.'

So he took him out for a run by the river, just for a few minutes, because the light was fading fast, and by the time they got home it was gloomy and Julia was in the kitchen with the girls giving them their supper and their evening feed.

'Tea?' he offered, knowing now that she liked to drink while she was feeding, and she smiled her thanks and settled down on the sofa with the babies.

He put her tea—with cold water—in reach, and sat down with his at the other end of the table and watched her feeding them while Murphy chased his bowl around the tiled floor.

'I might buy him a bowl with a rubber base,' she said ruefully, and Max laughed and sipped his tea and watched his wife and daughters, and thought that life had never been more complex or more challenging—or more fulfilling.

Happy families, he thought, and wondered how long it would last. He'd done his best—handed Yashimoto the deal of the century—but he didn't care and it made him feel good, because the man had worked hard to turn his old company around, and, given a leg up, he'd be fine now.

But that was just the tip of the iceberg, of course. There was a ton of other investments which still needed his serious intervention, and with his eye off the ball— Well, who knew what could happen to it? He'd had to rescue a situation this morning because he hadn't been on hand to deal with it, and Stephen had been tied up with Tokyo.

And for some reason Andrea hadn't flagged it up to him.

Oh, well. It was sorted now, but he wasn't sure how much longer he could pretend his empire could run itself.

'Are you hungry?' he asked her, watching as she detached Libby and sat her up.

'Starving. Why? What did you have in mind?'

He chuckled. 'Nothing with garlic. I was wondering if I should get something from the pub again.'

'Oh. That would be lovely. They do a really great thing with mozzarella and basil, a little tartlet. It's fabulous. And sticky-toffee pudding.'

'Stick— That sounds gross,' he said with a laugh.

'No. It's gorgeous. You ought to try it.'

'I'll try some of yours.'

'If I let you have any.'

'Oh, you will,' he said, taking Ava off her and wincing at the deafening burp. 'I'll sweet-talk you.'

'You can try,' she said, but her eyes were twinkling and he felt a sudden stab of longing. Damn. After the conversation they'd had last night, there was no way he was getting that close to her, so he'd be better off not thinking about it.

'Come on, pest. Let's take you up and change your nappy and tuck you up in bed, so your mother and father can have a little civilised conversation.'

'Better keep them here, then,' Jules said from behind him, and he turned back and caught her teasing smile, and felt desire lance through him again, hot and hard and needy.

It was going to be a long, long evening.

She lit the fire while he was over at the pub collecting their order, and by the time he came back the logs were blazing merrily behind the fireguard and the table was laid.

'Is that woodsmoke I can smell?' he asked, coming back into the kitchen, and she nodded.

'I've lit the fire. I thought maybe we could play chess again, or watch some of the baby DVDs.'

She saw his smile slip. 'OK. That would be nice,' he said, and made a valiant attempt to resurrect the smile, but it didn't fool her. And the first time they'd watched a DVD of the babies it had upset him. But why?

'Max?'

'Fancy a small glass of wine? There's a bit of white left, or I've bought some rosé.'

'Oh. Rosé would be nice. Thanks,' she said, and let it drop for now.

* * *

She was watching him.

He ignored her, handing her the stacked plates with their covers and swiftly twisting the cork out of the wine. By the time he'd poured it and sat down opposite her, she was busy concentrating on her food, and, with the smell of the sticky-toffee pudding drifting from its resting place on the side of the Aga, he thought he might have got away with it.

For now. But the DVD's were a minefield, making him feel raw, and he wasn't sure he could watch a film shot in special care. Not see how close they'd come—

'Wow, that was gorgeous. Thanks, Max.'

He put aside his black thoughts and smiled at her. She looked lovely tonight, her hair loose around her shoulders and her eyes warm and gentle. If only…

No. Not yet. She'd said so, with knobs on, but, if he could only get that close to her, maybe he could convince her to come back to him.

'It's a pleasure,' he said. 'So—how about letting me thrash you at chess again?'

She hesitated for a second, then gave him a mischievous grin. 'OK. If you don't mind being beaten. I've remembered how your mind works.'

'Faster than yours,' he pointed out, and she stuck her tongue out at him and stood up.

'Let's see, shall we?'

'Indeed. Best of three?'

'You think it'll take that many?'

'No. Two will be more than enough to have you whimpering off with your tail between your legs,' he retorted, following her with the dog in his wake.

That was a mistake, because he almost had her for the

second time when Murphy stood up and walked round the table, and, seizing her chance, Julia called him all excitedly, and his tail thrashed and cleared the board.

'Oh, dear, what a shame, we'll have to start again,' she said with a wicked grin, but he wasn't having it.

'I can remember where every piece was,' he said, and proceeded to reset the chessmen in place.

'Your knight wasn't there.'

'Yes it was.'

'No. It was there. Your bishop was there.'

'Rubbish. How could my bishop have got there? Let's face it, Jules, I've thrashed you,' he said, lounging back on the sofa and crossing his ankle over the other knee. 'Just admit it.'

'Never.'

'I never had you down as a cheat,' he said softly, and she stopped in her tracks and stared at him.

'I wasn't cheating! I was just teasing, Max. Trying to lighten the atmosphere.'

He swallowed. 'What's wrong with the atmosphere?'

'I don't know, but ever since I mentioned the DVDs you've been funny. Why don't you want to see them?'

'I do,' he lied. Well, it wasn't really a lie, but he was scared and sick inside, and emotions he'd buried too long ago were bubbling to the surface. And he didn't want to deal with them.

She got up and cleared away the chess pieces, folded the lid of the coffee-table over and straightened it, then dimmed the lights and switched on the television. 'OK, then,' she said quietly. 'This is the next one—the babies in hospital. We were about to watch it the other night when you walked out.'

'Just put it on, Jules,' he said gruffly, his left hand wrapped tightly round the stem of the wine glass, and, before he knew what she was going to do, she'd started the disc and had taken hold of his right hand, wrapping it in both of hers and snuggling up against his shoulder.

'OK, that's Ava. She was stronger. She was born first, and, although she was smaller, she was better developed and she's heavier now than Libby. And that's Libby. She had to have much more help with her breathing, and there were a few days when—when we thought we might lose her,' she said a little unsteadily, and he realised she was struggling just as much as he was. Her fingers tightened on his, and he squeezed them back, as much for himself as for her.

'They look tiny.'

'They were. Twins are always smaller. They've only got half as much room, so considering that they do pretty well, but by the time they were delivered my uterus had reached its limit and it was in danger of rupturing. They had to do two operations to free the adhesions, and then finally they couldn't release any more and they had to deliver them. But I hung on as long as I could.'

'It sounds awful,' he said, wincing at the thought. It must have been so painful. Why on earth hadn't she contacted him? Although God alone knows what use he would have been to her, haunted by his demons.

'It was. And I was so scared. I nearly called you. If you'd rung before, I would have done, but then my phone was stolen and all I could do was get by, minute by minute, and then the crisis was over.'

'I would have come,' he said gruffly.

'Would you?'

She turned and looked at him, and he met her gentle, searching eyes briefly before he turned away. 'Yes,' he said with conviction. 'I would.' Even though it would have killed him.

'Max, can I ask you something?'

He looked back at her, and his heart started to pound. 'Sure.'

'Who's Debbie?'

The wine sloshed over the rim of the glass, soaking his hand and running over the arm of the sofa. He leapt to his feet and got a cloth, dabbing and blotting and rubbing with it until she took it out of his hand and pulled him back down gently onto the sofa beside her.

'Max, forget that, talk to me. Who is she? Why was your mother so surprised that I'd never heard of her? And what did she do to you that's made you so shut down inside?'

He stared at her, his breath rasping, then he closed his mouth and swallowed. He could do this. He owed it to her—and he should have told her years ago.

'She was my girlfriend,' he said, his voice sounding strange to his ears. Rough and unused. Like his feelings. 'She was pregnant, and she got pre-eclampsia. They did a C-section, but she was fitting when they took her into Theatre, and she died. So did the baby. My son. He lived for fifteen hours and seven minutes. He was twenty-six weeks. That's why the DVD—'

He clenched his jaw, holding back the tears, keeping it all under control. For an age she said nothing, but then she dragged in a shaky breath and said, 'Did he have a name? Your baby?'

'Ye—' He swallowed and tried again. 'Yes. I called him Michael. It was my father's name.'

'Oh, Max.'

The tears welled in her eyes and splashed down over her cheeks, and she covered her mouth with her hand and tried to hold in the sob.

He couldn't look at her. Couldn't watch her crying for Debbie and their tiny son, or for him, so locked in grief that he couldn't even watch a film of his own daughters without replaying his baby's short, desperate hours. He couldn't watch it, or her, because, if he did, if he let the feelings up to the surface, they'd tear him apart like they had before, and he couldn't take it all over again.

'Oh, Max,' she murmured, and he felt her fingers stroke away the tears that he could feel running soundlessly down his cheeks.

'It's OK, Max, I've got you,' she said gently, and he realised that, far from tearing him apart, it felt good to let it go, because Jules was with him, and he wasn't alone any more.

And so with a quiet sigh he turned into her arms, and for the first time in fifteen years he let the tears flow unchecked.

CHAPTER SEVEN

HE SLEPT until nine the following morning, the only time she'd ever known him to sleep late.

Even jet-lagged, he'd never slept for so long, so she crept into his room at eight to check that he was still breathing and found him lying spreadeagled on his front across the bed, snoring softly. The covers had slipped off one side, but the room was warm, so even though he was naked he wouldn't be cold.

The urge to pull the covers up over him and creep in beside him and take him in her arms almost overwhelmed her, but instead she tiptoed out and went back downstairs and put the washing on, then let Murphy out into the garden for a romp. He brought her his ball on a rope, and she threw it for him a few times, but it was chilly out, and she didn't like to leave the girls. They were getting so adventurous, and even in the playpen she didn't trust them not to get up to mischief.

So she went back inside, and she put the radio on quietly and folded the washing that had aired overnight on the front of the Aga and made herself a coffee. Then, just when she was convincing herself he hadn't been breathing at all and she'd imagined it, she heard the boards creak and the water running in the bathroom, and she gave a sigh of relief and relaxed.

They'd talked for hours last night. He'd told her all about it; about how he'd met Debbie, and how excited they'd been when they'd found out she was pregnant. And he talked about little Michael, and how he'd held him as he died, and how he'd vowed then never to put another woman at such risk.

'So it wasn't that you didn't want children?' she'd asked, pushing him, and he'd shaken his head emphatically.

'Oh, no. I would have loved children, and the girls— Well, they're just amazing. The most precious gift imaginable. I just can't believe we've got them. But I don't know if I could have coped with the pregnancy.'

'So what would you have done if I'd told you?' she'd asked, and he'd shrugged.

'I don't know. I don't know if I could have gone through all those weeks of waiting, knowing it wasn't going to be straightforward, watching you suffer, waiting for something awful to happen. I think it would have torn me apart.'

'And if we were to have another?'

His eyes had been tortured. 'I don't know if I could take it. I'd rather not find out. We've been so lucky to have the girls. Let's not push it.'

Not that it was really an issue. She didn't really want to get pregnant again after the last time, and the doctors hadn't seemed to think it would be a good idea, but in any case, until their relationship was a great deal more secure, there was no way she was going to risk it.

Even assuming she let him get that close.

But one thing she knew. She wasn't going to let him

sweep it all back under the carpet again. She was going to make him talk about it—about Debbie, and the baby, and how he felt about it—if it killed him. He owed it to them not to let them be forgotten, and so their memory would be treasured, and kept alive, and their girls would know one day that, a long time ago, they'd had a brother.

Oh, hell.

She scrubbed the tears from her eyes and looked up as he walked in, and he took one look at her and sighed gently.

'Oh, Jules. Are you OK?'

'Sorry. I was just thinking about when we tell the girls, when they're older.'

He gave a strangled laugh. 'Talk about crossing bridges before you get to them. Anyway, never mind that. What does a man have to do round here to get a cup of tea?'

'Put the kettle on?' she suggested, and he put it on the hob and crouched down and said hello to the babies, who sat happily in the playpen chewing on blocks.

'I think they're teething,' he said in wonder, and she laughed and got up.

'Of course they're teething. They'll do little else for the next umpteen weeks. Apart from try and escape from whatever means of restraint we put them in.'

'We'll have to try handcuffs,' he said, and she put her hand over his mouth.

'Shh,' she said. 'Not in front of the children.'

And he laughed, the first real, proper laugh she'd heard from him in years, and then the laughter faded and their eyes locked, and he stopped breathing.

She knew that, because she could see his chest freeze, and his heart was pounding, the pulse visible in the hollow of his throat, beating in time with hers. And then he seemed to come out of the trance and dragged in a breath and looked away. Somehow that freed her, too, so she made tea and put bread in the mesh toast-holder that went under the cover of the hotplate, and when the water was boiling she made a pot of tea and put the wire holder under the cover to toast the bread—and all the time all she could think about was the sound of his laugh, and how the tears last night seemed to have freed his emotions.

Did that mean he'd be able to play?

She hoped so. She'd always known there was another side of him, one he kept shut down, and she couldn't wait to meet the other Max.

'So what are we going to do today?' she asked.

'What's it like outside?'

'Cold. Bright and sunny, but cold. The wind's chilly.'

'So—something indoors? How about going to find a better stairgate?'

'That's a good idea. And they could do with some more clothes, if we're going to one of the big shops. They're growing like weeds.'

'That'll be chewing the loo brush,' he said drily, and she stared at him in horror.

'What?'

'Ava,' he told her, and she looked down at her elder daughter in the playpen, happily gumming away on a plastic toy, and felt sick.

'When?'

'The other day in the bathroom. Don't worry, she didn't actually get it in her mouth,' he said, and she realised he'd been joking and felt her shoulders sag.

'Is that how it ended up on the window sill?'

'Yup.'

'Oh, the little horror. She's never done that before.'

'Probably because you're more efficient with them than I am. She was at a loose end for rather too long while I prevaricated about the temperature of the water. So—shopping?'

She stared at him. He sounded—good grief—almost enthusiastic. He'd *never* sounded enthusiastic about shopping before. He'd hardly ever *gone* shopping before. Except for clothes, and that was more a case of visiting his tailor for suits and shirts. She'd always bought anything less critical for him, and always in a stolen moment from the office during a meeting that he was attending without her.

Quite simply, there had never been *time* for shopping in their old life, and, if he was looking forward to it now, well, she wasn't going to waste the experience.

'Let's go to Lakeside,' she suggested. 'There are all sorts of shops there, and it's all under cover, so we don't have to worry about the babies getting cold. We can make a day of it.'

She hadn't been joking.

He hadn't really believed that there could be so many shops all selling similar things lined up row after row after row. Well, he'd known they existed, of course he did, but that they should be so heaving with people on a February week-day stunned him.

But they found a stairgate for the babies, and lots of clothes, nappies and toys—so many, in fact, that he ended up making more than one trip back to the car to offload them. And there was a special baby zone, where they were able to feed and change the babies, and for once he managed not to get too messy.

Then it was back to the fray, and he caught Jules looking longingly at a clothes shop. For women.

'When did you last buy anything new?' he asked, and she smiled wryly.

'What, apart from jeans and jumpers? I can't remember. But I don't need anything else.'

'Yes, you do,' he told her. 'Of course you do.'

'When for?'

He shrugged. 'When I take you out for dinner?'

'What, with the babies in tow?'

'No. When we get a babysitter.'

'I don't know a babysitter—well, apart from Jane, and she won't want to babysit for me in the evening. I usually take the girls round to her if I need to go somewhere where I can't take them.'

'My mother?'

'Linda? She lives in London.'

'She'd come up.'

'What—just so you can take me out for dinner? That's a bit of an ask.'

'We could stay there.'

In their old room? The one where they'd stayed in the past? She was looking doubtful, and he realised why.

'Sorry. I'm getting ahead of the game here, but—why not buy a dress? Something pretty. A top, maybe, if you don't want a dress, or some new trousers. You can always dress up at home, if you want to.'

'But I don't,' she said bluntly, and he blinked.

She was looking at him as if he'd suggested something

wrong, and it dawned on him that she was taking it as a criticism of her clothes.

'Oh, Jules, don't get uppity. I wasn't criticising. I just thought—if you wanted something pretty—' He broke off. 'It doesn't matter. Forget it. I'm sorry.'

And, without waiting for her response, he walked away.

Damn.

Had she misread him? Because she'd *love* to buy some new clothes, something pretty that fitted her new, different body and made her feel like a woman again instead of a milk machine.

Underwear. Pretty, sexy underwear.

For Max?

Maybe. God knows he wasn't seeing her in her nursing bras.

And a pretty top, and some nice, well-cut trousers that didn't cling to her lumpy thighs like glue. None of her old trousers fitted her any more. They were all too tight, but she'd been stick-thin when they'd been jetting all over the place, because there had quite simply never been time to eat.

But she had time now, and the inclination, to keep herself well, and so she had curves where she'd never had curves before.

She grabbed the hands of the baby buggy and ran after him. 'Max? Max, stop! Please!'

He stopped, and she caught up with him and tried a smile. 'I'm sorry. I misunderstood—and you're right. I'd love to get some new things. I actually *need* to get some new things. Can you bear it?'

'Only if I get to see them as you try them on.'

'Oh. I was talking about underwear, really.'

His eyes flared, then darkened. 'Even better,' he murmured, and she felt a soft tide of colour sweep over her cheeks.

'You can't—'

'Maybe not in the shop,' he agreed. 'But later.'

She swallowed. 'OK, forget the underwear,' she said hastily, and he pulled a face, but he laughed anyway.

'So, what else?'

'Just—tops, trousers. It won't take long.'

He snorted. 'I'm not that naïve. Why don't I take the kids with me and leave you to it for an hour or so? You can ring me when you're ready, and I'll come and pay.'

'You don't have to pay!' she protested, but he just raised an eyebrow.

'Jules, you're my *wife*,' he said firmly. 'And I will quite happily pay for your clothes. I've just paid several hundred thousand pounds for the sake of spending a little time with you. I don't think the odd top or pair of trousers is going to make a whole lot of difference.'

Oh, lord. She'd thought the Yashimoto deal was a bit hasty. Now she was beginning to realise just how much he'd invested in their relationship, and she looked at him with new eyes.

'I'm sorry. I didn't mean for you to do that.'

'Jules, it's fine. I'm happy with it. It was a good decision. And we're talking about a cut in profits, more than a deficit, so forget it. Now, my phone?'

'Oh. Yes.' She rummaged in her bag and found his phone, but, as she handed it over, there was a bit of her that wondered if he'd suggested this as a way of getting the phone off her.

'No. Trust me.'

Had she said it out loud? 'Sorry. Right, I'll be as quick as I can. Don't leave them.'

He gave her a look, then turned away and headed off into the crowd, leaving her feeling suddenly empty-handed and at a loss.

Come on, Julia, she told herself. Organisation. Underwear first, then a top, then trousers. And she headed into a large top-end department store, found the lingerie and started shopping.

'How long can she take, girls?' he asked, crouching down in front of the now-restless babies and trying to entertain them. 'She said she wouldn't be long.'

He gave a rueful little laugh, and Ava reached out her hand and gurgled at him. 'Da-da,' she said, and he felt his eyes fill.

'Oh, you clever little girl,' he said, struggling not to embarrass himself in public, but then she said, 'Mama,' and he realised she was just babbling.

Idiot him. Of course she was.

He straightened up and looked around. What could he do to entertain them? There was a book shop, so he headed in there, all ready to find books for them to suck and chew and hurl on the floor, but then he saw cookery books.

Books for idiots. Books for people who'd never lifted a spatula in their lives. People like him.

He'd cook for her. He'd find a book that seemed straightforward and comprehensive, he'd find a recipe, and they'd drop into the supermarket on the way home and he'd cook for her.

Fish. She loved fish. Fresh tuna? He thumbed through the recipe books, found one that looked promising, checked out tuna and discovered that it took seconds. Whap-whap on a hot griddle and it was done. Excellent. And he could serve it with salad and new potatoes. Even he couldn't screw those up.

He bought the book, hung the bag on the back of the buggy and then reached for his phone.

She was engaged. Damn. Oh, well, he'd give her a minute. She might be trying to call him. He was about to slip it back into his pocket when it rang, and he answered it instantly.

'You were on the phone!' she said accusingly, and he sighed.

'So were you. I was trying to call you. The babies are getting restless.'

'Oh. Sorry. I'm done.'

She told him where she was, and he looked at the map, worked out where he was and then made his way there through the teaming throng of happy shoppers.

Well, he was happy, too—or he had been, till she'd bitten his head off for nothing. Oh, well. He supposed she had some justification for thinking he was using the phone for work purposes, because he *had* made one quick call to Andrea. But only the one, and it had lasted three minutes tops, and it had been important.

So he couldn't get on his self-righteous high horse and rip her head off right back, because she'd been right. He had cheated, and she was probably right not to trust him.

He found her, standing near a till with an armful of clothes, waiting for him.

'I'm sorry,' she said, her first words, and he felt a little prickle of guilt.

'Don't worry about it,' he said. 'So—what did you buy?'

* * *

She didn't know what to wear.

He'd called into the supermarket on the way home, left her and the babies in the car, and run in to do a shop. He'd been less than five minutes, so she had no idea what he'd bought, but he had a small carrier with him.

'What's that?' she asked, and he grinned.

'Supper. I'm cooking for you.'

'Really?' Oh, lord, that sounded dreadful, but she could still smell the garlic on her skin after the paella, and she had no idea what he would go for this time.

'Don't worry, there's no garlic,' he promised with a wry grin, and she laughed self-consciously.

'Sorry. So what are we having?'

'Aha,' he said, tapping the side of his nose. 'I'm cooking. All you have to do is put on something pretty and be entertained.'

So here she was, washed and spruced, wearing a light touch of make-up for the first time in months, and standing naked in her bedroom contemplating her purchases.

A jumper, she thought, being chicken, but she'd heard him light the fire in the sitting room, and when she'd popped down for something for the girls she'd noticed he'd laid the table in the kitchen rather than the chilly and more formal dining-room.

So she wouldn't be cold.

So—one of the new tops? The lacy one with the tiny camisole underneath, perhaps? Or the silky one with the little collar and the fine embroidery?

Lacy, she decided, and that dictated the bra and pants set, because of the colour combination. She'd only bought one pair of trousers, but they fitted her so well she was delighted with them, and she put them on to complete the outfit, stood back to look at herself, and blinked.

Wow. That was a bit different.

Gone were the jeans with the slightly grubby knees from spending her life on the floor with the babies, and the jumper with a little stain on the front from some tomato-and-pasta baby food that didn't seem to want to wash out.

Gone, too, the dark rims round her eyes and the tired, straggly hair.

Instead she looked feminine, elegant and—yes—pretty. And it made her feel a million dollars.

In a fit of wickedness, she squirted scent into the air and walked through it, then slipped on her high heels and went downstairs.

He was sitting at the table flicking through a magazine, and he looked up and his jaw sagged.

'Wow,' he breathed, and, standing up, he put the magazine on one side and walked over to her, his eyes never leaving her. 'Turn round,' he instructed, with an edge in his voice, and she turned, slowly, and then came back to face him and met his eyes. His smouldering, fire-blue eyes. How could blue ever be a cold colour? Not on Max. Oh, no.

'Will I do?' she asked a little self-consciously, and his mouth twitched into a lopsided grin.

'Oh, I think you'll do,' he said, his voice slightly gruff and gravelly, the way it was when he was aroused, and the words stroked through her like fire, sensitising every spot they touched. He stood there for another few seconds, studying her, then with another crooked smile he stepped back and held out a chair for her. 'Would you care to take a seat, madam?'

'Thank you.'

She smiled up at him, laughing when he flicked a napkin across her lap with a flourish. It would have had more impact if it hadn't been a tea towel, but his mouth just twitched and he went over to the stove, set the griddle on it and watched it until it was smoking, then dropped two dark steaks on it.

She sniffed the air. Tuna? Her stomach rumbled, and she looked for the plates. Ah. There they were, just coming out of the bottom oven with a bowl of new potatoes. He put a knob of butter on the potatoes, sprinkled them with chopped chives and set them on the table, dished up the tuna steaks and set her plate in front of her with another of those flourishes which she realised were becoming part of the meal.

'Salad, madam?'

'Thank you. Murphy, in your bed, this isn't for you. Max, sit down.'

'I'm not sure that doesn't put me in the same category as the dog,' he said with irony, and she chuckled.

'Of course not. Good boy.'

Giving a little snort, he sat opposite her, and then got up, lit the candle in the middle of the table and turned down the lights. 'Better,' he said, and handed her the potatoes. 'No garlic, please note.'

'Chilli?'

He shrugged. 'Just a touch—sweet chilli and lime marinade. It shouldn't be hot.'

It wasn't. It was delicious, cooked to perfection and utterly gorgeous, and she was more than ready for it. The wine was a delicate rosé, not so chilled that the flavour was lost, and he followed it with little individual chocolate pots, ready made but wickedness itself, decorated with fresh strawberries and served with a dark, rich Cabernet that was the perfect complement.

'Wow, Max, that was fabulous,' she said, pushing her plate away and smiling at him in amazement.

To her surprise, he coloured slightly and gave a wry, self-conscious grin. 'Thank you. I just—read the instructions.'

'No, you did much more than that. You went to a lot of trouble to make it right, and it was wonderful. Thank you.'

His smile was warm and did funny things to her insides. 'It's a pleasure,' he said, and she could tell he meant it. 'Coffee in the sitting room?'

'That would be lovely.'

'Go on, then, go and sit down.'

'What about this lot?'

He shrugged. 'What about it? It won't come to any harm. Come on, out of here. I'll stack the dishwasher while the kettle boils, if that'll make you happier. Now, shoo.'

She shooed, going into the sitting room with Murphy and putting another log on the fire, then sitting down on the sofa to wait for him. Murphy was sniffing the table, and she pushed him gently out of the way with her foot and looked at the little dish he'd been investigating.

Truffles? Yum. She had one, just to pass the time, and then Max arrived with the tray and gave Murphy a chew to eat by the fire. 'I thought it might keep him out of the chocolates.'

'It will. But only till he's eaten it.'

'Well, we'll have to finish them first,' he said, taking the seat beside her and handing her her coffee. 'Here—open wide.'

And he put one of the wicked little truffles into her mouth.

'Mmm. They're gorgeous,' she said. Well, she meant to say. It came out a little more garbled than that, and she got the giggles, and he shook his head and slung his arm casually around the back of the sofa behind her and grinned.

'Oh, dear. Did you have two whole glasses of wine?' he teased.

'No, I did not,' she retorted, recovering her composure and poking him in the ribs. 'Cheeky.'

'Two halves, anyway. What did you think of them?'

'Lovely. They were really nice. I bet they didn't come from the bargain bucket.'

He chuckled. 'Not exactly. But I felt it was worth it.' He trailed a finger down her cheek, and smiled a little wryly. 'You know, I thought you looked gorgeous this morning, but now...'

His finger dipped, trailing round the neckline of her top, following the edge down towards her cleavage, and she felt the air jam in her lungs.

'Max.'

His hand dropped away and he straightened up, lounging back in his corner of the sofa and reaching for his coffee. She leant over and picked up a chocolate, and he said, 'My turn,' and opened his mouth. Just slightly, just enough so that, when she put the truffle in between his teeth, his lips brushed her fingers, the slightly moist surface catching her skin so that when she took her hand away his lips clung softly to her fingertips.

Her eyes flew up to his, hot and dark and dangerous, and she felt need flow like molten lava through her veins.

His hand came up and caught hold of hers, easing it from his mouth and placing it against his heart, and she could feel the pounding beat beneath her palm, the taut muscles, the coiled tension in him.

And she wanted him.

Now. Tonight.

'Max?' she whispered.

He was staring at her mouth, his eyes slightly glazed, and she could see the pulse beating in his throat. His eyes flicked up to hers and locked.

'Take me to bed.'

CHAPTER EIGHT

'ARE you sure?'

'Yes.'

With a sharp hiss of indrawn breath, his eyes flickered briefly shut, then opened, locking with hers, burning in their intensity, and he got slowly to his feet and held out his hand, pulling her up so she was standing facing him, just inches away but not quite touching.

'You don't have to do this.'

'I know.'

He closed his eyes and said something she couldn't hear, then turned away. 'We need to put this lot away and sort the dog out.'

'I'll do it.'

'No. We'll both do it. It'll be quicker.' He put everything back on the tray and carried it out to the kitchen, Murphy close behind him, and he took the dog out while she put the milk back in the fridge and checked that all the food was out of Murphy's reach. It was—all except the chocolates.

Max came back in with the dog, picked up the truffles and met her eyes. 'I'll bring these,' he said, and she was instantly taken back to another time, another place, when he'd brought chocolates to bed and fed them to her, one by one, as he'd made love to her.

She could still taste them.

'Don't look at me like that,' he said, his voice taut, 'or I'll lose it completely.' His lips quirked in a fleeting smile, but she could feel the tension coming off him in waves. It matched her own, and suddenly she couldn't wait any more.

Turning on her heel, she walked out of the kitchen, flicking off the light and leaving him to follow.

She heard him murmur to the dog, close the door, and then she could feel him right behind her, the warmth of his body just a breath away.

'Your room or mine?'

'Mine. It's further from the babies.'

Only just, but she wasn't at all sure, after so long, that she'd be able to keep a lid on her reaction to his love-making—and the shower at work hadn't been the only time he'd made her scream. Not by a long way.

She turned on the light, but he'd brought the candle, and he put it on the chest of drawers beside the chocolates, lit it and turned out the light. She was grateful for that, because it suddenly dawned on her that he hadn't seen her body since she'd had the babies, and, between the ravages of breastfeeding, the scar from the C-section and the gain in weight, maybe he needed a rather more subtle introduction to the new her.

But it seemed he wasn't in any hurry to take her clothes off after all. Instead he tunnelled his fingers through her hair, bent his head and touched his lips to hers.

Just a feather touch, the lightest brushing of skin on skin, but, as he moved his head from side to side, their lips clung, dragging gently, heightening the sensation, until she felt a whimper force its way out of her throat.

Oh, Max, kiss me, she begged silently, and, as if he'd heard her, he anchored her head more firmly with his hands and stroked his tongue across her lips, coaxing them apart.

They needed no coaxing. She opened to him, and with a ragged groan he slanted his mouth over her and plundered it, his mouth hungry on hers, searching, thrusting, his tongue duelling with hers, driving her wild.

Only when they had to break for breath did he lift his head, the air sawing in and out of his lungs, his eyes glittering in the candlelight. 'Jules, I need you,' he whispered, his voice rough and urgent.

'I need you, too—please, Max. Now.'

And without any further delay he stripped off his shirt, shucked his trousers and socks and heeled off his shoes in one motion.

The boxers hid nothing, the soft jersey clinging faithfully to his erection, and she felt her mouth dry. It had been so long. Her body was trembling, the need so great she could hardly move, but it was all right, because she didn't need to. He was there, his hands gently, carefully easing the top over her head—first the lace, then the little camisole—and when he saw the bra he closed his eyes briefly and she saw his lips move soundlessly.

'Thank God you didn't show me that in the shop,' he said at last, and she laughed a little breathlessly.

'There's more,' she said, and he groaned and slid the zip down on her trousers and eased them away.

She sucked her stomach in, but he tutted and ran his hand over it, his hot, dry palm flat against the skin, his fingers trailing fire. One finger flicked at the elastic of her little lace shorts. 'What are these?' he said, his voice unsteady.

'I thought you might like them.'

'You're going to kill me,' he whispered, and, drawing her into his arms, he brought their bodies into contact for the first time.

They both gasped, then sighed, and then eased closer, until finally he lifted his head and met her eyes.

'Jules—I have to have you now, or I'm going to die, I swear it,' he said unevenly. 'I need you so damned much.'

His eyes were bright with fire, and his chest was heaving against hers, the candlelight picking out the sharp defini-tion of his muscles and turning him to gold as he lifted her gently in his arms and laid her on the bed.

He followed her down, his eyes never leaving her face, and then finally he let them track over her, following the line of his hands as they stroked over her skin and left fire in their wake. He ran his knuckles over the edge of her bra, down the line of her cleavage, then turned his hand and cupped her breast, his thumb chafing lightly over her nipple until she thought she'd scream.

'I want to taste you,' he muttered gruffly. 'Every day I watch the babies suckle from you, and…'

She wanted it, too. Ached for it. She undid the catch—front-fastening, she'd thought, for convenience, but she wondered now if she'd had this in mind all along—and he eased the cups away, then slid his hand inside and lifted one breast to his lips.

Milk dewed on her nipple, and he caught it on his tongue and tasted it, then closed his mouth over her and suckled hard.

She gasped, a shaft of white-hot need lancing through

her with deadly accuracy, and he lifted his head, his eyes black now, his mouth taut.

For the longest moment they stayed like that, their eyes locked, and then with a desperate sound he stripped away her tiny lace shorts, ripped off his boxers and moved over her, his solid, muscled thighs hard against her legs as he nudged them apart.

'Jules,' he whispered.

And then he was there, inside her, filling her, and she felt the storm closing round them, the sensation overwhelming her until suddenly everything broke loose and her climax ripped through her.

He caught her scream in his mouth, trapped it against the savage groan that tore from his chest. And then he rolled her to her side and pulled her in close to him, their bodies still locked together, their hearts racing, and, when she finally opened her eyes, he was looking at her with wonder in his eyes, the lashes clumped with tears.

'I love you,' he whispered, and, drawing her close again, he tucked her head under his chin and wrapped his arms around her, his hands stroking slowly, rhythmically, against her spine until finally she fell asleep in his arms.

He'd missed her so much.

He'd never told her, hadn't revealed just how hellish the last year had been. Oh, he'd said a few things, but nothing compared to what was locked up in his heart.

But she was back now, and, if it killed him, he'd make sure he didn't fail her again.

His arm was going dead, but he didn't want to disturb her. He was just enjoying the luxury of holding her, and he wasn't sure how she'd be when she woke up. Distant? Full of regret?

Hell, he hoped not.

And then she stirred, opened her eyes and smiled at him, and he felt the tension ease out of him like a punctured balloon.

'Hi.'

'Hi,' he answered, and feathered a kiss across her lips. 'You all right?'

'Mmm. You?'

'Oh, yes. I'm very all right.'

'My leg's dead.'

'Snap. My arm's fallen off, I think.'

'It's going to hurt.'

'Uh-huh.'

She grinned. 'One, two, three—'

He gave a little groan and shifted further out of her way, then laughed and drew her back in to his side, so they lay with fingers intertwined and their heads together on the pillow. 'Better?'

'Mmm. Max?'

'Yes?'

'I love you.'

'Oh, Jules.' He rolled towards her, not caring about the pins and needles in his arm, and kissed her gently. 'I love you, too.'

'Good,' she murmured, and, a second later, he heard a soft, almost imperceptible snore.

He smiled. He'd tease her about that in the morning, he thought, and, shifting closer to her, he curled his hand over her hip and went to sleep.

* * *

The babies woke her, and she rolled to her back, opened her eyes and blinked.

It was broad daylight, and she could hear Max's voice in their room. Getting out of bed and wincing at the unaccustomed aches, she pulled her dressing gown on hastily and went out to them.

'Hello, my lovelies,' she said, going into the room, and they beamed at her from their cots.

'Am I included in that?' he asked, looking much too sexy for his own good in nothing but a pair of boxers, and she chuckled.

'You might be. How long have they been awake?'

'A few minutes. I've changed their nappies and given them a bottle of juice, but I think they want their mum and something rather more substantial.'

'I'm sure they do. Come on, my little ones. Shall we go downstairs and say hello to Murphy?'

She lifted Ava out of her cot and handed her to Max, and then pulled Libby up into her arms and nuzzled her. 'Hello, tinker. Are you going to be good today?'

'Probably not, if she's like her sister,' he said drily, and carried her downstairs. 'I'll do that stairgate this morning.'

'Mmm. Please. I'd hate anything to happen. Hello, Smurfs! How are you, boy? Find anything nice to eat?'

'I'm sure he will have given it his best shot,' Max said wryly. 'Won't you, you old rascal?'

Murphy thumped and wagged and grinned at him, and she laughed. 'He's such a suck-up. Horrid dog, aren't you? Horrid. Here, Libby, go to Daddy.'

'Da-dad,' she said, and they both stopped in their tracks.

'Did I dream that?' she asked, and he laughed and shrugged his shoulders.

'Only if I did, too. I thought Ava said "Da-da" yesterday, but then I thought she was just babbling.'

'Da-da!' Ava chirruped from the playpen, hanging onto the edge and grinning furiously at him, and Julia felt her eyes fill with tears.

'They said your name,' she whispered, pressing her hand to her mouth, and he swallowed and grinned, and looked as if he'd crow at any minute.

'Well, girls. How about that?' he said, and put the kettle on.

Breakfast was over, they were all washed and dressed, and Max was trying not to think about the fact that he couldn't take Jules back to bed for hours. Unless the girls had a sleep in the afternoon, of course.

'Shall we do some house-hunting?' he suggested to take his mind off it.

'Sure. If I get the computer we can do it in here. We've got wireless.' And she disappeared and came back a moment later with a laptop. John Blake's?

No. Don't get funny about it. He's given your family a home.

'Shove up,' she said, and settled herself down on the sofa with the laptop. She keyed in a password, and he hated himself for memorising it without thinking. Hell, she was right not to trust him, he thought.

'OK. I'm on one of the big property sites. What are we looking for, and how much?'

'I wouldn't put an upper limit on it. Start at the top and work down.'

'Really?'

'Well—yeah. Why not? Do you want to live in something horrible?'

'No! I want to live in something normal!' she retorted, and he sighed.

Wrong again. Two steps forward, three back, he thought, and wondered why he could never seem to get it right for more than a few minutes at a time.

'Just put in the area you're interested in, and let's see what there is.'

Nothing. That was the simple answer. There was nothing that wasn't either too small or too remote or too pushed-in or just plain wrong.

And nothing, but nothing, matched up to Rose Cottage.

'I wish I could stay here,' she said unhappily.

'He wouldn't sell it?'

'Would you want it?'

He smiled at her wryly. 'It's not really up to me, is it? We're talking about your home, your choice, somewhere for you and the babies. And I guess all I'll do is visit you.'

Her eyes clouded, and she looked hastily away.

Now what? 'Unless I work away during the week and come back for weekends. I'm not really into commuting. I'd rather work a short week.'

'What—only six days, you mean, instead of seven?'

He sighed. 'Can we start again?'

She looked away and bit her lips. 'Sorry. It's just—we seem to be getting on so well, and then the future rears its ugly head and there's no way round it.'

And the babies were fussing and bored.

'Let's dress them up and go for a walk,' he suggested. 'We could use the slings.'

They'd bought slings the day before, to carry the babies on their fronts so they could go for walks without taking the buggy, and so they sorted them out. He ended up with Ava and Julia with Libby.

They swapped them all the time, he realised, as if neither of them wanted to create a closer bond with just one of the twins. Odd, how it had just happened and they hadn't talked about it, but then it had always been like that with them. They'd hardly ever needed to discuss things, they'd just agreed.

Until now, and it seemed that sharing the babies equally was the only thing they could agree on.

Well, out of bed, at least. That, he was relieved to know, was still as amazing as ever. And he wasn't going to think about it now.

They strolled along the riverbank for a way, while Murphy rushed around and sniffed things and dug a few furious holes in search of some poor water-vole or other unfortunate creature, and then they walked back to the house.

'Do any of these barns belong to the house?' he asked, and she nodded.

'Yes, all of them. It was a farm—Rose Farm—but the farmland was all sold off and they took the name, so it was renamed Rose Cottage. Which is silly, really, because it's a bit big to be a cottage, but there you go.'

He looked around curiously. There were lots of buildings that were too small to do anything specific with, but others—like the range of open-fronted, single-storey brick cart-lodges—could be converted into office accommodation.

If only they could find something like it for sale, then there was a possibility that he could work from home. Not just him, but one or two other members of the team—a sort of satellite office. He knew lots of people who'd scaled down their operations and 'gone rural', as one of them had put it, but he'd never seen the attraction.

Until now.

'Come and see the garden,' she said, and led him through the gate at the side.

He'd been out there with the dog, of course, but he'd never really examined it, and, as she walked him through it and talked about it, he began to see it through her eyes.

And it was beautiful. A little ragged round the edges, of course, in the middle of winter, but even now there were daffodils and crocuses coming up, and buds were forming on the rose bushes, and, if he looked hard, he could imagine it in summer.

'I've got photos of it with the roses all flowering,' she said. 'It's stunning.'

It would be. He could see that. And he remembered what she'd said, on the day that she'd left him.

I want…a house, a garden, time to potter amongst the plants, to stick my fingers in the soil and smell the roses… We never stop and smell the roses, Max. Never.

Well, she had her garden now, and her roses. Watching her talk about them, he could see the change in her, the glow in her eyes, the warmth in her skin, the life in her. Real life, not just the adrenaline high of another conquest, but genuine satisfaction and contentment.

And what shocked him more than any of that was that he wanted it, too.

* * *

'Why don't you have a day out with Jane?'

'What?' She shifted forward on the sofa and stared down at him on the floor; he was lying at right angles to her with his hands linked behind his head and Libby sprawled asleep on his stomach.

'You heard. I'll look after the girls. We'll be fine.'

'Are you sure?' she asked doubtfully.

'Yeah, we'll be great. Don't you trust me?'

'Well, of course I trust you. I'm just not sure you know what you're letting yourself in for.'

'Undiluted hell, I expect, but I'm sure we'll all survive.'

She thought about it, and shook her head. 'No. But I might meet her for a coffee,' she suggested, toning it all down a little and going for something more manageable. 'Besides, she's got the baby, and the others will need dropping off at school and picking up again, and she's always really busy. But I'll ask her. When were you thinking of?'

'Whenever you like. Tomorrow?'

Tomorrow was Monday. One week since he'd arrived. It was two days since they'd ended up in bed. And it had been incredible, but she was letting herself get too addicted to it, and there were other things to think about. Like him in London and her here with the children.

Still, it could work. Lots of couples did it.

But she didn't want to! She wanted it all! And she was realistic enough to know she wasn't going to get it. Not with Max, and the thought of having a relationship with anyone else was just a joke. There was no way anyone could live up to Max. It wouldn't be fair to ask them to. And, besides, she loved him. Desperately.

She just had to find a way to make it work, for all their sakes.

'I'll go and ring her,' she said, tucking a cushion down next to Ava so she couldn't roll off the sofa, and getting carefully to her feet.

'Julia? How are you? I've been afraid to ask!'

'Oh, a bit like the curate's egg—good in parts.' Very good, but she didn't want to talk about those parts. And the bad bits—well, they were too difficult to contemplate. 'Look, Max has offered to babysit for me so we can grab a coffee. What are you doing tomorrow?'

'Nothing I can't cancel. I'm dying to see you and hear all about it. Where, and what time?'

'The Barn? Ten-thirty?'

'Fine. How long will you have?'

'As long as I want. He offered me the day, but I don't want him having a bad experience so he's put off for life.'

'No, absolutely not. Clever girl. Right, let's make it ten-thirty tomorrow, and I'll tell Pete I'll be home at one. He's at home, so he can babysit. Does that sound OK?'

'Fine,' she said, and hung up with a smile. She was really looking forward to it. It would be the first chance she'd had to see Jane on their own since she'd left hospital with the babies, and she was ridiculously excited.

She went back to the sitting room and found him lying on his front, with Libby on her back just under his head, giggling while he blew raspberries on her tummy. He looked round over his shoulder, and she stopped admiring his muscular bottom and smiled at him.

'It's all arranged. I'm meeting her tomorrow at ten-thirty at a coffee shop by a craft centre just a couple of miles away, and I'll be back at one. Is that OK?'

'Fine. Good. We'll be all right, won't we, half-pint?' he said, grinning and turning back to Libby, so Julia was free to admire his really rather gorgeous bottom without interruption.

'So tell me all! I've been so worried about you.'

'No, you just want the low-down,' Julia teased, settling down with a proper, decent latte and a properly indecent slab of chocolate-fudge cake.

'Well, of course I want the low-down,' Jane said, exasperated, and, reaching over with her coffee spoon, she stuck it in the cake and stole a huge chunk. 'Mmm. Oh, wow.'

Or something like it. Julia rolled her eyes and took a slightly less disgusting chunk for herself.

'Well?' Jane asked when her mouth was available again.

'Well—I don't know. Sometimes I think it's going all right, and other times— Well, he cheats a bit.'

'Cheats?'

'Not like that. We had rules. Two weeks—no phone calls, no Internet access, no sneaking back to London or staying up all night working—and most of the time he's been great. But he tried to sneak his phone back—he rang it from mine, and I think he was hoping to hear it and track it down, but I had it under my pillow on silent, and I answered it and told him off.'

'Oops.'

'Yeah. And we were looking on the Internet over the weekend for a house for me. Max is a bit funny about me living in another man's house, and if he wants to buy me one…' She shrugged. 'But we couldn't find anything round here that ticked all our boxes. Well, mine really, because, as he says, he'll be in London and I want to be near my friends. And that's the problem, of course. He won't live here—can't, really, working the hours he does—and I won't go back to London until I'm absolutely sure that he's in earnest about this and in it for the long haul. It's a bit like going on a crash diet—you can do it for a few days, but then something crops up.'

'Like chocolate-fudge cake,' Jane said, eyeing it longingly, so that Julia pushed it towards her and handed her the fork.

'Like chocolate-fudge cake, or an unmissable deal or a stock-market crisis, and he'll be off, I know he will. And I don't know if I can deal with it. I don't want to be a single parent, but I'd rather do that than live in a constant state of flux.'

'And have you told him that?'

'Oh, yes. But what can he do?'

Jane shrugged, stole another bit of cake and handed it back. 'Feel free to tell me to butt out and all that, but does he actually need to work? I mean, to live? For money?'

'No. Absolutely not. He doesn't ever need to work again. But he'd go crazy. He's an adrenaline junkie. He can't live without the cut and thrust.'

'Talking of which,' Jane said with a wicked twinkle in her eye, 'you're looking all loved-up at the moment. I take it *that* part of the reconciliation is going well?'

Julie felt a tide of colour sweep over her cheeks. 'That,' she said, stabbing her chocolatey fork at her friend, 'is none of your darned business.'

'That's a yes, then. Thank goodness for that.'

'Why?'

'Because he's the sexiest man alive! Don't get me wrong, I adore Pete, but your Max is seriously hot, and it would be such a wicked waste.'

She sighed. 'That's part of the problem, of course. If he looked like the back end of a bus and couldn't make love for nuts, it would be easier to leave him.'

'But you don't want to leave him,' Jane pointed out reasonably. 'You just want to live with him somewhere that isn't in the flightpath of his next plane out. You just have to work out a way to keep him with you.'

She rolled her eyes. 'And I can do that by…?'

'How about him moving the office out here?'

'What?'

'You heard. Lots of people are doing it. Or he could work from home.'

'If he could work from home, he wouldn't be in New York or Tokyo all the time.'

'Ah, but there's a difference between wanting to and being able to. He's able to work from home. He just hasn't wanted to yet. That's the crux of it. Are you going to eat any more of that?'

'You should have just had your own,' she said, sliding the plate back to Jane.

'Nah-ah. I'm on a diet.'

'Yeah, right. So—you think I should find a way to keep him in the country?'

'Mmm. Apart from just handcuffing him to the bed, which of course is the other option.'

She laughed into her coffee, splattering herself with froth and getting the giggles. 'You're incorrigible. It's so nice to see you again like this,' she said with a sigh, mopping up the last of the coffee. 'If only I didn't have to move so soon. You know John's coming back in a month or so, and I've got to find somewhere else to live?'

'No,' Jane said, shaking her head.

'Yes, he is.'

'No, he isn't. He's met someone. Hasn't he told you? Some guy in Chicago who's fifteen years younger and wants him to move out there permanently. But he's torn.'

'About the guy?'

'No, that's pretty certain. About Murphy, I think. If it wasn't for the dog, he'd do it, but you know how he adores him. And the cottage. But the dog's the real deal-breaker.'

'So—if he stays,' she said slowly, 'Then what will he do with the cottage?'

Jane shrugged. 'Sell it, I suppose. I don't know. I didn't speak to him, it was Pete who answered the phone last night while I was in the bath. That's all I know. It was pretty late, that's probably why he didn't ring you. Why don't you ring him?'

'I might,' she said. 'I might very well do that. How far behind us is Chicago? Is it six hours?'

'Something like that.'

'So, by the time I get home, it'll only be seven am. That's a bit early.'

'And you might want to talk to Max.'

'Or not. I might want to present him with a neatly packaged solution, and see how hard he tries to get out of it. It's easy to talk about in theory, but, when it comes to the crunch, I might get a more honest response if he can see it in black and white and has to make a decision one way or the other. If he feels cornered, then it won't work, and at least I'll know.'

And please God it wouldn't come to that.

CHAPTER NINE

THERE was nothing.

He pushed the chair away from the desk, glared at the screen in frustration and wondered what on earth he was going to do about finding them a house where they could all live while they sorted this out.

Although he had no real idea if he could sort it out. He'd need to get into some serious discussion with his team before he made any radical changes, but in the meantime—

'Gallagher.'

'Hello? Who's that?'

Max stared at the phone in his hand, realising he'd answered it on autopilot. 'Um—it's Max Gallagher. Can I help you?'

'Probably not. Can I speak to Julia, please?'

The voice was cautious, and he glanced at the caller display and saw it was an international call. Blake?

'I'm sorry, she's not in. I'm babysitting the girls. It's—ah—it's her husband.'

'I wondered. It's John Blake—she's housesitting for me.'

'Yes. Yes, I gather. Look, she'll be back at one, if you want to speak to her. She's gone for coffee with Jane.'

'Ah. Right. Well, in which case she'll probably know, but I was phoning to tell her that I'm not coming back. Well, I don't think so. There are—um—personal reasons, and— Well, I've met someone and I'm going to be living here, so I needed to discuss the house with her. And the dog.'

Murphy.

Max glanced down at him, lying on his foot as usual, and wondered what his plans were for the dog. He discovered, to his surprise, that it really mattered to him.

'I don't suppose you want to sell the house to me?'

'To *you*?'

'Yes—for Julia. We're—' Hell, he hated doing their washing in public, but he guessed Blake would know about their marital problems, at least in outline. 'We're trying to sort out—see if there's a way…'

'Is she all right with that?'

'Oh, there are rules,' he said with irony. 'We're halfway through a "no contact with the office" trial at the moment. But I can't just cut myself off from work, and I've been looking to see if there's anywhere around here where I can have a home office with a few staff, and a home with my family, so I can spend at least the majority of my time with them. And there's nothing.'

'And you think you could do that with my place?'

'Subject to the planners playing ball.'

'They like that,' John Blake confirmed. 'They don't like barn conversions for housing, but, for rural enterprise and business use, they're usually quite keen. And, if it's for your own personal business use, they might be very cooperative. In fact I've had some plans drawn up. They're probably still in the filing cabinet. You could have a look at them.'

'So—does that mean you'd consider selling to me?' he asked cautiously.

'I don't know,' the man said. 'I've got a problem with that. I seem to have a sitting tenant, and I want her to be happy with her new landlord, so I'd have to talk to her.'

He gave a soft laugh. 'Oh, I think she'd be happy. She's been saying that she doesn't want to move, and I can see that she really loves it here. And—there's the matter of the dog.'

'Yes.'

Max smiled thoughtfully. 'But we love Murphy, don't we, mate?' he said, rubbing the dog's ears so that he thumped his tail.

'Is he there with you?'

'He's always here with me. He's lying on my foot.'

'And you'd keep him?'

He laughed. 'I think Julia would kill me before she let anything else happen to him. And, besides, he's good company on a run.'

'Oh, you run? He loves that. He always comes with me when I go out.'

'So will you consider it?'

'We'd need to fix a fair price. Can you set that up—get a couple of the local agents round to value it?' He suggested two names, and Max jotted them down.

'Give me your number, too.'

He wrote it beside the names of the agents, then added, 'Can you do me a favour, John? Can you keep this a secret from Julia for a few days? Just to give me time to see if it'll work.'

'If you're taking the dog, the price is negotiable.'

He laughed softly. 'John, we'll take the dog whatever.

I can't imagine being without him, and I like the idea of her having a dog with her when I'm not around. I meant the planners. I need to get an unofficial nod from them, some kind of informal agreement that they'd consider it favourably before I could go ahead, but I don't want to raise Julia's hopes.'

'OK, I'll wait until I hear from you. But I have to warn you, I spoke to Pete last night so Jane may well have told her that I'm staying over here. Just so you know.'

'OK. I'll stall her—tell her there's plenty of time to think about it. I'll dream up something. Shall I get her to call you when she's back?'

'If you could. Thanks. And give Murphy a hug from me.'

He chuckled. 'Will do.'

He hung up, stared at the phone for a second and then grinned. 'Well, Smurphs, we might have got ourselves a house. What do you think of that?'

His tail thumped, and Max found the number of the local planning office and called them.

Ten minutes later, he had his unofficial answer, and it was a guarded and conditional yes. He punched the air, checked the babies, made himself another coffee, went back to the study and called Andrea.

'We need a meeting,' he said. 'I've got something to put to you. And I want Stephen there.'

'When are you thinking of?'

'This afternoon. Sort it.'

'What about Julia?'

'This is for Julia. I'm trying to find a way that we can be together, and that depends to a certain extent on you guys. You could do me a favour. Call her and tell her I need to get down to the office and sort out a major crisis. Make something up. I don't care, just don't tell her what this is about. I want it to be a surprise.'

'Andrea?'

'Hi, Julia. Look, I hate to do this to you, but I'm afraid I need Max back here at the office as soon as possible. There's a problem, and he's the only one with all the information to sort it out. You know what he's like for carrying things in his head.'

'Don't I just? It used to drive me mad. OK. I'll send him back to you. Do you need to talk to him?'

Max was looking at her curiously, and she shook her head at him. 'OK, Andrea. Thanks. I'll pass it on.'

She hung up and looked across at him again. 'Andrea wants you to go down—there's a hiccup. Apparently you keep too much in your head, so they can't sort it. Now where have I heard that before?'

'Can I go?'

She pretended to sigh, but secretly she was delighted. She wanted to call John, but she didn't want Max to know, so if he was out of the way...

'I think you have to, don't you? Go on, Max. Just go and get it over with.'

'You're a star. And I'm sorry.'

He kissed her goodbye, and it was only after he'd gone that she realised he seemed quite keen to go. Had he set it up with Andrea while she was out? She picked up the phone and looked at the last number called, but it was Jane. The only other phone was in the study, so she went in and checked on that one.

A local number, one she didn't recognise. She pressed redial, and discovered it was an estate agent.

'Sorry, I must have dialled the wrong number,' she said, and put the phone down again, smiling.

So Max was househunting, was he? Interesting. Well, she'd have to make sure he didn't do anything hasty. She could always veto anything he came up with if John was willing to sell. She just had to find that out.

She rang him.

'Hey, you old dark horse, I gather congratulations are in order!'

'Ah. Jane told you. Yes—and thank you.'

'So I take it you're happy?'

'Oh, yes. His name's Ryan, and he's forty-two and he's an architect. And he has an amazing house, and he wants me to share it with him. And we're going to have a ceremony, so, if you'd be able to join us, we'd be just over the moon.'

'Oh, John! I'm so pleased for you!' she said, her eyes filling. He was such a nice man, and he deserved happiness. 'Murphs will miss you, but I don't want you to worry about him. I'll keep him with me. The girls love him to bits, and I couldn't bear to part with him, so you can't have him even if you want him!'

John laughed. 'That's OK. Ryan has dogs, so I still get my share of dog hair in the food. I feel really at home.'

She chuckled, then bit her lip. 'John, I want to ask you something. My—um—my husband's back in the frame. Max. He tracked me down—I didn't realise it would be so hard to find me, and I wasn't really hiding, just avoiding the issue—but he's back with me, and we're trying to find a way forward. And I want us to have a home, out here in the country, near all my friends, because I know he's going to have to go away on business. But I was thinking, if you'd sell us the house, there are all the barns. He could have an office here.'

'Yes.'

'What?'

'Yes, I'll sell you the house. Of course I will, if it'll make you happy.'

'Oh.' That was quick. 'Really?'

'Really. And I'm really glad to hear you're getting back together. Just hearing you talk about him for the last year made me think you should be together. You obviously love him very deeply, and, if this helps you to find a way to overcome your problems, well then I'm with you all the way.'

'Oh, John, thank you. I can't tell you what it means to me.' She felt a flicker of excitement start deep down inside, and spread until her whole body was glowing with it. 'We'll have to have it valued. I could call some estate agents.'

'Don't bother. I've got a friend there with an agency. He knows the house well. He'll give us a fair figure, and I'm happy to go with that if you are. I'll get onto him.'

'Sure. Fine—of course.' And that meant she wouldn't have the problem of getting Max out of the way.

'Let me know the moment you've spoken to him, could you? And, if you ring and Max answers, don't tell him, will you? I want it to be a surprise.'

John chuckled. 'OK. I'll call you when I've got a figure. How are my babies?'

'Gorgeous. And into everything. Max has had to fix a staircase because they're crawling everywhere, and Ava's trying to walk—and I have to go, John, because she's trying to get out of the playpen! I'll speak to you soon. Love you.'

'Love you, too, chicken. Take care.'

She rescued Ava, picked up the phone again and tucked it in her pocket, picked Libby up and carried them both through to the sitting room. 'No climbing,' she warned them, and, tipping out a pile of toys on the floor, she sat on the edge of the sofa and phoned Jane to tell her the news.

'So—that's what I hope to do. And I know it's totally out of the blue—but, well, if it's not what you want I'll quite understand. I'll need a good, reliable team at my head office, and I don't know how realistic it would be to relocate everyone out to the country, so at the moment I'm just sounding people out.'

Andrea and Stephen were silent. They looked dumb-founded, and he realised he'd been jumping the gun, getting carried along on a tidal wave of theory again, not thinking about the effect it would have on everyone else.

He was good at that, he thought in disgust, and shook his head.

'Sorry. It's a crazy idea. Forget it.'

'Actually, no. I don't want to forget it,' Stephen said, suddenly coming to life. 'We don't need to be in London. Communication is worldwide and simplicity itself. And Dana's been talking about getting out of London. If it wasn't for the fact that the hours are too long for commuting, we would have done it before. But, now we've got the baby, we were talking about buying two places and shifting her and the baby out to the country with me joining them whenever I can. But this could be even better. This could really work for me.'

Wow. He nodded thoughtfully, and shifted his gaze to Andrea.

'Any comments?'

'I can't move. My daughter's about to have a baby, and she needs me close. She's disabled, so it's not easy.'

'And she lives in London?'

'Yes. Well, just outside. Her husband's a pilot. He flies out of Stansted. They live near Stratford, so I can get to them on the Tube.'

'Would they contemplate a move? Stansted's only an hour from the village, probably less. Forty minutes? It's only just in Suffolk, on the Suffolk-Essex border. It's not a million miles from here. And I'd make sure you had a generous relocation package.'

She frowned. 'And them?'

'All of you. Whatever it takes, Andrea. If we were to move the entire operation—and bearing in mind I want to cut back to something much more manageable, for all our sakes—then I'll need my key people.'

'I've only worked for you for six months, Max. How can I be so key?'

He gave a wry laugh. 'You have no idea,' he said drily. 'I am not an easy man to work for.'

She smiled. 'I had noticed. You just need managing.'

'So Jules tells me.' He glanced at his watch. 'Look, I need to get back. Can I leave it with you to think about? And, if you feel we can get enough key people on board, then I'll call a meeting and throw it open for discussion with the rest of the team. And I don't want Jules to know anything about this until I have something concrete to tell her.'

'So how can we contact you?'

He gave Andrea a sly smile. 'I have a new mobile number. I picked the phone up on my way here. If you could sychronise it with my database, and also get me a wireless-enabled laptop with the same info on it, that would be good. I'm just going to phone Gerry in New York.'

'Yes, what about New York?' Andrea asked, and he smiled again.

'I'll tell you when I've spoken to Gerry.'

'He can't move to Suffolk.'

Max chuckled. 'No, Stephen—but he can buy me out. He's been talking about it for years. I'll just keep a small stake in it as a silent partner.'

They stared at him as if he'd grown two heads. As well they might. The New York business was worth half their turnover.

Stephen whistled softly. 'You really are serious, aren't you?' he said, and Max nodded and stood up.

'Oh, yes,' he said firmly. 'I've never been more serious about anything in my life.'

She spent the afternoon with an architect to discuss the conversion of the farm buildings. He lived in the village and worked from home, and she'd met him on a few occasions, so she put the babies in the buggy and walked round to see him, and he came back with her, had a look and listened to her ideas.

'Well, it's possible,' he said. 'It won't be cheap, of course, barn conversions never are. But, depending on the size of what you're talking about, I should think the planners would be delighted. The buildings are falling into disrepair, and they hate that. So—yes, in theory, I think it could be done.'

'You couldn't do me a few quick drawings, could you?' she asked, and he chuckled.

'Really. I'll pay you.'

His smile was wry. 'Good. I don't like my invoices to go unpaid. It makes the bank nervous.'

She swallowed. 'Are we talking a lot? Thousands?'

He chuckled at that. 'Just to take a few photos and sketch you out an idea or two? No. Nothing like it. But, as it happens, John asked me years ago for my advice and I took some photos and used them as the basis of an artist's impression, to give some idea of how it might look, and drew up a few plans. You're welcome to borrow those, as a starting point.'

'Oh, Trevor, you're a star!' she said, and hugged him impulsively.

She went back with him to his house and collected the drawings, then after the babies were in bed she studied them until she knew them by heart. Some of the ideas wouldn't work, she thought, but on the whole the principle was good.

So, she just needed a value for the property, and she could draw up a plan of action, hang some figures on it and present it all to Max.

If he ever came home.

He was late. Very late. It was nearly ten—not that that was late for Max, but considering the rules…

She'd been happy to send him off at lunchtime, but now, thinking about it, about how keen he'd been to go, she wondered just how committed he was to this whole thing.

Would she be making a huge mistake to go ahead with it?

She put the plans away in a drawer in the study, checked on the babies and contemplated a shower. If only she knew how long he was going to be.

Oh, it was ridiculous. She knew him. If Gerry had a problem in New York, he could be talking to him for hours because of the time difference. It might be two or three in the morning before he came home. And she wasn't waiting up that late.

She told herself she was being unreasonable. Max had dropped everything for her, without warning. That was unprecedented. But it gave her an idea of what it might be like to be back with him. Even living here and working from home for part of the time, he could still be in London for much of the week. Was it unreasonable of her to ask for more than that?

So many women had two lives—one with their husbands at the weekend, the other during the week while their husbands were at work in the City.

But not her. She couldn't do it—not with Max, who would get sucked straight back in the moment there was any slack in the rope.

Oh, damn. Maybe a long, hot shower would help.

She stripped off her clothes and went into the bathroom, turned on the shower and stepped into it. Oh, that was better. She turned her face up to the water, eyes closed, and let it pour over her, washing away her doubts and fears.

He'd be home soon, and she'd feel silly for worrying.

But it was a warning, she realised, and she'd do well to take it seriously.

'Jules?'

There was no sign of her, but the lights were still on, and upstairs he could hear water running.

She was in the shower.

Fuelled by adrenaline, missing her after nearly a whole day apart, he ran upstairs, stripped off his clothes and walked into the bathroom. She had her back to him in the walk-in cubicle, and he stepped in behind her and slid his arms round her waist.

She gave a little shriek, then started to laugh, and he turned her in his arms and kissed her under the pounding spray.

'You startled me,' she said, pushing him away and coming up for air, and he grinned.

'Sorry,' he said, utterly unrepentant, and, reaching for the shampoo, he squirted some in his hands and massaged her scalp firmly.

'Oh, that's lovely,' she said, dropping her head against his chest, and when he was done he eased her back under the water and rinsed it until it was squeaky clean.

She wiped the water out of her eyes and smiled up at him. 'Well, don't stop,' she said, handing him the shower gel. And, with a quirk of his eyebrow, he put a little gel on his hands, worked them together and then spread it lovingly over her body—her breasts, her stomach, the soft, shadowed nest between her thighs.

'Max!'

'Shh. Come here,' he ordered softly, and, lifting her, he lowered her gently onto his aching erection. 'Oh, Jules.'

His mouth found hers, and, bracing himself against the wall, he started to move.

'Max!'

'It's OK, I've got you,' he said, and felt her climax start, the tightening ripples running through her, and, with an untidy groan, he followed her over the edge.

CHAPTER TEN

JOHN didn't come back to her with a value for the house.

Maybe he hadn't been able to get hold of his friend, she thought, or maybe he had other things on his mind. Love had a way of distracting you from the core business, and she should know. She'd let Max distract her all week.

Ever since Monday night, when he'd finally come back from London, he'd been distracting her with his lazy, sexy smile and promises.

'What's wrong?' she'd asked him, too familiar with his moods to trust this one. 'I know that look—you're plotting something.'

And he'd grinned that wicked, oh-so-sexy grin and tapped the side of his nose. 'Saturday,' he'd promised.

'So you are up to something.'

'Just be patient,' he'd said, and wouldn't tell her any more. But just now, when he'd told her he was going out for a run, she'd looked out along the valley from the bedroom window and had seen him standing with his hand held to his ear.

On the phone.

But she had his phone, as part of their deal, so he must have got himself another one, and he was using it in secret.

Cheating? Or planning a surprise?

In which case, why couldn't he just tell her that, since she knew already, and use the house phone out of earshot?

Because it was nothing to do with her, nothing to do with Saturday. Saturday, of course, was Valentine's Day. It would be most unlike him to remember that, but maybe Andrea had prompted him and he'd organised flowers or something.

They wouldn't be going out for dinner, because of the babies. Well, not unless he'd organised a babysitter, and she wouldn't be happy with that unless she'd screened the girl first—and it was Thursday afternoon now, so there wasn't a lot of time left to take up references and interview her.

And, anyway, taking her out for dinner wouldn't explain why he had this air of suppressed excitement about him that he always had when the adrenaline was running. She should know, she'd seen it enough times when he'd been about to close a deal, tying up the loose ends with some delicate negotiating.

He was brilliant at it, and it brought him to life, but it brought out a side of him that was impossible to live with.

And she had a horrible, horrible feeling it was happening again.

She nearly rang Andrea, but then thought better of it. She'd ask him instead. They were coming up to the end of their two weeks on Monday, so she'd see what he came up with on Saturday—this famous surprise he was planning— and then, if it turned out that he thought he could just ask her to go back to him and carry on as usual, well, then she'd have to say no.

Oh, lord. She didn't want to think about it. It made her feel sick, but something was definitely going on, and that made her feel sick, too. Apart from anything else, he hadn't mentioned househunting or moving or anything about it since Monday—and to be fair he hadn't mentioned it then, he'd simply called an agent and she'd only found out by accident. So it had been the weekend, then, when he'd been all for looking on the Internet.

And, since then, nothing about houses or the business or work-life balance at all, but he'd spoiled her all week, pampering her during the day, making her drinks, playing with the babies, taking the dog out for runs. And, every night, he'd taken her to bed and made love to her until she couldn't think straight. And, fool that she was, she'd been more than happy to let him.

On Tuesday, he'd taken them all to the beach again for another walk along the front, and this time they'd taken Murphy.

He'd got soaked in the sea, but he'd had a marvellous time, and Max hadn't seemed to mind the sodden, sandy dog in the back of his car at all.

Curious. He would have gone mad before, just at the thought.

And on Wednesday he'd pushed the vacuum cleaner round and washed the kitchen floor, and then they'd spent the afternoon in the garden working on the rosebed while the babies had slept. The weather had been gorgeous again, and they'd got a lot of weeding and pruning and tidying done.

And, today, he'd sent her off for coffee with Jane again while he did the babies' washing.

So much unprecedented behaviour. Because he loved her, or because he was trying to shmooze her back into his life without making the necessary changes? She stood there, watching him on the phone in the distance, and wondered if sending her for coffee with Jane twice this week had just been getting her out of the way. If, every time he'd taken the dog for a run, he'd been secretly on the phone planning a takeover.

She gave a heavy sigh and turned away from the window.

So much for scaling back the operation.

She thought of the plans for the barns, sitting quietly in the drawer in the study, and she felt cheated. They could have had so much, she thought, but he wasn't playing fair. He'd broken the rules, so he wasn't taking it seriously.

And she couldn't wait until Monday. She couldn't wait till Saturday. She wanted answers now. Tonight.

The doorbell rang, and she went downstairs and opened the door.

'Parcel for Mr Gallagher,' she was told by a helmeted courier. 'Sign here, please.'

'Sure.'

She signed, closed the door and put the parcel on the kitchen table, then made herself a cup of tea and sat and regarded it warily.

What was it?

It was only small, very light. A part of his Saturday plan? Or something to do with the business?

There was nothing on it to give away the sender, but it had come from London. That was all she could tell, and that was from the dealer's phone number on the courier's bike registration-plate. So even that might not be right.

She couldn't open it.

Or see through it, she thought wryly.

She had to stop herself from shaking it again.

'Jules?'

'In the kitchen.'

He came in, the muddy dog at his side, and Murphy ran over to her and rubbed himself wetly against her leg.

'Oh, you monster, you've been in the river!' she shrieked, and Max hustled him into his bed.

'Sorry about that. Murphy, stay. Everything OK?'

She met his eyes challengingly. 'I don't know, you tell me. What was your phone call about?'

Damn.

Damn, damn and double damn. She must have seen him. Oh, hell. He'd thought he was out of sight, but then he'd started pacing, like he always did when he was thinking, and he must have come back into range.

And she'd seen him.

'Sorry. It was Andrea.'

'I don't think so. She was contacting you through me.'

'It was urgent.'

'And you just happened to have another phone on you?'

He felt a tide of heat run up his neck, and looked away. 'Jules, there's been a lot going on. I didn't want to—'

'What? Stick to the rules? Don't lie to me, Max!'

'I'm not lying. I'm trying to sort things out.'

'I thought you had a team to do that for you.'

'They need support.'

'Do they? Good for them. You had a parcel delivered. I signed for it.'

She looked pointedly at the table, and he saw a small packet lying there.

The last element of his plan.

He left it there. At this rate, he might not need it. 'Thanks. Look, Jules, I'm sorry about the call—'

'And what about this morning? Were you on the phone then?'

The truth must have shown in his face, because she gave an exasperated sigh and stood up.

'I can't do this, Max. I can't live with your lies. Either we're giving this our all, or we're not. And you're not, so that's it. I'm sorry. I want you out. Now.'

Oh, hell. She was on the verge of tears, and all his plans were going out the window with knobs on.

He swore softly and reached for her, but she ducked out of his range and ran upstairs. He heard her door slam behind her, and then a moment later the awful, fractured sound of her sobbing.

And then one of the babies started to cry.

Damn.

And just when it was all starting to look so good.

He ran upstairs, went into the babies' room and scooped Ava out of her cot. 'Shh, sweetheart, it's all right. Come on, don't wake Libby.' But Libby was awake, and she started to grizzle, and so he picked her up, too, carried them downstairs and made them a drink, gave them a piece of squashy banana each to suck on and found them some dry nappies beside the Aga.

He didn't want to take them back upstairs, but he wasn't leaving, either, not while Jules was still crying, and hopefully not when she'd stopped. He could hear her overhead, and her sobs were ripping right through him. He wanted to go to her, but he couldn't leave the babies. They were too adventurous, and they'd pull themselves up and fall and hurt themselves, and he'd never forgive himself for that.

But the sobbing was agonising, and he couldn't leave her any more, so he ran upstairs, tapped on her door and went in.

'Jules, please. Let me explain,' he said.

'There's nothing to explain. You had a chance. You blew it.'

'One phone call!'

'Two—at least,' she said, sitting up and turning round, her face ravaged with tears. 'And those are just the ones I know about!'

'OK, three, actually. But, last time I checked, taking care of your business so your family didn't suffer wasn't a hanging offence—'

'Don't twist my words.'

'I'm not. I'm just pointing out that it was only a few calls—I can't stop working for ever, just because you've decided you don't want to play any more! And you knew what I did, what my job involved, before you married me.'

'But we've got the babies now.'

'And you left me before you knew you were pregnant, so don't bring them into this, they're nothing to do with it,' he snapped. And suddenly he realised he couldn't take it any more, and maybe she was right.

'I've done everything I can to make this work for us, and what have you done? Spy on me, fail to trust me to do my best for us, refuse to compromise. Well, I'm sorry, I can't do any more, and, as it's obviously not going to be enough for you—well, maybe you're right. Maybe I need to go back to London, and resurrect what's left of my business. And don't move out of this house,' he added, stabbing a finger in her direction for emphasis. 'I'll get my solicitor to get in touch. I'll make sure you're taken care of, but not for you. This is for the babies. And I will see them, and I will be part of their lives, but I won't be part of yours, and you'll have to live with that and so will I.'

And without another word he went into his room, threw his things into his bag and carried it downstairs.

The girls were sitting in their playpen and they looked up at him and beamed. 'Dada!' Ava crowed, pulling herself up, and he dragged in a breath and clamped down on the sob that was threatening to tear its way out of his chest.

'Goodbye, babies,' he whispered soundlessly, and, crouching down, he kissed them in turn, gave Murphy a pat and then let himself out. The keys for the estate car were on the side in the kitchen, but he threw his case into the sports car, slammed the door and shot off the drive before he could weaken and go back in, and beg her to change her mind...

He'd gone.

He really had gone. Taken his lovely, sexy little car and his clothes and gone away without a backward glance.

And he was right. She'd been terribly unfair, expecting him to make all the changes, give up everything so she didn't have to, and now she had everything except him, and she was devastated.

And, because she didn't know what else to do, she phoned Andrea and told her.

'Oh, Julia! Oh, no! Oh, I don't believe it! Didn't he tell you what he's been planning?'

'Planning? I thought it was something to do with Valentine's Day.'

'Oh, well, maybe that's when he'd planned to tell you. You know Max—he likes to do things his way. But, Julia, you have to give him a chance to explain. You have no idea what he's given up for you all—so much! We're all stunned. You have to hear him out—you have to give him a chance. Call him.'

'I can't. I've got his phone.'

'The new one?'

'No. But I don't have the number of the new one.'

'I do. Write it down, and ring him now, and, if you don't get him and he turns up here, I'll make him ring you.'

But he didn't answer, and he didn't call, and she couldn't let it go.

'Come on, babies,' she said, and, dressing them warmly in their sleep-suits and coats, she put them in her car, put Murphy in the back and set off for London, the parcel he'd had delivered on her front seat, together with the plans for the barns.

Just in case.

He went to the office, but after he'd parked the car he sat in it for several minutes before he realised he couldn't go in. Not like this. Not with his hold on his emotions so incredibly fragile.

So he went back to his apartment, threw open the door onto the roof terrace and stood there, hands rammed in the pockets of the jeans he'd never need again, and stared broodingly down into the murky waters of the Thames far below him.

It wasn't anything like the tiny, crystal-clear stream that ran along the lower edge of the garden of Rose Cottage. That was a real river, with minnows, newts and kingfishers, with badgers, foxes and rabbits drinking from it at night and herons fishing in it by day.

And he'd never live there with her now. Never have a chance to walk out of the office door at five o'clock and stroll across the drive and in through his front door, to be greeted by the dog and the children and his beautiful, beloved wife.

Oh, damn. He wasn't going to cry. He was done with that. He'd done it every night for a year. He wasn't doing it any more. It was over. Finished.

He had a shower, changed into something his tailor would have recognised and dropped his jeans in the bin.

No. That was stupid. He'd need them when he was with the girls, he thought, so he threw them in the laundry basket and walked out of the door.

He didn't know where he was going, or why, but he couldn't stay here and think about her any more.

He wasn't there, but his car was.

She'd spoken to the concierge and parked in a visitor's slot. He hadn't recognised her, but he recognised distress when he saw it, and she was plenty distressed.

He even gave her a hand to get the buggy out, unfold it and put the babies in it, and he held the dog until she was ready to go up.

'Is he expecting you, madam?'

'No, but I've got my key. It's all right. Thank you for your help.'

All the way up in the lift her heart was pounding, but, when she got there, the apartment was empty. He'd been home, though. She could smell soap, and his bag was flung on the bed, the contents tossed out all over the place.

The fridge was empty apart from a few bottles of white wine and some withered lettuce in a bag. Did he never eat? Or maybe he'd turned it out before going to New York, which was what he'd been supposedly doing last Monday.

Heavens, only ten days ago. It seemed much, much longer. So perhaps he'd gone shopping?

The girls were restless, and Murphy was running round and sniffing everything. She let him out onto the roof terrace and hoped he had the good sense not to jump over. Please God. She couldn't ring John Blake and tell him that.

Going back inside, she looked around the sitting room, and it was a minefield. If she let the girls out of the buggy, they'd get into all sorts of trouble. The glass coffee-table, for a start, had smooth, sharp corners and hard edges, and there were things dotted around all over the place that they could get hold of.

Remote controls, speakers, tall vases—and pieces of statuary that would rock over and kill them so easily.

And the polished wooden floor was less than welcoming to adventurous little girls. So they stayed where they were, in the buggy, and she warmed their supper in the microwave and fed them spoonfuls in turn, and then she lifted them out, one at a time, and breastfed and changed them.

She was just tucking Libby back into the buggy when she heard the front door open, and Max's feet stopped dead just in her line of sight.

She clipped the safety strap and sat back on her heels, and met his blank, expressionless eyes. 'What the hell are you doing here?'

She didn't know. Only that she'd been wrong, so she said the only thing that seemed to make any sense.

'I'm sorry.'

For a moment she thought he was going to walk out, but then he took a step towards her. 'What for? I mean, specifically?'

'Being a selfish, unreasonable, demanding bitch?' she offered tearfully. 'Refusing to compromise? Expecting you to make all the changes? Not trusting you? Not giving you a chance to explain? I don't know,' she said, her voice cracking. 'I just know I can't live without you, and I'm sorry if I've hurt you, I'm sorry if I've ruined everything for you. Andrea said she couldn't believe—'

'You've been talking to Andrea?'

She nodded. 'She gave me your phone number—the new one. I rang it, but it was off.'

'The battery's flat, and I didn't have the charger in my car. So—what did she tell you?'

'Nothing. Just how shocked they all were at what you'd done, but I didn't know what you'd done, you hadn't told me, and she didn't, so I still don't know, Max. What the hell have you done because of me that's so awful? What have I made you do? Please tell me!'

He gave a shaky sigh. 'You haven't made me do anything. I chose to do it. I wanted to. I was just lashing out, because it was all supposed to be so wonderful, and yet again it seemed I'd got it wrong.'

He turned away and walked over to the door, opening it and going out onto the roof terrace. 'Murphy?' he said, sounding surprised, and the dog lashed him with his tail and licked his hands, and he crouched down, put his arms round him and held on, while she watched and waited.

'Oh, Max, please tell me what you did,' she whispered,

and, as if he'd heard, he came back inside, sat down, took
the dog by the collar and held him still.

'This isn't going to work. There's nowhere for the
girls to sleep, and the dog's going to trash the place in
a minute, and I've already sold it—and anyway I want
to sit down with you and talk this through properly, so
let's go home.'

'Home?' He'd sold the apartment?

He smiled tiredly. 'Yes, Jules. Home.'

It was an awful journey, and only that word kept her sane.

Not that anything happened, but she was on tenterhooks
the whole time, longing to get back and find out what he'd
done, what he was talking about, and if, after everything
she'd said and done, they still had a chance.

The word 'home' kept echoing in her mind, though,
and the fact that he'd sold their apartment, and it sustained
her all the way back to the cottage.

They put the girls to bed, shut the dog up in the kitchen
and went into the sitting room. It was cold, but Max lit the
fire and turned down the lights, and, sitting on the floor
leaning back against the sofa, he drew her down beside him
and put his arm round her.

She could feel the heat of his body on one side, and the
glow of the fire on the other, and his hand was draped over
her shoulder and stroking it rhythmically. But she could
feel a tremor in it, and she knew he wasn't nearly as casual
about this as he seemed.

'Right. Let's imagine it's Saturday evening, and I've just
cooked you dinner, OK?'

'Oh, Max—'

'Shh. And we're in here with coffee and chocolates, and it's been a lovely day, and the babies are asleep. OK?'

'OK.'

'And then I'm going to make you a proposition, and I want you to think about it and give me your answer when you've had time to examine it and make sure it'll work for you. Still OK?'

'OK,' she echoed again. 'So—what's the proposition?'

'Well, first of all, John's selling the house.'

'I know. And—'

'Shh. Listen to me. And I've had it valued.'

'When?'

'On Tuesday, while we were at the beach, and today, while you were having coffee with Jane. Two agents. And I've spoken to John, given him the figures and we've agreed a price.'

'But—'

'Shh. You can have your turn in a minute. Anyway, John said he'd contacted an architect in the past and spoken to him about converting the buildings—actually, he said he had a set of plans and he thought they might be in the filing cabinet, but it's locked, so I can't look. Anyway, it's irrelevant, because they probably won't be right, but in principle the planners are prepared to look favourably on converting the buildings into offices so I can move the London office up here. And I've sold my share in the New York office to Gerry.'

She stared at him in confusion. 'You've sold New York?'

'I can't walk there, so it's too far,' he said with a slight smile. 'That was my benchmark. And I can't walk to London, so I'm moving the office up here, and everyone who wants to come. That's Stephen, his wife and baby, and Andrea, her daughter and son-in-law, and various other members of the team. And the others will get good references and a redundancy package to tide them over.'

She stared at him, dumbfounded. No wonder Andrea was shocked. 'New York *and* Toyko?'

His smile was wry. 'Ah, well, Yashimoto and I had already talked about it, and I was ready to let it go. Somehow—' He broke off and swallowed, and his fingers tightened fractionally on her shoulder. 'Somehow, after all the grief it caused us, I never really felt right about it. And I'd turned his company round, and it was working again, so it was successful in its own way. And I didn't exactly lose money, I just didn't rip him off when I sold it back to him.'

She tilted her head up and stared up at him. 'You really were already going to sell it to him? Because I've been feeling so bad about it, after all that work you put into preparing for the takeover, and with New York as well—'

He shook his head, pressing a silencing finger to her lips, then smiled. 'It's fine. I'm happy. So it's all down to you, now. Andrea says she'll come and help settle me in, but she can't work full-time, not with her disabled daughter about to have her first baby, and so this'll only work if you'll job-share with her. But the advantage is you'd have control of my diary,' he added with a grin.

'So, what do you think, Mrs Gallagher? Want to give it a go? Or is it still too much? Because, if you really want me to, I'll ditch the lot and take early retirement and learn to do macramé, if it means I get to be with you and the girls—because I realised today after I walked out on you that I couldn't do it, couldn't walk away, because I love you too much.'

His smile faltered, and she realised he was in deadly earnest. She lifted a hand and cradled his face tenderly. 'Oh, Max. I love you, too. And you don't have to learn macramé. And I'd love to get back into the business with you; I miss it. I just couldn't do that and that alone, to the exclusion of everything else in my life, but a job share— that sounds interesting. And I like the idea of the diary.'

He gave a shaky laugh and squeezed her shoulder gently. 'I rather thought you might.' He drew her closer against his side, and tilted her face and kissed her slowly and tenderly. Then he lifted his head and smiled down at her. 'There's one other thing, but I don't know where the packet is that was delivered earlier. I hope you've still got it.'

'It's in the car. I'll fetch it.'

And, scrambling to her feet, she ran out to the car, took the little parcel and the plans off the front seat and took them back inside, kneeling beside him.

'Here. And these are the plans. I got a copy off the architect the other day. He lives in the village, and I contacted him about it. And John was supposed to be getting me a price for the house so I could pass it on to you. And there's an estimated breakdown of the cost of conversion and fittings, too, but that was just for a small operation.'

He frowned. 'So—why have you got all these? I swore John to secrecy.'

She smiled at him. 'So did I—and he didn't say a word about you, except to say that he thought we belonged together and, if it would help us, he'd be only too happy to let us have the house. That was all. And I thought, if I presented you with the option of moving part of your operation up here so you could divide your time between here and London, then, if you felt trapped by it, it wouldn't be right for you, and then at least I'd know.'

He put the plans aside with a dismissive hand. 'I don't feel trapped,' he said firmly. 'Not in the least bit. I feel incredibly blessed. I know it's been a tough year, but it's over now, and we're back together, and I don't ever want us to be apart again.'

'Nor do I,' she murmured. 'And I'm so sorry I didn't tell you I was pregnant. I should have done. I wanted to, but I really didn't think you'd want to know. If I'd had the slightest idea about what you'd gone through with Debbie, I wouldn't have hesitated.'

He kissed her gently. 'I know. And that's my fault. And it's my fault you got upset today when you saw me sneaking around with the phone talking to John. If I'd only shared it all with you, but, no, you know what I'm like, I wanted to surprise you. I wanted to go, "Ta-da!" and pull it out of the hat like a damn magician with a rabbit, and it all backfired in my face. So no more secrets, eh? No more keeping our feelings to ourselves, no more suspicions. We have to trust each other, even if we don't know what's going on.'

She nodded slowly. 'I do trust you. I want to trust you. It was just—I know that look you get when you're about to close a deal, and you've been like that all week, so I knew, I just *knew* something was going on. Something big. Something important.'

'It was. I was planning our future. I can't think of anything more exciting than that. Here. I've got something for you.'

And he ripped open the packet and tipped out a little

box, then opened the box carefully and took out a tiny leather draw-string purse. Then he shifted so that he was kneeling, facing her.

'Put out your hand,' he said softly, and she held it out, thinking it must be a ring. He'd never given her a ring, apart from her wedding ring, and she'd had to buy that.

'Other way up.'

Oh. Not a ring, then. Suppressing her disappointment, she turned her hand over, and he tipped up the little bag over her cupped palm and shook something out. Something cool and brilliant, and utterly beautiful. Three somethings, in fact.

'Max?'

'You never had a ring,' he said gruffly. 'Only your wedding ring, because we got married so quickly and quietly that there wasn't really any time or need, or— Well, no, there was a need, but I just didn't see it at the time. But I should have done, and I should have seen the need to have a more public ceremony. But, since I seem to get everything wrong, I thought you should have a say in this, so I bought you three diamonds—one for us, and one each to celebrate our beautiful little daughters. And I don't know what you want to have made with them, but I thought maybe a ring, and a pair of earrings, or an eternity ring, or a necklace—I don't know. It's up to you.'

'They're beautiful,' she said, awestruck. 'Stunning.'

'They're flawless white diamonds. They were cut in Antwerp from the same stone, and, if you want more, we can get them—to make another ring, or something else. They've got other smaller ones from the same stone. But I thought we could have them set so that I can give them to you in June.'

'June?'

'When the roses are in bloom,' he said softly. 'I know it might seem a bit sentimental, but I really want to renew our vows. I nearly lost you, Jules, and it was only then that I realised how much you meant to me. I want a chance to tell our friends how much I love you, and how lucky I am to have you, and I want to stand with you, in our garden, and smell the roses.'

'Oh, Max.' Her eyes filled with tears. 'I said that to you.'

'I know. And you were right. We never made time to smell the roses, but we've got time now. We can do it every summer for the rest of our lives—if you'll have me.'

'Oh, Max. Of course I'll have you. I love you.'

He gave a fleeting smile. 'I love you, too—and I always will.'

And, cupping her hands in his, he drew her to him, bent his head and kissed her.

EPILOGUE

IT WAS a glorious June day—the day after Ava and Libby's first birthday—and all their guests were gathered in the garden of Rose Cottage to hear them make their vows.

And everyone who mattered to them was here. Linda, his mother, and Richard; Jane and Peter with their children; John Blake and his new partner; Andrea, her daughter and son-in-law, and Stephen, Dana and the baby, and all the other people from work who'd been able to make it. Even Gerry from New York and Mr Yashimoto had flown in, and the girls, dressed in their brand-new little dresses, were in the care of their new au pair and were being spoilt to pieces by all their friends and family.

Well, Max's family, since Julia didn't have any now. Not that it mattered, strangely, because she had so many very dear friends, and she had Max and the girls, and who could want more than that?

She was wearing her diamonds—the largest one set in a beautiful, simple necklace that hung just below the hollow of her throat, the others in a pair of matching earrings—and she had roses in her hair, to remind them both.

And now they were standing together under the rose

arch in the garden, and John Blake was calling everyone's attention. It was to be very simple. This was no formal ceremony, just two people who loved each other speaking from the heart, and neither of them had a script.

She should have felt nervous, but she didn't, because nothing had ever felt more right. Max was standing there in front of her, holding her hands in his, and his eyes held hers steadily, the love in them shining more brilliantly than any diamond.

'I promised to love you,' he said quietly but clearly. 'But I didn't know what love was until I nearly lost you. I promised to honour you, and I took your presence by my side for granted. And I promised to cherish you, and I didn't even notice when your heart was breaking. But I know the difference now,' he went on. 'And I vow, before all our friends and family, never to make the same mistakes again. I'll probably make others. They'll be genuine, but I'm only human, and I apologise in advance if I ever hurt you or disappoint you or let you down again. But I will always make time with you to stop and smell the roses,' he said with a gentle smile. 'And I will always love you, and nothing will ever change that.' He slipped his hand into his pocket and pulled out a ring—a hoop of brilliant-cut diamonds, a perfect match for the others he'd given her.

'Max?' she said soundlessly.

He smiled. 'They're from the same stone; they belong together—as we do. For eternity,' he said, and slipped it onto her finger so that it came to rest against her wedding ring, a perfect complement to its simplicity. 'I love you, Julia.'

He squeezed her hands gently, his smile encouraging,

but for a moment she couldn't speak. Then she lifted her head, looked deep into his heart, and smiled back.

'I love you, too. I always did, even when I hated you, when I hated what was happening to us. I never stopped loving you. I took away something I can never give you back—the birth of our daughters. And I'm so, so sorry for that. But I can promise you that I'll never hide anything from you again, that I'll never distrust you or withdraw from you or fail to find the courage to face our demons together, because together I know we can do it, and without you I'm nothing. You are my life, Max. My life, my love, my heart. And I will always love you.'

His eyes filled, and he closed them briefly, then opened them again and released her hands. But only so he could take her into his arms, and, with a tender smile, he sealed their vows with a kiss…

Expecting
ROYAL
TWINS!

MELISSA McCLONE

With a degree in mechanical engineering from Stanford University, the last thing **Melissa McClone** ever thought she would be doing was writing romance novels. But analysing engines for a major US airline just couldn't compete with her 'happily-ever-afters'. When she isn't writing, caring for her three young children or doing laundry, Melissa loves to curl up on the couch with a cup of tea, her cats and a good book. She enjoys watching home decorating shows to get ideas for her house—a 1939 cottage that is *slowly* being renovated. Melissa lives in Lake Oswego, Oregon, with her own real-life hero husband, two daughters, a son, two loveable but oh-so-spoiled indoor cats and a no-longer-stray outdoor kitty that decided to call the garage home. Melissa loves to hear from her readers. You can write to her at PO Box 63, Lake Oswego, OR 97034, USA, or contact her via her website: www.melissamcclone.com.

For Tom, Mackenna, Finn, Rose, Smalls,
Rocket, Spirit, Chaos and Yoda.
The best family a writer could have!

Special thanks to: Elizabeth Boyle,
Drew Brayshaw, Roger Carstens, Amy Danicic,
John Fenzel, Terri Reed, Robert Williams
and Camas Physical Therapy.

CHAPTER ONE

NIKOLA TOMISLAV KRESIMIR, Crown Prince of Vernonia, strode past his father's assistant and the two palace guards standing watch. As soon as he entered the king's office, Niko heard the door close behind him.

He grimaced.

Niko didn't have time for another impromptu assignment. His in-box was overflowing. The upcoming trade conference was turning into a logistical nightmare. Princess Julianna of Aliestle was patiently waiting to have lunch with him.

He was used to juggling competing demands, thrived on them actually, but the collar of his dress shirt seemed to have shrunk two inches since he'd left his own office three minutes ago. He tugged on his tie.

Not that it lessened his frustration level.

A summons from the king trumped everything else and often messed up Niko's schedule for the rest of the day, sometimes week. Not to mention the havoc royal protocol played with his priority of turning their provincial country into a modern nation. But he followed his father's orders out of respect and for the good of the country.

King Dmitar sat behind his large mahogany desk staring at a manila file folder in his hands. His once dark hair was now as white as the snowcapped peaks of the Balkans and Carpathians. His face, like Niko's own, was as rugged as those same mountain ranges. His wire-rimmed reading glasses rested low on his nose, making him look more like a professor than a soldier or a king who had spent the majority of his rule trying to unite his country against all odds.

Niko stood ten feet away, waiting.

A breeze blew through an open window, carrying the sweet fragrance of flowers from the royal gardens. A vast improvement over the acrid smell of gunpowder and sickening scent of blood that used to taint the air around here.

Five years had passed since the ratification of the peace treaty. Tensions between the two warring factions erupted occasionally, but peace prevailed. Niko intended to ensure it always would. A totally united Vernonia, however, seemed like a far off dream. A fairy tale, really.

Not wanting to waste more time, he cleared his throat.

His father looked up. Dark circles ringed his eyes.

"You sent for me, sir," Niko said.

The lines on his father's face seemed deeper, more pronounced, than they used to be. The conflict had aged him; so had grief. But still the corners of his mouth curved upward into a rare smile. "I have good news, my son."

The best news would be that Vernonia had been accepted into the European Union, but Niko knew they still had too many improvement projects to complete first. He stepped closer to the desk. "I've spent the morning wading through the demands of the trade delegations. Good news will be a welcome relief, Father."

"Your bride box has been located."

Not located. *Found.*

The unexpected news sunk in. Niko respected the past, but the fact something as important as his marriage was dependent on such on antiquated custom as presenting his wife a family heirloom on their wedding day irritated him. Traditions could only take his country so far. "You are certain it is mine?"

"As certain as we can be until we have the box in hand."

His bride box hadn't been seen in over twenty years. Not since the collapse of the Soviet Union brought turmoil to many Balkan countries. Vernonia had avoided the ethnic strife that ravaged many of its neighbors, but terrorist acts had led to a deadly civil war that tore the country apart and nearly destroyed its economy. "Where is the box?"

"The United States." His father adjusted his glasses and studied the folder. "Charlotte, North Carolina, to be exact."

"A long way from home."

"Yes."

The location wasn't really important. Niko would have the box back. Tradition—and his father—would be satisfied. Nothing would stand in the way of Niko's marriage to Julianna. He could finally fulfill his duty as his parents and people wished him to do. The marriage would give him the means and opportunity to do what he wanted—needed—to do with Vernonia.

Plans formed in his mind, but he couldn't get too far ahead of himself. Nothing could happen until he had possession of the box. "How was it discovered?"

"The internet." His father shuffled through papers in the file. "Someone posted on an antiques forum looking for the key. After a few exchanges verifying the seriousness of our interest, we were sent a picture that confirmed our suspicions. The box is yours."

"Incredible." Niko considered the number of private investigators and treasure hunters hired to find the heirloom. He laughed at the irony. "Technology to the rescue of an Old World custom."

"Technology may be useful at times, but our people desire tradition. You must remember that when you wear the crown."

"Everything I've ever done has been for Vernonia." Niko's family had ruled for eight centuries. The country was in their blood and hearts. Duty always came first. "But we must modernize if we are to succeed in the twenty-first century."

"Yet you have agreed to an arranged marriage."

He shrugged, but the last thing he felt was indifference. His marriage would act as a bridge between the past and the future. He might not be the United

Kingdom's Prince William, but Niko had the attention of royal watchers. The publicity surrounding a royal wedding would be good for his country's nascent tourist industry. He would use whatever he could to Vernonia's advantage. "I may not be a stickler for tradition, Father, but I will always do what is best for the country."

"As will I." His father placed the folder on his desk. "You have the key."

"Of course, sir." Niko always had the key. He had been wearing the damn thing ever since the decree that he could never take it off twenty odd years ago. The only thing that had changed since then was the size of the chain. He pulled the thick silver one from beneath his shirt. A key that looked more like a cross and heart welded together dangled from his fingers. "Can I finally stop wearing the necklace now?"

"No." The word resonated through the spacious office until the tapestries on the wall swallowed the sound. "You will need the key when you go to North Carolina tomorrow."

"Send Jovan. I can't travel to the United States right now. I'm needed here," Niko countered. "My schedule is full. Princess Julianna is here."

"The box is yours," his father said. "You will be the one to bring it home. The travel arrangements have already been made. Your aide will be provided with an itinerary and the necessary information."

Niko bit his tongue. Further resistance would be futile. The king's word was final even if it made little sense under the current circumstances. "Fine, but you do realize I have never seen the box."

"You have seen it. You were a child, so you don't remember."

What Niko remembered from his childhood and early adulthood was war, the one thing he wanted and hoped to forget. Keeping peace and modernizing Vernonia were his main goals now. Though the parliament wanted him to provide an heir. Might as well get on with that, now that nothing stood in his way of marrying. Speaking of which…

"Do you wish for me to propose to Julianna before I leave for America or upon my return, Father?"

The king's face reddened. "There shall be no official proposal."

"What?" Niko remembered the open window and the people on the other side of the office door. He lowered his voice. "We've spent months negotiating with the Council of Elders in Aliestle. Even the Separatists are in favor of the marriage since King Alaric supported them during the conflict. The only obstacle to marriage has been the bride box. A delay will send the wrong—"

"No proposal."

Frustration mounted. Niko had searched for a suitable bride for almost a year. He didn't want to have to start over. "You agreed Julianna is an excellent choice for a wife and the future queen of Vernonia. That is why finding the bride box has been a priority."

"Julianna is more than suitable to be queen, but…"

His father removed his glasses and rubbed his tired-looking eyes. "Are you in love with her?"

Love? Niko was surprised his traditional father had broached the subject. His parents' marriage hadn't been a love match. Niko had never expected one for himself after his older brother, Stefan, had been killed during the conflict.

"We get along well. She's beautiful and intelligent. I will be content with her as my wife," Niko stated honestly. He'd always known as crown prince he would marry for Vernonia's good, not his own. "The publicity surrounding a royal wedding will increase our visibility to the tourist industry. Most importantly, an alliance with Aliestle will give Vernonia the capital it requires to complete rebuilding. That will help our efforts to join the European Union."

"You've looked at all angles."

Niko bowed his head. "As you taught me, Father."

"And Julianna. Are her feelings engaged?"

"She…cares for me," Niko answered carefully. "As I do for her. She understands what is expected."

"But is she in love with you?"

Uncomfortable, Niko shifted his weight between his feet. "You've never spoken about love before. Only duty and what a state marriage would entail."

"You are old enough to know whether a woman has feelings for you or not. Answer my question."

Niko considered his outing with Julianna yesterday afternoon. They'd left their security detail on the shore and sailed on the lake. He'd kissed her for the first time. The kiss had been…pleasant, but Julianna

seemed more interested in sailing than kissing him
again. "I do not believe she is in love with me. In fact,
I'm certain she isn't."

"Good."

"I do not understand what is going on, sir. If something has changed with Vernonia's relationship to
Aliestle—"

"Nothing has changed there." His father's drawn out
sigh would have made the parliament members' knees
tremble beneath their heavy robes. "But a slight…
complication in regards to you marrying Julianna has
arisen."

Niko's muscles tensed. "What kind of complication?"

Inside Bay #2 at Rowdy's One Stop Garage in Charlotte,
North Carolina, a Brad Paisley song blared from a
nearby boom box. Oil, gasoline and grease scented
the air. Isabel Poussard bent over a Chevy 350 small
block engine. The bolt she needed to remove wouldn't
budge, but she wasn't giving up or asking for help. She
wanted the guys to see her as an equal, not a woman
who couldn't make it on her own.

She adjusted the wrench. "Come on now. Turn for
Izzy."

A swatch of light brown hair fell across her eyes so
she couldn't see.

Darn ponytail. It never stayed put. If she had any
extra money, she would get a short hairstyle so she
wouldn't be bothered anymore. She didn't dare cut it
herself. For years her uncle Frank had chopped her

hair with whatever was handy, scissors or razor blades. She'd grown up looking more like a boy than a girl. Not that any dresses hung in her closet today.

Izzy tucked the stray strands behind her ear. She struggled to turn the wrench. Her palm sweated. The wrench slipped.

Frustrated, she blew out a puff of air. "No one is going to let you work over the wall in the pits during a race if you can't loosen a little bolt."

She imagined the start of the Daytona 500. The roar of the crowd. The heat from the pavement. The smell of burning rubber. The rev of engines.

Excitement surged through her.

Being on a professional pit crew had been Uncle Frank's dream for as long as Izzy remembered. An aneurysm had cut his life short. Now it was up to her to turn his dream into a reality. He'd spent his life caring for her and sharing his skill and love of cars. More than once he'd had the opportunity to be on a pit crew, but he hadn't wanted to leave her. This was the least she could do for him.

As soon as she saved enough money, she would enroll in pit crew school. She wanted to put her days at dirt tracks and stock car circuits behind her and take a shot at the big leagues. For Uncle Frank and herself. She had bigger goals than just being on the pit crew. She wanted to be the crew chief. Izzy would show those kids who laughed at her grease-stained hands they were wrong. She would do something with her life. Something big.

She adjusted her grip on the wrench and tried again. The bolt turned. "Yes!"

"Hey, Izzy," the garage owner's son and her closest friend, Boyd, shouted to her over the Lady Antebellum song now playing on the radio. "Some folks here to see you."

Word of mouth about her skills kept spreading. She could not only fix old engines, but the new hybrids, too. Her understanding of the computer and electronics side of things coupled with a gift for diagnostics drew in new clients daily. Her boss, Rowdy, was so happy he'd given Izzy a raise. If this kept up, she could enroll in school in a few months.

With a smile, she placed her wrench and the bolt on the top of her toolbox.

Izzy stepped outside. Fresh air filled her lungs. Sunshine warmed her face. She loved spring days better than the humid ones summer brought with it.

In front of her, a black limousine gleamed beneath the midday sun. The engine idled perfectly. Darkened windows hid the identity of the car's passengers, but uniformed police officers stood nearby.

Not simply "some folks" wanting to see her. Must be a VIP inside the limo if police escorts were needed.

Izzy couldn't imagine what they wanted with her since the car sounded like it was running fine.

She wiped her dirty hands on the thighs of her cotton coveralls. Not exactly clean, especially with grease caked under her fingernails, but cleaner.

One of the police officers gave her the once-over, as

if sizing up her danger potential. A good thing she'd left the wrench in the garage.

A chauffeur walked around the car and opened the back door. A blond man exited. He wore a designer suit and nicely polished black dress shoes. With a classically handsome face and short clipped hair, he was easy on the eyes. But his good looks seemed a little bland, like a bowl of vanilla ice cream without any hot fudge, whipped cream and candy sprinkles. She preferred men who weren't quite so pretty, men with a little more...character.

"Isabel Poussard?" the man asked.

She stiffened. The last time anyone used her real name had been during her high school graduation ceremony when she received her diploma. She'd always been Izzy, ever since she was a little girl. Uncle Frank had taught her to be careful and cautious around strangers. He'd worried about her and been very protective. She knew he'd be that way now if he were here.

Izzy raised her chin and stared down her nose. The gesture had sent more than one guy running in the opposite direction. "Who wants to know?"

Warm brown eyes met hers. The guy wasn't intimidated at all. He looked almost amused for some strange reason. "I am Jovan Novak, aide to His Royal Highness Crown Prince Nikola Tomislav Kresimir."

Jovan's accent sounded European. Interesting since this was NASCAR country, not Formula 1 territory. "Never heard of him."

"He's from Vernonia."

"Vernonia." The name sounded vaguely familiar.

Izzy rolled the word over in her mind. Suddenly she remembered. "That's one of those Balkan countries. Fairy-tale castles and snowcapped mountains. There was a civil war there."

"Yes."

"Hey, Izzy," Boyd shouted from behind her. "You need any help?"

She glanced back at the bear of a man who stood with a mallet in his hands and curiosity in his eyes. A grin tugged at her lips. She appreciated how Boyd treated her like a little sister, especially since she had no family. Of course that made things interesting the few times she had a date pick her up after work. "Not yet, Boyd, but I'll let you know if I do."

Jovan looked like he might be in shape, but she could probably take him without Boyd's help thanks to Uncle Frank. When she was younger, he used to barter his mechanic skills for her martial arts class tuition. Now she worked out every day to get in shape for the work necessary by a pit crew member during a race.

"Isabel. Izzy." Jovan's smile reached all the way to his eyes. He bowed. "It is such a pleasure to make your acquaintance, Your—"

"Is this about a car repair?" He acted so happy to meet her. That bothered Izzy. Most customers limited their interactions to questions about their cars. Some simply ignored her. The men who went out of their way to talk to her usually ended up propositioning her. "Or do you want something else? I'm in the middle of a job."

Not exactly the most friendly customer service, but

something felt off. No customer would know her real name. And the guy smiled too much to be having car trouble.

"One moment please." Jovan ducked into the limousine.

Time ticked by. Seconds or minutes, Izzy couldn't tell since she wasn't wearing a watch. She used the clock hanging in the garage or her cell phone to keep track of time while she worked.

Izzy tapped her foot. She had to get the Chevy finished so she could work on the Dodge Grand Caravan. Somewhere a frazzled mom with four kids was waiting to get her minivan back. It was up to Izzy to get the job done.

Jovan stepped out of the limo finally.

About time, she thought.

Another man in a dark suit followed. Izzy took a closer look.

Smokin'.

The thought shot from her brain to the tips of her steel-toed boots and ricocheted back to the top of her head.

The guy was at least six feet tall with thick, shoulder-length brown hair and piercing blue-green eyes framed by dark lashes.

She straightened as if an extra inch could bring her closer to his height. Even then the top of her head would barely come to his chin.

But what a chin.

Izzy swallowed a sigh.

A strong nose, chiseled cheekbones, dark brows.

Rugged features that made for an interesting—a handsome—combination in spite of a jagged scar on his right cheek.

Talk about character. He had it in spades.

Not that she was interested.

Spending her entire life surrounded by men, car mechanics, gave her an understanding of how the opposite sex thought and operated. The one standing in front of her wearing a nice suit and shiny shoes was trouble. Dangerous, too.

The limo, expensive clothing, personal aide and police escort meant he lived in a completely different world than her, a world where she was seen as nothing more than a servant or wallpaper or worse, a one-night stand. Having to deal with mysterious rich people intimidated her. She wanted nothing to do with him.

But she didn't mind looking. The man belonged on the cover of a glossy men's magazine. He moved with the grace and agility of an athlete. The fit of his suit made her wonder what was underneath the fancy fabric.

Everyone else around him seemed to fade into the background. She couldn't remember the last time she'd had this kind of reaction to a guy. No doubt the result of working too much overtime. Time to take a night off and have some fun. That would keep her from mooning over the next gorgeous guy who crossed her path.

"You are Isabel Poussard." His accent, a mix of British and something else, could melt a frozen stick of butter.

She nodded, not trusting her voice.

His assessing gaze traveled the length of her. Nothing in his eyes or on his face hinted if he liked what he saw.

Not that she cared. Not much anyway.

A hottie like him would never be interested in a grease monkey like her. Still he was a yummy piece of eye candy. One she could appreciate.

Izzy raised her chin again, but didn't stare down her nose the way she'd done with Jovan. She wasn't ready to send this one on his way just yet. "You know my name, but I don't know yours."

"I am Prince Nikola of Vernonia."

"A prince?"

"Yes."

She supposed a prince would have a police escort as well as an aide, but this was just the kind of prank Boyd would pull and kid Izzy about for the rest of her life. She glanced around looking for a camera. "Am I being punk'd?"

Jovan grinned.

Nikola pressed his lips together. "No."

Yeah, on second thought, she couldn't imagine the police participating in a joke. But she still had a hard time believing royalty would come to Rowdy's. This wasn't the worst part of town, but it wasn't the best, either. "Am I supposed to call you Your Highness or something?"

"Niko is fine," he said.

Better than fine, but he probably already knew that. Men as attractive as him usually did. "So Niko, why are you here?"

Jovan started to speak, but Niko held up his hand and silenced his aide.

Nice trick. Maybe he really was a prince. Or maybe he liked being the one to talk.

"You posted on the internet looking to find a key to a box," Niko said. "The box is mine."

She stared down her nose. "I don't think so, dude."

He winced.

"The box belonged to my mother," Izzy added. "I'm just looking for the key."

"I know you want the key, but the box in the picture never belonged to your mother."

Oh, boy. Rowdy and Boyd had told Izzy if she posted on the internet she would get some strange replies. But she'd received only one email from a person who described the box so perfectly she'd sent him a picture of it. "You're HRMKDK?"

"That's my father," Niko explained. "His Royal Majesty King Dmitar Kresimir."

Like a king would ever email a total stranger about a wooden box. Sure it was pretty, but it was old. Izzy had thought the only value was sentimental. Maybe she was wrong about its worth. "I did correspond with your, um, dad, but I already told you, the box belongs to me."

"The box is technically yours, but only because I gave it to you."

What a ridiculous statement. The box was Izzy's only connection to her mother who had died when Izzy was a baby. That was why she was desperate to find the missing key and open the bottom portion to see if anything was inside. With Uncle Frank gone, she had no family, no connection to her past. She wanted to know something…anything.

Fighting her disappointment over not finding the key, Izzy squared her shoulders. "I've heard of Vernonia, but I've never been there. I'm certain we've never met. I've had the box for as long as I remember."

"You have had the box for twenty-three years," Niko said. "I gave it to you when you were a baby."

"A baby," she repeated, as if hearing it a second time would make more sense than the first time. It didn't. The guy wasn't that much older than her—that would mean he'd been just a kid. Ludicrous.

"Yes," Niko admitted ruefully. "I must sound crazy."

If he wasn't, then she was. "You do."

"I can assure you I'm not crazy," Niko stated matter-of-factly. He glanced at his aide standing next to him. "Isn't that true, Jovan?"

"Not crazy," Jovan agreed, though he continued to look amused by what was going on.

"I'm guessing you're paid to agree with him, Jovan," Izzy said, irritated.

"Yes, but I'm also a lawyer if that adds to my credibility."

"It doesn't." Maybe this was how good-looking, eccentric royals wasted their time and money. She wished they would go bother someone else. "I think you both must be certifiable."

The two men looked at her with puzzled expressions.

"Insane." Izzy glanced at the police officers. She couldn't imagine them wasting their time and tax dollars protecting some mental case claiming to be a prince. Surely they would have checked him out and asked to see his diplomatic papers or passport or something. "Let's pretend what you say is true—"

"It is true," Niko said.

She took a deep breath to control her growing temper. "Why would you give a baby the box? Is there some significance to the gesture?"

"It's customary."

It was her turn to be confused. "Huh?"

"Tradition," Niko clarified. "When a Vernonian prince gets married, he presents his wife with a bride box on their wedding day."

"That still doesn't explain why you would give the box to me."

"Because I am your husband."

CHAPTER TWO

"MY HUSBAND?" Isabel's voice cracked. Her expression would have been comical if this were not such a serious matter.

"Yes." Niko understood her shock. He even sympathized. Discovering he had a wife had sent his world spinning off its axis. But her feelings—his feelings—would only delay the annulment needed to remedy this "complication" so he could marry Julianna and help his country. "It is a lot to take in."

"Take in?" Sharp, brown eyes bore into him. "Okay, Niko or whoever you are, cut the bull and tell me what's really going on here."

He stared at Isabel with the dirty, baggy coveralls, lopsided ponytail and grease on her hands and cheek. She might be halfway attractive with her oval face, high cheekbones and expressive eyes, if she weren't dressed like a man and covered in motor oil.

"Come on, Niko." She placed her hands on her hips. "Spill."

He expected her lack of protocol and manners, but the strength in her voice surprised him, as did her take-no-prisoner tone. Most people kowtowed to him.

Few ever challenged him. He was…intrigued. "I am speaking the truth. I am your husband."

She pursued her full, unglossed lips and gave him a long, hard look. He was used to such a frank appraisal, but unlike most women, Isabel did not seem impressed by what she saw. He didn't know whether to be amused or annoyed by this woman who worked at a dilapidated garage fixing other people's broken-down vehicles.

"I told you. I've never seen you before," she said. "We can't be married."

"Indeed we can. You simply do not remember."

Isabel's gaze remained steady. "I think I'd remember getting married."

"Not if you were only a few months old at the time."

Her mouth formed a perfect O. "What?"

"I was only six years old when we married, and my memories are very vague."

Almost nonexistent, but he needed to convince Isabel of what had occurred twenty-three years ago, not add to the doubts shining in her pretty hazel eyes.

"Children marrying?" Isabel's nostrils flared. "There are laws against that kind of thing."

"Yes, and today it is illegal in Vernonia, but not twenty-three years ago."

"This is crazy." Her voice jumped an octave. "I'm an American."

"Your mother was American, but your father was Vernonian."

"My father…" Isabel's glanced toward Jovan as if seeking confirmation. At his nod, her hands balled into fists. "Now I know you're lying. My father's name isn't listed on my birth certificate. I have no idea who he is."

The hurt and anger in her voice suggested she was telling the truth. There was no reason for her to lie. She had too much to gain by accepting what Niko was telling her. His respect inched up. Opportunists or not, many women would have jumped at the chance to be his wife. "I have proof."

"You mean the box," she said.

"The bride box, yes, but also documentation and a photograph."

Curiosity flashed in Isabel's eyes. "What kind of documentation?"

Her interest loosened some of the tension in his shoulders. Maybe the paper would convince her of the truth. He motioned to Jovan, who removed a leather pouch from his inside suit pocket with a flourish and handed it over.

As Niko opened the flap, he noticed two tall men in coveralls watching them from the garage.

No doubt the limousine and police cars would attract attention. Niko wanted to avoid the media at all cost. The annulment needed to be handled quietly with no press coverage. Before departing for the United States, he had been upfront with Julianna about the situation, but others from Aliestle might not be as understanding about the sudden appearance of "his wife" on the front page of tabloids. He didn't want to risk losing her and what she would bring to Vernonia.

He glanced around. "I would prefer a more private place to discuss matters. Inside the limo perhaps?"

Isabel glared at him. "Do I look like the kind of woman who would get into a car with strangers?"

Niko assumed based on her reaction the answer wasn't yes. "I may be a stranger, but I am your husband."

"That remains to be seen."

She wasn't making this easy, but given her appearance he shouldn't be surprised. "Perhaps the garage or if there is an office—"

"Here."

He needed her cooperation. The last thing Niko wanted to do was upset her any more than he already had. He would allow her this much control.

"Fine. We shall remain here." He removed two folded pieces of paper from the pouch. "I took the liberty of having the marriage certificate translated."

She eyed him warily. "Marriage certificate, huh?"

He extended the papers toward her. "See for yourself."

Instead of reaching for the documents as Niko expected, Isabel wiped her hands on the thighs of her oversize coveralls. The same way she had when she'd walked out of the garage.

Not totally without manners, he realized, but a far cry from the grace and style of a woman like Julianna. "These are copies so it doesn't matter if they get dirty."

Isabel took the documents and unfolded them. As

she read, she flipped back and forth between the two pages.

Niko appreciated her thoroughness. Now all he needed was her compliance. Given how things were proceeding so far, that might take time. Especially since he hadn't begun to explain the situation to her.

"The certificate actually looks legit," she said.

"It is."

"But it's wrong." She pointed her oil stained finger to the line with her mother's name. "My mother was never married."

He hesitated.

This "complication" went beyond Isabel Poussard being his child bride and standing in the way of him marrying Juliana and obtaining her significant dowry and trade support from Aliestle. Isabel might think she was a full-blooded American, but she wasn't. She was also Vernonian, the last of the royal Sachestian bloodline. Her family came from Sachestia, a region in the northern part of the country. She was one of his subjects, one who knew nothing of her parents, her homeland or her past. Isabel deserved to know the truth, but a part of him felt awkward about what he had to do, say. He wished it were already over.

"Your mother, Evangeline Poussard, was an American college student. She was backpacking through Europe when she met Prince Aleksander Zvonimir." Yesterday, Niko's parents had explained what happened so he could explain it to Isabel today. "The two fell in love and eloped."

She looked at Niko as if he'd grown horns. "My mother was married to a prince?"

"Yes."

Isabel's mouth quirked. She looked as if she was trying hard not to laugh. "So I suppose next you're going to tell me someone who looks like Julie Andrews is not only my grandmother, but also the queen?"

Niko had no idea what Isabel was talking about. He knew who the actress was, but couldn't connect to the reference. He looked at Jovan for an explanation.

"The Princess Diaries," Jovan explained quietly. "A series of books and movies about an American who discovers she's a princess."

Niko had never heard of any such Princess Diaries, but at least he understood the context now.

"My mother is the queen," he said to Isabel. "Though she would be thrilled to be a grandmother, I can assure you she looks and sounds nothing like Mary Poppins."

Isabel didn't crack a smile.

So much for his attempt to lighten the mood.

She shook her head. "I just don't see how any of this can be true."

"The truth is not always clear, but that doesn't mean it isn't true."

As she studied the translated document, two lines formed above the bridge of Isabel's nose. He found the trait surprisingly endearing. It made her seem less in control and more open to possibility.

"Let's say my mother was married to this prince,

and he's my father," Isabel said. "Why would she give birth to me in America?"

"She didn't," Niko said. "You were born in Vernonia."

"My birth certificate says I was born in the United States. I have a copy." Isabel pursed her lips. "One of the documents is fake. I'm guessing it's yours."

"Guess all you would like, but yours is the fake," he said. "Given the political unrest in Vernonia when you were born, I wouldn't be surprised if your parents had another birth certificate made omitting both Vernonia and Prince Aleksander's name."

"You sound as if you believe all this." Disbelief dripped from each of her words. "That Prince Aleksander was my father."

"Yes," Niko said firmly. "I believe you are Princess Isabel Poussard Zvonimir Kresimir."

She scrunched her nose. "Do I look like a princess?"

"You look like a car mechanic, but that doesn't change the facts. You are a princess of Vernonia and my wife."

Isabel stared at the marriage certificate. "Then how did I wind up here?"

"That's what we'd all like to know," Niko admitted. "My father's staff have been trying to figure that out."

She arched an eyebrow. "Where did they think I was?"

He didn't answer.

"Where?" she pressed.

"Buried in your family's cemetery."

She gasped. "You thought I was dead?"

"Not me. I was too young to remember you, but all of Vernonia believed you were killed with your parents in a car bombing a month after our wedding."

Isabel lowered the papers. "A car bombing?"

"By a splinter faction of Loyalists who were nothing more than terrorists." The way her eyes clouded bothered him. "It was a…troubled time, with two groups aligned to different royal bloodlines. That is in the past now."

The two little lines above the bridge of her nose returned.

Good, Niko thought. Isabel was thinking about all that he'd told her. She would see she had to believe—

"Look. I get that you're somebody. Otherwise you wouldn't have the limo, lawyer aide guy, documents or a police escort. You know my mother's name, but you have the wrong person. The Evangeline Poussard who was my mother never went to Europe. She never married. She never would have married off her baby. And she died due to complications with childbirth, not in a terrorist attack."

"What about the box?" Niko asked.

"I don't know. Maybe there are identical boxes. Yours and hers." Isabel shoved the papers at him. "I don't have time to deal with this. I have work to do."

With her head held high as if she were the Queen of England and not a lowly mechanic, Isabel turned away from him and marched toward the garage.

Niko's fingers crumpled the edges of the papers. He

tried to remember the last person besides his father who had dismissed him so readily. "Isabel."

She didn't glance back.

What an infuriating woman. He wanted to slip into the limousine and forget he'd ever heard the name Isabel Poussard, except he couldn't. They were tied together. Legally. He needed to undo what had been done without their consent. "Wait."

She quickened her step. Most women ran toward him not away, but he had a feeling Isabel was different from the women he knew.

"Please," he added.

She stopped, but didn't turn around.

He forced himself not to clench his jaw. "Before you go, please look at the photograph."

Isabel glanced over her shoulder. "What photograph?"

She made him feel more like a peasant than a prince. Likening a wife to a ball and chain suddenly made sense to him if said wife happened to be a strong-willed woman like Isabel Zvonimir.

He removed the picture from the pouch. "The wedding photo."

She didn't come closer. "Look, I'm on the clock right now. My boss is watching. I can't afford to have my pay docked so you can pull a prank."

"This isn't a prank." The old garage needed a new roof and paint job. Niko wondered if Isabel's financial circumstances were similar to those of her place of employment. "I'll give you one hundred dollars for five minutes of your time."

She straightened. "Seriously?"

Now he had her attention. With the pouch and picture tucked between his arm and side, he removed his wallet, pulled out a hundred-dollar bill and held it up. "Quite serious."

She hurried toward him with her gaze fixed on the bill.

"You really are crazy, but for that kind of money you can have seven minutes." Isabel snatched the money from him and shoved it in her coverall pocket. "Hand over the picture."

Niko gave her the photograph. He didn't need to look at it again. After examining the picture so many times during the flight to Charlotte he had memorized everything about the twelve people in it. "You are the baby in the white gown with the tiara. Your mother is holding you. Your father is standing on the right of you. Your paternal grandparents are the two next to him."

Isabel held the photo with both hands. Niko watched her face for some sign of recognition of her mother, but saw nothing.

"This looks more like a picture from a baptism than a wedding," Isabel said.

"Only because of the baby." Niko repeated what his mother had said to him. "This is a traditional royal wedding pose with the bride and groom in the center and their families on either side."

Isabel narrowed her gaze. "You're the little boy in the suit with the light blue sash across your chest?"

"Yes."

She glanced up at him. "I don't see much of a resemblance."

"That was twenty-three years ago."

Isabel traced his boyhood image. "You don't look very happy."

Niko wasn't very happy right now. He wanted to be rid of this complication, of her. "I imagine a six-year-old boy would not be too happy about getting married."

"Who is the other boy?" Isabel asked.

"My older brother."

"Why didn't they marry the baby off to him?" she asked.

Niko noticed Isabel said "the baby" not "me." He took a calming breath to keep his patience under check. "Stefan was the crown prince and already betrothed."

She looked up. "Was?"

"Stefan was killed during the conflict seven years ago."

Her eyes grew serious. "I'm sorry for your loss."

Niko didn't want or need her pity, only her cooperation. "All Vernonians suffered losses during the conflict. I intend to make sure that doesn't happen again. I want to keep the peace and modernize the country."

"Worthy goals." Isabel refocused on the photo. "I'm sorry you came all this way for nothing. My uncle Frank had one picture of my mother that wasn't destroyed when their parents' house burned down. She looked nothing like this."

Niko recalled the dossier containing information

about Isabel. She didn't have any living relatives. Her mother had been an only child and orphaned at nineteen following a train derailment that killed her parents. The Zvonimir side of Isabel's family tree had been killed during the conflict. Nowhere on either side of her family tree had anyone named Frank appeared.

"Who is Uncle Frank?" Niko asked.

"Frank Miroslav," Isabel said. "My mom's older half brother. He raised me after she died."

Miroslav. Niko recognized the surname, but had no idea how it related to Isabel and her American mother. He glanced at Jovan for clarification.

"The Miroslavs served the Zvonimirs for centuries," Jovan explained. "There was a deep tie and strong loyalty between the two families even though the relationship was master-servant. Franko Miroslav was Prince Aleksander's chauffeur, and I would go as far to say his best friend. It is rumored that Franko introduced the prince to Evangeline Poussard."

Isabel's mouth dropped open. She closed it.

"That would explain how you escaped out of Vernonia and ended up here," Niko said. "If they used another driver and a doll for the baby after you left the country—"

"No." Her lips tightened. "The woman in the photo is not my mother."

"Are you certain the woman in the picture your uncle Frank showed you is your mother?" Niko watched the range of emotions crossing her face. The vulnerability in her eyes surprisingly pulled at his heart. "I apologize, Isabel. I know this is difficult for you."

"What you're saying is impossible. Who would let a Vernonian chauffeur into the U.S. with a baby? Where would they get forged American documents? It's just not possible." She looked at the photograph as if trying to discover a secret hidden in it. "Uncle Frank wasn't a chauffeur. He wasn't a servant. He was a car mechanic from a little town outside Chicago. The town where he grew up with my mother. His little sister. He was like a father to me. Why would he lie to me about this?"

Niko respected the way she stood up for the man who raised her. Loyalty to one's family was important and would serve her well. "Perhaps Franko, your Uncle Frank, withheld certain truths for your own protection. You were his princess. A faction in Vernonia would have tried to kill you if they'd known you lived."

A faction that had been loyal to Niko's father even if the king hadn't approved of the group's methods and violence.

"It's so unbelievable."

Niko was not going to convince her with words, but perhaps he could show her. "There is a way to find out if what I say is true or not."

Her gaze jerked up from the photo to meet his. "How?"

He pulled the chain from beneath his shirt. "We can see if my key fits the lock."

Please don't fit. Please don't fit. Please don't fit.

The mantra had been running through Izzy's mind for the last half hour, ever since driving home with Boyd and Jovan to retrieve the box. Now she sat in

Rowdy's office with the wooden box on her lap waiting for the others to join her.

That still doesn't explain why you would give the box to me.

Because I am your husband.

Her husband. Izzy's vision blurred. She felt light-headed.

She clutched the wooden box with its mother-of-pearl inlaid design. She didn't want to drop it onto the hard tile floor. All these years, she'd carted it around, carefully, but not overly so. The value had been sentimental, not monetary.

Now…

Izzy Poussard, a princess and a crown prince's wife?

No way.

Okay, some women—maybe many women—would be excited to discover they were a long lost princess from some faraway foreign land and married to a handsome prince. But not Izzy. Oh, sure, she wanted a happily ever after, but her fairy tale didn't involve enchanted castles, sparkling jewelry and Prince Charming. Her dream revolved around wearing a fire suit in team colors, working over the wall on a pit stop, becoming a crew chief and standing in the winner's circle with champagne being squirted everywhere.

The door to Rowdy's office opened. Niko, Jovan and her boss entered.

"It'll be just a few more minutes, Izzy," Rowdy said. "Duncan Moore is on his way."

"Thanks." Izzy had asked Rowdy to call one of their

customers who was a big-name attorney in Charlotte. She needed to talk to a lawyer before Niko and Jovan tried to take the box from her. To her surprise, Niko had offered to cover all her legal expenses. Izzy hadn't wanted to accept the prince's charity. She hadn't relied on anyone since Uncle Frank's death. But she didn't have extra money lying around to cover surprise legal fees. Duncan Moore wasn't only one of the best lawyers, he was also one of the most high-priced attorneys in town. Being prideful was one thing. Being stupid was another. "And thank you, Niko, for covering my legal expenses."

"You're welcome," he said. "I am not here to cause you grief or unwanted expenditures."

Izzy wanted to believe him. The corners of her lips lifted into a closed-mouth smile.

He smiled back.

Butterflies flapped in her stomach. Uh-oh. She'd better watch it. Being attracted to a man claiming to be her husband would only complicate things and might lead to her losing ownership of the box.

"Duncan's here," Rowdy announced.

Thank goodness, Izzy thought.

Duncan Moore, bald, in his late fifties and on his third marriage, strutted into the office. On any other man a polka-dot bow tie would have looked ridiculous with a suit, but it worked well on the successful attorney.

"Sorry for the delay, everyone. Izzy." Duncan looked at Niko and bowed. "Your Royal Highness."

Niko acknowledged Duncan with a nod. "This is my aide and lawyer, Jovan Novak."

Jovan shook Duncan's hand.

Unease crept down Izzy's spine. The seriousness of the situation ratcheted up a notch with two lawyers present.

"We may proceed now," Niko said.

The tension in the office quadrupled. Izzy's legs shook so much the box on her lap jiggled up and down. She placed the box on Rowdy's desk and opened the lid. She removed the velvet-covered tray so the keyhole showed. "I didn't realize the tray came out or there was a keyhole until after Uncle Frank died. He allowed me to look at the box, but never touch it."

"Did your uncle say the box belonged to your mother?" Duncan asked.

"No, but I assumed so." Izzy hoped her words wouldn't give more credence to the prince's claims. "Uncle Frank just said it was important."

Niko held the key he'd worn around his neck. "Let us see how important."

His hand was as steady as a neurosurgeon's. If it had been her, she would be trembling. Who was she kidding? She was trembling.

He inserted the key in the hole.

Izzy was tempted to close her eyes. She held her breath instead. She wanted to know what was inside the bottom portion of the box, but she didn't want anything the prince had told her to be true.

He turned the key.

Click.

"The key fits," Niko announced.

The air whooshed from Izzy's lungs.

No, this can't be happening. It can't be true.

The bottom portion of the box slid out. A hidden drawer.

"Would ya look at that," Rowdy said with a hint of awe to his deep voice.

Even though she had been waiting for this moment for a few years now, she was afraid to look. All her curiosity had vanished, replaced by trepidation. She didn't care what was in the box. She only wanted things to go back to the way they'd been before Prince Niko arrived.

"It's the same tiara," Jovan said from across the office.

No. Isabel didn't want to see so she squeezed her eyes shut. Her chest constricted. She shuddered.

Someone touched her shoulder and squeezed gently. Rowdy. Both he and Boyd could be big old teddy bears. She opened her eyes, but saw Niko with his hand on her instead of her boss.

"Isabel." Concern filled Niko's voice. "Would you rather wait?"

The tenderness of his gaze brought tears to her eyes. The situation, she rationalized, not him. Still she appreciated his gesture of comfort, drew strength from it, too. "No."

Straightening, Izzy looked into the drawer past the small diamond tiara to find papers, photographs and jewelry. Her uncle Frank could have found the box or bought it at a garage sale or even stolen it in desperation. Maybe that was why she had no key.

No, she was just being silly now. None of those things would explain the prince knowing her mother's name or his key fitting the lock. Isabel needed to accept what was in front of her, except…

Niko reached into the drawer.

"Wait, sir," Duncan shouted.

The prince drew back his hand.

"May I please take a picture of the contents before they are disturbed?" Duncan asked with a camera in hand. "I would like to document everything. For both Izzy's and your sake."

"Certainly," Niko said.

The flash of the camera reminded Izzy of lightning and intensified the emotions warring inside her. She hated storms. Uncle Frank had died during a lightning storm. She swallowed back a tide of grief.

Duncan backed away. "Thank you, sir. Please proceed."

Niko didn't. Instead he looked at her. "At one time your parents had a key to the bride box. They placed these contents inside. Only you should remove them."

Anger flared. She loved Uncle Frank, but he had kept her past a secret. Why? Why hadn't he trusted her? She wanted to know why this had happened.

"Isabel—"

"I'll do it." She couldn't decide what to do about

this until she knew more. "But only because I need to have all the facts."

Izzy felt four pairs of eyes staring at her. She was used to the attention. Not many people expected a female mechanic to fix their cars. This was different. Unsettling. But Uncle Frank had taught her to always hold her head high, no matter how uncertain she might feel inside. If only he were here now…

She scooted her chair closer to the desk. With a shaky hand, she raised the tiara from the box. "It's so tiny."

Niko nodded. "My parents had the tiara commissioned for you to wear at the wedding. The small diamonds represent all the towns and villages. The three larger diamonds symbolize you, me and Vernonia."

"It's hard to tell if it's exactly the same one in the photo," she said, knowing she was grasping at straws.

"It's the same one," Niko countered.

Izzy set the tiara on the desk. Next she removed foreign coins and dollar bills, a diamond pendant, an emerald bracelet and three stunning rings.

Those jewels would be worth a fortune if real. Maybe that was why Niko wanted the box back so badly. Money could make people do almost anything.

She picked up a photograph, a picture of a man and a woman.

"Those were your parents," Niko said softly.

Her parents. Izzy wasn't ready to believe it just yet. She stared at the handsome couple. They were smiling and holding hands. They looked happier than they did in the wedding photograph. "The woman is beautiful."

"You look like her," Rowdy said.

"I wish." Izzy's heart ached for some memory of the two people the prince claimed were her parents.

"You resemble your mother," Niko said. "But you have your father's eyes."

Izzy felt a rush of excitement. No one had ever seen a resemblance between her and Uncle Frank. She removed more photographs. Baby pictures, family portraits, casual snapshots, of people she didn't know taken in places she didn't recognize.

Next came an official looking piece of paper with foreign writing. "I don't know what it says."

"Allow me," Niko offered.

She handed it to him.

He glanced over the document. "It's your birth certificate. Evangaline Poussard Zvonimir is listed as your mother. Aleksander Nicholas Zvonimir is listed as your father. Your place of birth is Sachestia, Vernonia. That is in the northern part of the country."

Jovan placed the documents they'd shown her earlier on the desk. "In case you are concerned about the translation and wish to compare, ma'am."

"My name is Izzy," she corrected. "I would like to see a translation by an impartial person to confirm the document."

"How can you still not believe?" Niko asked.

"I'm simply being cautious," she admitted. "You've gone to a lot of trouble to find me. You could've just offered to buy the box and be done with it. And me."

"You are my wife," Niko said. "I cannot pretend you do not exist and be done with it or you."

Izzy grimaced. "Too bad there isn't some birthmark that would prove without a doubt that I'm royalty."

"Perhaps there is one." Wicked laughter lit Niko's eyes. "I would be happy to search for one."

Her cheeks warmed at the thought.

His faced reddened, too.

She hadn't been expecting that reaction from Niko, but his embarrassment made him seem less a dark, formal prince and more...human. That made Izzy feel a little more comfortable with him even if her heart pounded like a piston engine each time she noticed him staring at her.

She removed several pieces of paper stapled together. Again, the words were written in a language she couldn't read. She handed the pages to Niko.

He flipped through them. "This is your father's will naming you the sole beneficiary of his estate."

"I will need a copy of the will, sir," Duncan said.

"Of course." Niko handed it to the lawyer then turned his attention on Izzy. "Everyone believed you died with your parents so your father's estate went to—"

"You," she said without an ounce of doubt.

"As your husband, your inheritance passed directly to me."

"What kind of estate are we talking about, Your Highness?" Duncan asked.

Niko glanced at Jovan. "What is the approximate net worth?"

"Approximately twenty-five million euros," Jovan said.

She didn't know much about foreign currency, but she knew a lot of money was at stake here. "You're willing to give that to me for some box?"

"The box and an annulment," Niko clarified.

Rowdy whistled. "It's like winning the lottery, Izzy."

Yes, it was. She took a deep breath. That meant it was probably too good to be true.

"Let's not get too excited," Duncan cautioned. "We have no idea how the legal system works in Vernonia. Each country has its own laws for estates and inheritance. Something like this could be tied up in the court system for years."

"I would never keep anything that rightly belongs to Isabel," Niko stated firmly. "Vernonia might be a small country, but we have a parliamentarian government and a modern justice system. It will not take the High Court years to sort this matter out."

"Can't something like this be taken care of in the U.S?" Izzy asked.

"Your father's property is in Vernonia," Niko explained. "Besides, the High Court is private. There could be publicity if we used the court here in the United States."

She glanced at the lawyer. "Duncan?"

"I don't know anything about Vernonia's court system, but Prince Niko is correct about the publicity. America loves royalty. The press would have a field day if they found out you were an American princess."

Izzy frowned. "I'm not—"

"Come to Vernonia with me," Niko suggested. "We will appear in front of the High Court and have this matter resolved quickly."

Apprehension washed over her. She never went anywhere. "I don't have a passport."

"I can pull some strings," Niko said.

"Most definitely," Jovan agreed.

She bit her lip. "I don't know. Maybe I should take some time to think about it."

Silence filled the room. Outside in the garage bay an air compressor sounded. A horn honked. A car door slammed.

"There's a lot at stake, Izzy," Rowdy said. "Don't let that stubborn streak of yours get in the way."

Stubborn streak? She wasn't stubborn.

"Listen to Rowdy," Duncan advised. "Prince Niko believes you are Princess Isabel. He's willing to give you a multimillion dollar estate. What more do you need to think about?"

Her gaze bounced between Rowdy and Duncan. They made good points. Still she hesitated. Cautious. Nervous. Unsure.

"Something else is in the drawer, ma'am," Jovan said.

She glanced down and saw a note-size envelope

tucked away in one corner. The word Isabel was written on the front. The cursive writing looked feminine.

As she picked up the small envelope, her hand trembled. The flap had been tucked inside, not sealed. Carefully Izzy removed sheets of paper and unfolded the pages. She was happy to see words written in English.

"Our Beloved Daughter." Tears pricked Izzy's eyes as she read the words. No one had ever called her daughter. Not even Uncle Frank who she loved like a father.

She continued reading.

You are only a baby yet you are already a bride. Forgive us for sending you to America, but your father saw no other way to keep you safe. The marriage between you and Prince Nikola was supposed to protect you and keep peace among Vernonians. But that plan appears to have backfired and now you are in even worse danger. My greatest wish is that you never read this letter. I plan to destroy it when we arrive in the U.S. If you are reading this note now, then things did not go as your father and I planned. And for that, little princess, I am more sorry than you will ever know.

Your father is torn between the two sides wanting control of Vernonia. The Separatists first wanted to split into their own country, Sachestia, with your grandfather as king. Now they want to wrest full control from King Dmitar and take over the entire country, but your father would rather remain loyal to the throne and Vernonia. Your marriage, however, has unexpectedly antagonized both factions and made it impossible for him to support either side now. We must leave Vernonia as soon as possible. Your safety is our utmost concern. Once this craziness ends, we will happily return.

We do not dare leave the country together so we are sending you first. We are entrusting you to the care and protection of Franko Miroslav. He is your father's chauffeur, and our dearest and closest friend. He will do whatever is necessary to keep you from harm. We have arranged passage and paperwork so the two of you can escape to the U.S. We will follow the next day.

No one knows of our plan, including the king. He's a good man, but the fewer people who know your whereabouts the better. Your departure and location will remain a secret until it is safe.

Your father is telling me it's time for you to go. I must sign off now, Isabel.

We love you, our darling Izzy, and hope to be with you soon.

Love,
Mommy and Daddy

Izzy took several deep breaths as the words sunk in. She'd never felt anything toward the woman in the photo Uncle Frank had shown her, a woman who wasn't really her mother. But this letter written in her mother's own hand provided Izzy with a connection to the woman who gave birth to her. Something she'd longed for since she was little. Something she'd hoped to find by looking for the key.

"True." She sat back in the chair. The girl more comfortable in Shop class than Home Ec was a real-life princess with both a mother and a father. Everything the prince had said... "It's all true."

"I'm sorry," Niko said.

Izzy believed him. No one wanted to discover they were married to a stranger.

Married.

Her stomach roiled.

Marriage was only part of this. Everything she thought she knew about herself was wrong. Izzy wrapped her arms around her stomach. She wasn't who she thought she was. She had money. A title. A father.

Izzy recalled her parents' smiling faces from the wedding photograph. A mother and a father who had loved her. A mother and a father who had been killed before she could get to know them.

Emotion clogged Izzy's throat.

But it wasn't too late to fulfill one of their wishes. Her parents had planned on returning to Vernonia. That must have meant Uncle Frank planned on going back, too.

Come to Vernonia with me. We will appear in front of the High Court and have this matter resolved quickly.

Maybe seeing the place where she came from would

help her figure out who she was and what her future held. She could get the marriage annulled and receive her inheritance. Forget going to pit crew school. She could buy her own racing team.

Izzy rose. "When do you want to leave for Vernonia?"

CHAPTER THREE

When do you want to leave for Vernonia?

Sooner rather than later. Niko sat at the table in the recreational vehicle, also known as an RV, where Isabel lived. His concern over the press discovering the reason behind his unannounced trip to the U.S. continued to grow. But Isabel still had to shower, dress and pack. That would take time. They would be leaving later whether he liked it or not.

Isabel stood in front of the small refrigerator still wearing her bulky, stained coveralls. She rubbed her hands together as if nervous. "Would you like something to drink or eat?"

He appreciated her hospitality. Twenty-three years away from Vernonia hadn't erased centuries of innate good breeding. "No, thank you."

With a hesitant expression, she glanced toward the back of the RV. "It won't take me more than a few minutes to get ready."

A lump on the faded brown-and-orange plaid cushion behind his back made him shift positions. "The plane will not take off without us."

As she closed a partition that separated the back

portion of the motor home from the front section, Niko surveyed the interior with dismay. Warped wood veneer. Cracked cabinet and cupboard doors. Frayed carpeting. Cramped space. The RV had to be as old as Isabel.

What had Franko been thinking? Yes, the chauffeur needed to keep her safe, but why had he never contacted the king for assistance? Why had Franko allowed it to come to this?

Niko exhaled on a sigh.

Isabel was no damsel in distress. She'd impressed him with the way she'd dealt with her world being turned inside out. She hadn't been blinded by his title or money. She wouldn't accept his word as the truth without concrete evidence. Surprising, given she lived in near poverty in a shabby motor home with no family or resources. A princess of Vernonia deserved better than a life spent working long hours bent over a car engine and coming home to half a dozen barking, trembling Chihuahuas who lived next door.

She wouldn't be his wife for much longer, but he wanted Isabel to have the kind of life her parents intended for her to have. She belonged in a castle.

The partition jiggled like it was stuck.

"Isabel?" Niko asked, wondering if she needed assistance.

"I'm almost finished," she said from behind the thin wall.

He checked his watch. Five minutes. That had to be a world record. Then again, Isabel didn't seem to be a woman who primped or even cared about her appearance.

The partition jerked open.

As she walked out of the back toward him, he did a double-take. Her faded blue jeans fit like a second skin, clinging in all the right places, accentuating her feminine curves and long legs. The fabric of her T-shirt stretched across her chest. Her high, round breasts jiggled. Her shiny brown hair swung back and forth below her shoulders.

He met her gaze, captivated by her warm, brown eyes. An appealing mix of intelligence and caring shone in their depths.

This was his...wife?

"I'm ready to go," Isabel announced.

So was he. Niko was ready to follow wherever she wanted to go.

"I don't own a lot of clothes." Isabel motioned to the worn purple duffel bag she carried behind her. The bride box with all its original contents was in the limousine with Jovan. "What I have probably isn't nice enough to wear to court."

"I will make arrangements for you to go shopping once we arrive." He would head off any of her financial concerns. "Do not worry about the cost."

"You're already paying for a lot."

"I don't mind." Niko would enjoy seeing her in designer gowns with jewels adorning her graceful neck. He would enjoy removing those things from her, too. Too bad that would never happen. "You are my wife."

"Only until the annulment," she reminded.

"Yes, but until then it is my responsibility to take care of you."

Isabel pushed her chin forward almost defiantly. "I can take care of myself."

"I know that." He still wouldn't mind a turn. Most women wanted him to take care of them. It felt odd that Isabel didn't. He bowed his head in apology. "A poor choice of words on my part. I promise to make it up to you."

"No need."

As she brushed past him, an appealing mix of vanilla and jasmine filled his nostrils. The smell was a significant improvement over the motor oil one earlier. "I want to."

"That's okay." Her smile nearly knocked him off his seat. "I've already forgiven you."

Niko didn't want her forgiveness. He wanted… her.

Damn. The attraction to Isabel was unexpected and unwelcome. His duties and responsibilities always took priority. Niko was practically engaged to Julianna. He shouldn't be attracted to any woman.

Not even your wife? a voice mocked.

He balled his hands to gain control. His father had taught him to keep emotion reined in. Otherwise it became a weakness, one that others, particularly adversaries, would use to their advantage.

Niko focused his gaze on Isabel's pretty face. Maybe it would be better to concentrate on her forehead. "Is there anything else you need to pack for the trip?"

"No. I won't be in Vernonia that long."

"You might like it there."

She shrugged. "This has been my home since I was six."

He couldn't believe she'd lived like this for the past seventeen years. "That's a long time."

"When Uncle Frank bought the RV, he said we would never have to leave home again. We could always take it with us." She removed a carton of milk from the refrigerator and poured it down the sink. "I wonder if he was thinking about Vernonia when he said that."

"Possibly." Niko glanced around her hovel. "There are many other places to live than here."

"I know." Isabel rinsed the carton in the small sink. "This motor home is nothing more than an old metal shed compared to a lot of other places, but I've been happy here. A little lonely since Uncle Frank died, but it's hard to leave the good memories behind."

"You will make new memories."

"I need to come to peace with the old ones first." She stared off into the distance. "So many things about Uncle Frank are making more sense now. The lack of photographs. Wanting me to study martial arts. Keeping such a low profile. Being so protective. Even if he wasn't related to me by blood he's still family. The only I ever knew."

Niko nodded. "We shall honor Franko for the sacrifices he made by keeping you safe."

"Thank you." Gratitude shone her eyes. "Vernonia must have meant a lot to him or he would have never given up so much for me. I always thought he was satisfied living like this, and I'd be the one to leave someday. Now I know he didn't plan on living here forever, either. He would have returned...home."

Isabel's words eased some of Niko's concerns about her future. "Your father's estate will enable you to live wherever and however you want."

She sighed. "The thought of so many choices is intimidating."

"Think of only one choice at a time. It won't seem so...overwhelming."

"Good advice," she said. "Thanks."

Helping her pleased him. "Is there anything else you need?"

Isabel glanced around. "Boyd is going to check on the RV while I'm away so everything should be okay."

Niko remembered the tall man who had driven her and Jovan to retrieve the box. The same man had come out to check on her and watched her from the garage. A woman as attractive as Isabel was sure to have men after her. One who worked with her would have an advantage. "Is Boyd your boyfriend?"

"Boyd?" She scrunched her nose. "He's like a brother. Some people think we're a couple, but we're just friends."

The news brought an unfamiliar sense of relief. But Boyd wasn't the only man in Charlotte. "Do you have a boyfriend?"

"No boyfriend."

"But you date."

"Not nearly as much as I probably should. I work too

much overtime to have a serious relationship. And the boys at the garage can be a little overprotective when guys do drop by."

The news pleased Niko more than it should have.

"What about you?" she asked.

"No boyfriend."

She grinned. "Any girlfriends?"

He used to have girlfriends. He'd dated models to princesses. Julianna wasn't his girlfriend per se, yet she was the woman he planned to marry. Better to keep things simple than give Isabel too complicated an explanation. "Yes, I have a girlfriend."

"What's her name?"

"Julianna. We are planning to marry."

"Congratulations, Niko." Isabel locked a window latch. "I hope the two of you are very happy together."

Her enthusiasm surprised him. "You do?"

"Of course I do," she admitted. "Why wouldn't I? I may be your wife, but that was a choice neither of us made or would choose today."

Niko winced. Her words stung. He might not choose her, but he didn't see why she wouldn't choose him. He was a prince and quite eligible according to the tabloids and magazines. "Who would you choose to marry?"

"No one."

"You do not wish to marry?"

"I have a few things I want to do first."

"Tell me about these things."

"I'm planning to enroll in pit crew school, work on a pit crew and eventually be a crew chief."

Those were unusual goals for a woman. Unthinkable

for a female in Vernonia let alone a princess. "You like racing."

"I love racing. Open-wheel, stock car, go-kart, it doesn't matter as long as there's a checkered flag at the end."

The passion in her voice matched the light in her eyes and reminded him of Julianna when she sailed. Perhaps the two women had more in common than Niko had thought. "Your inheritance will allow you to do almost anything you want in racing."

"Yeah, I guess focusing on going to pit crew school now is like a Lotto winner who plans to keep their job." Isabel swung the strap of a blue backpack over her shoulder. She opened the door. "Ready to roll, Highness."

Then again, maybe she didn't have that much in common with Princess Julianna after all.

Across the tarmac at the Charlotte Douglas International Airport, jet engines roared.

This was unreal. Izzy stood on the landing at the top of the portable aircraft staircase with a gorgeous prince who happened to be her husband. She still couldn't believe what was happening.

Each beat of her heart slammed against her ribs. She'd never once dreamed of traveling to a far off destination except to attend a race. But here she was about to board a private plane and fly off to another continent...

An airplane sped down the runway.

She shivered. Soon that would be her plane.

Some might call this an exciting adventure, but not Izzy. Her misgivings were increasing by the minute.

Another aircraft taxied by. The silver, red and blue color-scheme seemed almost festive compared to Vernonia's solid white airplane with only an aircraft numbers, letters and a small coat of arms for markings.

A royal coat of arms.

A chill ran down her spine.

She could never have imagined this happening to anyone let alone her. A grease monkey who cared more about the Winston Cup standings than the lines of succession for European thrones was now a princess?

Below her at the bottom of the stairs, a local security detail stood watch. A custom agent checked paperwork with the security liaison officer who wore a uniform and seemed to be part of the flight crew.

The shock of discovery still had her reeling. Denial battled acceptance. In spite of the physical evidence, Izzy still found the truth hard to accept. Would she ever feel like Princess Isabel Poussard Zvonimir Kresimir? She doubted it.

Facing the open doorway, Izzy sensed rather than felt Niko standing behind her. She clutched the strap of her backpack.

"It's time to board," he whispered from behind her. His warm breath fanned her neck.

Awareness shot through Izzy. Her uneasiness quadrupled.

Hold it together.

She straightened, not wanting to appear weak. "I know."

Yet the open doorway loomed in front of her like a mysterious black hole. Her heart pounded so fast, Izzy thought her chest might explode.

All she had to do was step across the threshold and board the plane. Too bad her feet felt as if they'd been permanently attached to the staircase. But they knew what Izzy kept trying to forget.

This wasn't only about never having flown before. She had absolutely no idea what waited for her on the other side. Of the doorway or when she arrived in Vernonia.

She'd never had to face the unknown alone. Uncle Frank had always been there to pave the way. Even after his death, she'd continued working at Rowdy's, living in the RV and following the plan they'd dreamed up together. But now she found herself on a new, uncertain path with all her plans swept away.

Worse, there was no turning back.

Her life was irrevocably changed whether she boarded the plane or stayed in Charlotte. The realization made her light-headed.

The prince moved closer, crowding her from behind. He emanated strength and warmth. Her pulse skittered.

Uh-oh. Izzy needed to put a little distance between them. Not that she had much room to go anywhere. She shifted to the side until her backpack and hip hit the staircase railing. "Give me a minute."

Niko gently placed his hand on the curve of her back.

Izzy stiffened. The slight touch made her more apprehensive.

"You will have plenty of time once we board," he said.

She was losing control of this situation, of her life. "Things are happening too fast. I need everything to slow down."

"Everything will slow down when we are in the air. We have a long flight ahead of us."

A long flight that would carry her away from everything familiar. Nerves smacked into her like a rogue wave. Her stomach churned.

"Isabel," Niko said.

Another plane took off. The roar louder than any engine she'd ever heard at the racetrack. Goose bumps prickled her skin.

"I told you I needed a minute." The words came out harsher than she intended.

"It's been an eventful day," Niko said.

"You think?" She swallowed around the crown-jewel-size lump in her throat. "I doubt anyone else has ever had a day like today. I wish it were all a dream. But it's not. And now I'm stuck."

"Stuck?"

"Having to go to Vernonia to annul the marriage and get my inheritance," she admitted. "Unfortunately I have no idea what's going to happen once we arrive. I may have been born there, but it might as well be Mars."

Niko's assessing gaze made her feel like one of

Cinderella's ugly stepsisters. "Vernonia is different from what you are used to. Some would call the country old-fashioned. Others antiquated. Especially when it comes to gender roles."

Izzy half laughed with a mix of desperation and fear. "If you're trying to make me feel better, it's not working."

"I will not lie to you, Isabel," he said. "Your life has changed. But you will not have to deal with any of this on your own."

A sense of inadequacy swept through her. Izzy was used to handling everything on her own, but she was completely out of her comfort zone here and practically shaking in her held-together-with-super-glue tennis shoes.

"It will be my pleasure to help you," he offered.

Niko made a dashing knight in shining armor, but Izzy didn't like being cast in the role of damsel in distress. She didn't want or need his help. "Thanks, but I can do this on my own."

Please let me be able to do this on my own.

With a deep breath, Izzy stood and stepped through the doorway of the plane.

"Welcome aboard, Your Royal Highness," a male flight attendant with a crew cut and navy blue uniform greeted. "We have a seven course dinner for you as well as movies for your entertainment."

It took Izzy a minute to realize the man was addressing her. "Thank you," she muttered, wondering how he knew who she was.

The flight attendant smiled at her. "Would you like me to escort you to your seat, ma'am?"

"Thank you, Luka, but I will show Princess Isabel the way," Niko said before Izzy could answer.

Luka bowed. "Enjoy your flight, ma'am, sir."

"I thought you wanted to keep my identity a secret to avoid publicity," she whispered to Niko as she moved away from Luka.

"Only until after we appear before the High Court," he explained quietly.

As his male scent surrounded her, heat rushed through her veins. She hoped the High Court would be their first stop after they landed.

"Do not worry," he continued. "The crew is part of the Vernonian Air Force. They can be trusted with the information. As can the palace staff."

That seemed like a lot of people in on the secret, but he was the prince. "If you say so."

"I do."

Izzy made her way down the aisle, holding her backpack in front of her. The interior, a mix of warm beiges, browns and blues, created a welcoming environment. Couches and tables filled the first section of the cabin.

"This is the lounge area," Niko explained. "Feel free to come up here if you want to stretch your legs."

"I doubt I'll unfasten my seat belt during the flight."

The corners of his mouth lifted. "That may get uncomfortable if you have to use the facilities."

Her cheeks warmed. She hadn't considered that.

The second section of the cabin contained rows of seats. The wide leather seats looked comfortable and luxurious, not narrow and cramped and squished together as her high school classmates had described after their graduation trip to the Caribbean. Izzy hadn't been able to afford the trip, so had stayed home and worked at Rowdy's garage.

Times sure had changed. Mechanic Izzy Poussard was now Princess Isabel, the wife of the crown prince of Vernonia. She nearly laughed at the absurdity of it.

"This is where we sit for takeoff and landing, or, if you choose," Niko said, "the entire flight."

Izzy passed the row where Jovan sat. A few other seats were taken by people she hadn't seen before. She continued to the last row of empty seats before a divider.

Before she could sit, a female flight attendant rushed from the rear of the plane. The young woman wore a navy jacket and skirt. Her blond hair was neatly braided into a bun. "Good evening. Allow me to hold your backpack for you, Your Royal Highness."

Before Izzy could say a word, the backpack strap was lifted out of her hand. Every one of her muscles tensed, bunching into tight balls. She wasn't used to being catered to. It was disconcerting because she didn't feel like royalty.

She sat in the window seat and buckled her seat belt.

The flight attendant handed the backpack to Izzy.

"Would you care for something to drink or eat, ma'am?"

"No, thanks." Izzy didn't want to upset her stomach any more than it already was. Her nerves were getting the best of her. Over the flight, over Vernonia, over Niko. Maybe if she distracted herself...

She pressed a button that turned on the overhead light. She twisted a knob that regulated the airflow nozzle.

Niko sat next to her. "Are you certain you do not want anything?"

Izzy wanted this to be over with. "No, thanks, Your Highness."

"Call me Niko."

"I'm not sure I should get in the habit of calling you by your first name. As soon as our marriage is annulled I doubt you'd want to be on such familiar terms with a commoner."

"You are not a commoner," he said. "You are a princess by birth. Royal Sachestian blood flows through your veins."

"That may be true, but I was raised American. Royalty is something other countries have."

"Americans have unofficial royalty. The Kennedys, the Rockefellers, the Hiltons."

"I suppose, but a princess isn't something I aspired to be beyond the age of four or five. Wearing a tiara has never been a dream of mine."

"You may feel like an American, but you are a Vernonian." He spoke as if her being a Vernonian was the most important thing she could be. No one had ever spoken to her that way. Not even Uncle Frank. "You will be amazed by the history of your family."

Intrigued, she leaned toward him. "I have a family history?"

"Your lineage goes back centuries. Your father's family played an integral role in the formation of our country, when Sachestia in the north merged with the south to form what we now call Vernonia." He fastened his seat belt. "If you have questions about anything, please ask."

"I—" The lights in the cabin flickered. She clutched the seat armrests until her knuckles turned white. "What's that?"

"The APU, auxiliary power unit, coming on," he explained. "It powers the lights and air system while we are in flight."

"Oh, yeah. I should have remembered that."

The plane moved backward.

Oh boy, oh boy, oh boy.

"Do not worry." Niko covered her hand with his large one. His skin was warm, but not soft. Scars and calluses covered his hand and fingers. "The plane is being moved so the pilot can taxi to the runway."

Forget about the plane. His touch disturbed her more than it comforted. She tried to slip her hand from beneath his, but couldn't. "I'm sorry if I've acted like a wimp, but I'm okay now."

"You've handled everything remarkably well, Isabel. You should be proud of yourself."

He wouldn't let Izzy remove her hand from his, but his words made her sit taller. She wanted to be brave for him, but mostly herself. That was what Uncle Frank would have wanted her to be.

The engines roared to life. She sucked in a breath. *Nothing to worry about. Nothing to worry about.*

The words became a mantra.

The plane taxied to the runway. Out the window, she saw the airport lights shining in the darkness. Pretty, but she would rather be at home watching a television show than sitting on a luxurious private jet holding hands with a handsome prince.

Too late to back out now.

Izzy pressed her feet against the floor of the plane.

"We will be in the air shortly," Niko said.

All she could do was nod.

The jet lurched to a stop. The engines whined, the sound growing louder. She was too nervous to appreciate the speed of the rotor. The cabin shook like the crowd at Daytona when cars went three wide. Izzy held her breath.

Suddenly the jet speeded down the runway.

She glanced out the window at the world passing by her.

"Remember to breathe," he said.

She did.

Nikola squeezed her hand.

This time his touch reassured her. She met his eyes. Her gaze dropped to his mouth. She thought about kissing him until she couldn't think straight, but that seemed a little extreme. Maybe burying her face against his chest until this was over would be better. She closed her eyes instead.

"Look at me, Isabel."

She forced her eyes open. Her gaze locked with his intense green eyes.

"You are safe," he said. "As long as you are with me, you will always be safe."

The confidence and strength he exuded made her almost believe his words. But she knew *safe* didn't really exist. If it did her parents would be alive. Uncle Frank, too.

The vibrations increased until she thought the plane might break apart. The forward momentum pushed her back against her seat. Niko laced his fingers with hers.

The plane lifted off the ground.

The lights below grew smaller and smaller until they disappeared altogether. The plane climbed at a steep angle, as if it were a fighter jet not a passenger plane.

The aircraft jolted. She sucked in another breath.

"A patch of turbulence," Niko said. "Normal."

None of this was normal. Not the takeoff, not the prince sitting next to her. And certainly not this life-altering adventure she was embarking on.

After what seemed like forever, the plane leveled.

"We've reached cruising altitude." Niko kept his hand on hers. "Not too bad."

It wasn't a question.

"No," she admitted. "But we still have to land."

The corners of his mouth lifted. "Landing will be easier."

"Really?" she asked.

He nodded. "You'll be tired due to the time change. You may even be asleep when the wheels touch ground."

"I'm not sure I'll be sleeping after everything that's gone on. My mind's a big jumble right now."

"You should try to sleep," he encouraged her. "Tomorrow will be a big day."

"Are we going straight to the court?" she asked.

"The High Court is not in session on Saturday. We will go to the castle."

"Castle?"

"My parents want to meet you."

"I've never met a king or a queen."

"You have, but you don't remember."

"What's your father like?" Izzy asked.

"He's very…kingly."

"That's intimidating," she admitted. "I'm glad I don't remember meeting him or I might be more nervous than I already am."

"He only wants to reassure himself you are alive and well." Niko squeezed her hand. "You have nothing to worry about."

This time Izzy knew the prince was wrong. Dead wrong.

She had lots to worry about, starting with the tingles shooting up her arm as he touched her. But even worse was the realization that she didn't want him to let go of her hand.

Not now.
Not when they landed in Vernonia.
Not…ever.

CHAPTER FOUR

As THE plane cruised at thirty-three thousand feet, the interior cabin lights dimmed. The engines droned, but unlike the white noise device Niko usually traveled with, the sound did not soothe him. He couldn't sleep. Too many things weighed on his mind. But a busy day did lie ahead. He should at least try to rest.

Niko pressed the button on the armrest. The leather seat reclined into a comfortable position. He closed his eyes but couldn't stop the continuous stream of information flowing through his brain. Thoughts about Vernonia, Julianna, his father and most especially the woman sitting in the seat next to him.

Isabel.

Opening his eyes, he turned toward her.

She sat with her seat reclined and her head resting against a pillow. She'd fallen asleep after struggling against her heavy, drooping eyelids and drawn-out yawns for almost an hour.

Isabel's unwillingness to give in to her tiredness without a fight made him wonder if she turned everything she did into a battle. Her actions today suggested as much. But the political peace that came with her lineage could be good for the country.

Yes, Isabel seemed like a fighter. No doubt the Vernonian in her. Niko smiled at the thought that she would likely disagree with him. No matter, he would want her on his side. If he had a side. Thankfully those days were over. No one would be forced to choose who to support or who to fight again.

Once he and Julianna said the words "I do," Niko would have the financial resources and international support to bring his country into the modern age and, in time, the European Union.

Nothing could stand in his way now.

Not an antiquated custom. Not a childhood bride.

Niko's gaze focused on Isabel once again.

He'd been married to her for the past twenty-three years, almost all of her entire life and over three-quarters of his. If not for the missing bride box, he would have never known she existed. Things would have been less complicated for him that way. But once she received her inheritance her circumstance would improve dramatically. A better life was waiting for Isabel. The life her parents would have wanted for her. That made what he was going through more acceptable.

He worried what responsibilities would be thrust on Isabel's shoulders once she arrived in Vernonia. People would judge her. She would need training to be a princess. Stylish clothes and makeup lessons would improve her appearance. A manicure would help with her dirty, chipped nails though not much could rid her hands of the calluses, cuts and scars. Perhaps she could start a new fashion trend by wearing gloves.

In spite of Isabel's faults and disregard for etiquette and style, she was a refreshing change from the other royals he'd encountered over the years. She was not caught up in the tangled web of tradition. Even Julianna, as perfect as she was, came from a kingdom more out-of-date than Vernonia.

He admired Isabel for working on cars. He remembered what being a soldier was like. Living day-to-day, sometimes hour-to-hour. It was the closest thing to an ordinary existence he'd had. Even after she put her mechanic days behind her, she could relate to the people at their level.

Isabel might not know how to be a princess yet, but at least she was a contemporary woman, something rarely found in his country. He could use that to his advantage as he moved forward with his plans. Though right now she looked more like a schoolgirl than a woman with the cashmere blanket tucked around her shoulders.

The cover rose and fell with each of her breaths. Her hair fanned across the pillow, the brown strands contrasting with the white fabric. The slender column of her neck contradicted the stiff backbone she'd shown earlier. The curve of her cheek and fullness of her lips weren't diminished by the lack of makeup and lip-gloss on her face. She possessed a natural beauty.

Although Niko appreciated her spirit and self-reliance, he couldn't deny the appeal of this softer side. The defiant set of her chin and tight jaw had relaxed.

The result of sleep, but she looked so peaceful and serene. He wondered if she ever looked this way awake. He doubted it.

With her lips slightly parted, she almost appeared to be smiling. The result of a pleasant dream? A dream about him?

No. Her dreams were none of his business. Isabel might be his wife, but he should think of her like a sister. Anything else would be…inappropriate given his intention to marry Julianna.

Isabel shifted in her seat. The way she stretched reminded him of one of the feral cats who lived in the stable. As she settled into a new position, the top half of her blanket fell from her shoulders and pooled on her lap.

He could see the rise and fall of her chest better now. The V-neck collar gave a tantalizing view of creamy skin and lace. The fabric of her shirt stretched across her breasts. The cool cabin temperature beaded her nipples.

Niko covered her with the blanket and tucked the edge around her shoulders.

"Sir," Jovan said, standing in the aisle.

Niko jerked his hands away from Isabel, feeling as if the palace's renowned pastry chef had caught him sneaking a *tulumbe* from a batch soaking in syrup overnight.

"It is late." Jovan handed him a blanket. "There is nothing more to be done until we arrive in Vernonia. Please rest, sir."

Niko knew sleep was futile, but he placed the blanket

on his lap. Jovan was only trying to do his job. "The shopping arrangements…"

"Have been taken care of, sir. Princess Julianna has offered her assistance and expertise."

The future wife helping the soon-to-be former one? The thought of the two women, so very different, made Niko's temples throb. "That will be…interesting."

"Princess Julianna's sense of duty is matched only by your own," Jovan said. "She simply wants to help you, sir."

Niko only hoped Isabel accepted the help. That independent streak of hers might get in the way. "Julianna will make a fine queen."

Jovan nodded. "She will also be an excellent role model for Princess Isabel to emulate, sir."

"Yes." Niko glanced at Isabel to see if she was still asleep. He lowered his voice. "She will need all the help she can get."

Jovan smiled at the sleeping woman. "Princess Isabel is not what I expected, but she has…spirit. She puts on no airs. Plays no games."

"She is different and has a certain down-to-earth charm," Niko agreed. "In time she could become a role model herself."

Jovan's brows furrowed. "I do not think she intends to stay long enough for that to happen, sir."

"Once Isabel sees all Vernonia has to offer, she will want to stay. We can have her things shipped over."

"You sound certain, sir."

"I am," Niko stated. "You saw the hovel she calls

home. Her life in the United States leaves much to be desired."

"She doesn't seem to mind that life, sir," Jovan said. "And with her inheritance…"

"Perhaps she does not know any better."

Niko's gaze returned to Isabel's face. Her full lips still appeared to be smiling. He wouldn't mind a taste of them. A kiss.

No. He couldn't allow himself to go there, even if he was…tempted.

He focused his attention on his aide. "Staying in Vernonia is best for Isabel."

Just as Julianna was best for Vernonia, thus best for him.

"I wonder what Princess Isabel will have to say about that, sir," Jovan said.

"She may not have an Ivy League education, but she is intelligent. It won't take her long to realize where her future lies."

"If she disagrees, I suppose we can finally make use of the tower, sir," Jovan joked.

Niko laughed. "You've been spending too much time around my father."

"Isabel."

A man was calling Izzy's name, but she didn't open her eyes. Her alarm clock hadn't buzzed yet. That meant this must still be part of her dream, an odd mix of fairy tale and nightmare with a brooding, handsome prince holding her captive in a tower.

"Isabel," the man said again.

She liked the way the three syllables rolled off his tongue. I-sa-bel. She snuggled against the pillow, wanting more sleep and more of him.

The bed lurched, as if she were riding on a flying carpet that had come to a sudden stop.

"Welcome to Vernonia," the male voice continued. *Where?* And then she realized.

Izzy wasn't in bed dreaming. She forced her heavy eyelids open. Bright sunlight streamed through the window. She blinked. The plane had not only landed, but also parked. A small turboprop taxied by.

Every single one of her muscles tensed. Yesterday had been real. The box. Her parents. The prince.

She clutched the armrests.

"Good morning, Isabel," Niko said from the seat next to her.

Izzy saw nothing good about this morning. She was tired, surrounded by strangers and far away from home. She turned toward Niko to tell him as much, but her mouth went dry at the sight of him.

Hello, Prince Hottie. Heat pulsed through her veins.

The stubble on Niko's face made him look sexier, dangerous. Especially with his scar. A real bad boy. His clothes remained unwrinkled, as if he'd just stepped away from a photo shoot, not spent the night flying across an ocean and a continent.

"You didn't eat much dinner last night," he said. "Are you hungry?"

She wouldn't mind a bite of him.

Strike that. A serving of prince sunny side up wasn't

on the menu this morning. Or any morning, Izzy reminded herself. This wasn't just some guy. He was her husband. At least for another couple of days until the High Court was back in session.

Izzy toyed with the edge of the blanket covering her lap. "No, thanks. I'm not hungry."

"I will have a meal delivered to your room in case you are hungry later."

Room service? She wiggled her toes with anticipation. She'd never stayed at a nice hotel that offered room service. Maybe this trip would have some bright spots. "Thanks, but please don't go to any trouble. I can order my own food."

"It is no trouble," he said.

But it was for her. "I prefer to do things myself."

"Luka already came by with the warm towels," Niko continued as if she hadn't spoken. "If you would like one—"

"No, thanks. I'm good."

Tired, but good. Izzy yawned, hoping she wasn't breaking some princess protocol. She needed more sleep. A shower wouldn't hurt. Once she arrived at the hotel...

"Ready to see your homeland?" Niko asked.

Vernonia might be her place of birth, but she would never call it her homeland. "I suppose I can't stay on the plane all day."

"You could."

"Really?"

"You're a princess," he said, as if she knew all the rules about being royalty. "But you might get bored."

"I don't do well being bored."

"That doesn't surprise me."

She stood and placed the shoulder strap of her back-pack over her shoulder.

"The crew will carry your backpack," Niko said.

"I don't mind."

"The crew does. They consider it an honor to serve you."

"I'm, uh, not really comfortable with that. My wallet and ID are in it."

"It looks strange for a princess to be hauling around a backpack."

"It's my purse," she countered. "Besides I don't care what other people think of me."

A muscle flicked at his jaw. "You've made that quite obvious."

Niko pressed his lips together. The same way he'd done in Charlotte. He wasn't happy with her. He'd probably better get used to it for as long as she was in town.

"Just so you know," she said. "It bugs me when people try to tell me what I can or can't do."

She walked down the aisle before he could say any-thing else to annoy her.

The other passengers, who had been introduced by job titles, not names during the flight, had already deplaned. The flight crew, including the pilots, stood in a line at the front of the plane. Izzy thanked them and exited.

At the top of the portable staircase, she took a deep breath. The crisp air refreshed her.

The airport wasn't as large as the one in Charlotte and seemed to be built on a plateau. Everything from the control tower to the runways looked brand-new. Beyond the runways the flat landscape gave way to foothills and rocky mountains beyond that.

Niko joined her on the landing. He motioned to a black limousine at the bottom of the stairs. "Our chariot awaits."

Attached to the front of the car were two small blue and white flags with yellow emblems in the center. They fluttered in the cool breeze. Uniformed guards with large guns stood nearby. A man in a black suit unloaded the luggage from a cart. He carefully placed her battered duffel bag into the trunk as if it contained fragile Fabergé eggs, not thrift store bargain buys.

Feelings of inadequacy swept through her. Izzy was completely out of her league here. She clutched the metal handrail like a lifeline.

Niko extended his arm. "I'm only offering because you must be tired."

His gesture of chivalry brought tears to her eyes. Uncle Frank used to do the same thing before escorting her across the street or down a parking lot staircase. Izzy wiped her eyes with her hand.

Boy, she must really be jet-lagged to get so sentimental. But Niko was right. Her legs were stiff from the flight. Her shoes fit tighter, making her wonder if her feet had swollen. She couldn't pretend she wasn't feeling more tired by the minute.

Falling down the stairs was a distinct possibility in her current condition and would not be a good start to her visit to Vernonia. Forget making a faux pas. The stage was set for an epic fail. She couldn't let that happen.

Better safe than sorry. Izzy wrapped her arm around Niko's. "Thanks."

Together, they descended the stairs. He went slowly, shortening his long stride. For her sake, Izzy realized. Her thoughts about him being a knight in shining armor weren't too far off. Still she wasn't comfortable needing his assistance. She'd been standing on her own two feet for the last five years, ever since Uncle Frank died. Leaning on someone else felt odd and unnatural, even if it was only for the length of the portable staircase.

"You are not merely tired." His gazed remained focused straight ahead, never straying her way. A slight breeze ruffled the ends of his hair. Even the scar on his face suited him. He wasn't a perfect prince, but he wasn't that bad. "You are exhausted."

"Yeah." She struggled not to yawn. "Though I'm not sure why since I slept most of the flight."

"Jet lag. It's the middle of the night in Charlotte," he explained. "You need time to adjust. You can rest soon. Though not too long or your body clock will be thrown off even more."

"A short nap is all I need."

"A short nap you shall have."

His grin made her breath catch in her throat. Izzy wouldn't mind if he tucked her in and kissed her goodnight.

Her foot missed a step. As if in slow motion, she fell backward. Her right hand clutched the railing. Her left hand gripped Niko's arm. Somehow he caught her before her bottom hit the staircase.

"Are you okay?" he asked.

His strong arms righted her so she was standing upright. "Yes," she said grateful. "Thanks to you."

"Only a few more steps."

Thank goodness. Her entire body trembled. Not because of the near fall, but because of Niko. Looks aside, his compelling presence drew her in like a tow truck's winch. She needed to get away from him.

As soon as Izzy reached the tarmac, she slid her arm from his. The chauffeur opened the back door. She climbed inside. Leaning back against the leather seat, she stretched out her legs, relieved to be away from Niko.

He slid into the limousine and sat next to her even though the rest of the seats were empty. Darn the man. Didn't he understand the concept of personal space?

His thigh pressed against hers. Not on purpose, she thought. Still her temperature rose.

The prince might be a hottie, but he was off-limits. He was her husband, but he planned on marrying someone else. His heart wasn't on the open market. She couldn't allow herself to be attracted to him.

Izzy scooted away. She needed something to defuse her growing awareness to him. "Where's Jovan?"

"In the front with the driver." Niko pressed a button and lowered the dark glass separating the back of the limousine from the front. "Jovan is making sure everything will be ready for you to shop today."

"I don't have to go shopping today."

"I know you are tired. I wish you could have more time to adjust, but my parents expect you to attend dinner tonight."

"Tonight?" Her voice cracked. "That's, um, nice of them, but dinner isn't really necessary. I mean, in a few days, we won't even be married."

"Our parents were friends. They orchestrated our wedding," Niko explained. "You are and always will be a princess of Vernonia and should consider us family."

Family.

Izzy felt a pang in her heart.

The word family brought up all kinds of strange emotions. Ones she'd tried to ignore while growing up. She'd never had any family except Uncle Frank. "That's a generous offer, but I feel more like a serf than a royal."

"A royal serf," Niko said. "An oxymoron."

"How about a royal waif?" she suggested.

Laughter danced in his warm eyes. "Serf, waif or princess, you'll find acceptance here, Isabel."

The only people who had ever accepted her were back at Rowdy's garage, but she appreciated Niko trying to make her feel better. She stifled a yawn.

"After you rest, you will shop. Someone will help you select and organize the various outfits you'll need."

"Um, thanks." Izzy didn't know whether to be offended or grateful he was providing her help. She didn't care about what was in style or not, but she wasn't colorblind. "I don't need a lot."

"Most women like having several different outfits."

"I'm not like most women."

His gaze raked over her. "No, you are not."

She didn't think he intended that to be a compliment, but she wasn't offended. His words reaffirmed what she already knew. Izzy Poussard wasn't princess material. She didn't belong in Vernonia. She needed to take care of business, learn about her family and return home to Charlotte.

As the limo left the airport, Niko pointed out the window toward a town up ahead. "We're entering the capital city."

Izzy was surprised to see a city smaller and more compact than Charlotte with narrower roads. But the commotion on the streets suggested a busy, bustling town.

A crane lifted steel girders while men in yellow hard hats guided them onto the fourth floor of a construction site. Next door, scaffolding covered the front of a new office building and men painted. Across the street, a woman in a multicolored skirt, boots and long sweater pushed a baby stroller. Two teenagers kicked a soccer ball back and forth as they hurried past the woman and child. A man in a business suit glanced at the limousine before hurrying into a newer five-story building made of steel and glass.

"What do you think?" Niko asked.

"It's very modern for a country that allowed children to marry."

"I told you, that is against the law now."

"Yes, you did." She didn't see any garbage or graffiti

anywhere. That was quite an achievement. "Everything is so new and clean. Even the streets."

"This part of town was demolished by bombing," he explained. "Rebuilding takes time and money. Projects are being spread out to best utilize our resources."

The limousine drove into another part of town. This section consisted of smaller stone and brick rectangular buildings each painted a different color. Some were new, but many were older. Several had window boxes, but no flowers. "Is this a residential area?"

"Yes."

Izzy noticed one similarity among the colorful homes. Holes on almost every structure. Bullet pocks? she wondered.

A memorial sign hung on a pole. Flowers and pictures were attached. She shuddered.

"I can't imagine what living through a war must be like. Just watching the television coverage of 9/11 was difficult. Granted I was a teenager, but this…" A weight pressed down on her chest. "I hope this never happens again."

"I intend to make sure it doesn't," Niko stated firmly. "War is never pleasant, but fighting amongst your own is particularly brutal. Friend against friend. Brother against brother. Both the Loyalists and the Separatists accepted the treaty unanimously. Our postconflict elections have gone well. We are fortunate to have not faced some of the problems that have plagued other Balkan countries. I am determined to see that peace is upheld and good triumphs for all Vernonians. No matter what side they supported in the conflict."

Her respect for him rose. "Good luck."

"Thank you."

The limousine left the town behind and traveled up a steep hill. Tall trees lined both sides of the road and cast shadows on the pavement. As the car crested a bump, she saw a castle in the distance.

Her heart beat triple time.

A fairy-tale castle, so perfect it appeared to have been painted on a canvas of blue. Turrets jutted into the sky. Leaded glass windows sparkled. Silver roof tiles gleamed beneath the morning sun. She'd never seen anything so beautiful in her life.

"Wow."

"We are fortunate the castle remained in such good shape given the battles fought here," Niko said. "The wall took several mortar hits, but that was the worst of the damage."

"Thank goodness." Jovan turned around from the front seat. "The royal family stayed in residence during the conflict."

"When we weren't fighting," Niko said.

Izzy was surprised a royal would be out on the front line. "You fought in the war?"

"Yes." The one word spoke volumes. "Stefan and I fought with the loyalists to preserve the boundaries and traditions of all people."

Izzy could imagine Niko as a warrior, fierce and hard, defending his people to the death. That took courage and strength. She pointed to the jagged scar on his cheek. "Did you get that fighting?"

"Yes, we are all marked in some way by the conflict," he said. "Some scars are physical. Others are not."

Did Niko have other scars? Hidden ones? Izzy wanted to know, but didn't know him well enough to ask. She wanted to see if there was more to this seemingly in-control prince than met the eye. Curiosity about the man her parents had married her off to, she rationalized.

As the limousine approached the castle, the immense structure loomed in front of her. Was that a moat?

She peered out the window. Yes, it was. A river flowed underneath a bridge flanked by armed guards. One waved the limousine across.

Two minutes later, the car stopped in front of tall, wooden doors. A uniformed man stepped outside. His white dress shirt, creased pants and sharp jacket made Izzy feel totally underdressed in her faded jeans, T-shirt and ratty sneakers. No wonder the prince was so keen on her shopping.

"Your bag will be delivered to your room, ma'am," Jovan said before exiting the limousine.

"Wait a minute." Izzy's gaze locked with Niko's. "I thought I was staying at a hotel."

"You are legally my wife," Niko said. "You will stay here at the castle until the annulment has been granted."

"I want to stay at a hotel."

"No."

Darn the man. He hadn't listened to her before. If he had, he wouldn't be telling her what to do. "But—"

"The castle is the most suitable place for you to stay."

Izzy could rattle off a hundred reasons why she shouldn't stay here with him, the queen and the king. She settled on one. "I'd be more comfortable in a hotel."

"You will be more comfortable here," Niko countered. "Your every whim will be catered to by the castle's staff."

"I don't have any whims that need catering."

He set his jaw. "No hotel."

Her eyelids felt heavy. She needed to sit down. "I really—"

"This isn't up for negotiation."

Her tiredness was putting her at a disadvantage. She couldn't think fast enough. "Please."

"You will sleep better here than anywhere. Trust me."

Izzy didn't trust him. She couldn't.

"It's also better for you to stay at the castle for security reasons."

Okay, that she could accept.

"Fine. I'll concede on that point." She stared down her nose. "But just so you know, as soon as we get the annulment, I'm outta here."

I'm outta here.

Niko had one parting thought before he handed Isabel off to a maid.

Good riddance.

He kept the thought to himself, balling his hands

into fists instead. He would not lower himself to *her* level.

The woman was ill-mannered and brash. She had no idea how she was supposed to act. A month locked in the tower with only etiquette and protocol books might actually help her learn to be a princess. The room in the tower would be better for her than the rusty aluminum can she called home. Though she would probably miss the grease from the garage.

The sharp click from his heels against the wood floor as he strode through the hall echoed his irritation.

"Niko."

He stopped and flexed his fingers. He did not want his annoyance at his "wife" to affect his soon-to-be new wife.

Julianna stood in the doorway of the library. Her designer skirt and short-fitted jacket complemented her figure the same way her deftly applied makeup accentuated her features. Her long, blond hair gleamed under the lights. "Welcome home."

One word came to mind as he stared at her—perfection. He couldn't have found a better princess to be Vernonia's queen. Her beauty was matched by her intelligence. She spoke four languages fluently—German, French, Italian and English. She was an Olympic-caliber sailor and an excellent spokesperson. She had the necessary family connections and wealth, but her sense of duty set her above many of the other unmarried royals he'd met over the past few years. She knew what her country expected of her, and she fulfilled her duty without question. One hundred and eighty degrees different from Isabel.

"It's good to see you, Julianna."

"And you." She sounded genuinely pleased to him. That would bode well for their future together, if only he could stop thinking about…his current wife. "I hope your trip went well," Julianna added.

The hallway was empty, but that didn't mean people weren't listening. He didn't want to take any chance of someone overhearing him.

"Let's talk in the library where we will not be disturbed." Niko led her past floor-to-ceiling bookcases to a small meeting room in the back. He closed the door.

Julianna ran her fingers along the polished walnut desk. "I had no idea this room was even here."

Memories of pestering his older brother, Stefan, while he attempted to study surfaced. Niko pushed them and the pang of grief aside. "Thank you for offering to help Isabel with her shopping."

Julianna smiled softly. "It's the least I can do for you."

Niko had always put Vernonia first. He dated, but had never had a true partner to confide in or ask for help. Perhaps that would change soon. "Thank you."

"You're welcome, but it's not a hardship. I love to shop."

He wasn't about to criticize his current wife to his future spouse, but he didn't want Julianna blindsided, either. "You may find Isabel a reluctant shopper."

"I'm sure I can convince her a shopping spree is in order."

"It could be a challenge," Niko admitted. "Isabel does not want to be a princess."

Julianna smiled knowingly. "Every woman wants to be a princess, even if they would never dare admit it aloud."

"Not Isabel." His blood pressure rose thinking about her. "I've never met a woman who tried so hard not to be female."

Julianna furrowed her finely arched brows. "Isabel wants to be a man?"

"No, but she is a car mechanic. She works hard not to look like a woman. No makeup. Baggy coveralls. Very casual clothing. No dresses or high heels."

"You sound exasperated."

"She is exasperating."

"First impressions can be deceiving," Julianna counseled, making Niko wonder if this was how she spoke to her younger brothers. "Isabel must be in shock."

"The news has shocked her, but I don't believe my impression of her is far off." Niko thought about her parting words to him. "Isabel is young. She speaks without thinking. She has no sense of what it is to be royalty."

"She sounds refreshing."

"I thought so yesterday, but today we keep…clashing," he admitted. "She slept so peacefully last night, but when she awoke this morning she was more beast than beauty."

Julianna's mouth quirked. "Isabel is a beauty?"

"Not exactly," he backtracked. "Some men might find her attractive."

"Do you?"

"She's my wife. I don't think of her in that way."

Amusement gleamed in Julianna's eyes. "I see."

"There's nothing to see," he countered. "Fortunately Isabel agrees an annulment is the only option. She was excited to hear about our getting married."

Julianna sighed. No doubt relieved the upcoming royal engagement and nuptials faced no more obstacles. "We can add her to the wedding party. A royal wedding can never have too many attendants."

"That is thoughtful of you." Her thoughtfulness was another reason why Julianna was perfect for his country. "I doubt Isabel will want to remain in Vernonia that long."

"You must convince her to stay," Julianna insisted.

"You haven't met her."

"It doesn't matter," Julianna countered. "Isabel has a duty to fulfill here in Vernonia."

"I understand what you are saying, but Isabel is very—" he searched for a somewhat complimentary adjective "—independent. I don't think she is the type to fulfill her duty."

"She needs training," Julianna said. "I can help her."

"You don't know what you're offering to take on."

"Come now, you make her sound like an ogre."

"Not an ogre," he admitted. "Ornery."

"I have four younger brothers. I can handle ornery."

"See how shopping goes, then you can decide if you want to continue helping her or not."

"I can't wait to see what you think of her with a brand-new wardrobe complete with coordinating accessories, shoes and makeup."

Niko's shoulders tensed. No way would Isabel agree to a total makeover. "Just get her into a dress by dinnertime, and I'll be much obliged."

"Obliged enough for another sail tomorrow?" Julianna challenged.

The jaunt to America had wreaked havoc with his schedule. Niko had little to no free time right now. He appreciated Julianna's help because that meant he didn't have to deal with Isabel himself. The woman didn't need only a fashion makeover, she needed a complete personality transplant. Niko doubted even the capable Aliestle princess could do much with Isabel by dinnertime. But if Julianna was willing to try…

"If you can make her presentable to my parents, I'll gladly find the time to go sailing with you tomorrow."

CHAPTER FIVE

Izzy didn't want to like it here. She wasn't going to fit in no matter what she did. The less attached she got to anyone or anything during her short visit the better. But right this minute she wouldn't want to be anywhere else but Vernonia.

Nothing could beat floating on this cloud.

Okay, she was lying on a four-poster queen-size bed, but the mattress was truly fit for a king. Or a princess. No lumps, bumps or peas to be found. The feather pillow conformed to the shape of her head and supported it exactly right. The luxurious sheets cocooned her. She sighed in delight.

Best nap ever.

She never knew a bed could be so comfortable or sheets could feel so soft.

Izzy kept her eyes closed, wanting to linger on the cloud a little longer. But not too long. She didn't want to throw her body clock any more as Niko had mentioned earlier.

Niko.

He hadn't looked happy when he'd handed her off to a maid named Mare. Izzy hadn't been as polite as she could have been. Being tired had contributed, but she didn't like being bossed around. She wasn't one of Niko's subjects. He seemed to forget she was an American. He couldn't tell her what to do.

The image of his ruggedly handsome face formed in her mind. Those to-die-for blue-green eyes. That dark mane of hair. His killer...

What was she doing thinking about him? Izzy opened her eyes.

Darkness filled the room. That was weird. Some natural light had been filtering in through the large windows when she lay down.

Oh, no. Panic spurted through her. Had she slept too long?

Bolting upright, she glanced at the digital clock on the nightstand. Only two and a half hours had passed.

Relief washed over her. But why was the room so dark?

She glanced around, allowing her eyes to adjust. Her gaze rested on the closed yellow damask drapes. They'd been open before she fell asleep.

Izzy squirmed with uneasiness. She had lived alone for the last five years and wasn't used to anyone being around when she slept. A good thing she wouldn't be here long.

She tossed back the covers and slid from the bed. Her bare feet sunk into a thick, colorful rug covering the hardwood floors.

Talk about living large. The grandeur of the interior exceeded the castle's fairy-tale exterior. She felt as if she were staying in a museum with antique furniture, famous paintings and exquisite tapestries. Everything looked so expensive she didn't want to touch anything she could break.

Inside the expansive bathroom, Izzy found her toiletry kit sitting on the gold-veined marble countertop. Someone must have removed it from her duffel bag. Having people do everything for you was really weird.

A thick, plush white robe hung on a gold hook. She ran her fingertips over the soft fabric. The robe was nicer than any of the clothing she had brought with her. A good thing she was going shopping.

Izzy brushed her teeth in the gold sink. Everything was gold, from the faucets to the gold seals on the pretty soap wrappers. Even the fluffy white towels had gold embroidery on the bottom portion. Uncle Frank would have gotten a kick out of this big gold bathroom.

She felt a familiar tug at her heart.

Then again, he hadn't been a simple car mechanic. He would have been used to castles and bathrooms like this. Living in a motor home had been the opposite extreme. Had he been hiding her? Or maybe Uncle Frank had wanted to give her as normal a life as possible, not one with gold sinks. Izzy believed he'd kept the past a secret and raised her the way he did for a reason.

Aleksander and Evangaline Zvonimir might have been her birth parents, but Frank Miroslav had been Izzy's father. He had wiped her tears when she hurt herself, boosted her self-confidence when the kids at school teased her for being different, and taught her everything she knew and loved about cars. He'd saved her life by leaving his own family to raise her in another country. She was only beginning to comprehend what he'd given up for her. It was too late to say thank-you, but Izzy wanted to make it up to him somehow. Maybe she could find his relatives and tell them how wonderful he'd been to her.

Emotion clogged her throat. She shook it off. The way she'd learned to do these last five years.

A shower would make her feel better. She turned on the water. As she undressed, steam filled the bathroom. She stepped into the large shower.

Hot water pulsed down on her as if she were standing in a heated waterfall. She nearly sighed at the decadence of the oversize showerhead.

Okay, Izzy grinned, comfy beds and amazing showers were definitely perks to being a princess. She could even forgive the invasion of privacy while she slept. A shower like this could make her forgive and forget most everything.

Normally she finished showering in a couple of minutes due to the size of the RV's tiny water heater. This time, Izzy stayed in until her fingertips shriveled like raisins.

Best shower ever.

She turned off the water, dried off with a towel, slipped into the luxurious robe and combed her hair.

Out in the bedroom, she padded to her duffel bag. It wasn't where she'd left it.

Izzy looked around. Her backpack sat on the table, but her duffel bag was nowhere to be seen. That was odd. The purple would be hard to miss against the yellow and gold decor.

Maybe whoever placed her toiletry bag in the bathroom had put the duffel bag away. Izzy checked inside the gilded armoire. Empty hangers hung on the rack. She slid out the two drawers. No bag or clothing. She checked under the bed. Nothing there, either.

This wasn't good. She wanted to get dressed.

Izzy had the clothes she'd worn on the flight, but she didn't relish the thought of putting them on again. They were dirty, and she was clean.

Her cell phone was no use. Anyone she could call was half a world away and asleep. They couldn't tell her where to find her duffel bag.

She thought for a moment. Only one explanation made sense. Someone must have taken her bag. To wash the clothes, iron them, who knew why?

A castle this size had to have a large staff. She would flag someone down and ask how to contact Mare.

Izzy poked her head out of her room. The wide hallway was empty. Waiting for someone to appear, she shoved her hands into the deep pockets of the robe. No one came.

"Is anyone out there?" she half whispered.

No reply.

Come on. Izzy grew impatient. This was a castle for goodness' sake. Maids and butlers should be running around. She would have to find someone herself.

She tightened the belt of her robe

Stepping into the hallway, Izzy left the door to her room open. She wanted to remember which room was hers.

The farther she moved away from her room, the more antsy Izzy became. Walking around with wet hair, barefoot and wearing nothing but a robe was not exactly princesslike. A castle probably had rules. Ones she would know. Maybe she should go back.

She was about to turn around when a white-haired man exited a room. The older gentleman was tall, wore a nice suit and walked with a slight limp. On closer look, she noticed he had a prosthetic leg.

No matter what side you were on, we are all marked in some way by the conflict. Some scars are visible. Others are not.

Niko hadn't been kidding. Izzy couldn't believe an old man had to fight in the war. Maybe he'd been a soldier at the beginning. Unless he'd just been a casualty. Thinking about what these people had endured made her heart ache.

He headed in a different direction.

She ran up to him. "Excuse me."

The man stopped. His eyes widened when he saw her.

"Do you work here?" she asked.

He blinked. "I do."

"Finally."

He studied her with probing green eyes. "Who might you be?"

"I'm Izzy. I arrived this morning from the United States."

"Welcome, Izzy." His smile deepened the lines on his face. "I'm Dee."

"Nice to meet you, Dee." In spite of all the wrinkles, he was still attractive. He must have been really handsome when he was younger. She couldn't help but think of Niko. "I'm in a bind. My bag with my clothing has disappeared. I searched the room, but can't find it."

"Oh, dear, that is quite a predicament."

She nodded. "I don't imagine trickster ghosts haunt this place?"

"No, though we do have our share of skeletons in the closet."

"That's what I figured." She felt more comfortable with the staff than royalty. One more reason she wasn't cut out to be a princess. "I'm sure you have work to do, but would you please tell me how I might locate Mare? She was assigned to help me, and I'm wondering if she knows where my bag might be."

"Part of my job is making sure everything runs the way it is supposed to around here."

"Oh, you're the castle manager."

"Something like that." He sounded amused. "I don't know where Mare is, but I know where we can find your clothes."

"Great."

Dee extended his arm. "Allow me to escort you."

She took his arm. "Thanks."

He walked with a steady stride. His leg didn't slow him down. "What do you think of Vernonia so far, Izzy?"

"I didn't see much during the drive from the airport,

but this castle—" she looked up at a fresco painted on the ceiling "—it's straight out of a fairy tale."

"I hope the accommodations are to your liking."

"They are lovely. Thank you," she said. "I wanted to stay at a hotel, but Prince Niko wanted me to stay here. He said I would be more comfortable."

"I hope you are comfortable."

"I've only been here a few hours, but I've already had a nice nap and a wonderful shower."

"An excellent start," Dee said.

Izzy nodded. She wondered if Niko would agree. Earlier he couldn't wait to get away from her. No doubt he wanted her visit to be a short one. At least they agreed on something.

"I believe what you seek is inside here." Dee stopped in front of a pair of wide double doors and opened one of them. "These ballroom doors are heavier than they look."

She peered inside and gasped. This wasn't a ballroom. This was a clothing store.

Mannequins, decked out in elaborate outfits with matching accessories, fought for space on the parquet floor between racks of clothing and shoes. Stylishly dressed women bustled about in short skirts and high heels, carrying purses, lingerie and shoes. A mix of perfumes lingered in the air.

The room looked to be a pumped up, steroid-version of *What Not to Wear*. This was so not the kind of shopping Izzy had in mind. She struggled to breathe.

Some women might tingle with excitement at the thought of being let loose among all these clothes and shoes, but the sight filled Izzy with dread. Fashion didn't interest her in the slightest. She was into comfort, not style. Worse, these women had gone to all this trouble for her. Niko and Jovan, too.

Near a three-paneled mirror, she noticed a man who looked out of place among all the feminine finery.

Not just a man. Niko.

He'd showered, shaved and changed suits. He looked like he had at the garage—hot. She wasn't the only one who thought so. A few of the other women kept stealing glances.

Niko didn't seem to notice. He was engaged in a conversation with a gorgeous blonde supermodel. Feeling more out of place than before, Izzy crossed her arms over her stomach.

Dee cleared his throat.

Conversations stopped. Women froze in place. Heads bowed. Eyes lowered.

"What's happening?" she whispered and moved closer to Dee.

"Do not worry." He smiled down at her. "Everything is fine, Izzy."

Niko stared intently at her, making her question the fine part. "What are you—"

"Izzy's bag with her clothing disappeared from her room," Dee said, rather bravely Izzy thought considering the fierce expression on Niko's face. "I offered her my assistance."

"The women needed her sizes so they borrowed her bag, Father."

Realization hit Izzy between the eyes. She inhaled sharply. "Dee as in Dmitar."

"Yes, my dear," Dee said.

"Oh, no." Her cheeks burned. She pulled the robe tighter as if she could somehow disappear into its folds. "You're the king, the one who emailed me about the box, and I'm an idiot."

"Father—"

King Dmitar held up his hand the way Niko had done with Jovan.

Niko remained silent. Izzy had forgotten about that trick, but made a note to remember it for later.

"You're not an idiot, Izzy," King Dmitar said kindly. "You are delightful. I see the best of your parents in you."

Emotion tightened her throat. "Thank you, Your Majesty."

"As for my son…" King Dmitar turned his attention to Niko. "Izzy does not know our ways. She should not be left on her own and forced to figure out where her clothing disappeared to."

Niko bowed his head. "Yes, sir."

King Dmitar turned his attention back to her. "And a suggestion, Izzy."

"Yes, Dee." She cringed at her lapse. "I mean, Your Majesty."

"Queen Beatrice does not like the color pink. You may wish to keep that in mind while shopping."

"Thanks for the tip, sir." Izzy smiled, trying to make the best of the situation. "I'm not much into pink myself."

"Excellent." The king eyed the racks of dresses. "The queen does like the color purple. As do I."

"I'll remember that, sir. Thank you."

He focused on each person in the room until his gaze came to rest on the stunning blonde who had been talking with Niko. The king pressed his lips together for a moment. "I see you are in good hands. I will leave you to your shopping."

With that, the king departed.

As soon as the doors closed, the women went back to carrying accessories to the mannequins. The blonde, who had been speaking with Niko, supervised them.

Izzy blew out a puff of air. "I can't believe that was your father."

Niko stood next to her with an irritated look in his eyes. "Who did you think he was?"

"The castle manager."

The irritation vanished. Niko laughed. "I suppose that is one of his job responsibilities."

"You're not helping."

Niko raised a brow. "I didn't think you needed anyone's help."

Izzy made a face at him.

"You may have trouble finding an outfit to go with that expression," he teased.

"I'm sure I can find an outfit to match every expression as well as one to wear each hour of the day. I thought I was going shopping at a store or a mall." She motioned to all the clothing. "It's a bit…much, don't you think?"

"Not for a princess," Niko said. "There will be dinners, outings, appearances at the High Court."

"I won't be here that long."

"Long enough."

Izzy tried to take it all in. Tried and failed. "I think I'm beginning to understand what Cinderella might have gone through."

"Except in your case the shoe already fits."

"But we want to get it off as soon as possible."

"That is the plan."

He sounded excited. Izzy set her chin. "You know, dude, I want the annulment just as badly as you do."

Before he could reply, the supermodel hurried over, walking on high heels as if she were wearing tennis shoes. She probably taught Pilates, cooked like a gourmet chef and rescued orphans from third-world countries in her spare time. The woman smiled, showing off two rows of perfectly spaced white teeth. The boys at the garage would be comatose in her presence. "You must be Princess Isabel."

"Isabel," Niko said. "This is Her Royal Highness Princess Julianna Von Schneckel of Aliestle."

Julianna. Niko's girlfriend and future wife. She was also a princess. No wonder he couldn't wait to annul the marriage and marry a woman who exuded so much confidence and beauty even a *Sports Illustrated* swimsuit model would be intimidated.

Izzy was out of her element in every possible way. She forced her foot to stop tapping.

Julianna extended her arm. Everything about the princess was perfect right down to her manicured and polished fingernails. "It's wonderful to meet you, Isabel."

She shook her hand. Julianna's grip was firm and her hands rougher than Izzy expected them to be. "And you."

Niko watched them with interest. No doubt comparing his current wife to his future one.

A chilling thought inched its way down Izzy's spine. She hoped he wasn't planning to stay while she tried on clothing. This was going to be difficult enough without him here watching or, worse, providing commentary.

"Thanks for arranging all this, Niko." Izzy tried to sound as cheerful as she could. "But I'm sure you have better things to do with your time so don't feel you have to stick around. As your father said, I'm in good hands."

"You're in excellent hands," Niko said. "But I have a few minutes before my meeting."

Bummer, Izzy thought.

"You keep Isabel company, Niko," Julianna said. "I want to get everyone in their places."

People had places? Izzy took a deep breath and exhaled slowly.

"It won't be that bad," Niko said, as soon as Julianna was out of earshot.

"Want to trade places?" Izzy asked.

"My legs weren't meant for dresses."

"Mine, either. I mean, I haven't worn a dress since..." Uncle Frank's funeral, she realized. "It's been a long time."

"You'll look fine."

She shrugged. "New clothing isn't going to turn me into a princess."

"Whether you wear a pair of coveralls or a dress by Chanel, you are already a princess," he said. "But new clothing might help you feel more comfortable here."

She stared at the large crystal chandeliers hanging from the ballroom ceiling. "I don't think that's possible."

"You only just arrived."

"I'm not like her."

"Her?"

"Your girlfriend. Princess Julianna."

"I never thought you were like Julianna," Niko said. "You said you needed clothing so I arranged for you to go shopping."

"I should learn to keep my mouth shut."

"Perhaps." He sounded amused. "But this is a gift, Isabel. I appreciate you coming all this way to settle matters. Please indulge yourself shopping. Even if you never plan on wearing the clothing once you leave, you can always donate the clothes to a worthy cause."

That was some gift, Izzy realized. Royalty really were different than normal folk. "You're wasting a lot of money doing this."

"The expense is irrelevant."

"Maybe for you." Her gaze locked with his. "But for me, this would buy a lot of car."

A knowing smiled played at the corner of his mouth. "Noted."

Something held them connected. Izzy didn't know what, but she couldn't look away. Truth was, she didn't want to. She had no idea how long they stood like that, but it felt like forever.

"Are you two finished sparring so we can shop?" Julianna asked playfully.

As Niko looked away, Izzy felt an odd sense of rejection from the broken connection. It must be jet lag.

He focused his gaze on his future bride. "Yes."

"Then off with you." Julianna waved her hand toward the doors. "Your presence will make Isabel uncomfortable."

He nodded once. "Enjoy the shopping, ladies."

Izzy watched as Niko exited the room. "You need to teach me how to do that."

"I am going to teach you many things. How to handle a prince is only one of them."

"I don't think I could ever handle Niko like that."

"I believe you already have." Julianna smiled mischievously. "Ready to shop till you drop?"

"Not really." Izzy wondered what the princess had meant by her first sentence. Then again, maybe she was reading too much into things. "I'm not big on shopping and clothes and things like that."

Julianna's grin widened. "Then it's good you have me."

CHAPTER SIX

THAT evening, Niko stood in the dining room with Julianna, waiting for his parents and Isabel to arrive. Servants scurried about like mice only instead of carrying crumbs and cheese they carried pitchers of water and platters.

Anticipation filled the air. Even Niko felt himself caught up in it. Everyone wanted a glimpse of Princess Isabel. Unfortunately she was far from the princess they expected to see. She might be here by birthright, but she was clearly unhappy and didn't want to stay. The thought of her leaving brought a strange pang. Even if a wrench belonged in her hand, not a scepter.

He glanced at his watch. "Isabel is late."

"Isabel is not late." Julianna swirled her champagne flute. She looked lovely in a green cocktail dress and silver heels. Isabel could never pull off such an outfit. "A princess needs to make an entrance. Anxious to see her?"

"Anxious to know how much damage control I'll need to do tonight. Perhaps she has decided not to attend."

"Oh, believe me, she'll be here." Julianna smiled,

as if she knew a secret. "By the way, the wind should be lovely for a sail tomorrow."

"I'll believe it when I see it."

"The wind? Or your wife?"

Niko liked Julianna. There might not be any chemistry between them, but a friendship was growing. Friendship would be a good foundation for a marriage. Perhaps, in time, passion would enter into the relationship. Then again, passion never lasted, so perhaps friendship would be enough. "That role will soon be…"

Footsteps sounded outside the dining room. He glanced across the large room to the wide doorway.

A stunning woman wearing a lavender dress stood with a hesitant smile on her gorgeous face.

His heart rate kicked up a notch.

What a beauty. He gaze was immediately drawn to her expressive eyes. The rest of her was as appealing. Her brown hair was piled on the top of her head, secured by an invisible clip of some sort. Soft tendrils framed her oval face. But her eyes continued to mesmerize him.

"So what time should we leave on our sail tomorrow?"

"Time?" he asked yet couldn't take his eyes off the vision in the doorway.

Julianna laughed. "The makeover definitely worked."

Niko did a double take. "Isabel?"

"She cleans up quite well, don't you think?"

He'd seen her cleaned up, but not like this. All he could do was stare captivated. Isabel was…stunning.

"I can't believe you said she reminded you of a man," Julianna continued quietly. "She may not like the color pink and prefer motor oil to moisturizer, but she's quite feminine."

"I see that."

He liked what he saw. The above the knee hem of her dress showed off Isabel's long legs. He hoped she would be wearing more dresses. Legs like hers needed to be shown off, not hidden beneath coveralls, jeans and bathrobes.

"Though I will admit the rest of her princess transformation may take a lot more time," Julianna said. "Isabel says whatever is on her mind. That must stop or the media will take advantage of her."

"I have no doubt in your abilities now."

"I had fun. Izzy may not be a typical princess, but she's a charming young woman."

"Izzy?"

"That's what her friends call her," Julianna said.

Isabel had mentioned she liked being called Izzy, but he preferred her full name, liked the way it rolled off his tongue. Izzy sounded too…pedestrian. But there was nothing dull or unimaginative about her now. The lavender complemented her pale complexion. The style flattered her figure. She looked like a princess. "I doubt any of her friends would recognize her."

"You didn't."

"Shock."

"Nothing more?" Julianna asked.

Attraction, desire, lust. But he knew better than to tell his future wife those things. "Nothing else."

"Be a dear, Niko, and escort her into the dining room." Julianna sounded genuinely pleased with his reaction. "She's still trying to master the art of walking in high heels. I'd hate to see her make a mistake and berate herself over it."

He wasn't going to have to be asked twice. He smiled at Julianna, who looked almost smug with satisfaction. "I will be right back with your work of art."

As he approached Isabel, Niko was even more impressed by her transformation. The expert makeup application complemented her high cheekbones. Her glossed lips sparkled. Flecks of gold danced in her eyes. A complete change from the way she'd looked asleep on the airplane. Julianna had outdone herself. "You look lovely, Isabel."

"Thanks."

Niko caught a whiff of her vanilla and jasmine scent. That was the one thing that hadn't changed.

"I feel like a fraud," she whispered.

He didn't understand the agitation in her voice. She should be happy with the makeover. "Why a fraud?"

"I'm still me. Only the outer packaging has changed," she explained. "With all this makeup on, I feel like a clown. I'm sure in this dress and high heels, I must look like a corner hooker."

Niko winced. "No one would mistake you for anything but a princess."

Too bad she didn't act or speak like one.

"I appreciate that," she said. "Even if it's not one hundred percent true."

He extended his arm. "May I?"

"Royalty is big on escorting."

"It is part of our prince training."

"Is princess training available?" she asked.

"Yours has already started."

She pursed her glossed lips. "I was kidding."

He raised a brow. "I'm not."

She eyed his arm warily then placed her hand over his.

Niko felt a jolt of awareness. Perhaps it was just a shock from static electricity.

"Just so you know, I'm only doing this so I don't end up spread-eagled on the floor with my new lace thong showing."

Niko's gaze drifted to her round, delectable bottom and lingered for a second.

What the hell was he doing?

Abruptly he forced himself to look into her eyes. Anywhere else was unacceptable. He really would have preferred not knowing what type of lingerie she wore underneath her dress. The erotic image plastered across his brain would take time to erase. "I will make sure that doesn't happen."

For both their sakes.

Isabel took a step, teetering on her heels. "I don't know why anyone would choose to strap these torture devices to their feet."

"Why did you?"

"Because Princess Julianna told me I had to. A

closet full of shoes seems to be a prerequisite for being
a princess. But it seems as if none of them are allowed
to be comfortable."

He smiled at the exasperation in her voice and led
her into the dining room with nary a stumble or peek
at her panties.

She glanced around the room. "Wow."

Niko understood her look of awe. The room was quite
impressive with its marble fireplace, the gold damask-
covered walls, chandeliers and the long, rectangular
table set with fine china, sparkling crystal, freshly cut
flowers and a candelabra full of lit candles.

"No wonder you dress for dinner around here," she
added. "Black tie not optional."

Julianna joined them halfway across the room.
"Good evening, Izzy."

"Hey, Jules."

Niko noticed and liked the familiarity between the
two women. Shopping must quicken the bonds of feminine friendship. Perhaps Jovan had been correct about
Julianna being Isabel's role model.

"You look lovely," Julianna said.

Isabel smiled. "Thanks to you."

A waiter appeared with the tray of champagne flutes.
Niko took one and handed the glass to Isabel.

"No, thanks." She waved him off. "Tonight's going
to be hard enough without adding alcohol to the mix.
I doubt your parents would appreciate me dancing on
the table."

No, but Niko wouldn't mind too much. He did,

however, approve of her good judgment in refusing to drink.

Isabel studied one of the place settings. "I might have better luck dancing than trying to figure out what silverware and glass to use when."

"Go from the outside in," he said, remembering all the etiquette lessons forced on him even during the war.

"Watch what we do," Julianna added. "You'll do fine."

Two little lines appeared above Isabel's nose. She rubbed her hands together as if nervous. "Maybe I should get a plate to go."

A flurry of noise sounded in the doorway. Niko stiffened. "My parents have arrived."

"Don't worry." Julianna touched Isabel's shoulder. "Just remember what I told you earlier."

Isabel nodded, but she bit her lower lip. Uncertainty filled her eyes.

He almost felt sorry for her.

His father entered the dining room with a rare smile. He acknowledged Niko and Julianna before turning his full attention on Isabel. "What a lovely dress, Izzy."

Niko appreciated the way his father was trying to make her feel comfortable by using her nickname. King Dmitar could intimidate even the most seasoned statesman.

She curtsied. "Thank you, King Dmitar."

"I would like to introduce you to my wife, Her Royal Majesty Queen Beatrice." Dmitar presented his mother, who wore a floor-length ball gown, a diamond necklace and matching tiara. No one would mistake her for any-thing but the queen. "Beatrice, this is Isabel, but her friends call her Izzy."

Niko bit back a laugh. His mother would never call Isabel by anything other than her given name.

"We are delighted to have you back in Vernonia, Izzy," Beatrice said.

What? Niko stared in disbelief.

"It's a pleasure to meet you, Your Royal Majesty." Isabel curtsied again only this time she swayed on her heels like a tree in a windstorm. A soft gasp escaped her lips. Panic flashed in her eyes.

Niko grabbed her elbow so she wouldn't tip over.

She mouthed the word "thanks," and shrugged off his hand. She didn't look any steadier on her feet so he kept hold of her. "Isabel is still recovering from the long flight. I'm sure she would like to sit down."

"Of course." Dmitar motioned everyone to the table. "We have much to discuss."

"Yes, we do." Beatrice sat, and a waiter handed her a napkin. "But now that I've seen Izzy myself I agree with you, Dee. We won't have any trouble."

Isabel was seated across the table from him. She shot a questioning gaze to him and Julianna.

"Trouble, Mother?" Niko asked, curious what his parents had been discussing.

"Your father and I have been discussing Izzy's future," Beatrice said.

His mother's words set off an alarm in Niko's head. Waiters brought out the first course and set the bowls of soup on the table at the exact same time.

"That's really nice of you all." Izzy's smile looked forced. "But it's not necessary, Your Highnesses."

"But it is," King Dmitar countered. "All this must still be a shock to you, Izzy, but we are your family now. We don't have much time. We must make plans for what is to happen next."

"An annulment comes next, Father," Niko said. "We will go to the High Court first thing Monday morning."

Izzy nodded. "You don't need to waste your time planning anything, sir. My future is set."

"I appreciate your concern over my time." Dmitar's expression was earnest. "But I think it's time for a little history lesson."

Niko took a sip of his chilled eggplant soup. His father's lessons usually lasted until the wee hours of the morning.

Dmitar continued. "You, Izzy, are the last of the royal Sachestian bloodline that ruled the northern region for years before joining with the southern portion of the country to form Vernonia. For centuries, the Separatists have asked that your bloodline rule the north again. But the Loyalists have wanted the Kresimir bloodline to rule over all the land. The two groups hotly disagreed and fights would break out."

"A little like the Montagues and the Capulets?" Izzy asked.

"Only not so romantic," Niko said.

"But still quite Shakespearean," Beatrice said.

Julianna nodded. "History has shown a marriage between rival sides can ease strife and lead to peace."

"Excellent point, Julianna." Dmitar took a sip of water. "Over time, the arguments between the Separatists and the Loyalists intensified, Izzy. An official petition to separate the Northern portion of Vernonia circulated in the late 1980s. Civil war seemed imminent. Your father believed that a union between the two royal families would appease the Separatists and avoid war. His goal, our goal really, was to unite Vernonia once and for all with your marriage. But the civil unrest turned violent with terrorist acts. The people remained divided, and war broke out."

Silence enveloped the room.

Isabel toyed with her napkin. She hadn't tasted the soup yet. "It must have been a horrible time, Your Majesty."

"Horrible does not begin to describe it, my dear. Our country has been at peace for the last five years," Dmitar said. "But that was after the last of the Sachestian bloodline was killed during the conflict. The Separatists believed, they still believe, no Sachestian descendents remain. But now that you have returned like a Phoenix from the ashes—"

"So let's not tell them I'm back. No one has to know about me," Izzy interrupted. "I'm sorry for butting in, sir, but your country has been through enough. I don't want to cause any problems here. The truth is I really don't want to be a princess. Let's get the marriage annulled. If you can't transfer my father's estate we can figure something else out so I can disappear from Vernonia forever."

"That sounds like an excellent plan." Niko was proud

of her for speaking up and succinctly saying what needed to be said. That was one positive to Isabel's lack of princess skills. Julianna would have never said anything.

"I wish it were that simple," Dmitar said with regret. "We cannot pretend the Separatists do not exist or that their desire is not real."

"Julianna's father supported the Separatists during the war," Niko countered. "They support my marriage to her?"

"Yes, but they do not know about Isabel."

"Father—"

"Imagine you are a Separatist," Dmitar interrupted. "You have agreed per the peace accord to be a part of a new united Vernonia. You believe all the members of your royal family are dead, but suddenly discover one young princess lives. Oh, the joy. But then you learn the crown prince of your country has annulled his marriage to your princess so he can wed a different princess from another country. How do you think that will go over in this so-called united land?"

"You make it sound like I'm being slighted or something, sir," Isabel said. "I want the annulment. I don't want to be married to Niko."

Her firm tone left no doubt that she wanted out of the marriage as much as he did. She'd said that, but still the rejection surprisingly stung. Niko wasn't used to women not wanting to be with him. "Our marriage was only to avoid a civil war, Father. The war is over. There is no reason for us to remain married."

"Perception can be as strong a motivator as reality,"

Dmitar said. "Vernonians have quick tempers. Our loyalty is our strength, but our biggest weakness. We will cling to our causes until the bitter end. Whether right or wrong."

Niko stiffened in shock. "I hope you are not suggesting we remain married, sir."

Isabel's mouth formed another perfect O. Clearly she was aghast at the idea.

Julianna leaned forward with interest. Niko couldn't believe she was sitting here with their engagement on the line without saying a word.

Dmitar stared at him. "You have made it clear that is not an option."

Isabel's shoulders dropped. Her features relaxed. A smile tugged on the corners of her mouth.

Julianna leaned back against her chair, but her lips were pressed together.

Niko would have expected her to be happier. Perhaps she was nervous about his father's intentions. Niko would put her at ease. "Marrying Julianna is best for Vernonia. No offence, Isabel."

"None taken," she said.

"So you've said over and over again." Dmitar's gaze went from Julianna to Isabel to Niko. "That leaves me no choice but to find Isabel another husband. One she must marry the minute the annulment is granted."

"What?" Isabel shrieked.

"Why?" Julianna asked, sounding taken aback.

"Father." Niko had brought Isabel here. He didn't want the American to be forced into an arranged marriage. "You can't be serious."

"I'm very serious," Dmitar explained. "If Izzy is

married, the Separatists can be upset about the turn of events, but can do nothing to change the situation. If she remains single…"

Dread pulsed through Niko's veins. "They could demand we remarry or use her to rally against you."

"Yes," Dmitar said.

Niko thought he'd considered every angle. He believed the Separatists were content with their coalition in the government, that they were comfortable with his family as heads of state. He was so focused on modernizing that he never thought they would demand a marriage alliance in the face of improved economic development. But apparently he had been wrong. Because of that, Isabel would be the one to pay. She did not deserve to have her life plans derailed any more than they already had been.

"No." Isabel's face paled. "There has to be another way. Anything…"

He respected the way she stood up for herself. "Let us have time to think of an alternative, Father."

"The High Court convenes on Monday," Dmitar said. "You have one day to think of an alternative that will maintain peace. Otherwise Izzy must get married."

"Who do you plan to marry her off to?" Niko couldn't think of anyone in the kingdom that would be a match. The thought of some other man with her… whoa, he needed to reel in his thoughts.

"I've been working on that, dear." Beatrice stared at Izzy with interest. "Here's the list of eligible royals I've come up with so far…"

* * *

Talk about a living nightmare. Izzy's future was at stake. She had to think of something and fast.

Izzy lay in bed wide-awake. Her mind raced fast enough to capture the pole position at Darlington Raceway. Unable to sleep, she glanced at the clock. 2:04. No way she could sleep. Not with the conversations from dinner replaying through her mind like reruns of a TV show.

She imagined a show called *The Royal Kresimirs*. The preview would consist of shots of each of them. King Dmitar saying she needed to marry. Queen Beatrice rattling off a list of potential husbands. Prince Niko interjecting his opinion on each name his mother read. Princess Julianna smiling as she attempted to keep the peace. Izzy racking her brain to find a way out of being forced to marry.

But this was too far-fetched to be a television show. Something like this should never happen. Not in the twenty-first century. Not to an American citizen.

That gave Izzy an idea.

She could call the Embassy. Surely the State Department would help her out.

No, that would only solve her problem, not… Vernonia's.

Izzy wasn't attached to this strange country. Until yesterday she'd only heard of the place in the news, but Vernonia had meant something to her parents and to Uncle Frank. She wasn't selfish enough to ignore the war fought here or pretend another one couldn't happen again.

Her stomach growled.

She'd been so upset she couldn't eat dinner. She'd even turned down a slice of chocolate torte served for dessert. That had been dumb. Chocolate always made her feel better. Maybe a leftover slice was in the kitchen. That would raise her spirits.

She crawled out of bed, shrugged on the white bathrobe and stepped into the hallway. Still not sure which room was hers, she left the door open.

A few minutes and a couple wrong turns later, Izzy sat in the castle's deserted kitchen poking at a slice of chocolate torte with her fork. Her appetite was still missing in spite of her tummy's grumblings. She couldn't muster enough enthusiasm to take a bite of chocolate.

Pathetic.

"Here you are." Niko's voice cut through the silence and startled her. "I wondered where you had disappeared to."

"How did you know I was gone?"

"The door to your room was open." He walked toward her, past the wall of stainless steel refrigerators and around the massive commercial stoves.

"All the doors look alike." She noticed he wore the same dress shirt and pants as earlier, but he'd ditched the jacket and tie. He'd also unbuttoned the collar and rolled up the sleeves. The casual style looked good and made Niko seem approachable, more like a normal guy than a crown prince. "I left mine open so I wouldn't walk into the wrong room."

"Smart move. I called your name, but you didn't

answer." He sat in the chair next to her. "I thought you might have run away."

"Running away was the first thing I thought of doing." Izzy stared at the uneaten torte. "But I crossed it off the list."

"You have a list?"

"Well, yeah." She stabbed the fork into the torte and left it there. "I know this doesn't really affect you, but we're talking about my future. I'm not going to grab a splash of gas and hope I can make it to the end of the race. I need a full tank before I take an alternative to your father."

"What happens to you does affect me, Isabel." Niko's lips thinned. "Why do you think I'm still awake?"

She shrugged. "Just heading back to your own room for the rest of the night?"

"No." His jaw tightened. "I've been trying to come up with a solution myself. If I had thought this would happen, I would have never brought you back to Vernonia."

Izzy felt lower than pond scum. She'd accused him of having a midnight tryst while he'd been playing knight in shining armor trying to save her butt. "Sorry."

"No need to apologize. We need to find a way out of this."

We. Izzy didn't feel so alone. She didn't like needing help, but she liked having Niko with her now. She wasn't getting very far on her own.

He eyed her torte suspiciously. "Are you going to eat that?"

"No."

"May I?"

She pushed the plate toward him. "It's all yours."

"Thank you." He raised the fork. "What stopped you from running away?"

"Logistics," she admitted. "I can't get back home without a U.S. passport or cash."

"Ah, yes. You only have the temporary Vernonian passport Jovan arranged for you."

Izzy nodded. "But I don't have it. Jovan does."

"If you want it—"

"If I ran away, you wouldn't be able to get an annulment. That means you couldn't marry Jules without committing bigamy."

"Thank you for sticking around. I'm much obliged, as will Julianna be." He scooped up a forkful of torte. "I did think of one possibility. It's a bit extreme."

"I'm open to anything at the moment. Including extreme."

"How about faking your death?"

She stared at him in disbelief. "That's on my list."

The edges of his mouth curved. "Great minds think alike."

"It's a good idea," Izzy said. "I don't want to die, but if people thought I was dead, there would be no issues with the Separatists. No one would complain if you married Julianna. I would be free to live my life however I wanted."

"The logistics would be more complicated than running away."

She nodded. "There can't be a body."

"That limits the ways a person can die."

"I know."

"Fire," Niko suggested.

"Wouldn't bones and teeth be left?" she asked.

"Unless it was an inferno of some sort, but that might be dangerous."

"I wouldn't want anyone to get hurt."

"Of course not." He rubbed his chin. That sexy razor stubble had reappeared. "Drowning."

"Bodies disappear at sea never to be seen again."

Niko nodded. "Julianna is a world-class sailor. You could fall overboard."

"I like the drowning part, but do you really want to involve your future wife in something like this? I mean it's probably illegal."

"No, she should not be involved."

That meant it was just the two of them. Izzy felt like Niko was her partner in crime. "I could still fall into the sea somehow. Off a boat or a cliff."

"You will have to be prepared to say goodbye to Isabel Poussard forever."

Izzy thought about her life, of the people she'd come in contact with, known and loved. "You're right. I wouldn't be six foot under dead, but I would be dead to everyone who knew me."

"There would be no going back."

No going back. She would never be able to do anything racing related. But it was more than her dream she'd be losing. She thought of her friends back in Charlotte, of Rowdy and Boyd and the rest of the boys at the garage. Her chest tightened.

If she got married and had to stay in Vernonia or

another nearby country, her life would be different, but at least she could visit her friends. Faking her death would mean never talking to them again. "Honestly, I don't think I could lie to my friends about dying. Not after the hurt and grief we all went through when Uncle Frank died."

"I would rather not have to lie or break any laws, either."

She slumped in the chair. "We're right back where we started."

"We will think of something else."

Niko sounded confident, but a strange sensation settled in the pit of her stomach, one having nothing to do with not eating dinner. She had no way out of this mess. The reality of the situation seemed...undeniable. "I'm not sure there is anything else."

He set his fork on the plate. "Isabel—"

"Think about it." She fought the rising panic. "We've both been up half the night trying to figure this out. Faking my death is the best we came up with."

"We just need time."

"It's already Sunday." A lump formed in her throat. "We don't have much longer."

"That means…"

Tears stung her eyes. "I know what it means."

"You don't want to get married."

"No. But when I think what might happen if I don't…" This wasn't a debate about differences between two political parties and their views on the issues. People were willing to kill for what they wanted. Her parents had been murdered and her uncle Frank had given up his entire life because of the conflict between the Separatists and the Loyalists. Izzy had wanted to do something for her family. Maybe this was it. She blinked to keep the tears at bay. "I don't think I have any choice."

CHAPTER SEVEN

NIKO covered Izzy's hand with his. The warm touch was a harsh reminder to her that another man, a stranger, would soon call himself her husband and be the one touching her. Hot tears spilled down her cheeks.

She turned away so Niko wouldn't see her cry.

He cupped her chin and turned her face toward him. Gently he wiped the tears from her cheeks with his fingers. "I will not allow you to be forced into a marriage you do not want."

"Thanks, but this is bigger than you and me. People have suffered too much already. My parents and Uncle Frank sacrificed their lives. I won't be the catalyst for more violence and pain."

"I did not believe you had what it takes to be a princess, but you do," Niko said. "My apologies, Isabel."

The sincerity in his voice brought another round of tears. She would miss hearing him say her name.

"Thanks." Izzy sniffled. "I'm usually not so girly about things."

"I'm glad you're a girl," he said. "Or I couldn't do this."

Niko gathered her into his arms.

Izzy stiffened. She didn't need him, but she had no desire to back out of his embrace. The loneliness in her heart made her relax and lean toward him so he could pull her closer.

Pressing her cheek against his hard chest, she felt the beat of his heart, steady and strong. Invisible warmth enveloped her. For the first time in years, she felt safe. All the emotion she'd been holding in poured out.

Niko didn't try to soothe her with platitudes. He simply held her, rubbing her back. It was more than she had expected from him. It was all she needed at the moment.

She didn't know how long Niko kept his arms around her, but slowly her breathing settled. Her tears stopped. Izzy found the strength she needed in his arms. "I know what I have to do. It's just…I can't imagine having to spend the rest of my life married to someone who was forced to be my husband. It seems so wrong to me."

He brushed his hand through her hair. "You are not used to the concept. But arranged marriages aren't all bad. There's friendship, companionship, having a common purpose."

His closeness comforted her. Izzy could almost believe things would be better. "I only wish…"

"Tell me."

Izzy hesitated, but Niko had been so caring, so kind she had to tell him. "I wish instead of marrying some random royal with a fancy title I could marry for love. But at this point I'd settle for being able to choose who I married."

Niko continued to comb his fingers through her hair. "Whom would you choose?"

The thought of him popped into her mind then quickly vanished. The emotion of the situation, his compassion, was making her feel closer to him.

"Tell me who," he pressed.

None of her dates liked cars or racing the way she did. The guy she spent the most time with was Boyd. Building go-carts together, working at dirt tracks on pit crews, watching races. They shared the same interests and the same dreams. They just weren't...romantic. "Boyd," she decided.

"Your coworker?" Niko drew back to stare into her eyes. "You said he wasn't your boyfriend."

"He's not, but he's one of my closest friends. He wouldn't expect us to have, um, a real marriage."

"You mean sex."

Her cheeks burned. She shouldn't have said anything. "Yes."

"You would be satisfied with a marriage in name only?"

"It isn't about being, um, satisfied," she said. "We wouldn't have to be married for decades. Only a few years. Long enough for things to stabilize in Vernonia and for you and Jules to have a couple of heirs. Then we could divorce."

Izzy heard something that sounded like a gasp. She peered over Niko's shoulder. "What was that noise?"

"I didn't hear anything," he said.

She looked back again, but didn't see anyone. Must

have been the refrigerator or something. "Do you think your father would allow me to marry Boyd?"

"We can ask him," Niko said. "Would Boyd go along with the idea?"

"Probably. A lot of people have assumed we're a couple. We know each other pretty well." She pictured her coworker and friend. Boyd was an all-American, beef-fed Southerner. Down home and down to earth. Strong and rugged, but kindhearted like Niko. Not model handsome, but a lot of women found Boyd easy enough on the eyes. "I think he'd say yes because of our friendship, but if I told him I wanted to start a race team together that would most likely seal the deal. He's more car crazy than I am."

Niko's mouth twisted. "Would you be happy married to Boyd?"

"Marriage has never been on my radar screen, but…" She thought about her parents and Uncle Frank. Marrying a man she loved like a brother was nothing compared to the sacrifices they had made. She would do this for them. "If Vernonia remains at peace, then yes. I would be happy married to Boyd."

Niko let go of her. "We shall take this alternative to my father in the morning."

"That's only a few hours away." Izzy felt cold without his arms around her. She fought the urge to wrap her arms around herself to warm up. "Fingers crossed he says yes."

"Vernonia is indebted to you, Isabel." Niko's gaze met hers, and her heart bumped. "And so am I."

She didn't care about Vernonia, but him… His face

was so close to hers. Something—passion, perhaps?—flashed in his eyes, and heated her blood. He tilted his head.

Niko was going to kiss her.

Izzy's pulse rate skyrocketed. Her mouth went dry.

Heaven help her, she wanted him to kiss her.

She parted her lips in anticipation.

Niko held her hand, raised it to her mouth and kissed it. The brush of his lips was soft, a caress. She nearly sighed.

He lowered her hand. "If there is anything you ever need…"

She needed him to kiss her. Not her hand, but her lips.

Here. Now.

Niko released her hand.

Disappointment shot through her. No matter how much she wanted this moment to mean something more than one person comforting another, it didn't.

It couldn't.

Izzy might want her lips to be crushed by his, but it would never happen. Niko was too honorable. He would never hold her passionately. He would never share his dreams with her. He would never whisper words of endearment into her ears.

Those were things he would do with…Jules.

Niko was going to marry the pretty princess from Aliestle. And if the king said yes, Izzy would marry Boyd. She would return to the United States with a husband and a partner. They would join the world of racing, not as members of a pit crew, but as the owners of a new racing team.

Izzy would have everything she wanted. And so would Niko.

A happy ending for everyone involved, including Vernonia.

There was just one problem. Why didn't she feel happier?

The next morning, Niko sat next to Isabel on a settee in the king's private drawing room. His father stood across from them with a stern look on his face as he considered their request. The tension in the room was palpable. The silence increased Niko's discomfort level. He would rather be elsewhere, but he didn't want Isabel to have to go through this alone. She deserved his support for what she was willing to do for him and Vernonia.

Isabel rested her clasped hands on her lap. She wore a lime-green skirt and matching jacket. The heels on her shoes weren't as high as last night, making it easier for her to walk. She looked very much like a princess.

The only clue anything was wrong were the dark circles beneath her eyes. But he'd still place his money on her. The defiant tilt of her chin told Niko she was ready for a fight.

His father had no idea who he was dealing with. As Niko had learned last night in the kitchen, neither did he. Isabel was a strong and amazing woman. Beautiful and so much more than he imagined she could be.

Thoughts of her had kept Niko awake most of the night. Each time he'd closed his eyes he remembered the scent of her hair, the taste of her skin, the warmth in her heart. He never imagined feeling this way about her. Attraction explained part of it, but there was also his respect and admiration for her willingness to do what was best for Vernonia. All three were combining to a potent mix of affection.

Niko should be having these feelings about Julianna, not Isabel. He was anxious to get this matter resolved so he could refocus and not allow unwanted and unwarranted feelings for the American to cloud his thoughts.

Dmitar paced back and forth. "There is much to consider here."

Isabel's lower lip trembled. Only slightly, but the vulnerability Niko saw in that moment pressed down on him like a two tonne weight. She'd been uncomfortable crying in front of him. She liked handling things on her own. But he couldn't sit and do nothing now.

He reached out, covered her hand with his and squeezed.

The edges of her mouth lifted in a close mouthed smile.

His heart beat faster. He smiled back.

The lines on Dmitar's forehead deepened. Niko's shoulder muscles tensed until he realized the reason behind the change in his father's facial expression. He was staring at Niko's hand on top of Isabel's.

Niko pulled his hand away. Not that he should feel guilty. It wasn't as if he'd just kissed Isabel. He may have thought about kissing her last night, but today he'd simply offered a gesture of comfort. The fact he enjoyed touching her and holding her last night was of no consequence.

Gratitude, he rationalized. That was what Niko felt for Isabel. Appreciation for the sacrifice she was willing to make. Nothing…more.

"You are satisfied with this alternative, Izzy," Dmitar said finally.

"Satisfied is a relative term, Father," Niko answered. "This marriage is being forced upon Isabel."

Dmitar glared at him. "Your name is not Izzy."

Niko pressed his lips together.

"I admit I'd rather not have to marry at all, sir," Isabel answered honestly with her head held high. "But I will be more satisfied with this option than what was proposed at dinner."

Dmitar rubbed his chin. He usually made up his mind quickly. The decision wasn't that complicated yet was taking longer than it should.

That worried Niko. Isabel hadn't eaten breakfast. She looked as if she hadn't slept. She needed the situation to be resolved.

"Father," Niko said. "This alternative is the best option for Isabel. The choice of a husband should be hers."

"What's best for Isabel may not be what's best for Vernonia," Dmitar countered.

"Like Niko said, I believe this is the best option for Vernonia," Isabel said without any hesitation. "I've known Boyd for years. We like the same things. People we know won't think it's weird if we eloped. They will believe we're married, not trying to pull the wool over someone's eyes."

"That means the Separatists would believe it, too," Dmitar said.

She nodded. "If they thought it was a ruse, we'd be right back where we started."

"Plausibility is important," his father agreed.

Finally, Niko thought. Progress. "So you agree, sir."

"Are you in love with this Boyd fellow?" Dmitar asked.

"This is ridiculous." Niko stood, irritated and frustrated. "Love has nothing to do with it, Father. Please do not make this any harder on Isabel than it already has been."

Dmitar frowned. "I will not tolerate any more outbursts from you."

"I will stop when you cease toying with Isabel."

"Thanks, Niko." She smiled up at him, and his pulse quickened. "I appreciate you standing up for me, but I don't mind answering your father's question."

She sounded sincere. Niko sat.

"I love Boyd, sir."

Isabel's words hit Niko like a left jab. He felt an instant, squeezing pain. Something he'd never felt before. Surprise. That was what it must be. She had not mentioned this last night.

"Boyd is one of my closest friends," she continued. "He's like a brother. There are no, um, romantic feelings between us. The marriage would be in name only with the intention of divorcing when it was safe."

The tightness in Niko's chest eased with her clarification, but a small part of him envied Boyd for having such a relationship with Isabel. Niko had never had a close friendship with a man let alone a woman. At least not since the death of Stefan who had been big brother and best friend rolled into one. Now Niko's duty to Vernonia always took precedence over everything and everyone else. Including long-term romantic relationships. Short-term ones, too.

"That is quite a sacrifice you are willing to make," his father said.

Isabel shrugged. "Not really if you look at what my parents and Uncle Frank did. They gave their lives. I still get to be involved in car racing so I wouldn't call what I'm doing a sacrifice, sir."

Dmitar beamed. "You've thought this through, Izzy. Well done."

Niko's admiration for her grew. "I agree."

She looked up at him.

Isabel's hazel eyes appeared greener. It must be her jacket bringing out the color. He could still see the same gold flecks he noticed last night. Very pretty.

Dmitar cleared his throat.

Niko looked at his father.

"I accept this alternative," Dmitar proclaimed. "Isabel may marry Boyd."

"Yes!" Isabel pumped her fist. "Thanks, Dee. I mean, Your Highness. Majesty. Sir."

Not quite the perfect princess, but she was the perfect Isabel. Niko smiled.

"We will delay your appointment with the High Court until Tuesday to give Boyd time to arrive," Dmitar said. "Have Jovan prepare the necessary paperwork for the annulment, transfer of Aleksander's estate and a marriage license."

"He's already working on them, Father," Niko said.

Dmitar raised a brow. "Confident I would say yes?"

"Hopeful," Niko admitted. That and he hadn't been able to sleep knowing how negatively all this was affecting Isabel.

"Then we're all set," Dmitar said.

"Not quite, sir." Izzy stood, and Niko rose to his feet. "I still have to see if Boyd will marry me."

Dmitar chuckled. "He's a fool if he doesn't want to be your husband."

"Not only a fool." Niko liked the blush on Isabel's cheeks. "A complete idiot."

"Well, I hope Boyd is neither of those things, but I'd better find out." She curtsied. "If you'll excuse me, sir."

Dmitar dismissed her. As soon as she exited, he grinned wryly. "I never thought there would come a day when I'd hear you admit to being not only a fool, but also an idiot."

"I didn't."

"Not directly," his father said. "But you are married to Izzy and don't want to be her husband."

"It's not the same situation," Niko protested. "Julianna brings a large dowry, one bigger than Isabel's inheritance, Aliestlian trade support and investors, a royal pedigree that will provide alliances with other European kingdoms and the knowledge necessary to be queen. Even the Separatists support her. Isabel is an American, a mechanic. She doesn't know the first thing about being a princess or Vernonia. She has no qualifications to be queen."

"Isabel is honest, loyal, smart and has royal blood running through her veins," Dmitar said. "You say she has no qualifications yet this American mechanic is willing to marry someone she doesn't love for a country she hadn't stepped foot in until twenty-four hours ago."

Each word stabbed at Niko like one of the soldier's bayonets on display at the National Museum. He stared at the ground.

"You may want to redefine what makes a queen, my son," his father counseled. "Not only for your own sake, but your wife's. Otherwise you really will look foolish."

"Come on." Izzy checked the reception bars on her cell phone. Nothing. She shook the phone. "What's a girl gotta do to get coverage around here?"

The castle wasn't that far from town. There had to be a cell tower somewhere. She'd tried using one of the phones inside the castle, but couldn't figure out how to get a dial tone. If only Niko were here…

Strike that. She didn't need his help or those blue-green eyes of his to make her heart go pitter-pat.

Izzy walked past the garden and down three steps.

Her eyes burned from exhaustion. The stone path hurt the bottom of her feet. Her fault. She'd ditched her shoes ten minutes ago. But she couldn't give up.

The king had given his approval. Now she needed Boyd's.

Time was ticking. Izzy needed to make this call. She checked the display. No bars. "I bet this place still uses dial-up internet connections."

"A few villages in the mountains rely on dial-up, but the castle has a wireless network," Niko said from behind her.

"What are you doing out here?" She was surprised to see him. It was as if her thoughts had conjured him up like some magic wish. "I thought you had stuff to do."

"I do, but I thought I'd see if you had reached Boyd."

"Not yet." She held up her lousy excuse for a cell phone. "No service."

His smile turned to a laugh. "So that's why you were threatening to feed your phone to the fish."

"I—" Okay, she had said that, but he hadn't been there. "How did you know that?"

"A gardener warned the staff about a barefoot American screaming at her cell phone." Amusement danced in Niko's eyes. "I had a feeling it might be you."

Heat stole into her cheeks. "Jules said when you're

royalty someone is always watching even if you can't see them."

"Yes."

"But I wasn't screaming," Izzy defended herself. "At least not that loudly."

Grinning, he punched in a couple of numbers and handed his cell phone to her. "It's a satellite phone. I put in the country code for America. You're all set."

"Thanks." She appreciated Niko's help. It wasn't only the phone. He'd stuck up for her with his father this morning. If only Niko could make the call...

Nerves battered at her stomach. She swallowed, her mouth suddenly full of cotton. This was her future, so much depended on the outcome of this one call. She stared at the phone in her hand.

He rocked back on his heels. "I can give you some privacy."

"It's up to you."

"I'll stay."

Izzy figured he would. Niko took his responsibilities seriously. That included her, even if she was his wife in name only. She punched in Boyd's number and held the phone to her ear.

Niko watched her intently.

Izzy focused on the phone ringing. Once, twice, three times.

"Hey." Boyd sounded sleepy, as if she'd woken him up, but his voice came across strong and clear.

"It's Izzy."

"Good to hear from you, Iz. Is that prince dude treating you nice?" Boyd asked.

Her gaze met Niko's, and her pulse skittered. "I'm, uh, calling you on his phone."

"I don't like the way he looks at you."

Izzy glanced over at Niko, taking in his broad shoulders and athletic physique that his suit couldn't hide. His appreciative gaze traveled the length of her. She liked how he looked at her very much. "Don't worry about that, but…"

"What is it?" Boyd's voice sharpened.

She gripped the phone tighter. "I'm in a bit of a jam and need your help."

"You want my help?"

"You don't have to sound so surprised."

"Okay, but I am," Boyd said. "Doesn't matter, though. Whatever you need, my answer is yes."

"You might want to wait to hear what I have to ask you." As she smiled, her gaze met Niko's again. He gave her a conspiratorial wink. This time her heart stuttered. "It, um, might change your answer."

She needed to focus. Something she found hard to do with Niko around. But this was too important to let a pretty face distract her.

As Izzy studied a leaf on the ground, she explained to Boyd what had happened between the Separatists and the Loyalists in the past, what could happen in the future and how she had become drawn into the mess.

"So what do you need from me?" Boyd asked.

"I know it's a lot to ask, but I need a husband. Not forever. Just a few years." She took a deep breath. "Will you marry me, Boyd?"

* * *

Niko watched Isabel as she waited for Boyd's answer. Her toes wiggled. She kept readjusting the phone at her ear.

The man was a fool for making Isabel wait so long.

All of a sudden, a smile brightened her face. "Thanks, Boyd. You don't know what this means to me."

She laughed, a delightful sound that floated on the air. "Okay, you're on."

On what? Niko wondered. He would have liked to hear both sides of the conversation.

Izzy flashed him the thumbs-up sign. She was happy. Good. But he should be feeling relief, not the regret and disappointment playing ping-pong inside him.

"I'll have Jovan call you with all the details." She bounced from foot to foot. "Yeah, I know. I'll see you soon. Bye."

Izzy disconnected the call. She ran to Niko and threw her arms around him. "I don't have to marry a total stranger. Boyd said yes!"

Her soft curves molded against Niko. Heat pounded through his veins.

She hugged him tightly. "Thanks."

Niko wasn't sure what he'd done to earn this reaction. He didn't really care. He wrapped his arms around her. She fit perfectly against him.

"We did it," she said.

"Yes." The scent of her hair filled his nostrils. "We did."

He stared down at her face. She looked up at him.

Isabel's mouth was so close. Her lips were parted. An invitation?

He wanted to kiss her, more than he'd ever wanted to kiss a woman before. He wanted to know what her kiss tasted like. Sweet or tangy?

So tempting.

Longing filled her eyes. With each breath she took, each beat of her heart, it became clear. She wanted him to kiss her.

Yet he hesitated.

Julianna was ready to marry Niko.

Isabel was his wife, but another man had just accepted her proposal to marry her. Anything they did would be wrong. Illicit. Hurtful to the two people they'd agreed to marry.

Niko lowered his arms and stepped out of her embrace.

Disappointment pinched her face. Her smile faltered, but only for a moment. She handed him his phone. "I'm sorry for getting carried away with my celebrating."

"You do not need to apologize."

Izzy glanced around. "If someone saw…"

"You are my wife. We hugged. That is not a crime."

"Yeah, a hug." She sounded disappointed. "No big deal."

"Right." Though it had felt like a bigger deal to him. He missed her body touching his. Her warmth. The feel of her moist breath.

"Jules wants to work with me today." Isabel wouldn't meet his eyes. "Princess lessons."

He couldn't deny the chemistry between them, but that was a complication he couldn't afford. Whatever he was feeling was strictly physical. He hardly knew Isabel. "I have things to take care of myself."

"I'd better get going. I need to remember where I took off my shoes."

"If you can't find them…" He was about to offer to help her, but he couldn't. He needed to limit his time with her. "Ask one of the staff to assist you."

Izzy nodded. "See you later?"

She was a fair princess. And he didn't want her anywhere near him.

The words of—it might have been Shakespeare— swirled through Niko's head.

"Perhaps." Unless he could convince Julianna to join him for dinner after they went sailing. He needed her to take his mind off Isabel. "Otherwise, I'll see you tomorrow at breakfast."

Two hours later, Izzy walked through the library with a book on her head. Okay, "through" was a slight exaggeration. She only made it three steps before the book fell off and landed on the wood floor with a thump.

"I don't see why I need to do this." Izzy blamed her lack of concentration on not sleeping last night, but the real reason was Niko. She couldn't stop thinking about hugging him and wanting to kiss him. "It's not like anyone will ever be watching how I walk."

"Princesses need to have perfect postures," Jules said.

"But I'm not going to be a princess." Izzy stared at

the etiquette book she'd been balancing on her head. None of this stuff Jules was trying to teach her mattered. Not now anyway. "I'm going to marry my friend Boyd and go back to Charlotte. As long as I put my napkin in my lap at mealtime, I'll be good."

"Being good isn't enough. You must be the best. People have certain expectations," Julianna said, proving once again why Niko wanted to marry her. "You are a princess no matter where you live."

"Yeah, but if someone ever calls me by my title I might have to deck them."

Jules cringed. "Izzy…"

"I know." Izzy sighed. "Princesses don't punch."

"You are allowed to fight back if attacked."

What defined an attack? Since arriving in Vernonia, she felt as if she'd gone nine rounds. She was exhausted, confused and frustrated. Not to mention attracted to her soon-to-be-ex-husband and the soon-to-be-husband of her new friend. "I just want to go home."

"I'm so sorry, Izzy." Compassion filled Jules's eyes. "I know exactly how you feel."

The beautiful princess who would marry the handsome prince and live happily ever after as they ruled Vernonia had no idea how Izzy felt. No one could. Still she didn't want to be rude. That went against princess protocol. "Thanks."

Jules started to say something, but pressed her lips together. Niko and King Dmitar used the same gesture. Maybe it was a royal thing, stiff upper lip and all that.

"I'm good. Really," Izzy added. "At least I get to pick who I marry, right?"

"Yes. You are quite fortunate in that regard." Jules removed a heavier book from one of the shelves. "Try again. Remember…shoulders back, chin up and smile as you walk."

Izzy placed the book on her head. "I'm going to have the best posture of any mechanic east of the Mississippi."

"That's the spirit." Jules checked her watch. "I'm going sailing with Niko. Would you like to come along?"

Izzy remembered the "faking her death by drowning" suggestion, and a smile tugged at her lips. She would like to go, but she didn't want to be a third wheel. Jules was the closest thing to a girlfriend Izzy had here, yet she had wanted to kiss Niko. That went against princess protocol as well as the friendship code. She needed to distance herself from the prince. "Thanks, but I need to practice. Then I want to take a nap."

"You could sleep on the boat," Jules offered. "We'll be going out to dinner afterward. It should be fun."

"Sounds like it, but no thanks."

"You're sure?"

Was there a hint of disappointment in Jules's tone? No, Izzy had to be mistaken. The lovely princess was just clarifying her position.

You are allowed to fight back if attacked.

She remembered Jules's firm handshake. Izzy had a feeling the princess could hold her own in a fight especially when it came to another woman hitting on Niko. Not that Izzy would, but she didn't want to put Jules or herself in an awkward position by intruding on their evening. "I'm absolutely positive."

And maybe if Izzy repeated the words enough times, she might actually believe them.

CHAPTER EIGHT

THE next day, Izzy ate breakfast alone in the morning area. That was what she called the smaller dining room because the only time she ever saw it being used was in the morning. At least for the two she'd been here.

Izzy took a bite of the cheese blintzes covered with a raspberry sauce and swallowed. Delicious.

Add yummy food to the list of princess perks.

Jules entered and sat opposite Izzy. The princess looked stylish in a polka-dot, short-sleeve dress with her hair worn loose.

"Good morning, Izzy." A server filled Jules's cup with coffee. "You look more rested today."

"I am." Izzy had woken feeling a little more like herself. She'd realized her attraction to Niko was nothing more than a crush. Yes, he was gorgeous and had come to her rescue, so to speak. That had been fine with her world imploding yesterday, but she saw things more clearly this morning. "A little sleep can go a long way."

Or maybe it was common sense kicking in. She didn't want a man to see her as anything but an equal. Niko came from a totally different world and viewpoint.

She would never want to even try to be his equal. So why spend any more time thinking about almost-kisses or dreamy blue-green eyes?

Izzy sipped her freshly squeezed orange juice. "I hope you had a nice sail and dinner."

She squelched the pinprick of jealousy. She'd tried hard last night not to think of the two together out on the water. And she'd mostly succeeded.

She had more important things to think about. Boyd arrived today. Tomorrow her marriage to Niko would be annulled. She would receive her inheritance and marry her coworker and friend. She would return to Charlotte with more than she ever imagined. Perhaps not the same happily-ever-after Jules and Niko would share, but a good one just the same.

"I did. It was very enjoyable. Thank you." Another server placed a plate in front of Jules. "I love sailing. There's nothing I'd rather do."

"That's how I feel about car racing."

"We have more in common than you realize." The sincerity in Jules's voice wrapped around Izzy like a hug. "I hope you enjoyed your evening."

"I had dinner with the king and queen."

"And?"

Izzy recalled the conversation. Well, inquisition. "It was…interesting."

"How so?"

Her head and throat hurt thinking about all the talking she'd done. "They asked me so many questions I felt like a game show contestant."

Jules sipped her coffee. "What did they want to know?"

"Everything and anything."

"Intriguing."

"They may have been wanting to make me feel more comfortable," Izzy admitted. "I had a couple mishaps at dinner."

"Oh, dear."

She smiled. "That's exactly what the queen said. After my third mistake, Queen Bea was laughing along with King Dee and wondering if she was using the correct fork or not."

"Laughter makes everything better."

Niko stormed into the room with a stack of newspapers in his hands. His lips were pressed together, his eyes dark. "We have a problem."

Izzy had no idea what sort of problems could put so much worry on a prince's face, but it couldn't be good.

Jules set her fork on the plate. "What has happened?"

Niko opened one of the papers and showed them the front page headline written in English.

Princess Isabel Zvonimir Kresimir Lives!

Jules gasped. She covered her mouth with her hands.

Izzy stared at her name with a strange sense of detachment. It almost seemed surreal to see herself called a princess and her first name paired with two different last names. "What does the article say?"

"It's a complete biography of you, including your

return to Vernonia." He handed the paper to Izzy. "Whoever leaked this information to the press will pay."

"It'll be okay." Izzy wanted to put a positive spin on things. They had a plan. They didn't need to get distracted. "We knew my identity would come out at some point."

"We wanted to control when that happened." Niko tossed the rest of the papers on the table. "Read the article."

Izzy did. Each time she read the words wife or bride, she squirmed. The details in the story made the knot in the pit of her stomach grow. "Whoever leaked the information must have overheard my conversation with your parents last night."

Niko frowned. "We have never had any problems with the staff before."

"Some of the article is word for word what I said. It's also kind of strange." Izzy scanned the article once more. "There's very little about my life before I arrived in Vernonia. Your parents and I discussed my job, but nothing is mentioned. This article makes it sound like I was living the life of an exiled royal hiding out in North Carolina, not a mechanic working at a garage to make ends meet."

"That is good," Jules said. "People will only see you as a princess."

Izzy straightened. "There's nothing wrong with being a mechanic."

"No," Jules admitted. "But as King Dmitar said the other night, there's a perception."

Niko's frown seemed permanently etched on his face. "I would have rather they called you a grease monkey than my wife or princess bride."

Izzy winced. Okay, that hurt. "Why don't we head to the High Court now, then you won't ever have to hear that about me again."

Jules shot her a compassionate look. "I don't think Niko intended his words in that way."

His hard gaze met Izzy's and softened. His cheeks reddened. "No, I...I did not. I apologize. But the wording, especially the usage of husband and wife, suggests a closer, more intimate relationship than what we have."

"The article is slanted that way," Izzy agreed. "But once the annulment—"

"Jovan is at the royal offices in town," Niko interrupted. "People are assembling. The Separatist colors are flying in support of you. The people want you to be the next queen."

Her mouth gaped. "The people just found out about me."

His jaw thrust forward. "Word travels fast."

"You need to talk to them." Her eyes implored him. "Tell them Jules is going to be your wife. Explain how I'm engaged to Boyd."

Jules's gaze met Niko's. Some unspoken communication passed between them. "I cannot," he said.

The sudden silence increased the tension in the room tenfold. Izzy felt clueless. She struggled to put the pieces together.

The Separatists have wanted your bloodline to rule their portion of Vernonia.

Your father believed that a union between the two royal families would appease the Separatists and avoid war. His goal, our goal really, was to unite Vernonia with your marriage.

History has shown a marriage between rival sides can ease the strife and lead to peace.

I hope you aren't suggesting we remain married, sir.

Something clicked in Izzy's brain. The shocking realization made it hard for her to breathe. The weight of a people, a country, pressed down on her chest, on her heart.

She wanted to believe she was wrong. She had to be wrong. "There isn't going to be an annulment, is there?"

A muscle flicked at Niko's jaw. "The response by the Separatists this morning is similar to how the conflict began twenty-odd years ago."

Conflict. She heard the anguish in his voice. What he really meant was war. A bloody civil war that had killed her parents and caused a nation to suffer.

"The High Court and my father will not allow an annulment now," he added.

Vernonians have quick tempers. Our loyalty is our strength, but our biggest weakness. We will cling to our causes until the bitter end. Whether right or wrong.

Izzy trembled. She couldn't give in to the emotions raging through her. "You mean, for now."

Regret shone in his eyes. "I mean, ever."

Niko's words snuffed out her spark of hope.

No annulment. Niko would remain her husband. She would remain...here. Her life, her dreams...

She stared at the table, struggling not to lose it completely. And then she remembered. She wasn't the only one affected by this.

Guilt at her selfishness coated her mouth. Her gaze bounced between Niko and Jules. "What about the two of you?"

"A dowry can't stop a war. Only you can, Isabel," Niko said as if he were already resigned to his fate. "None of us want this, but for the sake of Vernonia, will you consider remaining my wife?"

That was romantic. Not.

"This is crazy. Our marriage didn't stop the war twenty-three years ago." The words poured from her lips like steam from an overheated engine. "We don't know that it will work this time or if it will even come to that. We shouldn't be forced to give up our dreams for a what-if."

Niko's eyes sharpened with disdain. Tight lines bracketed his mouth. "I will not risk my country and my people so you can return to America to play with race cars."

The abrupt change in him unnerved her, but she met his accusing eyes without flinching. "I was talking about you and Jules."

"I'm okay with this, Izzy." Jules sounded encouraging, but that was her nature. The princess wouldn't show how she really felt.

"Well, I'm not." Fighting her emotions, she stood.

"The two of you are perfect together. You're in love. You should be able to get married."

"Isabel," Niko said. "You should know—"

"I know enough." The desperation in her voice matched the way Izzy felt inside. She might be attracted to Niko, but that wasn't enough reason to marry a man who didn't love her, a man who wanted to marry someone else. "This country is completely whacked. I want nothing to do with it. Nothing at all."

She pushed back her chair, not caring that it clattered to the floor, and ran out of the room.

Izzy disappeared from sight before Niko could stop her.

Regrets assailed him. He had hoped she would eagerly do what was required of her, not get emotional and run away. He needed to make her understand what was at stake. "That did not go well."

"She is young. An American." Julianna stared into her coffee cup. "All this is foreign to her."

"I'll go after her."

"Give her a little time."

"Isabel is upset. She shouldn't be alone." He'd hurt her thinking she was being selfish. He needed to explain about his relationship to Julianna, too. "It's my responsibility."

Julianna sighed. "Izzy is not a responsibility. She's a person. Your wife. A woman can tell if you're there because you want to be or because you feel obligated."

"I do feel obligated." Frustration tightened the muscles in his neck and shoulders. "Isabel is not prepared to fulfill this role. Not the way you are."

"Isabel is not a typical princess, but her heart is in the right place."

"She does not want to be my wife."

"She is upset and frightened. Your behavior only served to make her more so."

His jaw tensed. He didn't like being called out on his behavior. "Isabel's feelings about arranged marriages are very clear."

"I will stay and help her adjust," Julianna said. "Perhaps if I do not return home, my father won't try to make another match for me right away."

Niko studied Julianna's face. Her eyes looked brighter. Her complexion had more color. "You're happy things turned out this way."

"Not happy. I would never wish this upon dear, sweet Izzy. But I am…relieved," Julianna admitted. "No one should be forced to marry someone they do not love. No offense."

"None taken." This side of her surprised him. "Yet you agreed to the marriage."

He cringed. His words sounded a lot like his father's.

She lifted her shoulder in a delicate shrug. "I was only doing what my father told me to do. What was expected of me. As I have always done my entire life."

Her words sounded similar to what Niko had said in the past. "I have done the same thing."

She raised a finely arched brow. "Are you certain about that?"

Her question offended him. He squared his shoulders. "Everything I have done has been for Vernonia."

"If that's the case, why would your parents go to the press about Izzy?"

"My parents would never—"

"They were the only ones who could have done this," Julianna interrupted. "While you and I were at dinner, they quizzed Izzy about her past. Her answers appear in the article. Isn't it strange that only positive information was published about her? The press rarely works that way."

I may not be a stickler for tradition, Father, but I will always do what is best for the country.

As will I.

Niko's stomach knotted. "I need to speak with my father."

Julianna rose. "I'll find Izzy."

He appreciated her help and her friendship. "You would have made a fine queen."

"Thank you." She bowed her head. "I have no doubt you will be an excellent king, especially with Izzy by your side."

If only he believed that could be true...

As if on autopilot, Izzy followed the directions given to her by a butler. The stone path should lead her to the garage. That was the only place she could think of at the castle where she might not feel so out of place, the only spot that reminded her a little of home.

The tower loomed above Izzy, as if mocking her.

The castle no longer seemed part of a romantic fairy tale. It belonged in a terrifying Gothic novel.

Would she ever be allowed to go back to Charlotte? If only to visit? Or would she be forced to stay in Vernonia forever, married to a man who didn't want her for his wife?

Izzy's insides twisted. She might have found Niko attractive. She might have wanted to kiss him. She might have even dreamed about him, too. But Izzy couldn't fathom spending the rest of her life married to a husband she didn't love, a husband who didn't love her.

She stumbled on a rock. Stupid heels. Somehow she managed to catch herself before falling flat on her face. Surprising since she felt as if she were carrying two tires—the hopes and dreams of Vernonia—on her shoulders. She was about to collapse from the load.

Izzy kicked her shoes off to keep from falling again.

Up ahead, she saw a rectangular brick building. That had to be the garage.

Welcome relief flowed through her. She quickened her step and entered through the side door.

The smell of motor oil greeted her like a long-lost friend. Tears pricked her eyes, but she wasn't going to cry. If she started, she might not be able to stop.

Izzy surveyed the interior: tools, tires, air compressor, an old truck and a limousine. She leaned against a wall and slid to the cement floor.

Her shoulders slumped. She closed her eyes.

Izzy had no idea how long she sat there. She didn't

care. Here in the garage, she belonged. She couldn't say that about any other place in the castle, not even the bedroom where she slept.

A door on the opposite side opened. The sharp staccato of heels echoed through the garage until Jules stopped in front of Izzy. "Rough morning."

Without looking up, she nodded.

Jules sat next to her on the ground.

Izzy shot her a sideways glance. "You're going to get dirty."

"That'll make two of us."

"I don't mean to be rude, but I don't feel like talking."

Jules wrapped her hands around her bended knees. "Then you can listen."

Izzy stared at the puddle of oil under the truck. Somebody needed to fix that leak.

"Niko and I aren't in love."

She looked at Jules. "What?"

"It was an arranged match. My third, actually," Jules explained. "Arranged marriages are the tradition in Aliestle, whether you are a royal or a commoner. My first match was made when I was seven, but he was later deemed unacceptable. Too bad because I really... liked him. My second was made when I was twenty-five. My marriage to Prince Richard of San Montico would have realigned our two countries after one hundred and thirty-nine years of feuds, but he was in love with someone else and married her. And then came Niko. He's honorable. Respectful. Attractive. But I'm not in love with him."

Izzy couldn't believe what she was hearing. "The two of you get along so well."

"We agreed to the match. We have common goals and a similar sense of duty."

"Duty?"

"I am a princess of Aliestle. My duty is to do what is best for my country," Jules said. "I am sure my father will make a fourth match for me as soon as he learns what has happened here."

"I had no idea, Jules. I'm so sorry." Compassion made Izzy reach out to her friend. "If I were you I would have run away by now."

Jules laughed. "I imagine you would have, but this is how I've been raised. Aliestle is more archaic than Vernonia when it comes to customs. But the land is rich with natural resources so we can afford to be... eccentric and backward with some of our traditions."

"But to marry someone you don't love..."

"I have dreamed about marrying for love since I was a little girl." Jules sighed. "The reality is an arranged marriage to best suit the needs of my country."

"That seems to be my new reality as a royal, and it sucks."

"Yes, sometimes it does," Jules admitted. "Duty and country first. But I'll tell you a secret. Even though I've always known I would be told who to marry, I've never given up hope that somehow I'd be able to marry for love. However remote the possibility."

"I hope it works out for you."

"Thanks, but I'm not holding my breath," she said. "I know it won't happen for me now."

"No, but Vernonia needs you, Izzy."

"Vernonia isn't my country."

"It was your parents' country and your uncle Frank's."

Izzy hadn't been thinking about them this morning. Only herself. That wasn't the way to honor the three people who had loved her so much and given up so much for her.

Guilt over her selfishness seared her heart. She needed to focus on what they would have wanted her to do in this situation, even if it wasn't what she wanted. "I only wish it didn't feel so wrong. I wish...I loved Niko."

"But you have feelings for him, yes?"

"It's been like a roller-coaster ride since I met Niko in Charlotte. I don't know what I feel for him."

"Remember, just because you don't love someone at the beginning doesn't mean you won't love them in the end. Love can grow over time."

"Do you really believe that?"

Jules smiled wryly. "Well, every time my father proposes another match I hope it's true."

Izzy couldn't ignore the bigger part in all this—Vernonia. People here, like people everywhere, deserved to live in peace. That was what her parents had wanted. That was what she believed her uncle Frank had wanted, too. Izzy's dreams of car racing seemed almost childish in comparison. Even if the High Court would grant her an annulment, she might be needed here in Vernonia. "I guess I'll have to hope it's true, too."

* * *

Niko stood in the king's office. Sweat beaded on his forehead and dampened the back of his shirt. He clenched his hands, struggling to control his temper. It wasn't working. "I can't believe you would betray me like this, Father."

"I didn't betray you, Niko. I spoke to the press for one reason and one reason only. To protect Vernonia. The Separatists want Izzy to be the next queen. We can't join the EU if we're having another civil war." Dmitar's lips thinned. "One day you'll understand the difficult decisions a ruler must make."

"If I am to rule, you need to treat me like the crown prince, not a pawn."

His father frowned, looking affronted. "I haven't—"

"You could have been honest about what needed to be done and explained your reasons. Not manipulate the situation the way you have." The words rushed out full of emotion and guilt at what his father's actions had done to two innocent women. "You have forced Isabel into a corner and hurt Julianna. Vernonia desperately needs the alliance with Aliestle. It's more than the dowry. The trade support and the influx of investment capital will enable us to modernize and join the European Union."

"Julianna is wealthy and beautiful, and even though her country has Separatist ties, she cannot unite the people the way Izzy will."

"Unite the people?" Niko stared at his father in disgust. "Have you not seen the gathering this morning? The Separatists' colors are already flying. It's history repeating itself. Isabel should be taken from Vernonia immediately."

"So you can marry Julianna."

"So Isabel will be safe. I fear for her safety. As should you."

Dmitar gave him a speculative look. "You like her."

"Excuse me?"

"Izzy." Amusement gleamed in his father's eyes. "I saw the way you touched her yesterday. The way you stared into her eyes."

Uncomfortable, Niko shifted his weight between his feet. He may like her, but that didn't mean they should remain married. "I hardly know her. I appreciate her sacrifice. I'm concerned about her well-being due to your underhanded tactics. The protests—"

"Izzy is safe," Dmitar interrupted. "These gatherings are different from the ones before. These are celebrations, my son. Unity. Finally."

Satisfaction sang in his tone.

Something more was going on here. Niko could feel it in his bones. Going to the press had only been one part of this. "You never planned on allowing Isabel to marry Boyd."

"I never planned on allowing you to annul the marriage in the first place."

Niko took a step forward. "How dare you?"

"I am the king. I do what is necessary."

"Necessary?"

"As soon as I saw the picture of the box and discovered Izzy was alive, I saw a real chance at lasting peace for Vernonia. A united country, all regions, all people. That is what Prince Aleksander and I hoped would happen twenty-three years ago with your marriage. I doubted you would go along so I used the annulment as bait to get your cooperation."

Fury infused Niko. "You can't play with lives this way."

"You were fine marrying Julianna."

"It was my choice. I've always been willing to marry without any preconceived notions of love," Niko said through clenched teeth. "But you've dragged Isabel into this with your machinations and lies."

His father shrugged. "The end is worth the means."

"No, Father. It is not." Niko squared his shoulders. "I have tried to fulfill Stefan's role. I've tried to live up to being crown prince and sacrifice for Vernonia, but you cannot continue to scheme and coerce a young woman into marriage. This type of action must stop. Now."

"A ruler must—"

Niko held up his hand, cutting off his father. "Be honorable in both thoughts and deeds. That is what you taught me. If Isabel refuses to remain married to me, I will support her decision, despite the dangers."

Panic flashed in Dmitar's eyes. "You must convince her. Vernonia needs an heir as soon as possible. A baby with both royal bloodlines."

"A baby?" Niko nearly choked. "Isabel doesn't want to be my wife. I doubt she will go willingly into my bed."

"Your duty—"

"I know my duty, sir," Niko said. "I've always known what is expected of me. I will talk with Isabel, but unlike you, Father, I will not manipulate her into marriage. The choice will be hers. And hers alone."

CHAPTER NINE

JULES headed back to the castle, but Izzy stayed in the garage. She wanted to repair the oil leak on the truck. She found tools and drained the remaining oil.

"You need a pair of coveralls so you don't ruin your outfit."

Izzy's heart lurched at the sound of Niko's voice. Pathetic. She hated the way she responded to him. He was only being nice because Vernonia needed her. She focused on the engine. "A little grease on my clothes won't hurt anything."

"I wonder what Tom Ford, Marc Jacobs and Stella McCartney would say about that."

She recognized the names of the famous fashion designers only because she now owned some of their clothing. "You mean Henry Ford."

Niko gave a short laugh. "I believe these belong to you."

His words forced her to glance his way. He looked out of place in the garage dressed so proper in a blue suit, white dress shirt and yellow silk tie. Her shoes dangled from the crook of his fingers. Out of place, but as sexy as a model in a magazine.

She wouldn't deny his physical appeal, but that didn't mean she would fall in love with him. Worse, what if she fell in love with him and he didn't fall in love with her?

She forced her gaze back to the truck and bent over the engine.

"I found one shoe in a bush and the other embedded heel down on the grass," he said.

"Keep 'em."

"They are not my size."

A smile tugged at her lips. She couldn't help it. "I'm sure you can find someone else they fit."

"They fit you, Isabel." He set them on the cement floor next to her. "Perfectly."

Izzy bit back a sigh. He was making an effort. The least she could do was meet him halfway. She straightened and stuck her foot in one of the shoes.

Niko kneeled to help her.

"I've got it," she said.

He stood, letting her do it herself.

She slipped on the other shoe.

"I am sorry for what I said earlier. For all of this," Niko apologized, his expression contrite.

She fought the urge to reach out to him. Self-preservation, not the grease on her hands, kept her from doing so. "Me, too. I shouldn't have run out like that."

"You had every right," Niko said. "We have been pawns in my father's game. His agreeing to let you marry Boyd was simply his own ruse to put his plans into action. He is the one who leaked the information about you to the press. He never intended to allow us to annul the marriage."

Dee had been so nice to her. The queen, too. "Why would he do that?"

"To unite Vernonia. That has been his goal as king. It's the same goal he shared with your father when they married us off."

Her father. Izzy's chest tightened.

"What do you want to do?" Niko asked.

"There's a choice?" She'd been trying to resign herself to her fate since talking with Jules.

His eyes darkened. "I hate what my father has done. I won't force you into…"

"Marriage."

He nodded. "I told you the first day I wouldn't lie to you. I don't want to coerce you into remaining my wife."

Izzy appreciated that. "I'm not what you wanted for Vernonia."

"No." His word, though honest and expected, jabbed her heart like a knife. "But it's what the country needs. Part of being a princess or a prince is putting your people first."

Niko believed that wholeheartedly. Jules, too. Izzy understood the necessity of peace, but not this duty they kept talking about.

That made her uneasy. Especially when she thought about the future.

How would Izzy know if Niko came to care about her or if he was simply doing his duty, the way he had been doing since the first day they met? The question left her as unsettled as the thought of unrequited love.

Still she appreciated his leaving it up to her. Too bad she really didn't have a choice.

"I don't like what your father did, but I will remain your wife. For Vernonia," she clarified, not wanting him to get the wrong idea.

"Thank you." He sounded relieved. "I know what you are giving up."

"Keeping peace is the most important thing. I couldn't live with myself if I was the reason for people being hurt." She fiddled with the engine to keep her hands busy. "I just hope your father is more honest and open in the future. Otherwise it will make things... difficult."

"I spoke with him about that." Niko seemed hesitant, uncertain.

"What?"

"My father believes Vernonia needs an heir. He wants one as soon as possible."

Her stomach knotted. "This will be a, um, real marriage?"

"I am the crown prince." A small smile played at the corners of Niko's lips, drawing her gaze. He had such a well-formed mouth, so inviting... "An heir and a spare are the minimum for any royal marriage. Real or not."

She blinked and forced herself to look away as heat crept up her neck. "Can't a person get used to one thing before having something else thrown at her?"

He placed his hands on her shoulders.

Warmth, delicious and oh, so inviting, emanated from the point of contact and flowed through Izzy. The entire dynamics of the situation seemed to change with the one touch. She focused on the word seemed. This was still an arranged marriage with a total stranger, who cared more about duty and country than anything else.

"This is not the kind of marriage you planned on having with Boyd," Niko said. "But we can make this work."

"How?" Izzy wished she shared his confidence. "It's not as if we're going to fall madly in love with each other."

"No, this isn't a love match, but that doesn't mean we can't have a successful union."

"Successful?"

"Providing the necessary heirs."

"So it's all about the baby making."

"That is a large part of it."

"I appreciate your honesty, but maybe you could sugarcoat it a little."

"You need to know what you're getting into," Niko said, as if he were an employer offering her a job, not a husband speaking about their relationship.

"Do we live together?" she asked. "I'm not sure how this kind of marriage will work."

"We have two options. A state marriage. That is living as husband and wife until we have the required number of heirs, then we live our separate lives, only appearing together at state functions or for our children's sake."

Izzy wasn't expecting a fairy-tale ending, but she hadn't been prepared for something so…calculated. "Would I be able to return home to live? To Charlotte, I mean."

He hesitated. "Possibly, but you must understand a divorce would never be allowed and custody arrangements might be tricky."

Niko was talking about children yet they'd never kissed. "What's the other option?"

"We live as husband and wife until death do us part."

"A together forever kind of thing?" she asked.

"As close to that as we could manage," he said. "In the old days, arranged marriages were quite successful. Why shouldn't ours be? We like each other, right? Besides, contemporary marriages based on love don't come with guarantees. Many people end up separating. Every marriage takes work if it's going to last."

"What kind of work?" she asked honestly. "I've never had a serious relationship before."

"Me, either," he admitted. "We will have to figure out what it takes together."

Izzy rested the palms of her hands on the car. A marriage based on respect and honesty wouldn't be bad. She was attracted to him. "If we can't figure it out, we can always just live apart."

A vein throbbed at his jaw. "If the marriage does work…"

"Then we'll owe your father a big thank-you."

Niko rocked back on his heels. "So it's settled."

"Not yet." Izzy straightened. "I don't see how we can begin to make a marriage work when I don't feel married."

"We are married."

"I know we got married, I saw the photograph and the marriage certificate, but I don't remember getting married. Maybe if we had a wedding ceremony, one we both remembered, I'd feel like your wife."

His gaze searched her face. "This is important to you."

"To feel married. Yeah, especially if we're going to, um…"

Amusement twinkled in his eyes. "Have sex."

This was *so* not what she wanted to be talking about with him. "Provide Vernonia with an heir."

"Do you enjoy sex, Isabel?"

Oh, man, he assumed she'd had sex. What was she going to say?

"I…" She looked around as if the answer would pop up on the hood or headlight for her to see. Of course, it didn't. Where was an enchanted castle when you needed one? "I don't know. I've never…"

She couldn't finish the sentence. He might be her husband, but that somehow made it more embarrassing.

"Never?" he repeated, sounding intrigued.

"Never." She felt self-conscious under his gaze. "I had the chance, more than once, but I always thought having sex after the first or second, even the third date was selling myself short. Uncle Frank said it should be an expression of love and commitment, not a way to cap off dinner or a movie."

Niko didn't say anything.

She flushed. "I'm a total freak, aren't I? I don't know how to be a princess. And I have no clue how to, you know."

"You are not a freak." He reached out to tuck a strand of hair behind her ear. "You're beautiful."

She shivered at the light touch. If only she felt beautiful.

"Do not worry. We have not known each other long, but there is a chemistry between us," he said in a husky tone.

Okay, at least he'd felt it, too. That had to count for something.

He moved closer. "I didn't pursue it because of Julianna."

"That was honorable of you."

Wicked laughter gleamed in his eyes. "But now that it is the two of us and you are my wife…"

Izzy stepped back until she hit the truck's bumper. "Look, I wanted to kiss you in the kitchen two nights ago. Outside near the garden yesterday. But now I don't want to do anything until I feel married."

He raised a brow. "Not even kiss?"

Temptation flared. A touch made her feel all tingly. A kiss might send her right over the edge. "No."

"We will have a wedding." His smile crinkled the corners of his eyes, and her heart beat like a drum. "We shall have a royal wedding complete with a fanfare of bugles, a packed cathedral and a horse-drawn carriage that would make Cinderella envious."

"That sounds so elaborate." And overwhelming. "I was thinking more along the lines as a quick trip to the courthouse."

"You need to think bigger," he said. "In fact, a wedding isn't enough. We will also go on a honeymoon."

Every single nerve ending stood at attention. She balled her hands so tightly her nails poked into her palms. A honeymoon implied romance, intimacy, sex. "That really isn't necessary."

"It is if we are to get to know each other and start our marriage right."

And, she realized with a sinking feeling in her stomach, conceive an heir. If that was all Niko wanted, their marriage really didn't stand a chance.

At precisely one o'clock in the afternoon the following Saturday, a flourish of trumpets announced the royal wedding procession. As fifteen hundred guests sat in the intricately carved wooden pews, the ancient stone cathedral's walls swallowed the music. An omen or poor acoustics?

Izzy shivered with apprehension.

The first of twelve bridal attendants, all wearing ice-blue strapless silk gowns, strolled out of the vestibule and into the church. She'd barely met any of the women, but at least Jules was her maid of honor.

Even though I've always known I would be told who to marry, I've never given up hope that somehow

I'd be able to marry for love. However remote the possibility.

Jules had received another reprieve from the altar. She'd also convinced her father to support trade and offer investment capital to assist Vernonia's rebuilding efforts. Izzy hoped the princess's generosity would be rewarded and she would be allowed to marry for love.

It was too late for Izzy, but things were improving between her and Niko. She'd been on her best behavior trying to learn all she could about being a princess from Jules. Niko seemed to be trying, too.

Would trying be enough to make a marriage work?

Izzy hoped so. She clung to the idea that love could grow over time. That they could have a forever kind of marriage, not a state one.

Music continued to play. Izzy recognized the song. Soon it would be her turn to walk down the aisle.

She remembered her princess instructions.

Shoulders back. Chin up. Smile.

Izzy could do this. She was a princess of Vernonia, even if she felt like a mechanic from Charlotte. She was doing this for her new country. For her parents. For Uncle Frank.

And Niko.

Her chest tightened at the thought of him.

He was waiting for her at the front of the church. Boyd, acting as his best man, would stand next to him. When she'd explained to her friend that marrying Niko was her choice and she liked him, Boyd had given her a strange smile and a shrug. Whatever sting he might have felt disappeared when the king offered to buy Boyd a new truck for his troubles.

Izzy took a deep breath and exhaled slowly.

Through her lace veil, she watched another attendant, the youngest daughter of a former Separatist leader, enter the church through the massive arched doorway. The oohs and aahs of the crowd floated on the air as they did during a fireworks display. The flashing of the camera bulbs and the web of electrical cords from the television crews made it seem more like a sports event than a wedding. Selling the television rights to the royal nuptials of the crown prince to the half-American princess had brought in more money than anyone had expected.

Rowdy, her former boss, cleared his throat. He stood next to her in the vestibule ready to walk her down the aisle. Sweat beaded on his forehead. He looked uncomfortable in the tuxedo. "You sure about this, Izzy?"

No. But she thought about Niko. He'd been honest about his reasons for marrying her. He'd been open about the need for heirs and the types of marriages they could have. But she'd also noticed the tenderness in his eyes when she caught him looking at her, the way he'd helped her since arriving and the love he had for his country. All those things told her he was a good, honorable man. "I'm sure."

Rowdy's eyes gleamed. "All your uncle wanted was for you to be safe and happy."

"I am. Honest."

"Then we're good to go." Her ex-boss sniffled. "You are a beautiful bride."

"Thanks, Rowdy." Izzy felt pretty, even though she'd had plenty of help to look so good. Since early this morning, she'd been fussed over, primped and pampered with a massage, manicure, pedicure and expert makeup application. Everything had been overseen and supervised by Jules. Three hairdressers had spent over an hour sweeping her hair up and through the diamond tiara that secured the cathedral-length veil. The last of the crystals and pearls had been hand-sewn on the bodice of her wedding gown only an hour ago by a dress designer named Delia.

Yes, the crew of wedding experts had transformed Izzy into a fairy-tale princess bride even though she'd been the prince's wife for the last twenty-three years. A happily-ever-after wasn't waiting for her after the exchange of "I dos." The birth of heirs would classify the match as a success or a failure, but would the union be full of love or loveless? That was the big question. One that wouldn't be answered for…years.

Two more attendants made the long walk down the aisle. In the vestibule, the remaining bridesmaids and six flower girls moved forward. Izzy had been introduced to all of them five days ago at a luncheon thrown by the wives of Parliament members.

Nerves escalating, Izzy gripped her all-white rose bouquet. She focused on the flowers' sweet fragrance.

Three more attendants made their way down the

aisle. The folds of their gowns swished like flags in the wind.

Shoulders back. Chin up. Smile.

Jules flashed her a smile and a thumbs-up before stepping into the church. The six flower girls, dressed in layers of white ruffles, played with the white rose petals in their baskets. One of them, the youngest daughter of a duke, giggled.

The tight-faced, headpiece-wearing wedding coordinator shushed her. "Quiet. It's almost your turn."

And then it would be Izzy's turn.

Her pulse rate doubled. She took a calming breath. Another. And another. But it didn't help.

In the old days, arranged marriages were quite successful. Why shouldn't ours be?

She clung to Niko's words, holding out the hope that they could spend the rest of their years together, not apart and married in name only.

The flower girls skipped into the church.

"It's almost time, ma'am," the wedding coordinator said.

Izzy's heart slammed against her chest. Each fierce beat reminded her of the cannon being shot off during the royal orchestra's performance of Tchaikovsky's *1812 Overture* at the Royal Hall on Tuesday night.

Another flourish of trumpets sounded. Rather, bugles, as Niko had called them. The signal. Her signal.

"Ready?" Rowdy asked.

Izzy would never be ready for this.

She glanced behind her at the massive wooden

church doors. Two royal guards flanked either side. The instinct to run had never been stronger. But where would she go? What would she do? And who would clean up the mess she left behind?

She might not be a fairy-tale princess locked in a tower, but she was a prisoner of circumstance as was Niko. The two of them were stuck with each other. Better just make the best of it.

Shoulders back. Chin up. Smile. "I'm ready."

Rowdy kissed the top of her hand. "You're the daughter I never had. I'm proud of you. I know Frank would be, too."

Tears stung her eyes. Rowdy's words filled her with warmth. "Thank you. Thank you so much."

She took hold of his arm. Somehow she managed to lift her heavy feet and step into the church without tripping on her gown and falling on her face.

Dignitaries, royalty, even movie stars stood to watch her, but the faces blurred. She focused on the altar.

Her step faltered, but thanks to Rowdy's strong arm no one realized her lapse.

Shoulders back. Chin up. Smile. And breathe.

Izzy needed to breathe or she was going to faint.

She neared the altar. Boyd wore a tuxedo and stood to the right in front of the pew where the king and queen sat.

Rowdy removed his arm from hers.

A tidal wave of doubt and apprehension surged down her spine. Izzy clutched the bouquet's handle so hard it bent.

Rowdy gave her other hand a squeeze. The gesture reassured her. Then he placed her hand into Niko's.

She stared at his neatly trimmed nails, smooth skin, strong hand. A husband's hand. The father of her children's hand.

His fingers clasped around hers. Tingles shot up her arm.

Breathe. Just breathe.

Slowly her gaze traveled to his sleeve—a gold braided cuff against black—and up his arm. He wasn't wearing a tuxedo, but a uniform with gold braiding at the shoulders and a light blue sash, one of the colors from the Vernonian flag, worn diagonally across his chest. A thin row of white from his shirt collar could be seen at the top of the jacket. Ribbons and medals decorated the left side. He wore a thin gold belt around his waist.

He looked like a prince from the movies. Long, thick lashes framed familiar blue-green eyes. His straight nose complemented high cheekbones. Full lips contrasted with the sculpted planes of his face. A mane of brown hair fell to his wide shoulders.

He smiled, and his rugged features softened. Even his scar.

Tingles formed in her stomach.

Niko was almost too beautiful for a man, for a mere mortal. Yet here he stood, as if crafted by the angels in Heaven especially for her. Her heart sighed.

And that was when Izzy knew.

There was only one reason she'd agreed to remain

married to Niko. He might not be Prince Charming, but that didn't matter.

This might not be a love match for Niko, but it was turning into one for her.

She was already falling for her husband. And falling hard.

Niko stared at the woman standing next to him at the altar. Isabel wasn't beautiful; she was stunning. With her light brown hair artfully arranged around a diamond tiara, she was the epitome of what a princess should look like. Her elegant white gown accentuated her curves and ivory complexion.

He should be happy. His people had rallied around this young American, but she wasn't the princess bride he'd been expecting. Wanted. All his hopes and dreams for modernizing Vernonia had rested on his marriage to Julianna. Thanks to his father, Niko could forget about gaining entry into the European Union for years, if ever. His most important duty now was to impregnate Isabel.

Not that he would mind the task, but the rest...

We will have to figure out what type of work it takes. Together.

Niko had no idea what working together with Isabel would be like. He'd never had the same girlfriend for more than a couple of months, and even then he hadn't had a lot of free time. His best friend and closest partner had been his older brother, Stefan, who had kept Niko out of trouble and saved his life on at least two occasions. He didn't know how to create a new relationship. Having seen his parents' arranged marriage would help, but Isabel...

He glanced down at her.

She stared up at him as if he were the sun, moon and stars rolled into one. He could barely breathe. No one had ever looked at him that way.

It had to be the emotion of the moment. Or her makeup.

Isabel came to this marriage out of duty, the same as him. She already had an escape route planned.

If we can't figure it out, we can always just live apart.

He hoped things didn't come to that, even though that was the way many of his peers lived once they had secured the necessary heirs.

The archbishop spoke.

Niko focused his attention on the celebrant, concentrating on the words of the opening prayer. He'd been too young to remember his first wedding ceremony. He should pay attention to this one. Unlike Izzy, he doubted an exchange of vows would make him feel more married. Only time and possibly a child would do that.

But no matter how he felt, Niko would put Vernonia first. He could still do his duty, as a prince and as a husband. And he would.

Even though Izzy was a continent away from home, the gestures and words of the ceremony were similar to weddings she'd attended back in Charlotte. That gave her an unexpected sense of familiarity. Comfort. The last things she'd expected to feel today.

Staring at Niko's handsome face, Izzy concentrated on the archbishop's words—love, honor, until death do you part.

"I do," she said when he'd finished speaking.

Niko released a quick breath.

Relief, she hoped. Not regret.

She knew exactly what she wanted. A real marriage. The together forever kind. But in order for that to happen Niko had to fall for her the way she was falling for him.

"Do you have the rings?" the archbishop asked.

As the ring ceremony continued, Niko repeated the necessary words. Izzy prayed they would come true. He slid a beautiful wide diamond and ruby encrusted gold band on her ring finger. A perfect fit.

She ran her fingertip along the gold band she would give him. The royal historian claimed the diamond, ruby, emerald and sapphire cross heirloom ring not only provided protection, but also brought truth to light. Those two things had made choosing this wedding band from the royal family collection an easy one. She gripped it hard, afraid she might drop it. "I give this ring as a token of my love and fidelity."

With only the slightest tremble, she slid the ring onto his finger. Once again, a perfect fit.

The archbishop declared them husband and wife. He smiled. "You may kiss your bride."

Their first kiss. Izzy tensed due to a mix of nerves and anticipation. And the thousands of onlookers.

As Niko lowered his mouth to hers, she closed her eyes.

His lips brushed hers and disappeared.

That was it? Izzy pushed aside her disappointment and opened her eyes. She thought Niko had wanted to kiss her.

Suddenly his mouth returned, pressing against her lips. Hard, demanding, as if seeking her very soul. The urgency and need in his kiss frightened yet excited Izzy. She'd never been kissed like this.

It took every ounce of willpower not to cling to him, but she couldn't forget where she was. And who was watching. Not only the guests sitting in the pews, but a television audience watching at home.

Niko drew back, but only far enough to whisper in her ear. "I cannot wait for tonight."

Anticipation buzzed through her. Izzy moistened her thoroughly kissed lips and glanced at the shimmering diamond ring on her finger.

She couldn't wait for tonight, either.

The reception passed in a blur. The guests seemed to be enjoying themselves with the free-flowing champagne and mouthwatering food. Or cuisine as the queen called it.

Unbelievably Izzy felt like a princess. She floated across the dance floor, whirling and twirling to the orchestra, with Niko's strong arms around her. He stayed at her side the entire time, introducing her to so many diplomats and dignitaries she couldn't begin to remember their names. Rarely did he let go of her hand. She felt special, cherished, and that eased some of her nerves about what would happen later tonight.

Their wedding night.

She was excited, but a little worried about the two of them alone. Together. In bed.

After cutting the cake, Izzy stood at the railing of the landing between two sets of curved staircases for the bouquet toss. She held onto the handle of her white rose bouquet. Anticipation filled the eyes of the women standing below her.

"Is something wrong?" Niko asked in a low voice that seeped through her like warm caramel sauce.

"No." She remembered being one of the single ladies called to the dance floor at a friend's wedding last summer. No matter their station in life, royal or commoner, women wanted to catch the bouquet. "Just taking it all in."

"Savor the moment," Niko whispered. "But you may want to put the women out of their misery sooner rather than later."

With a smile, Isabel turned her back to the railing. On three, she let the flowers soar into the air behind her. She whipped around.

Women reached for flowers. A few missed by mere inches. The petals grazed another's fingertips. The bouquet landed in Jules's hands. The lovely princess stared down at the roses in wide-eyed dismay and promptly dropped them.

Izzy laughed, but no one else seemed amused.

The wedding coordinator rushed to Jules's side, scooped up the bouquet and placed them in the stunned princess's hands. The royal photographer corralled Jules for a picture with the bride.

Izzy stared at the camera. "You're smiling, but your eyes don't look happy."

"Catching the bouquet might be a sign," Jules admitted. "I fear I may find myself matched to another royal in need of a wife before I return home to Aliestle."

The camera flash made Izzy blink. They struck a different pose for the photographer. "Stay here."

Jules sighed. "I wish I could."

"I'm serious," Izzy said. "We're spending tonight at the castle, but then we leave on our honeymoon. The king and queen won't mind. They like having guests."

"My father might mind."

"At least think about it," Izzy urged.

"I will," Jules said. "Thank you."

Hours later in the suite that would be the bedroom Izzy shared with her husband, servants helped her out of her wedding gown. All the while, she wondered why Niko wasn't doing this. Wasn't a husband supposed to undress his wife on their wedding night?

Mare combed out her hair. Another woman ran a warm bath. A third lay out Izzy's peignoir set. The lovely confection of thin white fabric, lace and ribbon had been a gift from Jules.

Izzy appreciated the women's efforts. They were just trying to do their jobs, but what was next? A mug of warm milk and a plate of cookies?

All this pampering felt odd. Off. The most important part of tonight was missing. Where could Niko be?

The future of their marriage didn't bode well when a husband blew off his wife on their wedding night.

Izzy dismissed the women. She didn't need anyone to add to her growing anxiety. She could put on her own nightgown. But after bathing and re-tying the satin ribbon on the robe for the third time, she wondered if she'd made the right decision. The bow was still lopsided.

Not that Niko would probably even notice.

Izzy paced barefoot across the large room. She noticed a television set inside an armoire and a bookshelf full of books. But she was not in the mood to watch TV or read.

She glanced at the clock.

I cannot wait for tonight.

His words during the ceremony had made her think of what would be happening when they were alone, not at their reception.

The flames of the lit candles flickered. Shadows danced on the wall. He was coming to their room, wasn't he?

Izzy walked to the French doors, opened them and stepped onto the balcony. Stars twinkled in the inky sky. A breeze, carrying the scent of roses from the garden below, ruffled her hair and nightgown.

This was her new home.

She wanted to be with her new husband.

She just wished he'd get his butt up here.

CHAPTER TEN

NIKO entered the suite with the bride box in his hands. He placed the wedding gift on the table next to two crystal flutes and a bottle of champagne chilling in a silver bucket. The box belonged to Isabel once again. The archaic custom had been fulfilled. He only hoped she felt like his wife now. If not, he would do his best to make sure she did by morning.

He was prepared. The kiss during the ceremony had only whetted his appetite and made him want to skip the reception. The room appeared ready, too.

Soft music played from an iPod docking sound system. Flickering candles provided a romantic atmosphere. The duvet and sheets had been turned down, ready for him to carry his virgin princess bride to their bed.

All he needed was Isabel.

Desire carried him to the bathroom in search of her. She wasn't there. Niko took the time to remove his belt, sash and jacket. He also kicked off his shoes and pulled off his socks.

Out in the bedroom area, he still didn't see her.

She wasn't the kind of woman to cower in the closet. That left…

Niko strode to the balcony doors with a sense of purpose that belied anything he'd felt about her, about any woman, before. Isabel consumed his thoughts. She invaded his dreams. Maybe once he had her that would stop. He hoped so. He didn't like being so distracted.

He opened one of the doors quietly.

She stood on the balcony facing away from him. Niko had no idea what she was looking at in the darkness. Niko only knew what he saw—a vision in white with a starry sky as her backdrop.

His heart beat a rapid tattoo.

The breeze toyed with the ends of her hair the way his fingers longed to do. The fragile fabric of her long robe and matching nightgown ruffled around her legs, hinting at the treasures hidden beneath. Treasures that would soon belong to him, and him alone.

Niko would show Isabel one of the perks of their forced union. He wanted to make this night, their wedding night, special for her. They might have been married for twenty-three years, but tonight they would unite as husband and wife. He wanted her to enjoy the physical side of their marriage, not see it as an obligation to provide heirs to the kingdom. That could go a long way in making their marriage successful.

He stepped onto the balcony. "Wishing on a star or reconsidering faking your death?"

"I must admit drowning isn't looking too bad, but now that my wish has come true I might have to stick around a little longer." She turned with an expectant look on her face. "What took you so long, Highness?"

Niko wanted to take her right there. But he inclined his head instead. "I was forced to play polite with too many heads of state. I apologize for my delay, Highness."

She stared down her nose at him, but even though she was ten feet away from him the desire in her eyes was unmistakable.

Anticipation sizzled. His blood heated and thrummed through his veins.

"I assume you will make it up to me," she said coquettishly.

Her unexpected playfulness hinted at the fun they would have tonight. "I won't stop until you are satisfied."

She walked toward him, but not close enough to touch.

The breeze lifted the ends of her hair again, brushing several strands across her face. His fingers itched to tuck the wayward strands behind her ear. To touch her.

Isabel's bare feet carried her closer until she was bathed in the soft light from the room. The silhouette of her breasts could be seen through the sheer fabric. His groin tightened.

"Promises, promises," she teased.

"I promise you will have no complaints, milady."

His words earned him a breathtaking smile. She reached for the satin ties on her gown. Her fingers fumbled. Not as cool and collected as she appeared to be. That endeared her even more to him.

He longed to undress her, to see her standing naked before him, but he would give her a little more time.

"Allow me." Niko tied the two pieces of ribbon into a neat bow. "There."

Her confused eyes stared up at him through her thick lashes. "Aren't you supposed to untie it?"

"I didn't know we were in such a hurry."

She flushed.

"Impatient?" he asked.

"Well, yeah." Isabel tilted her chin. "Given you're only wearing your shirt and not the full uniform, I figured you were ready for the green flag so we could start the race."

"You want to race through tonight?"

"No, I mean—"

Smiling, he swept her into his arms and cradled her snugly.

Her eyes widened. "What are you doing?"

Soft, feminine curves pressed against him. His body tingled with awareness. "Carrying you over the threshold."

"I didn't think you were a big fan of traditions and customs."

"A few have their place." As he carried her to the door, his gaze rested on her mouth. "Especially on a wedding night."

She trembled. "Okay, the nerves are starting to really kick in."

He held her tighter. "Better?"

"Actually, yes." Isabel ran her fingertip along the scar on his cheek. She shifted against him, stretching until she pressed her lips against the side of his face, against his scar. "So beautiful."

"Not as beautiful as you."

"I had help."

"With or without help, you're still beautiful."

He didn't want to rush, but he wasn't that patient, either. Unable to resist the temptation in his arms any longer, he lowered his mouth to hers. She arched to meet his kiss.

With no archbishop, no audience and no cameras watching, Niko could do what he had wanted to do at the cathedral—take his time. No racing to the finish line tonight.

He wanted to savor the kiss, to linger and enjoy. She tasted sweet and warm with a hint of chocolate, like fondue. The castle chef used to make the rich chocolate fudge sauce for Niko's birthday. Just as he had done when he was younger, he soaked up the taste.

As he pushed open the door with his shoulder, Isabel's eager lips pressed against his. Testing, tasting, hungry. Her arms circled around him. One hand combed through his hair. The other splayed against his back, between his shoulder blades, pressing him forward.

Nothing else mattered but Isabel. Sensation swirled through Niko.

She wanted this. Wanted him.

Heat flared.

Her tongue darted into his mouth to tangle with hers.

Exploded.

Niko moved toward the bed, never letting his lips leave hers. He couldn't get enough of her kiss, of her. But he had to stop, for just a moment. He lifted his mouth from hers.

Isabel's eyes opened, her gaze hot and languid, intense and soft. A mass of contradictions. Just like her, his mechanic, his princess.

His wife.

He struggled to remain in control. He wanted to dispense with the niceties, abandon decorum and push up the hem of her gown and take her. But, this was her first time. She deserved better. He needed to go slow, not overwhelm her with tangled limbs and sweaty skin and breathless sex.

Carefully, gently, he lowered her to the foot of the bed so she was sitting on the edge. He stood in front of her, watching her. Waiting for her to look away in shyness.

Her gaze never wavered from his.

Talk about a turn-on.

His chest tightened. His control slipped a notch. Maybe three.

Niko tugged on one of the ribbon ends to undo the bow he'd tied on the balcony. He pushed the chiffon robe off her shoulders and down her arms until it fell over her hands and onto the bed.

He bent over her, kissing her bare shoulder and showering more kisses along her neck and jaw.

Izzy leaned back her head, giving him better access to her graceful neck. He continued kissing her. He loved the smell and taste of her skin. Finally his mouth grazed her earlobe.

A soft moan escaped her lips.

She was ready for more. So was he.

Niko wanted to make her his wife in every sense of the word. He touched the thin straps on both sides of her nightgown, noticing the softness of her skin beneath the rough pads of his fingertips.

She pushed his hands away. "Not yet."

He stared down at her, confused.

Before he could say anything, Isabel kneeled on the bed. She reached for a button on his shirt. "It's my turn."

Kneeling in front of Niko, Izzy's insides quivered with anticipation as she worked with trembling hands to remove his shirt. Through the cotton, she felt the heat of his skin, the rise and fall of his chest. His breathing was no steadier than hers.

That made her feel better and quieted some of her nerves.

Izzy hadn't done this before, but she'd overheard the guys at work. She knew what was supposed to happen. She wasn't about to let Niko do all the work tonight. No way. No how. She wanted him to enjoy tonight, too.

Her fingers shook as she slid another button from its hole.

"It's taking a long time," he said.

She moved on to the next button. "We're still on the warm-up lap."

"My tires are warm. I'm ready to start the race."

Izzy placed her palm over his heart. "Not yet."

His muscles rippled beneath the fabric. So athletic. So strong. He made her feel cherished, special. His. It was all she could do not to sigh.

Was this how a wife was supposed to feel?

She wanted to be his, but she also wanted him to be hers.

Izzy's fingers fumbled as she undid the last button. She brushed his shirt open, her hands grazing his warm skin. Tingles pulsed up her arms.

A key on a silver chain hung around his neck. The key to the bride box.

Izzy fingered it. "You're still wearing it."

"Not anymore." He pulled the chain over his head and gave her the necklace. "The bride box is on the table next to the champagne. It belongs to you, my wife, once again."

She held the key. The bride box and its missing key had enabled Dee to force them together. But she didn't want to think about those things right now. "Thank you."

"You're welcome." His gaze practically caressed. "Now toss the key on the floor so we can get back to what we were doing."

Izzy did.

Inching closer on her knees, she pushed the shirt over his broad shoulders and down his strong arms, arms that had carried her so effortlessly across the threshold as if she weighed nothing.

Her pulse skittered.

Izzy stared at his bare chest and tight abs in awe

and admiration. She wanted to memorize everything about him. His arms, chest and back showed the scars of war from his time as a soldier. Like the ribbons and medals he'd worn earlier, these were his badges of honor. He'd fought to protect Vernonia. She had no doubt he would fight to protect her. A dizzying current of desire traveled through her.

She touched his chest, tracing the length of a scar running from his shoulder to his waist. At the end of it, she opened her palm over his ribs, her thumb rubbing another, smaller scar under his sternum.

He drew in a sharp breath.

She pulled her hand back. "Sorry."

"No, it's fine."

"I'm not sure what I'm supposed to do next."

"You don't have to worry about that. It's my turn." Niko raised her hand to his mouth and kissed each of her fingers. "You're overdressed."

He reached for the strap of her nightgown.

"The lights?"

With a swoop of his arms, Niko lifted her off the foot of the bed and carried her toward the head of the bed. He set her on her feet so she was standing right in front of him.

He bent over and pressed a button on the nightstand. The lights went off, but the candles around the room provided a romantic glow. "More comfortable now?"

Izzy nodded, feeling shy. She was not like the other women in his life, the polished, beautiful princesses and models he must have dated.

He pushed the straps of her nightgown off her

shoulders and down her arms. Izzy's cheeks warmed. The gown fell to the floor, leaving her exposed to his view.

Slowly his gaze raked over her. Appreciative. Seductive. Possessive.

Her heart jolted.

"You are stunning. Enchanting." His hands moved over her body. Shivers of delight followed his touch. "Captivating."

His words melted her insides.

He ran his finger along the curve of her hip. "No lacy thong."

"I thought it, um, might get in the way."

"Fast learner."

"When it comes to some things." She winked, feeling more brazen. "Kiss me."

His lips captured hers again. This time with urgency and need. He needed her. The realization made Izzy's heart sing. She returned his kisses with reckless abandon.

There was no turning back. She wanted him.

As they kissed, he placed her hands on the waistband of his pants.

Excited, nervous, her fingers undid the hook, but fumbled with the button the same way they had with his shirt. Finally she got it and his zipper. He stepped out of his pants and briefs.

Izzy cast her gaze downward. Oh, my. She swallowed. Hard.

Her fingers reached out and gently touched him.

He inhaled sharply again. Captured her hand before

easing her onto the mattress. Her head rested against a pillow.

He climbed onto the bed, the mattress dipping under his weight. As he lay over her, his hair fell forward, the long ends teasing her skin like a feather. The tantalizing scent of him surrounded her. He lowered his head until his lips brushed hers.

Each touch, each kiss, each brush of his body sent shivers of pleasure radiating outward. He made her feel so desired, so sexy. She wanted to make him feel the same.

Boldly Isabel explored his body with her hands again. A low sound emerged from Niko's throat. She had no idea what she was doing, but his response gave her the courage to continue.

"We just started the race," Niko said. "But if you keep that up, I might have to black flag you."

His use of a racing term made her stomach tingle. "Why would you want to send me to the pits?"

Sweat dampened his forehead. "Breaking the rules."

"Forget the black flag. You can't penalize me for not knowing the rules." Her confidence spiraled. She continued touching him. "We have way too many laps to go to finish the race."

"Yellow then."

"Caution?"

He placed his hand over hers. "Slow down. Otherwise you won't be able to avoid the debris on the track."

She ran her hands over his hips and up his chest. "Better."

A flash of humor crossed his face. "For you."

She laughed. "What's it going to take to get the green flag again?"

"Ready to race?"

She nodded enthusiastically. "You?"

"I think you can answer that question." He drew a line along her jawline. "I don't want to hurt you, but since it's your first time…"

If she had done this before, she would be more comfortable, confident. She would be more like the women he was used to. But in spite of her nerves she was happy she had waited until tonight. Until him.

Her hand was still on his chest. She felt the beating of his heart beneath her palm. "I trust you."

Something flashed in his eyes. "I lapped you. Let's get you caught up."

Niko kissed her again until she thought her pounding heart might burst out of her chest. But he didn't stop there. It was his turn to touch her. His fingers sent pulsations of pleasure radiating outward.

A fire ignited inside her, and she arched toward him. She wanted more, so much more.

Her heart swelled with happiness and something she'd never felt before. She pulled back enough to look into Niko's eyes. "Just so you know, the bride box is now mine and so are you."

He slid between her legs, and her body, awash in sensation, welcomed him.

Niko was the only man Izzy wanted. The only man she would ever need. The only husband she could ever imagine having.

* * *

Lying in bed the next morning, Niko stared at Isabel asleep. She curled against him, her legs wrapped around his. He needed to untangle himself so he could get out of bed, but he didn't want to wake her.

If Isabel woke, she would want to know where he was going. Niko had no idea. He only knew he wanted—needed—to get away from her to think.

He pulled one of his legs out from under hers.

The sex had been great. Better than he expected. Isabel's curiosity and eagerness had made up for any lack of experience. He'd been powerless to resist her. She'd left him satisfied, spent and wanting more.

Wind blew into the room from an open balcony door.

Damn. He had been in such a hurry to get Isabel to bed he hadn't thought to close the door. Privacy was always an issue here at the castle. He was usually more careful. But with Isabel, he lost all control during the kiss at the ceremony.

Niko couldn't remember the last time he had allowed that to happen. He didn't like how losing control felt. He had wanted to make Isabel his wife, but she'd made him her husband. He wanted her again this morning. His body ached for her and his heart…

He raked his hand through his hair.

No. His heart needed to remain immune to his wife's charms, her humor, her beauty, her seduction. Diving into the marriage *heart* first would not be a smart idea.

Niko understood how falling in love with a woman

he had to be married to made sense, but he wasn't ready to be in love. He didn't know when he'd be ready.

Isabel may have come willingly to his bed last night, but their marriage was a direct result of his father's underhanded tactics. Niko was not going to lie to her about his feelings, but would she be as straightforward with him?

He had no idea if Isabel was committed to this marriage or not. Loving his wife wouldn't harm Vernonia, but she'd had no qualms about divorcing Boyd once their in-name-only marriage had served its purpose. She might feel the same way about this marriage. About him.

Niko wasn't ready to risk that.

He needed to keep an emotional distance and not become too attached. Losing Stefan had been difficult enough. Having Isabel walk away…

Niko would not put himself through that again, no matter how physically attracted he was to his wife. He had done his duty and married her. He would continue to do his duty and get her pregnant. He would do whatever it took to make their marriage successful.

But emotions had no place in this marriage right now. No place at all.

Izzy didn't want to open her eyes. She was sore and tired, but she wanted to spend the rest of the day in bed with her husband.

Her husband.

Heat rose as Izzy remembered how she'd responded to Niko's kiss, his touch, him. Ready for more, she reached toward Niko, but her hand found only empty space. She opened her eyes. He wasn't there. "Niko?"

No answer.

She hadn't expected to wake up alone this morning. She wrapped herself in the sheet and checked the bathroom and the balcony. Not there, either.

A knock sounded.

Why would Niko knock to enter his own room? Izzy exchanged the sheet for her robe and opened the door. Mare stood with a tea cart containing breakfast. "Good morning, ma'am. The chef has prepared breakfast for you."

A breakfast for one based on the tray and silverware, Izzy noted. That added to her unease. "Have you seen Prince Niko?"

"Yes, ma'am." Mare wheeled the cart into the room. "He's in his office."

Working, Izzy realized with relief. She shouldn't have been surprised given they were leaving on their honeymoon today. Niko must have wanted to get a few things done before they left. How responsible of him. Another trait she liked about her husband.

Izzy enjoyed her meal on the balcony. The scent of the roses from the garden smelled fresher. The sun in the sky shone brighter. The smile on her face felt wider.

And her heart…

She closed her eyes and looked up so the sun's rays kissed her face. The heat against her skin reminded Izzy of Niko. He cared about Vernonia with a fierce loyalty and love. She hoped he would come to care the same way about her. And she intended to do whatever she could to make that happen.

Two hours later, Izzy walked next to Niko toward the helipad. She cast a sideways glance at him. This was the first time she'd seen him all morning. He looked stylishly casual in his polo shirt, khakis and leather loafers. The man always looked good whether in formal attire or his birthday suit. She smiled at the image that brought to mind. "Where are we spending our honeymoon?"

"You'll see soon enough."

"I hope I packed the right clothes."

His brows furrowed. "Mare should have packed for you."

Izzy shrugged. "I like doing it myself."

"You must embrace your role as a princess of Vernonia, Isabel."

Niko didn't sound upset, but he wasn't smiling. Maybe she could fix that. "I'd rather embrace Vernonia's crown prince."

He didn't smile, but his eyes no longer looked so serious. "You must embrace both."

The helicopter traveled north. A majestic mountain range with snowcapped peaks rose sharply into the clear blue sky. The terrain, rugged and etched, reminded her of Niko. A feeling of warmth welled inside her. Her husband shared so many similarities with this land he loved. "It's beautiful."

"Yes." Staring out the window, he seemed preoccupied. Eager to make a connection like the one she'd felt last night while in his arms, Izzy placed her hand on top of his.

He turned toward her though the smile on his face didn't reach his eyes.

She smiled back, sure she was mistaken.

But he didn't lace his fingers with hers and hold her hand. That was...weird. After last night, she expected them to be closer, but he seemed almost ambivalent.

"Is something wrong?" she asked.

"No."

"Too much work you didn't get to?"

"No."

"Tired?"

"I am fine," he said stiffly.

"You don't seem fine." His aloofness annoyed her and set off alarms in her head. "You're acting different."

His jaw thrust forward. "I am the same as I always am."

No, he wasn't. He'd been nicer, friendlier the day they met than he was right now. She pulled her hand away. He didn't even seem to notice. Hurt burrowed in deep.

Was the honeymoon already over before it began?

Apprehensive, Izzy stared out the window and told herself to give him more time. She concentrated on the scenery. Villages dotted the landscape both in the mountains and foothills and valley floor as beautiful as a painting.

She glimpsed a castle in the distance. Smaller than

the one the royal family lived in, but just as fairy tale worthy with a tower and spires jutting into the sky.

As the helicopter traveled toward the castle, the structure came into clearer view. Her breath caught in her throat. A wall made of stones surrounded the grounds. Paths crisscrossed a carpet of lush green grass. Tall trees surrounded a crystal blue lake.

Izzy pressed her forehead against the window for a better look. "I love that castle."

"It's yours," Niko said.

She looked his way. "Mine?"

"That is where you lived with your parents," he clarified. "It's your family home."

Her home? Izzy stared out the window in disbelief. "This is where we're going?"

"Yes," he said. "Not quite as warm as the beach."

"It's a million times better than the beach." Maybe she was overanalyzing Niko's words and actions. He'd obviously put some thought into where to spend their honeymoon. "It's perfect. Thanks."

The castle turned out to be even more spectacular in person with more bedrooms than she could count, an obliging staff—many of whom were related to Uncle Frank—and a large six bay garage that had the potential to be a mechanic's dream hangout.

As the days passed, Izzy and Niko explored the property, toured various villages and visited with residents. She was enjoying herself, but she continued to sense a difference in Niko. Oh, he was polite, even solicitous, but he acted more like her friend than her husband no matter how hard she tried to initiate a deeper emotional connection.

Maybe that was how marriage was supposed to be, except…

When they were in bed, Niko couldn't seem to get enough of her. He gave her a taste of the intimacy she desired; a glimpse of how wonderful all parts of their marriage could be not just the physical side. They spent their nights and mornings learning about each other and sharing themselves. It whetted her desire for more. But once they left the bedroom, the closeness vanished as if an invisible wall had been erected between them.

"You like it here," Niko said three days later as they strolled through the grounds.

"I do," she admitted. "I love it here. The castle. The people. The villages."

You.

Izzy wanted to lose herself and her heart in Niko, but was too afraid to tell him how she felt. He'd told her he wouldn't lie to her. She wasn't prepared for that kind of honesty. Not on their honeymoon. But she could be honest about other things.

"This place—" she inhaled the fresh mountain air, trying to quell her uneasiness "—it feels like…"

"Tell me."

"Home."

"That's because Sachestia is your home," Niko said. "You can return whenever you wish."

You, not we. The one word changed everything she had convinced herself could happen. Maybe not today or tomorrow, but someday. Disappointment squeezed her heart.

The hope of love blossoming in her marriage was withering. The promise of "until death do us part" was turning into nothing more than a dull ache. Izzy might want more, but she resigned herself to not needing more than the physical intimacy Niko offered. She had a feeling that nothing would make him love her. Not even time.

The next day Niko rowed Isabel across the lake in a small boat. The days they spent together seemed to drag compared to the nights that were over much too quickly. He remembered the swing of her hips and the look in her eyes this morning. All her enthusiasm and energy seemed to have disappeared out here in the light of day. "You look...tired."

"I'm...not."

Niko waited for her to say more. She didn't.

That was his fault. His trying to distance himself from her was finally working. At first she wouldn't let him push her away, but lately she no longer seemed to care if they talked or remained silent. Except when they were having sex. Then everything between them worked perfectly. If not for the security detail watching from shore, he would take her now. "You're not very talkative today."

Isabel shrugged. "We only have a couple of days left here."

A bird flew overhead. Somewhere nearby a frog croaked.

The smell of freshly mowed grass from the lush lawns bordering the lake hung in the air, but Niko would rather inhale her vanilla and jasmine scent. "It's too bad we can't stay longer."

She perked up. "Really?"

"Yes." He wasn't sure about marriage yet, but he liked being on a honeymoon and spending time with her. "I haven't relaxed this much since…I can't remember when."

Her shoulders sagged again. "Me, either."

He didn't like seeing her this way. "You don't look relaxed."

"I'm worried about what things will be like after we leave."

Niko could kiss away her worry, but he wanted to be honest with her. "Things will be different when we return home."

She trailed the tips of fingers in the water. "No more great sex?"

"I promise the great sex will continue no matter where we are." He shook the rowboat. "This seems sturdy enough."

Isabel gave him a resigned smile, but he saw no invitation in her eyes.

"Once we are back, we won't spend the same amount of time together as we have here." An unexpected look of relief crossed her features. A look Niko didn't understand nor like. "You'll be expected to assume your role as a princess of Vernonia."

"Right away?"

"How does tomorrow sound?" Perhaps if Isabel had

something more to do she would be happier. "Regional officials have requested our presence at a village celebration. This will be a perfect introduction to the duties you'll have when we return home."

She shook her head. "We're on…vacation."

"Yes, but they only want us to participate in the parade. It shouldn't take long."

"I'm not sure I'm ready for that."

"All you have to do is smile and wave. The parade will be an excellent way for people who remember your parents to see you as their princess."

She wrung her hands. "What if I fall on my face?"

"You'll be sitting in a carriage."

Isabel stuck out her tongue at him.

He grinned, relieved her playfulness had returned. "If you fall, I'll catch you."

She stared at him with an unreadable expression in her beautiful eyes. He wished they would twinkle the way they had earlier in the week. "I guess it would be okay."

He'd hoped for more enthusiasm, but at least she was taking her place as a Vernonian princess seriously. That pleased him. "Thank you, Isabel."

Her gaze grew serious. "Is this what my life will be like when we return? Parades and whatnot?"

"You will be expected to take a public role making appearances, going on outings, attending openings. You'll get used to the routine after a few times."

Her gaze cut away. "Sounds like a lot of fluff. Princess waving and cutting ribbons."

She made the tasks sound so trivial. "There is some fluff involved, but participating in events is expected by the people and an important part of our duties."

"Duty or not, I'm not a fluff person," she said. "I prefer to do a task. Help people. Accomplish something. That's one reason I like being a mechanic."

"What's another reason?"

"Cars are awesome." She splashed him. "Which you would know if you ever drove one instead of being chauffeured around all the time."

Niko splashed her back. He'd missed this side of their relationship. He might not want things too serious between them, but that didn't have to take away all their fun. "You will be able to accomplish many things and help people with your solo agenda."

Her arms dropped to her sides. "My what?"

"Good Works," he clarified. "The social issues, charities and causes you want to focus your energies on apart from the ones we work on together."

"Are these Good Works another one of my duties?" she asked.

He nodded. "The entire country will follow what you choose to do."

She stared off into the horizon. The twinkle returned to her eyes and loosened the knot in his stomach. "I could bring a Formula 1 race to Vernonia."

Niko dug the oars into the water to take a deeper stroke. He needed to steer her away from that idea. "Grand Prix is an interesting thought, but I'm sure you will come up with something else."

"Think about it." Two little lines formed above her

nose. "A race sponsored by a long lost American princess would give Vernonia lots of good press and tourist dollars."

"Most princesses work on things like education or health issues. That's why they call them Good Works."

She slid him a furtive glance. "I'm not like other princesses."

"I know, but you're working on that, right?" he half teased.

She didn't look amused. "Cars and racing are my things. Why can't I combine those with Good Works?"

"Having your own interests is fine, but you are still Her Royal Highness Crown Princess Isabel of Vernonia," Niko explained. "You will become a role model."

Isabel frowned. "So you don't think I can be a role model now."

"You'll be a stronger role model if you take your contemporary outlook and make it more appealing to the masses."

Isabel crossed her arms over her chest. "So I'm not appealing, either."

"That is not what I meant."

"What do you mean?" Her voice rose and not in a good way. "You talk about wanting to modernize Vernonia yet you cling to all these outdated stereotypes. You should show Vernonians that things are changing."

"Show, yes, but we cannot shock people into progress."

"My working as a mechanic is not shocking. Neither is bringing an F1 race to Vernonia. It's a pretty darn good idea actually. You shouldn't dismiss it without at least considering it."

"Change takes time." Niko knew Izzy had a stubborn side. He didn't want her to dig in her heels about this. "Before you become too attached to this race idea, consider what Julianna might do if she were in your shoes."

Isabel winced. "You want me to be like Jules?"

"She would be an excellent role model for you to emulate when it comes to the choice of Good Works."

Anger flared in Isabel's eyes. "I don't know what Jules might choose to do, but I know something she wouldn't do."

"What?" he asked.

Isabel grabbed one of the oars and threw it into the water on the starboard side of the rowboat.

Forget stubborn. Now she was being ungracious. Niko reached for it. "You're not being nice."

Isabel stood. "I'm only getting started."

He didn't know what she had in mind, but her voice had an edge to it he hadn't heard before. "Sit down before you fall overboard."

She leaned over toward one side. The boat tipped.

"Isa—"

Niko splashed into the cold water. Isabel, too.

He tried to reach her so he could help her back into

the rowboat, but she dodged his arm. "Come here," he shouted.

She lay on her back and kicked, putting more distance between them. "Jules is my friend, but I don't want to be like her. I want to be me."

With that, Isabel swam toward shore. Each long, graceful stroke took her farther and farther away from him. The security detail on shore scrambled into the water.

Niko gathered the oars, climbed back into the rowboat and watched her with a sinking feeling in his gut.

The honeymoon wasn't scheduled to end for two more days, but it was definitely over now. Niko rowed back to shore. He had no idea what this meant long-term. He wasn't sure he wanted to know.

CHAPTER ELEVEN

THE next day, an overcast sky hid the afternoon sun. Emil, the castle butler and Uncle Frank's cousin, predicted rain would fall on the parade. The weather wasn't ideal for the village's celebration, but it matched Izzy's mood perfectly.

She had barely spoken ten words to Niko since the incident on the lake. He'd slept in another room last night. He'd skipped breakfast this morning. She hadn't seen him until an hour ago when they left the castle for the village.

An icy silence filled the limousine during the drive. Izzy didn't know what to say to Niko. If she had ever had a disagreement with a guy she dated, she just never went out with him again. Fighting seemed like such a waste of time and energy. But that meant she'd never learned how to deal with conflict.

"Ready?" Niko asked as they took their seats in a horse drawn carriage decorated with fresh, colorful wildflowers.

The space on the bench seat between her and Niko felt as wide as the infield at the Indy 500. She forced a smile for the villagers' benefit. "No, but I think it's too late for them to cancel the parade. Unless Emil is right about a rainstorm."

"The people would be disappointed," Niko said flatly.

Villagers lined the narrow street, waving every imaginable size of Vernonian flags. "It reminds me of the Fourth of July parades back home except there isn't any red, white and blue."

"Each of the colors in the Vernonian flag has meaning. The light blue represents the sky, that our country may be as tranquil as the heavens above. The white stands for purity of heart and action. The yellow crest is the color of the sun, as it faithfully raises each day we pledge our loyalty to remain faithful to one another."

"That's beautiful," she said. "I don't know whether the story behind the colors of the U.S. flag is fact or fiction."

"If this was the Fourth of July, you would be eating hot dogs and hamburgers."

"Yeah, but the grilled spiced meat with onions cooking in that booth over there smell pretty good." She motioned to her designer skirt, cropped jacket, hat, gloves and high heels. "Though I would never be dressed like this. I'd have on jeans or shorts and a T-shirt."

"People came to see a princess today."

A Sachestian princess. The future queen. Anxiety fluttered. "I know."

She didn't want to disappoint them which was why she'd worn the clothing the maid had put out this morning. But even though she wore fancy clothing and answered to Her Royal Highness or ma'am, she was still the same Izzy inside. Nothing would change that.

Not a new wardrobe.

Not princess lessons.

Not a prince for a husband.

If only Niko understood that and could accept her as she was. Then their marriage might stand a chance. As it was…

Izzy adjusted her white gloves and focused on the people. The friendly smiles and waves from the villagers lessened her apprehension.

Ahead of their carriage, a pickup truck pulled a float carrying folk dancers dressed in traditional costumes. Music played by the marching band behind them filled the air. The boom of the bass drum matched the beat of her heart, a combination of the anxiety over the parade and her marriage.

She waved and smiled, as did Niko. But once again, his smile didn't reach his eyes. He remained silent, as did she. The villagers didn't seem to notice the strain between them. For that, Izzy was thankful.

The carriage came to a sudden stop. The driver set the brake. The two horses whinnied and pawed at the ground.

She noticed the float in front of them had stopped, too.

A local official rushed up to the carriage.

"What is happening?" Niko asked.

"The truck pulling the dancers' float has broken down, Your Royal Highness. We are summoning a mechanic."

Finally, Izzy thought, a chance to be useful. She hopped out of the carriage without any assistance from the security.

Niko followed her off. He stood next to her on the street. "What are you doing?"

She straightened her skirt. "They need a mechanic."

"You are a princess."

"Why can't I be both?" Izzy kept her voice low and a smile on her face. Jules would be so proud.

"It's inappropriate," Niko said, under his breath. "Unacceptable."

She removed her white gloves. "The parade must go on."

"Don't do this, Isabel. The people—"

"I am more like these people than you."

"No, you are not. Do not do this. There will be consequences."

"You're overreacting." Izzy thought about Princess Diana, who had been known as the People's Princess. Diana hadn't been given that title by sitting around and waiting for others to take charge. "I know what I'm doing."

He pressed his lips together.

Annoyance flared. "Would you please stop with that royal stiff upper lip thing you always do?"

His eyes darkened. "I don't know what you're talking about."

As Izzy hurried past the float with the dancers, she tucked her gloves into a pocket on her jacket.

An official fell into step with her. "How may I be of assistance, Your Royal Highness?"

"I'm going to see if I can fix the truck."

The man gasped. "We need a mechanic, ma'am."

Izzy raised her chin. "I am a mechanic."

And a damn good one, she thought.

The hood of the truck was already opened. Several people stood there contemplating the inner working of the vehicle.

"The engine didn't die," the truck driver said, scratching his balding head. "But the truck won't move."

"Excuse me," Izzy said, nudging her way through several festively clad dancers.

The group parted for her like the Red Sea. The scent of motor oil from the engine smelled better than perfume, but the truck had to be older than her. She climbed on the grill to look inside. It even had a carburetor. She checked the hoses and the fan belt. Grease dirtied her hands. One of her fingernails chipped. For the truck to just stop moving, something must have broken or come undone. And that was when she saw it. "A-ha. A broken throttle linkage to the carburetor."

Izzy sensed rather than felt Niko move right behind her.

He whispered, "Let someone else fix it."

"I know how to do it." She looked at those standing around. No one was smiling. "I need a pair of glasses. Sunglasses would work, too. Wire rimmed ones would probably be easiest. I promise to replace them."

One of the officials stepped forward. Disapproval filled his eyes, but he handed her a pair of glasses.

"Thank you." Izzy broke off one of the earpieces.

She threaded the piece through the linkage and twisted the ends together. She lowered the hood and stepped out of the way. "That should do it."

The truck driver shifted into gear. The truck rolled forward. "It worked."

The crowd was so quiet. No one cheered or waved flags. The people stared with a look of shock and disappointment in their eyes. She didn't understand. The parade could continue, but the only ones smiling at her were the children.

There will be consequences.

An old man shook his head. Two men frowned. A group of women whispered and motioned to her.

Izzy hurried back to the carriage and climbed aboard. She brushed her dirty hands together, wishing for a wet wipe. Grease stained her skirt.

A crisp white handkerchief appeared at the end of Niko's extended arm. His tight jaw and narrowed lips told her he wasn't happy. He could join the club.

Izzy took it and wiped her hands. "I don't see why everyone is so upset."

The carriage lurched forward.

"People came expecting to see a princess, someone special not like themselves." Niko snatched the handkerchief from her and wiped her chin. "But instead they see a woman who doesn't care enough to keep her clothes clean for them. Your hands are dirty. Your fingernails chipped. They feel cheated and disrespected."

Heat burned her cheeks. "I wanted to win the people over by helping."

"You could have accomplished that by walking out to the crowd and visiting with them while the truck was repaired. You could have told someone what to fix instead of insisting you do it yourself."

Humiliation flowed through her veins. She glanced down at her still dirty hands and put on her gloves. "You never told me."

"You never gave me a chance, but can you honestly say you would have listened to me?"

She stiffened with shame, but she continued to wave and smile at the villagers along the parade route. The people, however, didn't return the gesture. "This is who I am," she said quietly.

"You are not a commoner, Isabel." Niko waved at a small girl holding a green balloon. "You are the special woman willing to sacrifice your future, your dreams for her country. You are Royal Highness Crown Princess Isabel of Vernonia. It's time you started acting like her."

As she blew a kiss to a little boy sitting on his father's shoulders and holding a small American flag, Niko's words sunk in. A horrible realization washed over her. "You're never going to accept Izzy Poussard, mechanic and race car fanatic."

"It is time for you to leave the past behind and move on," he said.

"The way you want Vernonia to move on without changing your own outdated views."

"I told you change takes time." His gaze met hers. "I know what Vernonia needs."

My father believes Vernonia needs an heir. He wants one as soon as possible.

Her worst fear was turning out to be true. Niko hadn't wanted to go on a honeymoon to start the marriage off right. He'd only wanted her to get pregnant. No wonder things were so great in the bedroom, but not anywhere else.

This marriage had been a sham from the very beginning.

"You never really wanted a wife." Her insides twisted. "The only thing you want is a baby. You said you'd be honest, but you're no different than your father."

The silent ride from the village seemed to push Isabel farther away from Niko. He longed to reach out to her, but he couldn't. Not when he was so on edge. He'd never been in a situation like this. Anger, frustration, hurt and something unfamiliar he couldn't define swirled inside him. He needed to keep the emotions in check so he wouldn't lose control.

The limousine stopped in front of the castle. Niko stepped out. Isabel followed. Without a look back, she marched into the castle like a soldier on a mission.

Niko felt the same way. He followed her up to their bedroom and closed the door.

She took a deep breath. "This was all a big mistake."

Relief washed over him. She understood that she had let him down—and had let herself down. That explained her outburst. "Send a formal apology to the village. Tell them you're sorry for your lapse in judgment and inappropriate behavior during the parade today."

Her mouth gaped. "I'm not talking about the parade. I'm talking about our marriage."

All the emotion he'd been holding in exploded like a volcano. Anger surged. "You mean the marriage I was trapped into?"

"It's not like I wanted to marry you!" she lashed back. Her eyes glistened, but she didn't cry. "I want to be in an equal partnership with someone who will accept me, love me for who I am, not for who they want me to be. I want to be a wife, not a duty or obligation that has to be juggled with a bunch of other responsibilities. I don't want to be married to a man who keeps me at arm's length and only wants to have sex with me because he needs an heir."

Each of her emotionally charged words jabbed at him like pummeling fists. Niko could barely think above the uproar in his head. He didn't know if he could give her what she wanted. He resented her for wanting more already. "We just got married. We've only known each other a few weeks. This was never supposed to be a starry-eyed romance or a love match."

Her mouth twisted. "You've made it quite clear that's not what you want."

"Would you rather I lie and tell you what you want to hear?"

"I want you to be honest, Niko."

"I have been honest!" His voice sounded harsh, raw. He didn't know how to handle all this emotion. "I've tried to be honest with you since we met."

"It's my turn to be honest." Her gaze bored into him. "I'm not sure I can do this state marriage the way I thought I could. I just don't get this whole duty thing. I'm not sure I ever will."

His heart skipped a beat. "Isabel—"

She held up her hand, and he stopped talking.

"I'm never going to be the perfect princess you want for Vernonia." Her voice cracked. "I don't want to be a royal broodmare, either. I need time to think, to figure out what I want to do."

His lungs constricted. He struggled to breathe. "Do?"

"Whether I remain in Vernonia or return home to Charlotte."

Her words stunned him. Whatever difficulties had come between them, Niko knew Isabel had a large heart. She must really be hurting to consider returning to the U.S. "We agreed to figure things out together."

"The only place we're really together is in bed. Sex won't solve anything." The pain in her pretty eyes was undeniable. "We need to figure things out on our own before we can do anything together."

"No."

"It's time for you to go."

Unfamiliar panic flared. He didn't want to leave her. Lose her.

Feelings overwhelmed him, overcame his tentative control. In a swift move, he pulled her to him and crushed his lips against hers in a brutal kiss. Isabel didn't back away, but kissed him back. He didn't know the right words to express how he felt, didn't even understand how he felt, but he could show her. Niko poured all his emotions, all his feelings into the kiss until she clung to him.

Finally, regretfully, he drew back. He saw the same passion, the same confusion in her eyes that he felt. "I'll leave you now."

The weeks passed. Izzy remained at her family's castle. The only contact with Niko had been a month ago when a package of documents arrived transferring her father's estate, including ownership of the castle, to her. He hadn't emailed, texted or called her.

Maybe that was why she'd felt so tired and crummy lately. A broken heart. She hoped not.

Izzy hadn't figured out what she should do or where she should go. She couldn't stop thinking about that kiss Niko had left her with. His desperation had been so real, palpable, but if that was the case, if that was how he felt, why hadn't he contacted her?

She decided to stay in Sachestia a little longer to learn more about her father's family. She spent her days visiting the various villages in the area, meeting the people and even working the land as a harvest came around. Not exactly princess behavior, but slowly she began making some inroads with the villagers after the parade fiasco.

The older generation seemed to have fixed ideas like Niko about what royalty should do, but the teenagers and children didn't. They accepted her as she was. They wanted to know more about cars so she offered to teach them about basic car repairs. Fifteen children showed up. The village official had told her to expect five.

During the class, she felt light-headed and had to sit down. One of the students, the daughter of the village's doctor, insisted Izzy see her father right away. Before she could say a word, the children were escorting her across the street to a small medical clinic.

The doctor turned out to be in his mid-forties, very nice and quite thorough with the tests he ran. She sat in the exam room alone waiting for the results.

"I have good news, ma'am," he said on his return.

"I'm healthy?"

"Yes, but you're also pregnant."

Pregnant. With Niko's child. She sat frozen, too stunned to feel anything.

"How…?" She'd been so overwhelmed and stressed that she hadn't thought about her period. It had never been very regular before, but still… "I mean, I know how, but how far along?"

"I'd like to do an ultrasound so we can figure that out."

Izzy nodded, unable to speak. She could easily narrow down the dates to the week, the only week they'd spent together as husband and wife. That would make her seven, possibly eight weeks pregnant.

The royal broodmare had fulfilled her duty without even trying. Izzy didn't know whether to laugh or cry.

A baby.

A surge of love, strong and protective, flowed through her. She hugged her stomach. If only Niko were…

But he wasn't.

Would you rather I lie and tell you what you want to hear?

No, but still Izzy's heart splintered. The baby she carried was as much his as hers. Keeping the news from him would be cruel and unforgivable.

As soon as the ultrasound was completed, she would call him with the news. Even if he were the last person she wanted to talk to.

Niko sat behind his desk in his office. The words on the monitor blurred. He rubbed his eyes.

The long hours were starting to catch up with him. But work was the only thing that had filled the void these past weeks.

Not void, he corrected. The empty space next to him in bed. But work couldn't touch the empty space in his heart.

Niko's forehead throbbed. He massaged his temples to stave off another headache.

In the outer office where Jovan worked, a phone rang.

Niko looked up, stretching the cords of muscles in his neck. When he finished he saw his aide standing in front of his desk.

"There is a call for you, sir," Jovan said.

"You deal with it."

"It's Princess Isa—"

Niko grabbed the receiver off his desk. "Isabel."

His aide walked out of the office with a smile and closed the door.

"Hey, Niko."

Hearing the sound of her voice for the first time in seven weeks filled him with an odd mixture of relief and regret. "You received the estate transfer paperwork."

"Yes, thank you."

Uncomfortable silence filled the line.

He'd always known what to say, especially when it came to women, but Isabel left him as tongue-tied as a schoolboy with a crush on his teacher, instead of a crown prince who had dated some of the most beautiful women in the world. But only one woman haunted his dreams now.

"I—"

"I didn't call about that," she said at the same time.

"Excuse me," he said. "Tell me why you phoned."

"I—I'm pregnant. With twins."

Her news stunned him. "Twins."

"Yes," she said. "An heir and a spare."

He would have laughed except for the serious edge to her voice.

"I hope you are happy," she said, her voice devoid of any emotion.

"I'm thrilled." And he was. The pregnancy would get them back on track. "I'll be there tomorrow to bring you home."

"This doesn't change anything."

"But you're pregnant."

"Pregnant, Niko, not sick," she said. "At least not yet. The doctor warned me morning sickness could happen."

"You need to be seen by a physician at the university hospital."

"I'm satisfied and happy with the village doctor."

"But—"

"I'm staying here, but I thought you should know about the babies."

At least she was in Sachestia and hadn't returned to the United States. For that he was grateful. She sounded different, more mature. The pregnancy? he wondered. "Thank you."

"I'd rather the news remain within the family and close members of the staff until the first trimester, just in case I miscarry. You never know what might happen this early."

His chest ached. He wanted to be with her. "Is the doctor concerned?"

"No, but I'd rather not have to deal with something like that publicly."

Good thinking. "I understand."

"Thanks." She cleared her voice. Perhaps she wasn't so unaffected by this as she sounded. "My next appointment is in a couple of weeks if you want to come."

"Yes," he said without hesitation, thankful for the invitation. "I will make sure my calendar is clear that day."

"I'll send the information to Jovan."

To Jovan. Niko's insides twisted. He hated this wall between them. "Fine."

"Okay, then."

He wasn't ready to let her go. "If you need anything…"

"Goodbye, Niko. See you at the appointment."

She hung up before he could reply.

Emotion roiling through him, Niko rose from his desk, exited his office and made the familiar walk to the king's office.

His father's assistant looked up from his computer monitor. "The king—"

"Will see me now." Niko walked past the royal guards, opened the door himself and entered his father's office.

King Dmitar hung up the phone. "Niko—"

"Isabel is pregnant with twins."

"Even better than I hoped for." A wide grin lit up Dmitar's face. "When does she arrive home?"

"She is staying in Sachestia. She must still be trying to figure things out."

"Have you figured anything out?" his father asked, as if remembering what Niko had told him when he returned alone from the honeymoon.

"I don't like fighting the way we did. I want to be with her, but she may not want what I can offer her."

"You have a duty—"

"To Vernonia."

"You also have a duty to your wife and your children." Dmitar rose and walked around to the front of his desk. "I know I've told you to control your emotions and do what is best for Vernonia, but I'm not sure that is the advice I want you to give my grandchildren."

"What?" Niko stared, sure he hadn't heard his father correctly.

"A united Vernonia has been the goal of kings for centuries, but united at what cost? Stefan's life? All the other sons and daughters and mothers and fathers who died during the conflict?" Regret filled Dmitar's voice and darkened his eyes. "I wouldn't allow my own feelings to influence my decision-making. I kept telling myself what my father had told me. Emotion is a weakness. So I brushed aside my concerns over you and Stefan. Your mother's worries, too. Now every time I look at the damn map of Vernonia on the wall over there, I wonder."

"Wonder what?" Niko asked, barely able to breathe.

"If I'd let the Separatists go, would Stefan still be alive today?"

Niko had never heard his father like this before. He stepped forward, unsure what to do. "Father—"

"That's why I had no choice but to see this through to the end and make sure you and Izzy remained married. I have to know if a united Vernonia is worth all the sacrifices made. Especially your mother's broken and grief-filled heart."

"It will be, Father."

"I regret losing Stefan, but you are a good ruler, Niko. You will be a fine king."

He stood taller. "Thank you."

"But I am concerned," Dmitar admitted. "You speak of modernizing the country, yet you hold a few old-fashioned notions. Especially your ideas of what a princess should be."

Isabel had said something similar. Uncomfortable, Niko shifted his weight between his feet.

His father continued. "Izzy might not be a clone of every other princess out there, but she can still be who she is and the love of your life. The two are not mutually exclusive even if your marriage was an arranged match."

Niko considered his father's words. "The people—"

"She's more than made up for the lapse at the parade. The people have forgiven her. They love her."

"You've been spying on her."

Dmitar raised a brow. "And you haven't?"

"I may have sent a couple royal guards north to Sachestia on a brief...scouting trip."

"Thought so." Dmitar laughed. "You've always done whatever was asked of you, but it's time you were selfish. Forget everything else. Save your marriage and keep Izzy in Vernonia, not through manipulation as I attempted, but through love and loyalty freely given."

"You want me to go after her."

"That's your decision, not mine," Dmitar said. "But if you have any feelings for her, do not allow anything to keep you apart."

Niko had never allowed himself to be vulnerable with anyone before Izzy. He'd opened up with her, but she wanted him to be vulnerable beyond the bedroom, to trust her in a way he'd never trusted anyone before. He didn't know if he could do that. "What if I still don't know how I feel?"

"Figure it out. Fast." His father's gaze rested on a

photograph of Stefan that hung on the wall. "Life can change in an instant, Niko. You don't want to have to live with that regret. Trust me."

CHAPTER TWELVE

Figure it out. Fast.

His father's words replayed in Niko's mind the rest of the day and evening. He wanted to figure it out. *Had* to figure it out.

Later that night, he tossed and turned, drifting in and out of sleep. Images of Isabel, twins, his father and Stefan collided into a half-awake, half-dreamlike state. The bed lurched, as if someone had shaken the entire wooden frame. Or bumped into it in the dark.

Could it be Isabel had figured things out herself and returned on her own? Hope mushroomed in his chest like a nuclear blast.

Niko bolted upright, instantly awake. He glanced to the spot on his left. Still empty.

Disappointment squeezed his heart. So far the only thing Niko had figured out was that he missed her. He missed her smile, her laughter, her kisses, her warmth. He even missed the grease under her nails. He missed every fiber of her being, especially the twin babies she now carried.

Wait. He looked around the room. If Isabel hadn't shaken the bed... Something else must have caused it.

As if on cue, a knock sounded on his door.

"Enter," Niko said.

Jovan in a dark navy robe and slippers rushed into the room, concern etched on his face. "There was an earthquake. They believe 6.8 on the Richter scale. The epicenter is in the north in Sachestia."

Niko's gut knotted with fear. "Isabel?"

"We cannot contact the castle. All communications in the area are down."

He jumped out of bed and rushed to his closet. "I must go."

"The helicopter will be here in forty minutes."

"Too long." He changed out of his pajama bottoms and into clothing. "Activate the emergency plan."

"Notifications went out as soon as confirmation of the earthquake was received."

His emergency response project was working properly, but he didn't care. All his thoughts were focused on Isabel. On her well-being. Her safety. She had to be all right. And the babies. He buttoned his long-sleeved shirt. "I am going to see my father. I will meet you at the helipad."

He ran through the hallway toward his parents' suite.

Niko's stomach churned with fear and worry. Isabel could be lying in the rubble of the castle, injured and alone. If anything happened to her...

Life can change in an instant, Niko. You don't want to have to live with that regret. Trust me.

No regrets. Niko understood that part. He only hoped he wasn't too late.

He didn't know if he could give Isabel the kind of marriage she wanted, but he would give all he could, and love her. He hoped, if she were safe and gave him the chance, what he offered would be enough for her.

"Fill the truck with food, water and blankets," Izzy instructed her staff, who bustled to and fro from the castle carrying supplies. Some were dressed. Others wore their pajamas and robes. A chill hung in the night air. The sun wouldn't rise for at least two more hours. She zipped up her jacket. "Hurry. We need to get up to the village ASAP."

"ASAP?" Emil asked.

"As soon as possible." She bent over to pick up a case of water. "I want to leave in five minutes."

"No, ma'am," Emil took the case from her hands and placed it into the back of a truck. "I will see that the supplies arrive safely. You must stay here."

He sounded so much like Uncle Frank.

"I'm pregnant, not sick." Isabel had told a handful of the staff members what was going on in confidence. She patted her tummy. "The twins are safe and warm in there. I know what I can and can't do."

Emil eyed her warily. "The doctor—"

"Said I could continue all my normal activities. Helping others in need is a normal activity."

Worry creased Emil's brow. "Prince Niko would not agree."

"Then it's good he's not here." Just hearing his name made the emotions swirl inside Izzy. Her eyes implored

Emil. "I'm sure supplies and help will be coming, but we're the closest to the village. We must go."

Emil nodded, respect gleaming in his eyes. "Your father and Franko would be proud of you, ma'am. I believe Prince Niko would be, too."

She doubted the latter, but appreciated Emil's words anyway. "Thanks."

Duty was important to her husband. He seemed afraid to let himself go and lose control, or rather had been afraid until their fight after the parade. Izzy couldn't forget the kiss he'd left her with. Full of emotion, brutal and punishing, the kiss seemed to betray the way he was also so strict with himself as prince. She was beginning to wonder if he'd held back his affection from her for that reason. Heaven knew she'd held herself back. She'd never told Niko she loved him. A mix of fear, pride and stubbornness had kept her from declaring her feelings.

There's a lot at stake, Izzy. Don't let that stubborn streak of yours get in the way.

Maybe she had been too stubborn. But there wasn't time for that now. She jumped into the truck. "Let's go."

Isabel's castle was deserted. No vehicles remained. It looked as if a tornado had ripped through the pantry and linen closets. Broken vases, glasses and sculptures. Tipped over bookcases and display cabinets. But no bodies. No blood.

Relief flowed over Niko.

Isabel must have evacuated and taken the staff with her, but where?

There were so many villages he couldn't begin to guess where she might be. He prayed she would remain safe wherever she was.

Hours later, Niko stepped through the rubble of one mountain village with a two-year-old child in his arms. The boy had cuts and bruises, but thankfully no broken bones.

The boy cried. "Mama."

Niko didn't know what to say to the distraught child, who had been sleeping under his bed when the earthquake hit. A neighbor had heard the boy's screams and pulled him from the rubble. They were still searching for the rest of his family. "They are looking for your mama."

The big, fat tears stopped rolling down the child's face. He stared up at Niko. "Papa?"

"They are looking for him, too."

Gratitude filled the child's eyes. He rested his head against Niko's chest.

Niko swallowed around the lump of emotion in his throat.

A nurse appeared in sweat-stained surgical scrubs. "I'll take him, sir."

Reluctantly he handed the injured boy to the nurse. "His family is missing. Please…"

Don't lose him was what Niko wanted to say given the number of people needing help and the chaos around here.

She nodded in understanding. "We will take good care of him, sir."

With that the nurse hurried into a hospital tent that had just been erected next to the medical clinic.

Help continued to arrive. The sound of helicopters and heavy machinery filled the air.

His father was in another village helping, but Niko hoped the king saw what he saw. A united Vernonia.

Whether Separatist or Loyalist during the conflict, people worked side by side in this mountain village, searching for survivors in the rubble and helping those that had been injured. Differences in point of view no longer mattered; they were all fellow Vernonians. Niko couldn't be more proud of the people.

If only he knew where Isabel was... That she was safe...

He noticed a familiar looking man up ahead. "Emil!"

The man turned and bowed. He had a can of oil in his hand. "Sir."

"Where is Isabel?"

Emil glanced around, looking uncomfortable. "She is safe, sir."

Safe wasn't good enough. Niko wanted his wife to be with him. He felt like a better man when he was with her. The past no longer mattered. The future seemed brighter. "Take me to her. Now."

The butler led Niko back toward the medical tent. "Princess Izzy is attempting to fix the medical clinic's generator, sir. I tried to stop—"

Niko raised his hand. "I've learned nothing can stop my wife once she sets her mind upon something."

She wanted him to trust her, to let her figure out how to be a princess herself, but he hadn't known how to do that. He was ready to try now.

Emil grinned. "A true Vernonian."

"Yes, she is." And the love of my life.

Years of dirt and grime coated the clinic's generator Izzy had found in the destroyed storage area in the back of the clinic. Villagers had carried it into an open area, eager for her to fix it with the tools they'd cobbled together. Izzy doubted if the generator had run in years or if it would have run under the best of circumstances. Her determination faltered, a combination of futility and frustration. Not to mention fatigue.

No. Izzy pursed her lips. The people were counting on her. She had to do this.

Kneeling, she checked a fuel line. "Come on. Show Izzy what's not right."

"Isabel."

The sound of Niko's voice washed over her like a ray of sunshine after a morning thunderstorm. She wasn't surprised to see him here. He was the crown prince. He should be here. But the vise grip on her heart wouldn't allow Izzy to even peek in his direction. She kept focused on the motor.

"You shouldn't be here," he said firmly.

Still telling her what to do. Well, she always knew Niko wasn't Prince Charming. Izzy blew out a puff of air.

"Don't worry, your heir and spare are safe." Her voice came out harsher than she intended. "I would never do anything to risk the babies."

Izzy knew he cared about the babies. She wished he cared about her. The hurt stabbing her heart was beyond tears.

The sounds of banging, shovels and axes surrounded them.

Izzy tightened a loose coil. On the next try, the generator started. Thank goodness. She stood and wiped her hands on the coveralls that Boyd had sent her with an embroidered name tag that said Princess Izzy in cursive writing. A way of saying thanks. Boyd really liked his new truck.

"I know you would never intentionally put our children at risk," Niko said.

Izzy could see his feet walking toward her, and she hated that her pulse quickened.

Niko stopped. "But I cannot stand the thought of anything happening to you."

"Me?" Hope flared, but she tapped it down. She wouldn't be swayed by charm-laced words or his pretty face or his wide shoulders or blue-green... "You only married me because you had to."

"I could say the same thing about you."

At least he admitted it. She tucked the thought away and marched past him. "Come on."

He followed her as she negotiated her way around the rubble.

She picked up two shovels and handed him one. "Know how to use one of these, Highness?"

"I do."

Izzy forced herself not to look at him. With so much work to be done, she needed to remain detached. She gestured with her own shovel. "Clear the rubble from the clinic's door."

"I want to talk to you."

She shut out any awareness of him. She couldn't afford the distraction. "Not now."

"What are you doing here?" He took her elbow with one hand.

"I'm doing what we're supposed to be doing." She shrugged away from him. "Helping our people."

With that she walked away, forcing herself not to look back.

Hours passed. Izzy worked, clearing, comforting and repairing. She even managed to get another generator started.

Taking a break, she rubbed her lower back. All the bending and kneeling had taken its toll.

The sun was starting to set. It looked as if a bomb had exploded in the village square. Only a few buildings had survived intact. Most had walls missing. Some had collapsed to the ground in a heap of rubble. But help kept arriving from every direction. More survivors continued to be rescued.

Niko handed her a bottle of water. "Drink."

She thought of the children in the hospital tent. "Someone else might need it."

"You need it." He shoved the bottle into her hands. "More supplies are on the way. Aliestle, San Montico and the U.S. are sending assistance. Vernonia is not on our own. We have help, and we will recover."

"The people will need to hear you say that." She sipped from the bottle. The refreshing water slid down her dry throat. "Okay, I did need that."

"You've worked hard, Highness."

"So have you."

Izzy glanced Niko's way. His pants and jacket were ripped and dusty. Drops of red—blood?—were spattered on his sleeve. Stubble covered his dirty face. His hair was tangled.

He'd never looked more like a prince than he did now.

She swallowed a sigh and drank more water.

When she finished, Niko took her grease-covered, dirty hands in his. Her heart hammered. "You look so much like the mechanic who walked out of that garage in Charlotte and stole my heart."

Her breath caught in her throat. "What?"

His eyes shone with affection. "You are the most perfect princess I could hope to find."

"Yeah, right. I look nothing like a princess."

He gave her a lopsided grin. "Exactly."

She stared at him confused. "Huh?"

"Isabel, Izzy, Princess, Your Highness, my wife. Your name doesn't matter." Niko pointed to her heart. "What matters is here. You have the heart of a princess."

Izzy was both excited and aggravated. "So why didn't you tell me this sooner?"

"I didn't know. Maybe I wasn't ready to admit it until

today," he said. "I wanted to be honest with you, but I wasn't honest with myself. I thought I knew what I was doing with my life. I had everything mapped out, and then this strange, kind, determined woman was thrust into my way and turned everything upside down."

"Strange?"

"Strange and beautiful." His smile sent tingles shooting through her. "You changed everything and left me uncertain how to act. Until now. I realize what a tremendous gift you are."

"When Uncle Frank died I holed myself up and stuck with what was comfortable." She stared up at Niko. "You thrust me into this whole new world and I've been trying to forge a path."

Niko squeezed her hand. "You won't have to forge it alone."

Izzy looked around at the devastation, but amid the rubble she saw signs of life, of love. "I know what Vernonia means to you. The land. These people. I'm here now because I understand this duty you are so attached to."

His gaze met hers. "A duty you are attached to also."

She nodded.

"Our duty isn't only to Vernonia. It's to each other and our children." Niko's words made her heart sing. "I want you with me, Isabel. Always. I offer all that I have and all that I am. I hope that is enough."

The choice was hers. She could take what he was offering or leave it.

Izzy stared at the man in front of her. Her heart

overflowed with love. "I miss you, Niko. I let my fears and pride get in the way of us being together, but no longer. I love you. I've loved you since our wedding day. I'm not sure what my role is supposed to be, but I'm ready to embrace it. With your help, maybe I won't fall flat on my butt."

"You won't. I won't let you fall."

Niko gathered her into his arms. She went willingly, eager for his touch and his warmth. He lowered his mouth to hers, reclaiming her with a slow, hot kiss.

Her heart danced, dipping and twirling as if on a ballroom floor and not a disaster zone.

"You are the only woman I want," he said, his voice so full of love she could barely breathe. "The only one I need. I love you. I want to marry you."

Izzy sunk into his embrace. "We've already married. Twice."

"This time I want to marry you out of love, not duty or obligation. Nothing fancy. Just us." He placed his hand over her stomach with an almost reverent touch. "And these two."

"Yes! I'd like that very much." Laughter spilled from her lips. "Maybe the third time we'll get it right."

"If not, we'll try again until we do." He looked her straight in the eye. "Just so you know, I'm never letting you go, Highness."

"You can't even if you want to, Highness." She grinned. "In case you forgot, your bridal box, the key and you are mine."

EPILOGUE

Izzy cradled His Royal Highness Aleksander, the future heir to the Vernonian throne, in her arms. Contentment and peace flowed through her. The baby slept with a serene expression on his beautiful face, a face that reminded Izzy of her beloved husband. She kissed her son's tiny forehead, inhaling the baby scent she never imagined could smell so good.

Niko carefully adjusted a little blue cap on His Royal Highness Franko's head.

Her heart overflowed at the sight of her loving husband and two healthy sons. Izzy exhaled on a sigh. Life couldn't get much better.

This was only the beginning, but she understood what happily ever after meant. She was living the fairy tale and felt blessed by all she'd been given from Vernonia, her people and Niko.

"Franko is asleep," Niko said quietly, as he stared lovingly at the child in his arms.

She glanced down. "So is Alek."

Their eyes met in unspoken understanding. Between all the nursing and diapering, getting both babies to sleep at the same time was quite a coup.

Niko's gaze clouded with concern. "The noise—"

"The pediatrician assured me that we're high enough from the crowd that the decibel level won't be a problem."

"I was more worried about them waking them up."

"They eventually will need to get used to noise and the attention," she said.

"The boys are lucky to have such a knowledgeable princess as their mother." Niko's smile made her heart leap. "And I am the most fortunate man in the world to be able to call you my wife."

She winked. "Just so you know, the feeling's mutual, Highness."

Desire gleamed in his eyes. "If only we didn't have to—"

"But we do. Duty calls." She walked toward the arched balcony doors of the Parliament building. "It's time to introduce Vernonia to their new princes."

Niko smiled mischievously. "You know what I'd rather do."

He eyed her like a man lost in the desert would look at a glass of water, leaving no doubt in Izzy's mind what he wanted to do. Even with the extra weight from the babies and breasts that leaked milk at the most inopportune times, Niko desired her. But her doctor said they needed to wait two more weeks. "It won't be much longer."

Niko's gaze went to each of their sons then rested on her. "Definitely worth the wait."

"Good answer."

"I'm learning."

"Yes, you are. You can swaddle and diaper like a pro now."

"As can my father."

Dee and Bea both wanted to take active roles in the twins' daily lives. The castle had never been so busy. Izzy couldn't imagine what it would be like when the boys started walking.

"What do you think of having some princesses or some more princes in the future?" Niko asked.

She pursed her lips. "I suppose you can never have too many spares."

Niko kissed her, as she had wanted him to do. A quick brush of the lips, but it would do. For now. His blue-green eyes gazed deeply into hers. No way would she ever doubt his love for her. Not for a second.

Izzy smiled up at him. "And I know you can never have too much family."

Miracle:
TWIN BABIES

FIONA LOWE

Fiona Lowe loves to read! As a child in Papua New Guinea books were *the* entertainment, so she didn't really learn about TV until she was eight and by then her love of reading was truly entrenched.

The real world intruded on her life and she was forced to pull her nose out of a book and earn a living. Nursing became Fiona's career and her favourite areas of hospital-based nursing are midwifery, Accident & Emergency and Theatre. But she enjoys being her own boss and so she headed into community health and health education. Seeing people taking control of their own health and avoiding hospital gives her a real thrill.

Fiona currently lives in southern Victoria, Australia with her supportive husband and two gorgeous redheaded sons. In the decade it took to get published she has lived in two countries and three different cities. When she's not writing she's working with teenage girls and volunteering as a school counsellor. She enjoys playing tennis, reading, gardening, attending the theatre and is *always* planning her next holiday adventure, which always seems to end up in a book. She loves to fire up the BBQ and invite friends over for a casual meal, a swim in the pool and lots of conversation.

And like most women she juggles way too many balls and falls in a heap now and then. Luckily she has a generous husband who picks her up, dusts her down and suggests she 'go read a book' for a bit to recharge.

Fiona would love you to visit her at www.fionalowe.com.

CHAPTER ONE

OXYGEN stats are dropping! Tube him!
More blood, he's bleeding out!
Flatlining. Stand clear, now!

A lone kookaburra's raucous laugh vibrated the hot, torpid summer afternoon air, mocking Nick Dennison's thoughts. Thoughts that were firmly fixed in the past, over one and half years ago before everything in his life had gone pear-shaped. Back in a time when being a doctor had defined him and life had been work, and work had been his life.

Resting back on his haunches after being bent over pulling weeds, he pushed against the trowel and stood up, stretching his back. Sweat ran down his cheeks and he wiped his face against the tight sleeve of his T-shirt, leaving a trail of rich black earth against the soft cotton.

Through the shimmer of the eucalypt-oil heat haze he could see in the distance the small fishing town of Port Bathurst, affectionately known by the locals as Port. Snuggled into the curve of white sand and turquoise water, protected on one side by a treacherous reef and on the other side by a granite-flecked mountain, Port was a glorious work of nature and far from the man-made inner-city life he'd always known.

A wet nose nuzzled his ankle as a ball dropped next to his foot. He glanced down at the intelligent and loving eyes of his blue heeler. 'Have you rounded up the chooks yet, Turbo?'

The dog cocked his head to the side, picked up the ball and sat down, hope and expectation clear in his expression.

Nick rubbed the cattle dog's black ears. 'I take it that's a yes.' He accepted the saliva-covered ball and hurled it off into the bracken, watching the dog tear after it. He had once talked to a hundred people a day—now he was conversing with a dog and talking to his vegetables. He'd craved solitude and simplicity for a long time. Now he finally had it.

He heard the phone ringing through the open window of his cottage and instinctively glanced at his watch. Tuesday. Five o'clock. His mother would have just got in from her midweek ladies' tennis match. He let the phone ring out. Being asked a hundred questions about his health and his lack of future plans wasn't conversation.

He grabbed a shovel and started spreading manure, losing himself in the joy of being able to do physical work again, closing his mind to everything except the rhythm of the movement.

Dr Kirby Atherton jogged down the long Port Bathurst pier just as the last tinges of orange faded from the cloud-studded sky. Another hot day was on its way, which would make the holidaymakers visiting town happy, but distress many of her elderly patients. She'd only been in town a few weeks but her early morning run was part of her routine. She lacked control over many things in her life, but keeping fit—*that* she could control. Running both exhausted and exhilarated her and helped keep the demons at bay.

'Morning, Doc.' A wide grin sliced across a weather-beaten face.

Kirby jogged on the spot next to a stack of crayfish pots and looked down at Garry Braithwaite, sluicing his fishing boat. 'Morning, Garry.'

'Everyone calls me Gaz, love.'

She noted his request for next time she greeted him. Acclimatising to Port was a lesson in letting go of city ways and shortening every long name and lengthening every short one. 'Good catch?'

'Not bad.' He indicated a large white plastic trough filled with crawling crustaceans. 'These beauties will be in Japan before you're in bed tonight.'

'That's amazing.' She glanced behind her at the fish co-op which was ablaze with lights. This was its busiest time of day as it accepted the catches of the local fleet. She turned back, a wistful tone in her voice. 'Are they all going to Japan? Not even a few to the farmers' market?'

'Just the ones the co-op rejects. I've got about five.' He started to wind up the hose, his expression cheeky. 'Do you have a special dinner guest tonight, Doc? Perhaps you should talk to Deano and get some abalone.'

Kirby ignored the inference. In some ways coming to Port had been like stepping back in time. It appeared to be the small town's opinion that no matter how qualified, successful or independent a woman was, if she was young and single she must be looking for a husband. A few months ago Kirby might have agreed. 'Save me a small cray, Gaz, and I'll catch you at the market in half an hour.'

She turned and switched on her MP3 player, and with her feet matching the thumping bass beat she ran toward the

aroma of freshly brewed coffee, the sweet smell of fruit
muffins straight out of the oven and the scent of rich brown
earth clinging to freshly picked produce.

She'd been trying to get to the market for the last three
Saturdays but each time a sick patient had derailed her plans.
Coming to Port was supposed to be the commencement of her
GP training but within a week of starting as the town doctor,
her mentor had fallen ill. Without supervision, Kirby was
flying by the seat of her pants.

It was still early in the season but if the last weeks had been
a typical Port Bathurst summer then she really needed some
extra help as well as a mentor. She didn't want to have to move
again and find another GP programme, and returning to
Melbourne was *not* an option. Surely there was an experienced doctor with a family who wanted to have an idyllic
summer by the sea?

But Port Bathurst wasn't Lorne or Sorrento, it didn't have
designer clothing shops, the mobile phone coverage was inter-
mittent and the dial-up internet was really more down than up.
The glory days of it being a gold-rush port had faded. Today
it sat at the end of a very long road, with a large chunk of wild-
erness between it and the nearest town. Although all these
things had been part of the charm that had drawn Kirby to the
historic town, it seemed to put most people off. No one had
answered her advertisement.

Kirby surveyed the slowly building crowd. It was still early
so there was a marked absence of teenagers but plenty of
empty-nesters clutching well-planned lists, examining the
fresh produce and enthusiastically haggling over prices.
Toddlers and preschoolers full of energy zipped up and down
between stalls, way ahead of their half-asleep parents. A man

in his thirties walked past, pride radiating off him as he held his wife's hand and wore a baby sling on his chest, his newborn snuggled against him fast asleep.

Family is everything. She steeled herself against Anthony's uncompromising voice but it wasn't enough to stop the ache that throbbed inside her whenever she glimpsed such a scene. She swallowed against the tightness in her throat, rolled her shoulders back and kept walking. Forget eating healthy—right now she needed hazelnut coffee and a hot jam donut.

She unexpectedly paused, derailed in her quest by the sight of an old wooden trestle table groaning under the weight of bountiful vegetables. Arranged in groups for effect, the vivid colours of nature demanded attention. The red and green skins of the capsicums shone, the plump white ends of spring onions contrasted stunningly with the healthy dark green tails, and the ruby tomatoes promised an old-fashioned, rich flavour. The vividness of the colours astounded her and she was struck by how lush and enticing everything looked. These vegetables glowed with good health and were positively sexy.

'Can I help you?'

The deep voice vibrated the air around her, moving it across her skin like a silk caress and leaving behind a tingling trail of unmet need. Completely stunned by her body's reaction to a disembodied voice, she glanced up.

Emerald-green eyes, the colour of the bay, gazed down at her, swirling with hints of blue and dancing with undiluted charm. An indistinct memory stirred.

'Anything take your fancy?'

You. She bit off the word that thundered hard and fast through her head and found her voice. 'I've never seen vegetables like this before. The colours are amazing.'

He smiled and dimples carved into his cheeks, seeming to darken his early morning stubble. Surprisingly deep lines for a man who looked to be in his early thirties bracketed a wide mouth, and unexpected fine lines radiated from his eyes toward short dark hair streaked with silver. 'Thanks. They're my first crop of organic vegetables so I feel like a proud dad with his children.'

She raised her brows. 'Except you're selling them.'

He grinned. 'Every kid has to go out and make their way in the world.'

She laughed. He was the most gorgeous farmer she'd ever met. Not that he really looked like a farmer despite the fact he had a cattle dog sitting quietly beside him. There was no sign of a battered hat and his pressed stone-coloured shorts contrasted with a fresh blue-and-white-striped short-sleeved shirt—smart, casual weekender clothes, the type that a man of the city would wear. A gym-buffed man of the city.

Working out in a gym could have given him his broad chest and wide shoulders but not the sun-kissed skin. Skin stretched over taut muscles and was covered by a smattering of golden hair which was in stark contrast to his darker head hair. No, this man's body emanated a base power generated by sheer physical hard work.

She studied his face. Something about him seemed familiar and yet nothing about him prompted recognition.

His brilliant green eyes danced at her. 'If you tell me what you're thinking about, perhaps I can suggest a vegetable to match?'

Horrified that he'd caught her out staring at him as if he was on display like his stock, she randomly pointed to a stack of vine-ripened tomatoes. 'I'll take two, please.' She noticed small white scars on the back of his hand as he reached across the table.

Long, tanned fingers picked up the red, round fruit and placed them lightly against her palm. 'I recommend you spread hot, grainy toast with the local goat's cheese in virgin olive oil, and then top it with thin slices of tomato covered with freshly ground pepper and some of my basil. You'll be licking your lips and fingers to soak up every last wondrous morsel.'

An image of him languorously licking her fingers spun through her, making her dizzy. She'd obviously been working way too hard if her mind could just shoot off on dangerous tangents like that. She'd come to Port Bathurst to start over and to protect herself, and that didn't mean melting into a puddle of lust at a stranger's feet.

'Right, thanks. Organic food and recipes, too. Awesome!' *Can you hear yourself? You sound inane.*

He shot her a crooked smile. 'Enjoy. It's the small things in life that are worth holding on to.'

'A farmer *and* a philosopher?'

A shadow flickered across his gaze for a moment before being absorbed by a world-weary smile. 'Something like that. Enjoy your weekend.' He accepted her money and turned to serve his next customer.

A flash of something akin to rejection spiked her, which was illogical and ridiculous. This wasn't a social situation. He was a stallholder and she was a customer and he had a line of customers behind her waiting to be served. *No man is worth it, remember!* Her indignant and wounded subconscious kicked her hard, reminding her of Anthony's betrayal.

Reminding her of why she'd come to Port Bathurst in the first place. A new start—keep moving forward and never look back.

But repeating her mantra didn't stop a deep line of disappointment rolling through her. A disappointment which was completely out of proportion to the situation. Man, she must be tired, but then again, working flat out for a month would do that to a girl. She tucked some flyaway strands of hair behind her ears and took a deep breath. *Just keep moving forward.* She turned and walked toward the coffee cart, needing the java jolt and sweet taste of hazelnut more than ever.

The queue for coffee was long and congenial and she chatted to people about the weather, signed a petition to save the old bridge, and listened to concerns about how the new fishing quotas would affect the town's main industry. Getting to know Port was all part and parcel of being a country GP.

'There you go, Doc. One skinny hazelnut latte, super-sized.'

'Thanks, Jade. It smells divine.' Kirby gripped the cup and headed toward a free table. She put her tomatoes and coffee down and slid into the chair. Carefully easing the tight-fitting plastic lid off the top of the cup, she admired the foamy froth, took a deep anticipatory breath and lifted the coffee to her lips.

The frantic barking of a dog and yelling voices stalled her sip and she turned sharply toward the commotion.

Jake, Gaz's ten-year-old son, came running toward her, his chest heaving and his face pinched and white. 'Dr Kirby, Dad can't breathe!'

She leapt to her feet and yelled out to Jade in the coffee cart, 'Get the St John's kit from the hall.' Then she ran, following the boy back toward his father. The crowd opened up around them, easing their passage through the closely lined stalls. She hurdled some packing cases and in the distance she could see Gaz leaning forward, coughing violently and trying to breathe.

His solid height and weight obscured the person who was helping him. Someone had his right arm around Gaz's waist and his hand pressed firmly against the fisherman's chest. Thankfully someone who obviously knew first aid. Kirby hoped he was giving a sharp blow to Garry's back at chest level.

Kirby ducked around the craft stalls, concentrating on her feet missing cables and desperately wishing for a more direct route to get to her patient. She looked up again. Gaz continued to cough, but his colour was fading from bright red to white.

As she got closer she saw the first-aider was her farmer. He'd just placed both his hands under Garry's armpits and thrust inwards. Surprise washed through her that he knew this newer and less damaging technique. Most first-aiders still used the older Heimlich manoeuvre. She prayed that whatever was choking Garry would be projected out of his mouth soon.

Just as she reached them, Garry slumped forward, his face blue. Instinctively, Kirby threw herself at him, her shoulder catching him on the chest, preventing him from falling. 'I'm—'

'Help me get him down.' The farmer's voice held an unexpected authoritative command and a tone that brooked no argument. 'I'm a doctor, just do as I say.'

Kirby staggered under the unexpected words and Gaz's weight as she tried to grab his arms. A farmer-cum-doctor? But she had no time to think about that strange combination. All her concentration was on the fisherman who struggled for every life-sustaining breath.

'Doctor!' Jade ran up clutching the first-aid backpack which Kirby immediately put on the ground and opened.

'I need the pocket mask,' the doctor and Kirby both said at the same time.

Questioning green eyes framed with thick brown lashes appraised her as she helped him lower Garry onto the ground. 'I'm Kirby Atherton, the town's doctor.'

'Excellent. I'm Nick. Let's get him onto his side and I'll try more lateral chest thrusts.' He knelt next to their patient, placing his hands firmly over the ribcage. Using his weight, he pressed with a downward and forward movement.

'I'll check his airway.' Kirby rolled a now blue Garry onto his side and put her finger inside his mouth, hoping desperately to feel a foreign object.

'Anything?' The word held hope and dread.

'Nothing.' She rolled him back, checked his carotid pulse and chest movements, and called out to Jake. 'What was Dad eating when he started choking?'

The trembling boy tried to speak. 'St-stra-strawberry. He threw it in the air and catched it in his mouth.'

'It will have lodged in his trachea.' Nick voiced her exact thought.

'Starting mouth-to-mouth.' She applied the pocket mask over Garry's mouth and lowered her head. He needed air but she had no idea if she could she manage to force any past the obstruction.

'Find me something I can put down his throat that will grip. Try the jewellery stall.'

Kirby heard Nick's mellow voice instructing Jade as she counted and puffed five breaths into the unconscious man.

The moment she raised her head, Nick applied the same pressure again over Gaz's ribs, thrusting downward and forward.

Kirby rechecked Gaz's airway, hoping to feel the firm fruit.

Her stomach rolled. 'Still nothing.' She gave Gaz another five breaths, panic starting to ripple through her. If they couldn't secure his airway soon, he'd go into cardiac arrest.

'I've got these.' Jade came running back and handed Nick a pair of long, thin pliers.

Kirby's fingers detected a faint beat. 'Pulse, weak and thready. He's going to need an emergency tracheostomy to bypass the blockage and avoid arresting. Jenny, pass me the scalpel blade.'

'Hang on a mo.' Nick spoke quietly but decisively. 'Give me half a minute with these sort of forceps and see if I grab the strawberry.'

Kirby didn't want to waste any more precious time. 'But we don't have a laryngoscope for you to visualise the trachea.'

Green eyes flashed with ready understanding. 'I've done it before in EMD.'

A blurry image played at the edge of her mind but immediately faded, overtaken by her focus on the emergency. 'What do you need me to do?'

'Steady his head for me.'

'Will do.' His confidence reassured her and she placed her hands over her patient's ears, two fingers still resting on his carotid pulse.

The scream of the ambulance's siren broke over the tense crowd, the sound both urgent and comforting as it brought the medical equipment they really needed.

'Here goes.' Nick shot her a look that said, *Nothing ventured, nothing gained*, and lowered the thin, silver pliers into the slack throat of the unconscious man. 'Can't feel anything, damn it.' His long fingers carefully controlled all the minute movements with stunning expertise.

Kirby kept her gaze on Nick's hand, willing it to find the obstruction. Time spiralled out, each second an agonising wait. Garry's pulse suddenly faltered under her fingers. 'No pulse. Get out now. I'm starting CPR.'

Nick immediately pulled his left arm back, and a soft, half-dissolved strawberry hung limply from the tip of the forceps. 'Got it. Roll him over.'

Kirby moved her patient's head to the side as he started coughing violently and vomited up a stream of pale pink liquid onto the ground.

Relief surged through her as she checked his pulse. 'Pulse back, patient breathing.' She looked up into Nick's face, as the worry lines on the bridge of his nose faded. She experienced a sense of déjà vu. 'Lucky save.'

He nodded, a slow smile appearing through the stubble on his jaw. 'Very lucky.'

'Kirby!'

She turned to see Theo and Richard, the ambulance officers, running toward her. 'Great timing, guys. We need all your gear.' She grabbed the black oxygen cylinder with its distinctive white top and quickly unravelled the pale green tubing. Gently, she lifted Garry's head and looped the elastic over his ears, adjusting the Hudson mask. 'This will help you breathe.'

The sick and bewildered man gripped her arm. 'Thanks, Doc.' His voice rasped out the words. 'I couldn't breathe… It scared the hell out of me…worse than being on the boat in a storm.'

She smiled down at him. 'I'm glad I was here, but really it was Dr…' She realised she didn't know his surname. 'Nick? I didn't catch your surname.'

He finished attaching the Lifepak electrodes and scanned the ECG tracing before looking up and speaking straight to Garry. 'I'm Dr Nick Dennison, and I'm just glad I was two stalls over.'

Nick Dennison. Kirby did a double-take so fast she almost cricked her neck, the name having instant recognition in her brain. But the man in front of her looked nothing like how she remembered Melbourne City Hospital's up-and-coming emergency care specialist. What on earth was he doing in Port Bathurst, selling organic fruit and vegetables?

CHAPTER TWO

NICK concentrated hard, keeping his gaze firmly on the cannula he was inserting into Garry's arm, immensely glad of the distraction. Kirby Atherton's sky-blue eyes sparkled hypnotically, like light dancing on water. It had been the first thing he'd noticed about her when she'd walked up to his stall, quickly followed by her willowy height and the way her running gear clung deliciously to every feminine curve.

But it had been her eyes that had really drawn him. He had the craziest sensation that if her eyes were deep pools of water and he dived into them, he would emerge changed somehow. He tried to shrug the irrational feeling away. Not even on his worst days last year, when he'd hardly been able to get out of bed and the drugs he'd been taking had made him despair, had he experienced such foolish thoughts.

And prior to being sick, when life had consisted of work and a revolving door of beautiful women, he'd *never* thought twice about a set of eyes. Perhaps his mother was right. Maybe he had been out of social circulation for too long.

Brushing away the unsettling thoughts, he released the tourniquet, watching the flow of saline, checking for problems, and refocusing on far more straightforward things. 'We're going start you on antibiotics, Garry.'

The exhausted patient just nodded from behind his mask.

The two burly paramedics lowered their stretcher in preparation to transfer Garry from the ground to the slightly more comfortable but narrow gurney.

'Do you need a hand?' Nick taped the drip firmly in place.

'We'll be right, thanks, Doc. We do this all the time so we're in the swing. Best help you can give us is to just step back out of the way.' Theo locked the brakes of the stretcher with his foot.

He stood up and moved to the side at the same moment as Kirby. Much of her fine blonde hair had escaped its pink elastic hair tie and strands blew across her flushed cheeks. Her scent tantalised his nostrils, a blend of exercise and glowing health overlaid with a swirl of flowers and berries. He breathed in deeply.

'I'm going to ring through to Barago Hospital.'

Her words brought him back to the task at hand and he caught her sideways glance—the look quick but questioningly intense—as if she thought she should consult with him.

Her mouth opened ready to speak and then her teeth suddenly dragged across her bottom lip, momentarily flattening it before the skin rebounded into shape—full, soft and rose red.

Blood pounded through his veins with an unexpected rush and it took every ounce of concentration to stay connected to the conversation. Hell, what was wrong with him? Had he stepped back so far from his previous life that he'd disconnected from things and lost the ability to focus? He ran his hand though his short hair, missing the satisfaction of being able to tug at its length. Once he'd been known for his single-mindedness and right now he wanted that back.

She spoke again, this time her words less certain. 'I think he should be evacuated and have a bronchoscopy.'

She reminded him of a resident who knew her stuff but lacked confidence in her judgement. It was a scenario he was used to but today it surprised him because as a country GP she must be used to making decisions all the time. Glad to be back on familiar territory, he moved to reassure her.

'It's a good call. The choking might have been an accident but he's at an age where you need to rule out multiple sclerosis or other muscular conditions.'

'Let's hope it was just an accident, Nick *Dennison*.' She raised light brown brows at him. 'You are *the* Nick Dennison, youngest appointed head of Emergency Medicine in Australia?'

He studied her pretty features, looking for something that would spark his memory, but nothing did. Surely if they'd dated or worked together he would never have forgotten those eyes. He shoved his hands in his pockets, knowing there was no point denying the truth. 'That's me. I'm sorry, have we met before?'

She shook her head. 'Not really. I attended one of your lectures when I was a resident at Prince William Hospital. I was on duty that night and wasn't able to go to the dinner afterwards, but I think you met a friend of mine, Virginia Charters.' She shot him a knowing look. One that said, *You didn't call.*

He had no recollection of Virginia Charters but then again, that entire lecture tour had been a blur of cities, lecture theatres and women eager to date him. He loved women and he loved dating. He just didn't love or date one woman.

He took a punt on the type of women he'd accepted invitations from, women he'd wined, dined and satisfied before his world had imploded. Before he'd lost complete interest. 'Ah, Virginia…brunette and vivacious?'

He caught the surprised and almost disappointed look cross her face that he sounded like he'd remembered.

'Yes, that's Virginia. I'm sorry I didn't recognise you but you look very different from how I remember.'

He grinned, wanting to keep things light. He had no intention of telling her what had happened to him. He had no intention of anyone in Port ever knowing. His time here was all about wellness and no way was he looking back. 'It's the lack of a suit, a lectern and the slide presentation glowing behind me.'

Her mouth immediately widened into a broad smile that soared to her amazing eyes. Eyes that filled with coloured prisms, the many hues of blue which spun and twirled like the shards in a kaleidoscope.

His heart jolted hard in his chest and his breath stalled as a flicker of almost forgotten heat surged deep inside him.

Lust?

Yes! He wanted to whoop with delight.

His libido had vanished the day his world had changed but today it was back, albeit dusty and creaky. Four months of opting out of the mainstream and concentrating on his health was paying off. His body was back.

Suddenly his fascination with her eyes, her mouth and her curves made sense. It wasn't Kirby Atherton per se. She just happened to be the first pretty woman he'd come across that coincided with his recovery. He relaxed into the knowledge as his world came reassuringly back into kilter.

Kirby briskly went through the motions of handing over Garry's care to the Barago Hospital and organising Jake into

the care of his aunt. Four phone calls and an hour later she
had it all sorted but throughout the process her mind had
buzzed continuously with the fact that Melbourne's most
well-known ER doctor, the man aptly dubbed 'the playboy
doctor', was in sleepy Port Bathurst.

The stories about him said he worked hard and played
hard and he was well known for hitting the trendy clubs and
bars until the early hours. He and her friend Virginia had
shared an intense twenty-four hours and Kirby had been the
shoulder Virginia had cried on when he hadn't called afterwards. She'd also been the voice of reason, pointing out that
Ginny had virtually thrown herself at him and to give the
man credit, he'd never promised her anything other than a
good time. That he'd apparently delivered.

At the time, Kirby had had the advantage of distance
because she had been cheerfully engaged, blissfully happy
and busy planning her future of marriage, motherhood and
medicine. Although she could appreciate the model good
looks of urbane and sophisticated men like Nick, she'd always
fallen for the guy-next-door type—the home-town handyman
slash family man.

*Anthony only talked about fixing things, remember? Then
he hired someone else to do it.*

She shoved away the unwanted thought that reminded her
of how blind she'd been and refocussed on the memories of her
friend. Ginny had been the one to go for tall dark and handsome.
Except Nick hadn't been dark then, he'd been blond, which was
part of the reason she hadn't recognised him. Today his hair was
shorter and darker and physically he was thinner but more toned.

She ran her fingers through her hair. Nick Dennison and
Port Bathurst just didn't match. Port didn't have a cutting-

edge emergency department and as for nightlife, well, the recent crazy whist night at the tennis club had pushed the envelope. Lasting until midnight, the hall had rocked because someone had brought along their CD player and got people up to dance after the cards had finished. Nick in Port was like the translated instruction booklet that came with her new bookshelves—it made no sense. Her mind went round and round, stuck in a loop.

Who cares why he's here? He's a doctor with a wealth of experience.

The truth sliced sharply through everything else, stripping away all irrelevancies. Nick was a doctor and she needed a doctor *and* a mentor. The equation balanced perfectly. Nick working in Port alongside her meant she could stay in the town.

It didn't matter that he was a party boy, a smooth-as-silk charmer and heart-stoppingly gorgeous. She'd given up men and men like Nick had never been her type anyway. No, this would be a professional association only and keep her GP training on schedule.

The only thing left to do was ask him if he would work the summer season with her. Rolling back her shoulders, she headed toward the market to professionally proposition Dr Nick Dennison.

She arrived at Nick's stall and her heart skipped a beat as she watched him in complete control but cloaked by a lazy charm. Out of his suit and white coat he looked much more like the sort of guy she'd once been attracted to. *Breathe. This one is not for you. No man is for you.*

He was serving a customer, his amazing green eyes and his total attention completely focussed on Phyllis Gutherson, Port's resident naysayer. But her usually sour expression had vanished and in its place was a girlish smile. She looked twenty years younger.

Waiting her turn and shaking her head in wonder at how he'd achieved such a miracle, Kirby bobbed down next to Nick's dog and scratched his ears. 'Your master could charm diamonds from jewel thieves, couldn't he?'

Large brown eyes gazed adoringly up at her as the dog laid his head in her lap.

'Turbo, stop it.'

At the sound of the deep, commanding voice, both the dog and Kirby looked up.

A smile met her gaze. A smile that fizzed intoxicatingly through her like the bubbles of champagne. Her bent knees liquefied and she wobbled slightly as she rose to her feet.

He leaned casually against the stall table. 'That dog will turn on the charm if he thinks it will get him something.'

'Gosh, and I wonder where he learned that from.' She shook her head, laughing. 'You just managed to make Port Bathurst history by getting Phyllis Gutherson to smile, and charming her into buying your last item of produce. I mean, who eats radishes?'

This time his grin had a tinge of guilt to it, not dissimilar to that of a kid caught out sneaking biscuits too close to dinner. 'I will concede I might have used a well-placed compliment or two to move the radishes but, hey, I just sold everything I harvested for my first market.' He raised his hand as his eyes danced with elation—joy, pure and simple.

Without thought, she raised her hand to meet his, drawn completely by his enthusiastic aura that seemed to wrap around her, pulling her in. Her palm connected with his in a slap of celebration.

Heat tore through her hard and fast, ricocheting from skin to muscle to deep tissue and fanning out until every cell vibrated with its legacy and she tingled all over. Tingled in a way she never had before, not even with Anthony, the man she'd loved and thought she'd be spending the rest of her life with. Horrified, she jerked her arm back to the safety of her side.

Remember why you're here. She swallowed hard and cleared her throat. 'That's fabulous. Congratulations. Can I buy you a cup of coffee to help you celebrate and to say thank you for your help with Garry?'

'Thanks for the offer, but I have to pack up here first and I don't want to hold you up.' He picked up some boxes and stowed them into the back of a ute.

Kirby hauled her gaze away from his rippling biceps and tried to keep her focus on why she was actually here. She didn't just want to blurt out, 'Please work with me.' The situation needed more finesse than that. 'How about I give you a hand and then we go for coffee?' *Don't sound so needy.* 'If that suits you.'

Emerald eyes studied her for a brief moment. 'OK, it's a deal.' He tipped over the wooden trestle and grabbed the old metal supports, his broad palm wrapping deftly around them.

Kirby had a sudden image of a leather tool belt sitting flat across his washboard abdomen and him fixing all her sticking sash windows. *Stay focussed. He's a doctor, not a handyman.*

'Excellent.' She passed him boxes and watched him stack them as if they were a mathematical problem. 'How long have you been in Port?'

'Technically, I'm not in Port because I don't live here.' He slid the long trestle into the ute.

Kirby's gut went into freefall. With his vegetable selling

she'd assumed he lived here. Her plan depended on him living close by.

He paused in his stacking and extended a muscular arm out toward the mountainous rainforest area behind the town. 'My property's Riversleigh, thirty K out, near Sheep-wash Corner.'

Her gut steadied. She was still in the game—just. Sheep-wash Corner was pretty isolated, even more out of the way than Port. Nick Dennison hadn't just left Melbourne for Sleepy Hollow, he'd gone bush, a tree-change. But why? The situation got even more intriguing. 'How long have you lived out there?'

His cheerful open face suddenly closed, and the dimples in his cheeks smoothed over. 'Four months.'

He handed her one end of a tarpaulin. 'What about you?'

She caught the deft change, the power switch in the conversation, and she pulled the tarp tight, just like her mother had taught her as a child when she folded sheets. He didn't want to talk about why he was here. 'I've been here since the start of the month.' She walked up to him to match her corners to his.

'Is this a long-term plan for you?' His fingers slid over hers as he moved to accept the tarp.

The sharp tingle of sensation almost made her drop her corners and she found herself gripping them instead of releasing them into his hands. The moment she let go, she flexed her fingers, willing the shimmering away.

Since the age of twelve Kirby had been tall and she was used to being a similar height to many men. But she had to tilt her head to look up into Nick's face. It disconcerted her. *He* disconcerted her. 'It's a summer plan to start with. I'm doing a six-month GP rotation.' *Six months to pull herself together.*

'A summer by the sea. Sounds relaxing.' His dimples reappeared, deepening as he smiled.

Her heartbeat seemed to skip. How could one man's smile make her feel almost dizzy? *This is your opening—grab it.* The practical words broke into the haze that enveloped her brain. 'Actually, apart from a run along the pier in the mornings, that is as close as I've got to the beach.'

He slapped his palm down on the tailgate of the ute and Turbo immediately jumped onto the tray, turned around and lay down. 'Quiet Port Bathurst been keeping you busy?'

'It's hardly quiet! Between the residents, the work with Kids' Cottage and now the tourists arriving, I can barely get to the laundrette on a Sunday to do my washing. I had easier days back at Royal William.' She stared straight up at him. 'I'm surprised the hospital board didn't approach you when you moved down here.'

His hands stilled for a fraction on the tailgate. 'Until this morning, the hospital board didn't know I was a doctor.' He slammed the back of the ute shut and wiped his hands on an old towel. 'No one did.'

His words stunned her. 'Why on earth not?'

A shadow passed through his eyes, like a cloud scudding across the sun. 'Because I didn't come here to practise medicine.'

Her plan, so clear and perfect in her head, took a massive broadside hit, but she wasn't letting go just yet. 'But you're a talented doctor and Port needs you.'

Dark brows drew together, causing a crease at the bridge of his nose. 'No, it doesn't, Kirby. Port's got you. Besides, I'm an accident and emergency specialist, not a GP, and right now I'm really not interested in working.'

She wanted to stamp her feet. She had the ideal mentor in front of her and he didn't want to work. She chewed her lip as her limited options ran through her head. With a deep breath she played the only card she had left in her deck.

Honesty. She raised her gaze to his and spoke from the heart.
'Without your help, I can't work here.'

Over the last couple of months Nick had said an enthusiastic 'No' to five job offers from hospitals around the country
with barely a second thought about his decision. But one
glance from Kirby's blue eyes, swirling with honesty and
tinged with pleading, and suddenly every reason for not
working was teetering on unsteady foundations. 'What do you
mean, you can't work here without my help?'

'How well do you know Port?'

'I don't really know it at all. I come here for the market but
I use Barago as my centre for supplies as it's bigger.'

She laced her fingers, moving them back and forth against
the backs of her hands. 'Soon after I arrived in Port,
Christopher Grayson, the town's GP, fell ill.'

Ignoring the wavering feeling, he stuck firmly to the facts.
'When is Grayson due back?'

Her gaze held his with a steady look. 'He's not. Unfortunately, he had a stroke and he's currently in rehab.'

He shoved his hands in his pockets, empathy weaving
through him for a man who had a battle on his hands. But this
wasn't his problem and there was another solution. The foundations steadied. 'So you advertise for another doctor to help
you with the workload.'

She sighed, tucking stray hair behind her ear. 'It's not just
the workload. I came to Port as part of my GP rotation.'

The image of her tugging at her bottom lip when she was
deciding to send Garry to Barago beamed against his brain.
His chest tightened. Suddenly her hesitancy and lack of confidence made sense. 'Please don't tell me this is your first six-
month GP rotation.'

'It is.'

Damn it. He slammed his right fist into his left hand. 'So without supervision you can't practise?' But the question was rhetorical, he knew the answer.

'Not in Port, no.'

He wasn't ready to work in medicine just yet. He'd promised himself six more months, just savouring being well. Hell, surely he deserved that after everything he'd been through. He ran his hand across the back of his neck, trying to sort out his thoughts. He had no connection with this woman, no reason to turn his plans upside down to help her. The obvious solution shot into his head. 'You could go elsewhere to do your rotation or back to Royal William.'

A shudder of tension moved through her. 'Royal William isn't an option I want to pursue. Look, Port has already lost one doctor, so it can't afford to lose me.' She tilted her head and the brilliant blue of her eyes flickered over him, pulling hard at his sense of duty. 'And you wouldn't do that to a rural community who's so enthusiastically embraced your organic vegetable venture, would you?'

The words hit like a flyball, hard and unexpected. The woman in front of him with her long, blonde hair, honey-gold skin and an air of vulnerability had suddenly transformed from a pleading porcelain doll to a steely blackmailer. He could turn down large hospitals where there were plenty of other contenders for the job but she had him backed into a corner where his 'no' would impact on many hard-working people.

He wanted to kick the tyres on the ute, he wanted to be back on the farm digging over beds filled with fragrant soil, he wanted to be anywhere but here, dealing with an unwinnable ethical dilemma. He crossed his arms and took in a deep breath. 'That's true, no town deserves to be without a doctor.'

'So you will work in Port this summer?' Expectation and enthusiastic anticipation filled her voice.

A flood of heat collided with frustration. Well, she wasn't getting everything her own way. 'I'll mentor you and give you the supervision you need, but I'm warning you now, I'm a tough teacher and I'll expect one hundred and ten per cent.' The words came out on a growl—the one he'd perfected to keep his interns on their toes. 'But as for working, well, it will be with *strict* conditions.'

He waited, expecting to see signs of anxiety at his mild threat about being a tough teacher, and he certainly expected to see both disappointment and hear questions about the conditions he planned to impose.

But her mouth widened into a smile that raced to her eyes and seemed to dance around her like the white light of sparklers. 'That's fantastic. You won't regret this, Nick, it will be a fabulous summer.'

But every single part of him regretted it already.

CHAPTER THREE

KIRBY sat and stirred her coffee at an outside table, looking down and watching the white foam of her latte blend into the hot milk. Nick sat opposite her. Usually she chose this table so she could admire the view of the bay and enjoy gazing at the pelicans, fascinated by the way they lowered their feet in preparation for a water landing.

But today she'd caught herself admiring the way Nick's thick brown eyelashes almost touched his cheeks when he blinked and how the new streaks of silver against his temples gave him a look of authority. Unwanted tendrils of attraction had tightened inside her and she'd glanced away. It was a lot safer to stare at her coffee.

Nick moved the straw of his smoothie up and down through the dense blend of fresh fruits. Apparently he didn't drink coffee. This was yet another surprise as every doctor she knew considered coffee a vital part of their day, but absolutely nothing about this man fitted the picture of the doctor she'd expected. However, despite everything being at odds with expectation, he'd offered to help her and that was all that mattered.

'You're missing out on an amazing flavour just for a superficial caffeine buzz.' He winked at her as he drank his fruit concoction, his Adam's apple moving rhythmically and hypnotically against his taut muscular neck.

A rush of heat burned her cheeks and she dragged her eyes away. 'It's not just the buzz, it's the flavour of hazelnut.' She already had a buzz and she hadn't even taken a sip of her coffee. It had started simmering inside her from the moment he'd said he would mentor her. It felt oddly strange and yet deliciously wonderful and she was pretty sure it was relief.

You can call it relief if you want to.

She immediately took an indignant sip of her coffee and turned a deaf ear to the voice inside her head. Of course it was relief. Her search for a doctor was over and now she could stay in Port for her full six months. *Stay a long way from Anthony and Lisa.*

'Tell me about the demographics of Port Bathurst.' Nick pushed his large shake container off to the side, his eyes fixed firmly on her and filled with businesslike intent.

Kirby relaxed under his professional gaze. This was the working relationship she'd anticipated when she'd asked him to mentor her. 'Fishing and farming are the main industries but life is tough in both. Many young people are leaving town, although the mayor was telling me that recently there's been a push to increase tourism. A new diving business has opened in the main street, along with charter fishing trips, "Surf the wave" classes and catered cycling holidays.'

He nodded. 'I sold vegetables from the farm gate to a family on a Gypsy Caravan adventure the other week. They'd started out from Port and were taking the back roads. Regeneration is really important for rural communities like this.' He leaned back in his chair. 'So, how does all of this impact on the medical services?'

'It keeps us busy. The clinic is attached to the hospital and there are six acute beds and a small emergency centre plus midwifery. Major traumas get airlifted to Melbourne after being stabilised here and elective surgery goes to Barago. We have a large elderly population and the hospital has a nursing-home wing which is currently full. Oh, and then there's Kids' Cottage.'

His eyes darkened slightly. 'What's that?'

She leaned forward as her enthusiasm for KC spilled out. 'It's a fabulous holiday camp for children. They have camps for sick children with chronic illnesses, they have camps for healthy kids who have siblings with chronic illnesses or disabilities, and they have camps for kids whose families are struggling emotionally or financially and just need a bit of breathing space.'

Nick's fingers started to unroll the rim of the shake container. 'But Kids' Cottage would have their own medical staff, right?'

She shook her head. 'No, the town has always provided medical assistance since it started one hundred years ago. It's something that the locals are very proud of.'

A muscle twitched in his jaw. 'That's one of my conditions.'

Laughter bubbled up inside her. 'Are you going to fight me for first dibs on working with the kids?' A nurturing warmth filled her, tinged with regret. 'But I know what you mean, the cottage was a big drawcard for me to come to Port.'

His mouth firmed into an uncompromising line. 'There'll be no fight. I don't want to work at the camp so you can happily keep all that work for yourself.'

She blinked, completely startled. 'But the camp is so much fun. Why on earth don't you want to work there?'

The waxy cardboard unravelled in his hands, pulled apart by rigid fingers. 'I said I'd help you but there'd be conditions. This is one of them.'

His usually mellow voice was suddenly brusque and for the first time she caught a glimpse of the 'doctor in charge', the doctor used to issuing orders and being instantly obeyed without question. It caught her by surprise and a jolt of anger speared her. She tilted her chin—she wasn't a green first-year resident. 'What do you have against working with children?'

A streak of something she couldn't really define flared in his eyes for the briefest moment, before being cloaked by a spark of irritation. 'I didn't say I had anything against working with children, I'm just exerting my right not to.'

His arrogance astounded her. 'I suppose you had a paediatric registrar to save you from such work.'

'That's right.'

The blunt words hit her, their uncompromising tone harsh and decisive. 'Well, there's no paediatric registrar in Port so what about children who come into the clinic?'

His mouth flattened into an obdurate line. 'On the unlikely chance you're not available, I'll see them.'

'Well, that's reassuring.' The sarcastic words leapt off her lips as a fizz of frustration spread through her. 'Do you have any other demographic groups you refuse to work with? Any other conditions I should know about before we start?'

His eyebrows rose in a perfect arch at her mockery, but when he spoke his tone was all steely business. 'This is how I see it working. Each weekday morning I'll meet you at seven a.m. for the nursing-home ward round and I'll work half-day clinics Monday to Friday with lunchtime case-review sessions as part of your supervision. I'll be unavailable on Saturdays because I'll be at the market.' He extended his arm toward her, every part of him vibrating with tension. 'Deal or no deal?'

She recognised the adversarial glint in his eyes as a

thousand questions hammered in her head and poured into her mouth, demanding instant answers. She couldn't understand why he wouldn't work at the camp. Why he would prefer not to see the children at the clinic—none of it made sense, but she swallowed hard against every single question, forcing them down deep. If she quizzed him too closely on why he wouldn't work at KC he would walk, and she couldn't risk that. He had her well and truly cornered and she had no choice.

Slowly, she stretched out her right hand and slid her smaller palm against his. Work-hardened calluses scraped gently over her softer skin in a tantalising caress as his fingers wrapped around her hand. His heat poured through her, racing along her arm, radiating into her chest, tightening her breasts and then burrowing down deep inside until every part of her had liquefied with desire. Yet a dangerous vixen-voice betrayed her, demanding even more.

No, no, I'm not doing this. I am immune to men. But her body disagreed. His touch was unlike any handshake she'd ever known and she breathed in sharply, trying to grasp control of her wayward and wanton body which longed to drape itself over the chair and purr with pleasure. She finally found her own voice and hoped it sounded firm and business-like. 'Deal.'

A smile roved across his face, creating twinkling dimples in his cheeks, sparking emerald lights in his eyes and completely eliminating all signs of his previous tension. 'Deal it is, then.'

'Wonderful.' The word came out horrifyingly breathy, the vixen having gained control. Suddenly the deal that would keep her in Port, well away from Anthony and her shattered dreams, was no longer the 'get-out-of-jail-free card' that she'd expected.

* * *

'But, Doctor, are you sure you've seen enough?' Mrs Norton's rheumy blue eyes sparkled as arthritic fingers fumbled over the pearl buttons on her crocheted bedjacket.

'Let me help you with that.' Nick smiled as he quickly buttoned the jacket on the elderly woman who would have been a stunning beauty in her younger days. 'If you can flirt with me, Mrs N. then you're doing just fine, but I have adjusted the diuretic so that should make breathing a little easier.'

'Thank you, Doctor.' She touched his hand as he finished latching the last button. 'And when will you be in to see me next, dear?'

'Tomorrow morning.'

'I'll be ready.' She gave him a wave as he left the room.

Mrs Norton was the last nursing-home patient on his morning round's list and over the last hour he'd met all the residents. Every female patient had held his hand and flirted with him as well as showing him pictures of their grand-daughters and great-granddaughters. *'She's a wonderful cook, Doctor, and you could do with some fattening up.'* The male patients had gruffly given him fishing tips, shaken their heads at his choice of football team and told him the 'sure-fire' solution to aphids—*'garlic and soapy water, Doc.'*

After working in emergency medicine for years, he'd expected to find a nursing-home round slow and boring work. He didn't know if it was because he hadn't worked in almost two years and today he was just enjoying being back in the field, but he'd been surprised at how much fun he'd had chatting with them all. The moment he got home he was going to make up that aphid-fighting mixture and use it on his tomatoes this afternoon.

He glanced at his phone and read a text from Kirby asking

him to meet her at the clinic. She hadn't made it to rounds, having been called out at six a.m. to Kids' Cottage.

He'd had no idea the town had a kids' holiday camp dating back a hundred years. When he'd initially said he would have conditions attached to working here, he'd been thinking about how he would juggle the farm with practising medicine and still have precious time for himself. He hadn't realised he would need to use the 'conditions' banner for anything else, but no way was he going to be the medico for a kids' camp.

He shuddered as the memory of his father's voice suddenly sounded in his head. *You have to go, mate. You'll enjoy it if you give it a chance.*

He'd hated the enforced time he'd spent at camps as a kid and he sure as hell wasn't spending time there as an adult. This time he had a choice and he was choosing to say no.

Suddenly the vision of Kirby's wide blue eyes aimed squarely at him and full of disapproval shoved his father's voice out of his head. Damn it, *he* was the experienced doctor and he had the right to say where he would work without giving a full-on explanation. He was so *not* revisiting his childhood, especially not with a woman whose eyes threatened to see down to his soul.

Better that she thought him a jerk than to go there.

Yeah, right. You go ahead and think that if it makes you feel better.

He ran his hand across his hair, short spikes meeting his palm, and he grunted in frustration. Hell, he didn't even have to be working in Port! This time here was supposed to be all about wellness and focussing on himself. He was the one doing *her* the favour.

Shaking his head to clear it of unwanted images, errant

thoughts and the eminently reasonable voice of his father, he strode toward the clinic, which was attached to the small emergency department of Port Bathurst Bush Nursing Hospital. Pushing open the door, which was covered in healthy-lifestyle posters, he stepped into the waiting room.

'Good morning. You must be Dr Dennison. Welcome!' A woman who looked to be in her early fifties with spiked, short red hair walked toward him, extending her hand. 'I'm Meryl Jeffries, the practice nurse, and it's wonderful that you're here.' She pumped his hand firmly and didn't draw breath. 'The whole town is talking about how you used Cheryl's jewellery pliers to pull that strawberry out of Garry's throat, and thank goodness you were there. Anyway, Kirby is just giving Theo the scoop on young Harrison, who thought that he'd start the day by jumping off the top bunk and fracturing his tib and fib so she'll be here in a minute and, well, here she is now so I'll let her give you the tour as I've got my baby clinic.' She threw her arm out behind her toward the reception desk. 'But if you need anything just ask because Vicki and I have been here for years.'

Vicki, who looked a bit older than Meryl, glanced up from the computer and smiled at him over the top of her bright purple glasses. 'Lovely to have you here, Dr D., and, like Meryl said, just yell. My only rule is that you bring the histories back to me as you greet your next patient so they can be filed or else things get lost. Oh, and I made you a ginger fluff sponge and it's in the kitchen so help yourself to as much as you like because you do look a bit on the thin side, dear.'

He opened his mouth but words escaped him. It was like work had just collided with his mother—instructions and praise all rolled into one with a slightly disapproving look thrown in. 'Ah, thank you for the welcome and the cake.'

They both nodded and smiled and then Vicki returned to her computer screen and Meryl disappeared down the corridor.

'I see you've met Meryl and Vicki.' A familiar tinkling laugh sounded behind him.

He turned around to find a smiling Kirby walking toward him. Her hair moved in sync with her body, brushing across her shoulders and floating around her face. On Saturday she'd been wearing Lycra running gear. Today she wore a summer dress with a close-fitting scoop-neck top that hugged her waist before opening out into a short full skirt that showcased her shapely long, tanned legs. Bright red painted nails peeked out of strappy sandals.

Heat poured through him and zeroed in on his groin, making him dizzy. His reaction to her was so much stronger than two days ago and that made no sense at all. On Saturday she'd had a bare midriff and figure-hugging clothes on so of course his body had reacted. Hell, he'd been pleased it had because it meant things were finally getting back to normal despite the fact he'd always preferred brunettes.

But today far more clothes covered Kirby's body and yet the hidden curves tantalised even more. He dragged his gaze up from the hint of creamy breast back to her face and prayed she hadn't noticed his lapse of professionalism. He might have been known for dating many women but he'd *always* kept work and pleasure distinctly separate. He never dated someone he worked with directly so he definitely needed to get back into the work saddle again if those lines were blurring.

He rubbed his jaw. 'Those two are like a hurricane. Are they always like that?'

'Always.' A more serious expression played around her mouth. 'But don't be deceived—they really know their stuff and the clinic runs like clockwork. Vicki's children are adults and living in Melbourne now so I think she's missing mothering and she's making up for it with us.' Her eyes danced, softening the indignant look that streaked across her face. 'Although I've *never* had a cake made for me.'

He answered without thinking. 'You can have as much as you like. I really don't eat cakes.'

'First no coffee and now no cake?' She tilted her head enquiringly, a glint of interrogation in her eyes. 'Next you'll be telling me you don't drink.'

He smiled, falling back into old habits in an attempt to deflect her. 'I do drink but only top-shelf wine on special occasions.' He didn't really want to talk about why he'd given up cakes and cream. 'So how about you show me around the clinic and the emergency department of the hospital and then I can get started.'

Work. After all, that was why he was here. He itched to throw himself into a busy day because working seemed a heck of a lot safer than talking about himself or ogling a colleague's décolletage.

'Can I run something past you?' Kirby caught Nick between patients.

'Sure. What's up?' His eyes darkened to the colour of moss as he swung around on the office chair, his gaze fixed firmly on her.

A gaze so intense that her skin tingled. *Get over yourself. You asked the man a question and he's giving you his undivided attention, just as a colleague should.* She gripped

Melinda Nikoloski's history and focussed on the facts. 'I've got a thirty-five-year-old woman with general fatigue, enlarged glands, persistent cough, raspy voice and episodes of shortness of breath.'

'On bare facts alone it sounds like summer flu.' His mouth tweaked up on the left in a thoughtful smile. 'But you wouldn't be running it past me if you thought it was flu.'

She slid into the chair next to his desk, grateful for his intuition. Grateful that he was here. Leaping into this job a year before most people started a GP rotation had stretched her, but she'd been desperate to leave Melbourne, desperate to distance herself from everything that reminded her of what she'd lost, and Port had been desperate enough to accept her. 'The previous doctor saw her a month ago, made a diagnosis of flu and prescribed bronchodilators for the shortness of breath.'

He tapped his silver pen on a notepad. 'So how is she now?'

'Not much better.' Kirby chewed her bottom lip in thought. 'She could be anaemic, like many women in their mid-thirties are, so on Friday I ordered a routine full blood examination and those results should be back shortly, but even so, I have a nagging feeling about it. Totally non-scientific, I know, but nagging none the less.'

Understanding lined his face. 'Listening to your gut feeling is an important part of being a good doctor. Out here you don't have access to the full weight of diagnostic tests that you get in a large hospital.'

He sat forward, his hands flat on the spun cotton of his summer trousers which so casually covered what she imagined to be solid, muscular thighs. 'A persistent cough and shortness of breath can too easily be attributed to asthma. As we've got an X-ray machine, let's do a chest X-ray. It's a simple test and hopefully we can rule out a lung mass.'

'But she's not a smoker and has no other risk factors.'

He shrugged. 'There are *other* masses that can be found in the chest. But that said, it's important to remember that non-smoking females are dying from lung cancer because it's being missed in the early stages of the disease. Granted, the air down here is cleaner than other places but you don't know what she's been exposed to.' He tugged on the hair just behind his ear, his voice rising slightly. 'Hell, we don't know half of what we're exposed to in the air or in our food.'

His heartfelt reaction surprised her. He sounded more like an environmentalist than a doctor. But, then again, he did grow organic vegetables and he didn't drink coffee. Two things she knew he hadn't done two years ago because Virginia had basically told her everything about this citified man who'd loved the good things in life. 'OK, I'll organise a chest X-ray. Thanks.'

'No problem, it's what I'm here for.' He spun back on his chair, his attention returning to the article he'd been reading when she'd walked into the room.

Familiar disappointment slugged her and she tried to shrug it off because there was *no* reason to feel like this. Nick had done his job well. Very well. *He's the mentor, you're the student. That's what you want and that's what you're getting.*

She continued to remind herself of that against the strange hollow feeling in her gut as she walked back to her consulting room. Glad of something to do, she picked up the phone and called Melinda, asking her to come in for a chest X-ray.

Melinda sat in the chair, her face pale with black smudges under her eyes. She rubbed her knee. 'I think I should have got an X-ray of my knee as well as my chest. It's been sore for the last week.' She sighed. 'I really hope the chest X-ray will tell you what's wrong with me because I'm sick of feeling like this and I think I'm getting worse, not better.'

Kirby silently agreed with her patient—Melinda had the pasty pallor of someone extremely unwell. She slid the black and white film onto the light box and flicked on the light. Using her pen she outlined the image. 'Your heart is here and it's the normal size, and if there was any fluid on your lungs or infection that would show up as white on the film. But your lungs are pretty clear, which is why they look black.' *And you don't have a tumour, thank goodness.*

'But I feel so awful.' Tears welled up in the woman's eyes. 'I'm so grumpy, the kids and Dev are avoiding me and all I want to do is sleep but I keep going hot and cold and my joints ache.'

'Just hot at night?' Piece by piece she tried to match up the vague symptoms. She rechecked the X-ray but there was no lower lobe consolidation, no sign of pneumonia.

Melinda wrung her hands. 'Sometimes during the day too.'

'Are you still menstruating?' Menopause was unlikely but Kirby had learned the hard way that sometimes the unexpected happened.

Her patient grimaced. 'Oh, yes, I'm doing that too well— flooding, in fact.'

Which led Kirby back to her initial thoughts from Friday. Menstruating women were often anaemic—lacking in iron could make you feel pretty low. *But not give you hot flushes.* The words nagged at Kirby. Perhaps she needed to run a test for hormone levels and do blood cultures as well.

She glanced at her watch and picked up the phone to speak to Vicki. 'The courier should have arrived with the results of your blood test and hopefully the results will say I need to prescribe you my famous orange-juice-and-parsley iron-boosting drink.

'If that's the case, in two weeks you'll feel like a new woman and we can discuss your options to reduce your menstrual bleeding.' She smiled, trying to reassure her patient despite an enveloping sense of gloom that Melinda's condition would not be that simple and neither would it have such a straightforward solution.

But she *had* to be wrong. Right now she didn't trust her gut at all, given the way her body melted into a mush of pulsating need at one smile from Nick. How could one smile from a man she knew to be a womanising charmer undermine everything she'd learned at the hands of Anthony? *Face it, Kirby*, he'd said. *You can't give me what I need.*

She knew better than to get involved again—this time she knew in advance what the outcome would be and she wasn't putting her hand or heart up for another brutal and soul-destroying rejection. No, now she was a lot wiser and she knew better than to let attraction blind her to a handsome man. But her body wasn't listening to her brain and it betrayed her every time she clapped eyes on Nick. No, she definitely didn't trust her gut, because right now her radar was really out of whack.

A knock sounded on the door and Nick walked in, holding a printed piece of white paper with the familiar logo of Barago Hospital's pathology department. The smile on his face didn't quite reach his eyes and the lines around his mouth looked strained.

'I brought you this.' He handed the report to Kirby and immediately turned his attention to Melinda. 'I'm Nick Dennison. I hope you don't mind me barging in like this but as I'm working with Dr Atherton I thought I'd introduce myself.'

Recognition moved across the sick woman's face. 'Oh, you're from the market. When I bought those strawberries from you on Saturday I didn't realise you were a doctor. Mind you, I didn't get to taste any of them, the kids ate them all before we got home!'

Kirby heard the warm burr of his voice reply to Melinda but her whirling brain didn't decipher the words. At first astonishment that Nick had brought in the report drowned out the conversation then shock rocked through her, muting everything around her, and finally aching despair obliterated all sound. She read the pathology report three times and finally closed her eyes against the words. But they lingered against her retina as if burned there. Melinda had leukaemia.

Slowly the conversation between Nick and her patient sounded in her ears again and she sucked in a deep breath, turning to face them both. Nick had pulled up a chair, his casual demeanour tinged with an alertness she hadn't noticed before. She realised he'd read the report and that was why he'd brought it in.

She shot him an appreciative look—she hated giving out bad news. It wasn't something a person got better at with practice and it certainly never got easier. 'Melinda, the results of your blood test are back and I'm afraid it's not good news.'

Melinda instantly stiffened, fear clear in her eyes. 'What do you mean?'

Nothing Kirby could say would soften the truth. 'Your white blood cells—the ones that fight infection—are abnormal and that means you have a form of leukaemia.'

Melinda's hand shot to her mouth before falling back to her lap. 'You mean cancer of the blood?'

Kirby nodded slowly. 'That's right. We need to get you to

Barago hospital this afternoon for a series of tests, including
a bone-marrow biopsy so that we can get an accurate diagnosis and start chemotherapy.'

But Kirby knew Melinda hadn't heard a word since she'd
confirmed leukaemia was cancer.

The petrified woman started to breath quickly, short,
shallow breaths, her hands gripping the sides of the chair.

Kirby reached for a paper bag but Nick grabbed it first.

'Melinda.' He squatted down in front of her and took her
hand. Looking straight into her eyes, he spoke slowly. 'I need
you to breathe into the paper bag and try to slow your breathing. I'm going to count to help you.'

Melinda's gaze fixed on Nick like a drowning woman
seeking a life preserver in a choppy sea. Her hands trembled
against the paper bag.

The timbre of Nick's voice vibrated reassuringly. 'Breathe
in…breathe out… Breathe in…breathe out. That's fabulous,
you're doing really well.'

Kirby stood up, needing to do something, and gently touched
Melinda's shoulder. 'The dizzy feeling will fade with the deep
breaths.' She felt so inadequate. This woman had just been told
awful, life-changing news and her battle was only just beginning.

She caught Nick's steady gaze, filled with empathy, but she
couldn't see any trace of her own feelings of powerlessness
and frustration there. Had he given bad news so often that it
no longer got to him? She immediately dismissed the uncha-
ritable thought but she couldn't fathom the rock-solid determination that took up residence in his eyes.

Slowly Melinda lowered the brown paper bag onto her
lap, her pupils, large and black, almost obliterating her hazel
irises. 'I'm going to die, aren't I?'

Nick kept his hand on Melinda's arm as he sat back in his chair. 'You're about to start the biggest challenge of your life but many people successfully go into remission and go on to lead long and happy lives.'

A sob escaped Melinda's lips. 'But you can't tell me I'm not going to die.'

Nick spoke quietly, his voice steady and firm. 'Right now we don't know enough about your condition to tell you any more than what Kirby already said. This is why you're going to Barago for an accurate diagnosis and then probably to Melbourne for treatment.'

He leaned closer and the dappled sunshine streaming through the window caught his profile, emphasising the silver in his short hair and the unusually deep lines around his eyes and mouth. 'But I can tell you this—leukaemia will test you and force you to dig deep to release a strength you never knew you had. It will make you question everything about your life, force you to prioritise and give you the opportunity to truly know what is important to you.'

Kirby watched Melinda visibly calm under Nick's words and she wished she'd been able to express herself so eloquently but she was still back at 'It's so not fair'. She'd never heard any doctor speak about cancer like that. Usually, it was sticking to the bare facts about treatment.

As he picked up Melinda's hand, sunlight struck the backs of his hands, making the scars whiter than ever. 'I know you didn't put your hand up for this and it's a journey you don't want to take, but I can guarantee you there are parts of the trip that you won't regret.'

'Can I hold you to that?' Melinda's pain-tinged words sliced through the air.

Kirby's heart hurt and anger surged through her that a young mother of three had to deal with this illness and all the unknowns a disease like cancer generated.

'Absolutely, and I'm here to talk to any time.' Nick smiled but, unlike his usual charisma-laden grin, this smile simply conveyed serenity. 'And once you're home, I'll be keeping you supplied with vegetables.'

How could he be so calm? She railed against the unjust diagnosis. Melinda had leukaemia! How on earth could he be talking about vegetables?

Organic vegetables.

Something urged her to really study him while his attention was fully fixed on Melinda and slowly information started to slot into place. He was an experienced city doctor now growing vegetables in the country and avoiding talking about why. His shorter than expected hair grew darker than the blond it had been two years ago and the premature streaks of silver in his hair matched up with the deep lines around his eyes and mouth. White marks on the backs of his hands matched the type of scars left by an intravenous cannula.

Her lungs emptied of air and a shard of pain cramped her heart as all her unanswered questions about Nick lined up. She'd just solved the puzzle. She'd bet her last cent he was talking to Melinda not as a doctor but as a fellow traveller. Nick Dennison had experienced cancer.

The only question still needing an answer was what type of cancer. *No, there's one more. Has he won the battle?*

The thought that he might not terrified her more than it should.

CHAPTER FOUR

NICK bit into the sweet nectarine, savouring the complex but delicious summer flavour on his tongue, and marvelling at the taste. Once he wouldn't have given that a second thought.

'That looks good.' Kirby walked into the staffroom, her usual cheerful demeanour completely absent, dented by the morning's work and Melinda's diagnosis.

This woman confounded him. She lurched from being in charge and confident to needing more reassurance than he would have thought necessary. She reminded him of a junior resident, which was nonsense as she must have far more experience than that if she was doing her first GP rotation.

'Catch.' He tossed her a nectarine and pulled out a chair.

'Thanks.' She bit into the fruit she'd neatly caught and juice dribbled down her chin. Her pink tongue darted out, stroking her skin and licking at the sweet juice.

The image of her tongue against his chin, against his lips, in his mouth, beamed in 3D depth. Colours exploded in his head as blood drained to his groin. He silently started chanting the names of all the bones in the body and blood slowly and regretfully returned to his head.

Now fully back in control, he risked looking at Kirby with

the eyes of a colleague. Right now she needed a mentor and that was his job. He sat down and gave her an encouraging smile. 'If you're going to take everyone's problems on board like this then you're not going to last very long as a GP.'

Her large doe-like eyes reflected sadness, and a sigh rolled over her plump bottom lip. 'But it's just so unfair.'

He took in a thoughtful breath and wondered if she was one of those people who had lived a charmed life untouched by misfortune. 'Life isn't fair, Kirby. Surely you've worked that out by now.'

Her sparkling eyes, always so fill of vibrant colours and movement, suddenly filled with pervading emptiness. The change both startled and disturbed him and something inside him ached.

A moment later she shook her head and gave him a tight smile. 'I know I'm a hopeless case but when something happens outside the realm of what is expected in the circle of life, I find myself railing against it. If Melinda was seventy-eight I'd feel sad but she would have raised her kids and lived a full life.'

Memories of a parade of eyes filled with resignation and expressions of grief and fear hammered him. 'She still can.' His words sounded overly firm but he hated the way people assigned a death certificate to a diagnosis of cancer, which was why he refused to talk about what he'd been through.

A flash of understanding and purpose streaked across her face. 'Oh, don't get me wrong, of course she can and I hope she will, but I wouldn't wish that *struggle* on anyone.' Her gaze hovered on him for a moment, her expression intent. 'Would you?'

The hairs on his arms rose for a moment as he met her unsettling stare. He leaned back casually and placed the pit of his nectarine on a plate that sat between them, striving not to give anything personal away. 'Of course not. But although her treatment will be tough, she'll appreciate parts of the process.'

'Really?' Her brow creased in lines of confusion. 'How so?'

'She'll learn a lot about herself.'

'More than if she wasn't sick?'

He relaxed as the discussion stayed centred on Melinda. 'Absolutely. In general, human beings don't like change and most of us don't put our hand up to experience it. Cancer barges in and railroads you so you have no choice but to meet it head on and change.' He learned forward, warming to his topic. 'You drop the non-essentials and you see things with a clarity not everyone gets the opportunity to have. It's probably the only advantage of the disease.'

'That's an interesting perspective.' Kirby put the pit of the nectarine down on the plate and then leaned forward on her elbows, her chin resting on the palms of her hands, her gaze fixed directly on him. 'I've never heard it explained like that before but that's because it's happened to you, hasn't it? That's why you're here in Port, growing vegetables, instead of slaying even bigger career dragons in Melbourne.'

His chest tightened at her soft-voiced but accurate assumption. Damn it, he'd walked right into her question and he didn't want to answer it. He wanted his time in Port to be free of everything he associated with illness. He didn't want to see sympathy for him shining from those large bluer-than-blue eyes, and he didn't want her to start tiptoeing around him like people had in Melbourne. He just wanted things to be as they had been right up until this point. Shrugging, he bluffed. 'Perhaps I just wanted a tree-change.'

She shook her head. 'I *might* have believed that on
Saturday. After all, growing veggies and living in the bush
could have been because you'd burned out from years of fast-
tracking up the professional ladder, but even then it was a
stretch. Now too many things add up—your hair, your vice-
less diet.' Her fingers reached out toward his hand and with a
feather-soft touch they traced a jagged white scar. 'The marks
of an infected IV.'

A fire-storm of sensation detonated under her touch, rolling
through him fast and leaving smouldering desire in its wake.
Desire he could no longer pretend didn't exist. 'Why is this
so important to you, Sherlock?' He trapped her hand with his
free one, sandwiching hers between his.

Her pupils dilated into inky discs and a pulse fluttered in her
throat as she took a long deep breath, making her breasts strain
against the fitted bodice of her dress. 'Because you're a puzzle.'

He recognised her body's response to him, the marks of
desire matching those of his own. Their attraction for each
other ran between them like a vibrating wire.

It had been months and months since he'd held a woman's
hand, hell, since he'd really held a woman. Like so many
things in his life, he'd taken for granted the touch of a woman.
He loved women. He loved their company, their scent, their
curves—everything about them—and now his body craved to
hold a woman in his arms again. He ached for it. These
feelings he understood. Mutual attraction. Undiluted lust.

And he read them in Kirby's pink cheeks, her slightly open
mouth and in the lift of her breasts. He read enough to want
the buzz of the chase.

But without warning the heat from her hand surprisingly
morphed from scorching fire to cosy heat, warming him,

swirling around in sweet tendrils, licking at his self-imposed silence.

'And I can't resist solving puzzles.' She smiled a long, slow, knowing smile, which wound across her face, bringing it alive, the way colour invigorated a black and white canvas.

A smile that promised something good, something wonderful. A smile that called to him unlike any smile ever had. Right there and then, not telling her became harder than keeping his own counsel.

'So you can't resist me?' He traced a circle on her hand with his thumb.

Kirby's body shivered as his caress sent waves of delicious need pounding through her. *Remember Anthony, remember the hurt.* She forced out a laugh and pulled her hand out from under his, ignoring the chill that followed. 'See, this is the puzzle. You're known for flirting charm.'

'But not for growing vegetables. Fair enough.' His guarded expression unexpectedly melted. 'I can see why me being in Port is a puzzle because for years I worked hard and played hard.'

'So what changed?' She tried not to sound as if she was interrogating him but she badly wanted to know what had happened more than she probably should.

'Just under two years ago I couldn't shake off a virus. I felt like I had treacle running through my veins and I was constantly tired and my skin seemed to itch like mad. Then I discovered a pea-sized lump just behind my ear.' He tilted his head, his deep green eyes questioning. 'What do you think, Doctor?'

He'd just turned his story into a teaching session. She ran the symptoms through her mind. 'A type of lymphoma?'

'Well done, Dr Atherton. I had stage-one non-Hodgkin's

lymphoma so I stepped down from Melbourne City and started seven months of IV chemotherapy.'

She schooled her face not to show any emotion but to keep it focussed on a teaching session, as that was obviously the way he wanted to go. 'How was that?'

'What do you think it might be like?'

She spoke from the heart. 'Bloody awful.'

He laughed a rich, body-shaking laugh. 'That pretty much sums it up.' He flattened his hands out against the table. 'And you're pretty observant, Sherlock. I did have problems with infections on my hands so I ended up with a chest tube and a natty scar.'

He raised his brows and shot her a look of pure, unadulterated flirtation—a classic Nick Dennison look. 'But you didn't know that because you're *yet* to see me with my shirt off.'

Her mouth dried at the thought of all that exposed golden skin but despite the fog of lust that encircled her brain she managed to see through his ploy. She rolled her eyes. 'You can't derail me that easily.' *Liar!* 'I want to hear the whole story. Did you have radiation therapy as well?'

He ran his hand through his hair and frustration raced across his face. 'Yeah, I did and losing my hair really sucked, not because I minded being bald for a while but because I realised that when things get to me I run my hand through my hair. When there is no hair to tug on there's no satisfaction in it at all.'

'You could have invented a new action.'

He smiled, his eyes sparkling and dimples scoring his cheeks. 'Ah, but old habits are very hard to break.'

Just like flirting. It was second nature to him—see a woman and flick into flirting mode. 'It won't be long before you can really bury your fingers in your hair.' Her fingers tingled, wanting to do that very thing, and she quickly laced them together. 'But generally treatment takes about seven months. How come you didn't go back to work?'

He pushed back his chair, walked to the water filter and flicked on the tap, pouring two glasses of water. 'I went onto oral chemotherapy and I felt awful. If I'd worked at a desk job perhaps I could have managed it, but not A and E.'

She stood up and walked over to him, calculating the elapsed time since his diagnosis, still confused. 'Are you still on chemo, still battling the lymphoma?'

He immediately stiffened. 'No. The chemo is finished and I'm in remission. I'm not battling non-Hodgkin's lymphoma. I'm surviving it.'

His words shot out harsh and uncompromising and at that moment she understood exactly why he hadn't wanted to talk about being sick. He was focussed on his future, not his past. 'And Port and growing vegetables is part of that?'

He passed her the glass of cold water and leaned back against the bench next to her. 'When you spend a year feeling like death warmed up, you get sick of yourself and you get sick of the role of being a patient. You also get weary of well-intentioned people asking you how you are.' His eyes narrowed slightly, as if willing her to understand and warning her at the same time. 'I wanted some time out between being a patient and going back to work, time to just enjoy being well.'

'But why did you decide to grow vegetables?'

'When you're faced with the possibility of dying, you make changes you never expected to have to make. Taking a break from work was one, changing what I ate was another. Until I got sick it was easy to dismiss the link between food and illness but I can feel the difference in myself. I couldn't do "nothing" for nine months and I was growing my own veggies so I just extended it, and the markets are fun. I came out there because no one up here knew me—' He gave a wry grin, resignation clinging to him. 'Well, almost no one.'

She bit her lip, realising that by pushing him back to work she'd interrupted his plan. 'Sorry.'

He leaned into her, his shoulder nudging hers in a friendly bump and his arm lingering against the length of her own. 'No, don't be sorry, it's all good. I'm enjoying myself and in six months' time when I go back to the city I won't be rusty.'

His body warmth swam through her, making her dizzy. *In six months' time.* At least he had a plan. She'd rushed to Port so fast she really couldn't see past tomorrow. All she knew was that everything she'd expected to be happening in her life right now wasn't. Every plan she and Anthony had made lay scattered in a million irreparable pieces and her love for him had been returned, stamped unacceptable.

Her world spun on an unsteady axis and the only thing about her future that she truly knew was that it would not be happening with Anthony. *Not happening with any man.*

'You OK?' Penetrating eyes bored into her.

She shoved her gloomy thoughts of heart-breaking loss back down where they belonged, plastered a smile on her face and spoke the first thing that came into her head. 'I'm still having trouble seeing you as a farmer.'

'Come see me in action, then.' He pulled his keys out of his pocket and walked toward the door. 'I'm working in the veggie patch every afternoon.'

The unexpected invitation was tantalisingly tempting. She

strove for feigned interest and casualness. 'I'll keep that in mind if I'm ever out that way on rounds.'

He nodded. 'You do that. Around three is a good time to drop by.'

'Is that when you take a break?'

He stared straight at her, his eyes shimmering like sunshine on water, backlit with teasing intent. 'It's the hottest part of the day and usually the time I lose the shirt.' He gave her a knowing wink and disappeared.

Indignation at his perceptive wink, the one that said he knew she enjoyed looking at him, floundered against the surge of hot, delicious longing that shook her to her toes and left her wanting more.

He's your colleague and mentor. But the words sounded hollow. She dragged in a deep breath, determined to make the words count. They had to mean something. They had to protect her because, no matter how much she wanted to see where he lived, no matter how much her body craved to see him shirtless, she wouldn't allow it to happen.

She couldn't. She refused to allow herself to get close to another man again and have him find that her perfect body was so internally flawed. No way was she going to expose her faulty body to any more derision and heartache. She lived with the heartache every day already.

Nick took a long slug of water from his water bottle and then took off his hat and squirted some over his head, enjoying the coolness of the liquid against his hot skin. Turbo gave him a baleful look from under the tree. 'Hot, mate, isn't it? Only mad dogs and Englishmen go out in the midday sun, eh?'

Turbo barked.

'Sorry, I see what you mean. It's three o'clock and you're under the tree so you don't qualify as mad.' He jammed his hat back on his head and toyed with the idea of stopping but he needed to get this fertilising done now that his mornings were taken up with the clinic.

He caught himself glancing down the dirt track that doubled as his driveway. Heat haze hovered, making the metal of the closed gate look crooked. It had been four days since he'd issued his invitation to Kirby, suggesting she visit the farm.

Four days since she'd sat opposite him, her cheeks flushed, glistening lush lips and a sultry voice that rumbled through him every time he thought about it. She hadn't been able to hide her attraction to him and he'd expected her to drive up the track the following day. But she hadn't shown up and she hadn't mentioned the invitation since he'd extended it.

It was probably a good thing. *I don't think so.* He ignored the voice, overlaying it with reason. He'd been high on the joy of lust when he'd issued the invitation and had broken his self-imposed requirement of keeping work and play separate. Two years of celibacy could do that to a bloke.

The professional colleague part of him was pleased that at least she was the one being sensible but despite knowing that he still glanced at the gate each afternoon. It niggled that he did that. It niggled even more that she hadn't come. Two years ago he'd never been stood up and he wasn't that sure he wanted to get used to the feeling.

Two years ago and for years before that he'd dated women—lots of women. He loved the chase, the variety, the conversations and the sex. Unlike his parents, who'd been high-school sweethearts and had married each other at twenty-two, he'd avoided anything that came close to a committed relationship.

And cancer hadn't changed that. A committed relationship meant marriage and children. He didn't particularly have anything against marriage per se, but children, well, no way was he going to be a parent. Not when he'd lived through his parents' unresolved grief—he had no intention of reliving that same nightmare or exposing himself to that sort of loss again.

I just want a normal sister. His twelve-year-old self jetted up from the depths he normally kept sealed.

Plunging his shovel into the enormous pile of mushroom compost, he threw himself into the work and pushed his childhood back where it belonged. But he couldn't get the usual buzz of satisfaction that hard labour gave him because Kirby kept dogging his thoughts. Kirby with a mouth designed for kissing and a body made for pleasure, but who'd been professionally friendly at work and had kept every conversation strictly about patients. No matter what topic he tried to bring up she always neatly brought the conversation back to work. The level of supervision she was demanding bothered him.

By now in her career she really should have a lot more confidence in her diagnostic ability and treatment options, and only be using him as a sounding board for difficult cases. Instead, she seemed to want his review of all her cases. He needed to talk to her about that.

He lifted the shovel, dumping the contents into the wheelbarrow. He'd do it tomorrow but he'd have to be ready because every day this week, at the end of their lunchtime meeting, Kirby had jumped up and said, 'You'd better head off so you can enjoy your afternoon,' and she'd walked briskly out of the staffroom door, back toward her office.

His body absorbed the rhythm of the shovelling, his mind unravelling and roaming free. He suddenly realised that all week Kirby had been leaving the meeting abruptly the moment the last case had been discussed. She never lingered just to chat. No chatting and she hadn't visited. Was it possible she didn't want to spend any time with him?

Nah, not possible.

Laughing at the resurgence of his now healthy if misguided ego, he laid his shovel across the wheelbarrow and lifted the handles, ready to push his load to the vegetable garden.

Turbo barked and jumped up.

'Rest time's over, is it?'

Instead of running over to Nick, Turbo stood stock still, his black ears standing up, alert and listening. He ran part way down the track and then returned, barking all the time as if to say, *Come on.*

Nick put the barrow down and listened. Faintly in the distance he could hear the vroom of an engine. Using his hand as a shield against the sun, he saw a familiar, once-white, now red-dust-covered four-wheel drive round the bend and pull up at the gate.

Everything comes to those who wait. The gorgeous Kirby had arrived and for the first time ever they were going to be truly alone. He couldn't stop the broad smile rolling over his lips.

CHAPTER FIVE

YOU'VE still got time to turn around. Kirby braked at Nick's gate, already regretting the impulsive decision to drive along Nick's road in the hope of checking out his house. Why hadn't she just kept driving straight back into Port? Checking over her shoulder, she threw the gear stick into reverse, anxious to get back to the safety of the main road. With a quick, final glance around to check all areas were clear before she pressed down the accelerator, she looked up—straight into lush-green smiling eyes filled with a wicked glint.

Nick. Her mouth dried, and her tongue automatically moistened her lips. He'd seen her and now there was no turning back.

He moved forward with the easy grace of a panther and with a practised hand lazily swung the gate open and walked toward her car, his gait easy and rolling—a farmer's walk complete with a faithful dog trotting by his side. This time he really did look like a farmer from the tip of his battered hat down to his worn elastic-sided boots. Thankfully a shirt still covered his chest but as he got closer she realised it was wet.

Damp cotton clung to well-defined pectoral muscles and solid biceps, outlining them in perfect, taunting detail. Her heart thundered so hard in her chest that she could hear it. Could he? For all that the shirt didn't hide, it may as well have been off. *Why* had she pulled the wheel hard right at Sheep-Wash Corner? After all, her concern about a patient could have waited until tomorrow morning.

But that's not really why you're here, is it? You caved in and gave in to wanting to see where he lived. Gave in to wanting to see him.

Her palm connected hard with the top of the steering wheel and she welcomed the jarring sensation thudding painfully all the way to her shoulder. She was really starting to hate that challenging voice. She knew she should have just kept driving but she hadn't so now she needed to salvage the situation.

Wanting to be on the front foot, she flicked the switch that operated her window and watched it wind down, determined to get in the first word. 'Hello.'

He leaned forward, his arms resting casually on the door. 'G'day. Glad you could make it.'

His slow, drawling delivery stroked her skin, stoked the banked heat inside her. She swallowed hard as his scent of rich earth, hard work and soap washed over her, tugging at a basic need. In her search for control she blurted out, 'I was on my way back from visiting Tom Lenders and I wanted to ask you something.'

Dark brows rose, overriding the first crease of a frown as a flicker of disquiet appeared in his eyes. He pushed back from the door, the corded muscles in his arms thick like rope. 'Put her in gear and I'll meet you up at the house.'

'Are you sure?'

He nodded and slapped the cab of the vehicle with his hand as if to say, *Go through now.*

With her gut churning she drove through the gate, but Turbo soon had her smiling as he bounded forward, racing the car up past an enormous fenced vegetable garden. Glancing in the rear-view mirror, she saw Nick swing and latch the gate shut before turning and jogging back along the track. Pulling her eyes back to the road, she took the curve and a house came into view.

Wonder chased by regret immediately poured through her. A freshly painted weatherboard miner's cottage with a corrugated-iron roof stood in front of her, its plain Victorian lines offset by the simple decorative carving at the top of each veranda post. She slipped out of the four-wheel drive, her feet crunching on gravel, and Turbo immediately dropped a ball at her feet, panting at her in enthusiastic anticipation.

Distracted, she patted his head, her gaze still fixed on the house. *Whatever you want, my darling. Nothing will ever be too much for my wife and family. You know family is everything to me.*

She swallowed hard against Anthony's duplicitous voice and walked slowly up the box-hedge-lined path that led to the centre of the veranda and the front door flanked by matching aloe vera plants in heritage green wooden planters. Her shoes sounded loud on the hardwood boards as she stepped up from the worn bluestone step. Two wicker chairs sat invitingly on the veranda, with a low table in front of them. A sheaf of papers had been weighted down by a jug covered with an old-fashioned doily that kept flies from touching the contents. A well-thumbed novel lay face down, its spine deeply creased down the centre.

If there'd been a discarded scooter or skateboard nearby and some balls and a chalkboard, it would have been exactly as she'd pictured the house Anthony had promised her. The one she'd envisaged sharing with him and raising their family in.

Don't go there. Anthony doesn't want you. It's over, you know it's over.

Taking a deep breath, she plastered a smile on her face and turned at the sound of Nick's footsteps on the crushed white-rock path. 'Great house.'

'Thanks. I like it, although I wouldn't want to spend a winter without installing some heating.' He grinned at her. 'Open fires are all very romantic but they don't keep you very warm. It's definitely a summer house.'

He pulled off his work gloves, dropped them onto the table and poured two glasses of what looked like lemon cordial from the jug and passed her a glass. 'Grab a seat.'

Tendrils of warmth flicked through her veins as she lowered herself into the wide, comfortable chair. 'Is that the plan after this summer? To use it as a holiday house?'

He leaned back in his chair, his long legs stretching out in front of him, his left arm hanging down the side of the chair as his fingers rubbed Turbo's head. 'Probably. I love it down here but, like you, it's just a short-term plan.'

She stiffened as the horror of returning to Melbourne merged with all her insecurities. 'Why would you assume my plan is short term? Don't you think I can cut it as a country GP?'

He levelled a prosaic stare directly at her. 'You said this was your first GP rotation. That means you have to do a second one somewhere else.'

'Oh, right.' *Dumb, dumb, dumb.* She really should learn to think before she spoke. She took a slug of her drink and changed the subject. 'This is delicious—what is it?'

'Home-made lemon cordial.' He trailed his finger around the rim of his glass. 'You said you wanted to ask me something about Tom Lenders?'

Thankful to be back on safe territory she grabbed onto the topic with enthusiasm. 'Tom is a seventy-five-year-old man with hypertension and has recently been complaining of shortness of breath.'

'Any history of asthma?'

'No, and his chest X-ray is clear. There's no sign of cardiomyopathy or congestive cardiac failure but he has an audible wheeze and his peak flow is lower than expected.'

He tilted his head, intelligent eyes scanning her. 'So, what are *your* thoughts?'

She sat a bit straighter, feeling confident of her answer. 'I'm thinking that he has a form of asthma precipitated by the betablocker he's been taking for four years.'

Frown lines formed across his brow. 'And you brought this case to review why?'

She caught the slight tone of censure and was puzzled by his reaction. 'I wanted to be sure I didn't miss anything.'

He nodded, his lips pursing together firmly. 'You haven't missed a thing *but* I think you're missing the hospital system.'

His words sailed far too close to the truth for comfort and she smiled tightly. 'It takes a bit of getting used to but, no, I wouldn't say I was missing it.'

One black eyebrow rose enquiringly. 'Really? You've come from an environment where every decision made by a resident is reviewed by the registrar and every decision made by the registrar is reviewed by the consultant.' He put down his glass. 'Although by the time third year's over, most consultants are giving registrars a large amount of free rein.'

'Hmm.' She nodded and tacitly agreed. After all, what he said was true even though it hadn't actually happened to her.

He leaned forward. 'You would have found that?'

His gaze seemed to rivet itself to her mouth and she realised she was gnawing her bottom lip. She *so* didn't want to talk about this. Didn't want talk about how her life had fallen apart and she'd left her position at Prince William's way too early.

She tried a politician's tactic. Nodding, she gave another 'Hmm' and raised her arm. 'What do you call that tree over there?'

His head didn't move and his eyes didn't even flicker in the direction of the solid tree with the unusual seedpods. 'A banksia.' His gaze narrowed and his jaw tightened. 'You did finish third year?'

His accusatory tone lingered between them and his razor-sharp investigative look not only cornered her, it pinned her to the wall. Every instinct had her wanting to flee and she willed her phone to ring, wanting something, anything, to happen that would get her out of here. Adrenaline poured through her, the fight-and-flight response going into over-drive, and her body responded violently with a flush of non-sexual heat.

Horrible, unwanted heat washed through her, starting in her toes and building in intensity until all her skin burned so hot and tinder dry it felt like it would peel. Sweat immediately followed—drenching her, running in rivulets under her breasts, settling in the creases of her skin, threatening to soak her vest top. She gave thanks it was a hot summer's day and the flush and sweating would go unnoticed.

You're twenty-seven! What did you do to make this happen? Anthony's bitter voice boomed in her head. She downed her drink, forcing away the unwelcome voice, willing the hot flush to subside and steeling herself against the painful reminder of what it really meant.

Nick rose in one fluid movement and silently refilled her glass before settling back into his chair. His quiet voice rumbled deeply around the veranda, laced with tough resolve. 'As I'm acting as your mentor, I need to know how much experience you really have. You need to be honest with me, Kirby. I need the truth.'

The truth. Her heart pounded in agitation. He'd caught her out. She'd been double-checking everything because she hadn't had enough experience as a senior medical officer. But the moment she told him she'd left Prince William's early he'd ask why and the truth involved so many things she didn't want to tell.

The truth, the whole truth and nothing but the truth. The words read to a witness in court echoed in her mind. Suddenly a tiny shaft of light pierced the darkness and she knew she could tell Nick the truth. She sent up a silent vote of thanks that he hadn't asked for the whole truth. That she wasn't prepared to give.

Nick waited, watching a battle of emotions on Kirby's oval face. She really didn't want to tell him but he wouldn't let her get away without telling him. He would have to write up a report on her and for an accurate assessment he needed to have a starting benchmark. But he didn't want to sound like an inquisitor.

After all, she'd come out here to visit and he wanted it to be social more than work. He wanted a chance to be alone with her. He stood up and extended his hand. 'How about we walk and talk? There's a place I'd like to show you.'

Her already large eyes seemed to expand and her pale face flickered with gratitude mixed with resistant resignation. 'If you insist.' Her hand slowly slid into his.

'I do.' He pulled her to her feet and her reluctance seeped slowly into him, tagged by slowly building heat.

The moment she stood, she eased her hand out of his and walked toward the veranda steps.

Inexplicable loss streaked through him and he forced down every desire to grab back her hand. He strode after her. 'This way—the path goes from the back of the house.'

They walked in silence for a few minutes and he finally broke it. 'Come on, Sherlock, fill me in.'

She ducked under a low branch of a casuarina tree, her footfall hushed against the pile of dropped needles. 'You're right. I didn't finish my third year. In fact, I only completed seven months.'

He held up another branch for her and gave in to his need to breathe deeply, inhaling her wildflower scent as she passed by. 'That goes some way to explaining things.'

She gave a tight smile. 'Good.'

With the set of her mouth and the line of her shoulders he knew she was holding back more than she was giving. He took a calculated gamble to get her to tell him the story. 'Were you asked to leave Prince William?'

She came to an abrupt halt, indignation streaking across her face. 'No, I was not asked to leave. In fact, I was asked to re-consider my resignation.'

'But you didn't.'

'No.' She sighed and kept walking. 'I left for personal reasons.'

The path ended as they arrived at a creek lined with vibrant green tree ferns. Large fronds bent low toward the water, which burbled and rushed over and around granite boulders worn smooth by its action. Getting Kirby to tell him her story was like getting blood from one of the creek's stones. 'They must have been pretty big reasons if you left a job to come to this one before you were one hundred per cent ready.'

Her hands balled into fists and hung by her sides. 'If breaking off an engagement constitutes big, I guess it was.'

Her words surprised him, mostly because he hadn't expected her to have been engaged. He'd never considered marriage, it wasn't part of his life's plan, but he could empathise. 'At least you broke it off before it involved the full catastrophe of property and children.'

She swung away from him, an agonising sound starting to break from her lips.

The sound stopped abruptly but not before it tore at something inside him. He reached out and touched her arm. 'Hell, Kirby, I'm sorry, I just assumed it was you who broke it off.'

She turned back slowly toward him, her expression so full of hurt that it was the most natural thing in the world to pull her into his arms. With his forefinger he traced a line down her cheek. 'He didn't deserve you.'

As she looked up at him her voice cracked. 'He didn't want me the way I am.'

More than anything he wanted to banish the look of empty desolation that hovered in her beautiful eyes, haunting him. He tipped his head forward, feeling the caress of her breath on his face. 'More fool him.'

She stared straight at him and snagged her bottom lip with her teeth.

Desire thundered through him so hard it almost knocked the breath from his lungs. With his hand gently cupping her jaw, he lowered his mouth to hers, fusing his lips against her waiting softness and claiming what he'd dreamed about for days. She tasted of sugar tinged with citrus, of searing heat and need, and he lost himself in her, like a parched man stumbling into an oasis.

He trailed his tongue across her lips, touching, tasting and seeking entry, needing to bury himself in her heat and tang. Needing to absorb her essence, feel it in his veins.

Her mouth opened slowly under his and with a moan of need he accepted her unspoken invitation and deepened the kiss. Like an early voyager he explored and then he plundered, eagerly taking everything and still not getting enough. His arms tightened around her, moulding her soft curves to his toned body, treasuring the feel of having a beautiful, supple woman in his arms again. Stunned by how it far exceeded any memory.

Pulling away the loose band that barely held her hair in place, he breathed deeply, taking his fill of the aroma of cinnamon apples. His fingers splayed through her silky strands, revelling in the way their softness caressed his skin. As his mouth played over hers, he explored all the contours and dips, the peaks and hollows and left behind a firm imprint of himself.

The sound of the racing water of the creek, the songs of the birds and the rustling of the breeze through the ferns slowly retreated. All that existed was the feel of Kirby in his arms, the touch of her mouth against his and the way his blood pounded through him until every cell vibrated with the bliss of being alive.

'Nick.'

Her voice seemed a long way away. 'Hmm?' He started to trail kisses down to her jaw.

'Nick.' Her voice sounded louder, insistent, and her hands gripped his upper arms.

The pressure acted like a brake. He lifted his head and looked at her through dazed eyes, her image slowly coming into focus. Her fine hair cascaded around her face in complete disarray, her lush lips were wet, pink and swollen, but it was the startled look in her eyes that centred him with thudding brutality.

What the hell had he just done? He'd always prided himself on his finesse with women, of giving rather than taking, and yet right now, without any thought for her or her comfort, he'd kissed her senseless like a frustrated and randy teenager. He pulled back, mortified. 'I'm sorry, I shouldn't have done that. I shouldn't have kissed you.'

She stiffened slightly and her eyes, normally so clear, suddenly clouded, but then she shook her head. 'Please don't feel bad, it's not you, it's me. I just can't do this right now.' She drew in an unsteady breath and rested her palm on his forearm. 'I know it sounds really clichéd but what I really need is for you to be a colleague and a friend.'

A friend.

His blood drained from his groin and tried to perfuse his brain. A beautiful woman stood in front of him asking for his friendship. He'd never really done friendship with a woman and every part of him recoiled. He wanted her in his arms, he wanted her naked, and he wanted her wrapped tightly around him. Hell, he just wanted her.

He silently cursed the complete irony of the situation. His body had finally come roaring back to life, pulsing with virile good health, and the one woman he wanted didn't want him.

Somehow he managed to smile. 'Sure, I understand.'

Relief streamed across her face. 'You do?'

'I do.'

The hell you do, he told himself.

But he had to pretend he did. He had no other choice.

CHAPTER SIX

'HEY, Dr Kirby, I bet you I can race you to those big trees.'. Cooper pointed to the large Norfolk pines at the far end of the big asphalt car park at the back of Kids' Cottage.

'You're on.' Kirby stooped down and tightened her shoe-laces, smiling to herself. Three days ago Cooper had been withdrawn and sullen but the Port sunshine and the fabulous staff at KC had drawn him out. 'But do I get a handicap?'

Cooper flexed his fingers which extended from gloved palms. 'Nah, that's mine and today I'm not sharing.'

She grinned at the determination on his face. 'You're a tough opponent.' She put her left foot forward on an imaginary line as Cooper dropped his hands. 'Ready, set.'

'Go!' Cooper thrust forward, the wheels of his wheelchair spinning quickly as he propelled himself down the slight incline and toward the trees.

Kirby ran hard, needing to put in some serious effort to keep up, and she arrived at the pines seconds after him, panting for breath.

A beaming boy full of the flush of a win gave her faint praise. 'You did OK, Doc, better than my camp counsellor. I beat him by heaps!'

Too breathless to laugh, she rested her hands against her thighs. 'Thanks, Cooper, I like to keep fit.' She caught her breath and then headed back toward the main building, leaving Cooper at the archery range. Glancing at her watch, she increased her pace as she'd promised to do story time for the younger campers.

She loved spending time at KC and couldn't understand why Nick didn't want to do any work here. Why he really preferred not to work with children at all. She wondered if it was because Melbourne City was so very close to the Royal Children's Hospital so not many children came through Emergency. Perhaps he hadn't worked with many kids and paediatrics put him out of his comfort zone. But that reason didn't quite gel with her because Nick Dennison had a bring-it-on attitude to life and nothing seemed to faze him.

It really shouldn't bother her but it nagged at her because it was yet another part of the unsolved puzzle that was Nick, and she hated to admit it but the man fascinated her. He shouldn't because he wasn't her type at all. No man could be her type now.

Still, Nick not wanting to work at KC meant she didn't have to share the kids with anyone. She treasured that, visiting most days, even when she wasn't needed for her professional services. Although there was a large group of diabetic children visiting this week, not all the kids had a medical condition and many campers came to give their parents a break and a chance to sort out issues in their own lives. Often these children needed a lot more TLC than the kids who had a medical condition they'd grown to accept.

She loved children—loved their unbridled enthusiasm, their abundant curiosity and the sheer joy they could get from the simplest things. Her work here kept her busy, but it also kept her sane, filling a big hole in her life, filling a need.

Nick fills a need.

Nick. A vivid image of sea-green eyes filled with the simmering heat of desire flooded her, making her swallow hard.

Two weeks had passed since she'd called at Riversleigh and visited Nick at home. Two weeks since he'd kissed her senseless, reducing her to a quivering mass of pulsating need that had driven every coherent thought from her head. She'd revisited that kiss every day from every angle, from every blissful touch. She'd lost herself completely—melting into his arms and giving herself over to the intoxicating way his mouth had roamed deliciously over hers, sparking trails of glorious sensation that had spun and wove, tantalising her until she'd vibrated with pleasure and yearned for more.

Pathetically, it had only taken the touch of one kiss for her to ignore every promise she'd made to herself. She'd caved in completely and returned his kiss with the fervour of a lust-struck adolescent and taken as much from him as she could get. She'd absorbed his touch, savoured his earthy taste and revelled in the cocoon of his arms, never wanting the kiss to end.

But as the pressure of his mouth had lessened and his lips had trailed gloriously along her jaw, the slight change in his touch had been enough for a tiny but rational fissure to pierce her desire-fuelled haze. Panic had immediately surged. She'd pulled back, half hating what she was doing but knowing it was the right thing.

No matter how she'd once imagined her life playing out, she knew that dream was dead and that getting involved with any man was impossible. She knew that to be an irrefutable truth just as she knew the world to be round. She couldn't offer a man the future he would want—a future that she longed for but knew could never happen.

That was why Anthony had trashed her heart and left her, and why all other men would eventually leave her too. No way was she ever risking her bruised and shattered heart again to such wrenching pain.

Instead, she threw herself into caring for kids because it was as close as she was going to get to a child of her own.

She opened the library door to shrieks of, 'Read this one, Kirby,' and four enthusiastic pre-schoolers mobbed her, each clutching their own choice of book. Laughing, she collapsed onto the bright cushions and beanbags and gathered the children in close. 'We can read them all. Let's start with this story about the hare and his nut-brown baby.'

Warm bodies snuggled in, heads rested on her shoulders and her lap, and podgy hands touched her. She breathed in deeply, knowing intrinsically that she needed the comforting touch of these children as much as they needed her time and care.

The loud clang of metal against metal roused them all from their fourth story. Kirby finished reading the sentence, placed a bookmark between the pages and closed the book. 'That's the dinner bell, gang. Let's skip to the dining hall.'

'I want to hop.' A small but determined five-year-old stood with her hands authoritatively on her hips.

Kirby smiled and adopted a mediating approach. 'We can do that too but maybe we should hold hands.'

With lots of giggles and squeals, they made their way across the quadrangle to the mess hall, where the girls' camp counsellor waited to take them into dinner. 'Wash your hands first.'

As the girls obediently lined up at the taps at the base of

the stairs, the counsellor smiled at Kirby. 'Thanks for doing story-time. It gave me a chance to telephone their parents and reassure them that all is well.'

A real sense of community rolled through her. 'It's my pleasure. I think I enjoy the stories more than they do.' She glanced at her watch. 'But I'd better get going or else the supermarket will be closed and I'm getting tired of tinned spaghetti on toast.'

With a quick wave to the girls, Kirby ducked behind the old, grey, salt-weathered buildings and made her way back toward her car. She'd just pressed the auto-unlock button when she heard someone call her name and she turned toward the voice.

Hurrying toward her was Judy Dalton, the woman in charge of KC, her round cheeks pink with exertion. 'Oh, I'm so glad I caught you. Ben Hadley, one of the diabetic boys, has just vomited everywhere and he's looking a bit pale and wan.'

'Vomiting before dinner? Has he had his before-dinner insulin?' Kirby opened the boot and pulled out her medical kit, a thread of concern weaving through her.

Judy gave a quick nod. 'Yes, he'd just come up to sick bay to have it, which is why I left Phillipa with him, trying to encourage him to eat a jelly snake, and I ran to catch up with you.'

'I'm glad you caught me.' Kirby slammed the boot closed, hoping she could reach the boy before he had a hypo.

They jogged to the sick bay and found thirteen-year-old Ben lying on the bed, his face very white—even his freckles looked pale. Beads of sweat lined his forehead, dripping into his hair, and he'd pulled his legs up under his chin. Shaking, he gripped a large monometal bowl and promptly vomited into it.

'That's the third time he's vomited.' Phillipa quickly exchanged the bowl for a clean one. 'He can't have much more left in his stomach.'

Kirby pulled out her glucometer machine. 'I gather he wasn't able to hold down the snake.'

The woman shook her head. 'No, that came up too.'

'Hey, mate, sorry you're feeling sick.' Kirby knelt down beside Ben and put her hand on his forehead, her fingers hot from the heat radiating from his skin. 'Because you've vomited just after having insulin we need to give you some glucose to prevent a hypo. I'm going to put in a drip so you don't get dehydrated, and when your blood-sugar levels are sorted, we'll work out what's making you sick, OK?'

'OK.' The word came out in the familiar resigned tone that kids with chronic medical conditions often used.

'Finger jab first.' Kirby gave Ben a reassuring smile, quickly pricked his finger and carried out the glucometer reading. As expected, his blood sugar was too low. 'I'm going to give you mini-dose glucagon injection and then insert the drip.'

'My stomach really hurts.' Ben tensed up as a spasm hit him.

Kirby chewed her lip and swallowed a sigh. Vomiting in children could be due to so many different things—appendicitis, urinary-tract infection, meningitis. The list ran through her head as she injected the glucagon so the insulin had something to work on.

'Phillipa, can you please take Ben's temperature with the ear thermometer while I insert the IV?' Kirby handed the instrument to the woman and quickly primed the IV tubing.

'Thirty-nine point one.' Phillipa tossed the disposable earpiece into the bin.

'I thought he felt hot.' Kirby added an antipyretic to her list of drugs for Ben. Wrapping the tourniquet around his arm, she quickly found a vein, which was reassuring as often kids dehydrated really quickly. 'Hold still, Ben, it will be over in a moment.' She slid the IV cannula home and turned the drip onto a medium rate and gave him some Maxalon for the vomiting. 'Right, well, that combined with the rescue dose of glucagon should keep your blood-sugar level above five as well as keeping you hydrated. I've given you something to help the nausea and the fever but now I need to examine you. Tell me where your tummy hurts.'

'Everywhere.' Ben's voice broke on a sob.

She stroked his forehead. 'You poor old thing. I just need to have a gentle feel, OK?' Lifting his T-shirt, she started a gentle palpation of his abdomen, half expecting to find some guarding and rebound tenderness on the right side. Acute appendicitis presented with fever, vomiting and pain.

'Kirby.' Judy walked into the room, supporting a boy who was shivering violently. 'We've got another customer.' She laid the boy down on the other bed in the room. 'This is Cameron and he's diabetic as well.'

'I'm gonna puke.' Cameron heaved.

With the skill of experience Kirby managed to push a bowl under his chin just in time. She wiped his mouth and gave him a sip of water. 'When did you start to feel sick?'

'During dinner.' The boy laid his head back down on the pillow.

Kirby took his temperature. 'Thirty-eight five. You've got a fever, just like Ben. I need to check your blood-sugar levels, OK?'

'I can do it.' Cameron tried to sit up and fell back.

'Are you feeling dizzy?' Kirby asked the rhetorical

question as she quickly pricked his finger. Deftly placing the drop of blood neatly on the stick, she inserted it into the machine. 'Two point seven. I'm giving you a glucagon injection into your thigh right now.'

But Cameron was too drowsy to reply.

'Judy, can you do a glucometer check on Ben for me while I insert a drip into Cam?'

Judy nodded. 'Sure. Do you think they've both picked up a virus? They're in the same bunkhouse.'

Kirby concentrated on locating a vein. 'I had thought Ben might have appendicitis but his examination doesn't match up with that and now with Cameron I'm wondering if—'

Phillipa rushed in. 'I've got four more boys, all with the same symptoms.'

Kirby taped Cameron's IV in place, a sense of foreboding settling in her chest. 'Are they all diabetic?'

'Yes.'

She had kids dropping like flies. Running her hand through her hair, she marshalled her thoughts. 'Is anyone else at camp other than the diabetics starting to get sick?'

Phillipa shook her head. 'Everyone else is hale and hearty, chowing down to dinner as usual.'

She turned to Ben, who was more alert than Cameron. 'Ben, have you eaten anything today that didn't come from the KC kitchen?'

Guilt streaked across his cheeks and he dropped his gaze. 'Maybe.'

Kirby kept her voice light. 'I need you to tell me, mate, so I can work out what is making you and the other boys so sick.'

'I had…I ate a chocolate bar.' The mumbled words were barely audible. 'I'm sorry, I didn't think it would make me hurl.'

She patted his arm. 'I don't think a chocolate bar would cause you to be this sick. Did you eat anything else?'

The sick boy's gaze darted between Kirby, Judy and Phillipa, anxiety and fear duelling with a need to tell the truth. 'We…we sneaked out to the Greasy Spoon.'

Kirby recognised the name of the take-away shop about half a kilometre away and suppressed a sigh. 'Who's "we"?'

He swallowed hard. 'Unit C.'

'And what did you eat?'

'Chicken and chips. The lady gave it to us cheap.'

A vision of hot food sitting in an old bain-marie for longer than the allowed time took residence in Kirby's mind. A cooling chicken would be the perfect vehicle for hosting salmonella. And the boys had the vomiting, nausea and abdominal pain that fitted the picture. She suppressed a groan at the thought of the diarrhoea that would inevitably follow.

She swung around to Judy. 'So we have six boys so far. How many boys are in that bunkhouse?'

Judy grimaced. 'Fourteen.'

'Fourteen?' She couldn't keep the rising inflection of horror out of her voice. Fourteen vomiting diabetics. Fourteen kids at risk of hypoglycaemia. Not to mention other members of the public who might have eaten at the shop. Her mind started to race with the logistics of dealing with this outbreak.

The hospital only had six acute beds and based on what had happened so far they could expect more than double the current number of cases. She needed to set up an isolation ward, get extra medical supplies from Barago and organise an urgent courier to rush samples to the lab for an accurate diagnosis. As Port's medical officer she had to notify the health department and shut down the Greasy Spoon pending investigation and testing. But most importantly she would probably be treating and monitoring fourteen really sick children. Their care came first. How the hell was she going to divide herself up to meet every demand?

Judy and Phillipa looked at her expectantly. 'So what's your plan and how can we help?'

Nick dangled his legs over the edge of the Port Bathurst pier, a fishing rod in one hand and the other resting on Turbo's collar. The dog was crouched down, calculating how to round up the seagulls who hovered close by, ever hopeful of a free feed.

'Fishing is supposed to be relaxing, Turbo. You have to give in to the joy of sitting and waiting.'

Quizzical brown eyes met his gaze and Nick gave an ironic laugh. 'Yeah, well, that's the theory.'

Con Papadopoulos, one of his nursing-home patients, had told him that the pier at the turn of the tide was *the* place to catch dusky flathead. Fishing wasn't something that Nick had ever really done but right now he was looking for new experiences, looking for anything that took his mind off a blue-eyed, blonde-haired beauty with a smile that sent his blood racing.

Fishing didn't seem to be cutting it. Neither had cold showers, ten-K runs or fifty-K bike rides. No matter what he did, thoughts of Kirby roamed wild and free in his mind. He was used to getting what he wanted with women and the fact that she didn't want him in her bed ate at him.

Friendship. The word tasted bitter in his mouth. How could she only want friendship when their desire for each other vibrated palpably between them?

He reeled in the line for the fifth time to find the hook bait-less yet again. He sighed—so far he'd only managed to feed the fish and feed them well. He opened the bait box to try again and his phone vibrated in his pocket. Wiping his hands on his jeans first, he pulled out the phone, a crazy jolt of joy making his heart skip when he read the display. *Kirby*.

Kirby ringing at six o'clock when clinic was over and the evening was looming—perhaps she'd had a change of heart. Pressing the phone to his ear, he answered the call. 'If you're offering to take me out to dinner, I accept because not one single fish has landed on my line.'

'It's not a dinner invitation.'

The serious tone of her voice quickly dispatched all ideas of flirting and he immediately shot into professional mode. 'What's happened?'

'I need you out at Kids' Cottage—'

He cut her off, memories from his childhood flashing at him like a neon sign. 'I told you I don't work at the camp.'

'Well, today you do.' Her voice unexpectedly whipped him. 'I've got a suspected outbreak of salmonella poisoning and so far all the cases are diabetics.'

Hell! He raked his free hand through his hair as his pulse picked up. Sick diabetic kids. This was more than just maintaining fluids and electrolytes. This was complicated by either hyper- or hypoglycaemia. It didn't matter which way he looked at it, didn't matter how he felt about the camp, Kirby was right. This time he didn't have the luxury of choice. As a doctor he had to be there.

Forcing down uncomfortable memories, he sighed. 'I'll be there in ten minutes.'

'Make it five.'

The phone went dead, the silence deafening in its censure.

CHAPTER SEVEN

THE sharp electronic beep of Nick's watch signalled three a.m. as he walked slowly and softly along the long row of beds, the old wooden floorboards creaking in protest as he checked all their patients. Low night lighting illuminated the beds along with the silvery beams of a waning moon and he didn't need to use his torch.

Every bed was predictably identical, although these beds with their laminated pine bedheads and built-in drawers underneath the mattress were a lot more flash than the old metal beds he'd slept on at similar camps around the country. The same brightly coloured doonas lay on each of the eighteen beds and fourteen of them had sick pubescent boys huddled underneath, fitfully sleeping. Four beds contained sick adults who'd also eaten at the Greasy Spoon, their pale faces looking slightly at odds with the 'superpowers' doona tucked under their chins.

Kirby had created an isolation ward in one of the dormitories in the grounds of KC and everyone affected by the outbreak was being treated here rather than at the hospital. It made sense seeing that he and Kirby had been frantic—treating children non-stop for the last nine hours. They'd just managed to go one full hour without admitting a new case and hopefully no one else in the community had eaten the contaminated food.

They'd divided the care of the patients evenly and both of them had been so busy they'd hardly spoken to each other all night, but he'd known exactly where she'd been in the dorm at all times. Her sweet scent wafted on the air and when she spoke to her patients he could hear her reassuring and gentle voice. An immature part of him wished he was sick so he could feel her hand on his brow and hear such care for him in her voice. He ignored the thought as he'd learned long ago to take no notice of errant thoughts generated by long hours and fatigue.

Kirby's manner with the kids was the perfect blend of caring mother and objective professional and he couldn't help but be impressed. *The cottage was a big drawcard for me to come to Port.* He wondered if he should talk to her about pursuing paediatrics.

Judy Dalton touched his arm. 'Phillipa and I are back from a break. I've just convinced Kirby she needs to take one and so do you.'

Nick looked up the dorm toward Cameron.

Judy followed his gaze, understanding on her face. 'I promise I'll call you if he needs you.' She gave him a gentle push. 'Go.'

'You've got my mobile number?'

She nodded patiently. 'You're not going to be far away and I've got your number plus my phone is on and charged. Worst-case scenario, I can yell really loud.' She pointed to the door and mouthed, 'Go now.'

Part of him felt he should stay but most of him wanted to

take the chance of leaving the claustrophobic brown walls of the dorm. He hadn't had a break since he'd arrived.

'You OK?' Kirby greeted him as he walked into the kitchen, her voice soft.

'Fine.' Nick avoided meeting her far-too-observant gaze as he accepted the proffered mug of hot, steaming tea. Instead he stuck to the much easier topic of medical supplies. 'Has more saline arrived from the hospital yet?'

'Theo just rang and it's on its way.' She stifled a yawn but she couldn't hide the dark smudges under her eyes.

'You look completely whacked.' His hand tightened around the mug, tensing against the powerful urge to wrap his arms around her and pull her against him while he stroked her hair and let her sleep on his shoulder.

Her brows rose as her mouth twitched. 'I'd heard you had a way with words.' Laughter threaded through her voice. 'Now I can see why women lined up to date you.' She rested her chin against her palm. 'You look pretty exhausted yourself. How are your boys doing?'

'Fair.' He sipped his tea, welcoming the comforting warmth. Being inside the dorm had brought back far too many uneasy memories—massive homesickness, feelings of abandonment—and Cameron's grip on his hand and the baleful look in his eye had reminded him too much of himself at that age.

He leaned back and swung his feet up onto a chair. 'It's a fine line between too much and not enough insulin, and Cameron's levels keep swinging but at least he's stopped vomiting. I'll be a lot happier when Barago rings in the blood results.'

'Hypernatraemia is always a worry, isn't it?' She slid a covered plate toward him, a plume of steam curling up from the hole in the top of the silver cover. The aroma of garlic and onions filled the room.

He smiled at her rhetorical question that a couple of weeks ago would have been a real question. He was really pleased that she'd started trusting her judgement rather than second-guessing every decision. 'It is. We'll do another round of bloods at six a.m. and check everyone's electrolytes, including potassium.' He lifted up the food cover, suddenly hungry, realising it had been hours since he'd eaten.

She gave a quiet chuckle as she tucked into her spaghetti bolognaise. 'Poor Constable Masterton. This is his first posting after graduation and I think he came to Port hoping to crack an international abalone ring, and we've got him transporting blood samples between here and Barago.'

'Hey, he got to use the siren so he's happy.' Nick couldn't fault the way Port had pulled together to deal with this crisis. The paramedics had transported equipment, the nurses had all come back on duty and spread themselves between the hospital and KC, and now the camp kitchen was working all night keeping the staff well fed.

But it had been Kirby who'd organised everything. 'Three weeks ago I would have doubted you could have handled this sort of challenge but you've aced it. You're one hell of an organiser—I doubt anyone would have been brave enough to say no to you.'

'You tried.' She tilted her head and stared straight at him, her eyes lit with undisguised curiosity. 'I don't get it. Why haven't you wanted to work here?'

Damn it, how had a compliment to her suddenly become all about him? He tried a flippant response. 'You love kids so I was giving you free rein.'

Her stunning eyes narrowed. 'You don't like kids?'

He willed his facial muscles to adopt a neutral expression. 'I don't have anything against them.'

A ripple of irritation skated across her cheeks. 'What sort of answer is that? I saw you in action tonight and you were thorough and caring so I know that you not wanting to work here has *nothing* to do with a lack of medical knowledge, unless…'

He caught the moment her mind made the connection and his stomach clenched.

Her forehead creased with an expression of complete bewilderment. 'Why wouldn't you want to work at a wonderful place like this?'

His sister Sarah's contorted face, her contracted muscles and wasted body beamed through his brain, taking him back twenty-odd years in an instant, the images clogging his mind. His heart hammered against his ribs as voices-past jumbled in his head, loud and discordant.

Your mother needs a break, Nick. This way everyone gets a holiday.

I hate it here, let me come home.

Sweetheart, we love you. Camp will be fun.

'Nick. Nick?'

Kirby's voice broke through the cacophony of sound as he became aware of the clink of the spoon against china. 'You've gone all white. Here, I've added some sugar to your tea.' She pushed the mug into his right hand and covered his left hand with her own. 'It's KC, isn't it?'

She'd done it again. For years he'd spent a lot of time with a lot of women and not one of them had read him like Kirby could. She managed to get under his guard every single time. Her warmth trailed through him, slowing his racing heart, calming him. He finally met her gaze, the pull of her concern drawing him in. 'Yeah, it's the camp, Sherlock. Not this camp specifically but all camps like it. I spent a lot of time in them as a kid.'

Surprise lit up her eyes. 'Not good memories?'

He laced his fingers through hers, the need to touch her overwhelmingly strong. 'If a kid wants to come to a place like this then, like you say, it's going to be a great experience.'

'But not for you?'

He shook his head. 'I didn't want to be there and I resented that I had to go.' His fingers brushed the back of her hand, absorbing her softness. 'My younger sister, Sarah, had severe cerebral palsy. She'd been born at twenty-six weeks, was blind, severely contracted and needed twenty-four-hour care. I was five when she was born and I remember the hushed voices, the strained and grey faces of my parents and grandparents, and an overwhelming feeling that everything had just changed. It was weeks before she came home and when she did, she understandably absorbed my parents' time.'

'But at five you wouldn't have understood.' Kirby's keen eyes shone with empathy.

'No. As a kid I was consumed by a feeling that I had lost something huge but I didn't have the words to describe it. As Sarah got older and was permanently in a wheelchair, I realised she was never going to be any different and it was like a wound that never healed. Growing up I was both acutely embarrassed by Sarah and fiercely protective of her, especially if kids made crass remarks, but I just wanted to have a normal, healthy sister and be a normal kid. I craved a regular family, one where I could chase Sarah around the garden, tease her like a big brother is supposed to, and argue in the back seat during long car journeys.'

'And coming to camp just marked you as different.'

His head snapped up at the words that so aptly described what he'd been through. 'That's right. I always felt different. While my friends were off holidaying with their family or even getting to stay home and ride their bikes around the cul-de-sac, I was shunted off to camp.'

The vivid blue of her irises suddenly darkened. 'Or were you given the opportunity to have some freedom from your family?'

Her Pollyanna words gnawed at him, pulling at the child within. 'All I know is that had I ever been a father, I wouldn't be sending a kid to camp if he didn't want to go.'

'*Had* you ever been a father?' She leaned forward, her face earnest. 'You're thirty-three, with loads of time to become a father.'

He shook his head. 'Not after chemo, I don't. Chemo-therapy doesn't differentiate between healthy cells and malignant ones, and it nukes sperm. One of the side effects is infertility.'

Her brows drew in, carving a deep V above her nose. 'I knew that. But surely you would have banked sperm before you started treatment?'

He folded his arms across his chest. 'I chose not to.'

'What?' Incredulity lay thick and heavy on the word. 'Why on earth would your doctors have allowed you to make that decision?'

'Allowed me?' Anger flashed inside him at her lack of understanding. 'I wasn't some naïve twenty-year-old, I was thirty-one and I knew what I wanted. I lived through my parents' unresolved grief after Sarah died so young and I saw the effect it had on their lives, felt the effect it had on my life. I want control over my life and I'm not taking any risks of having a disabled or sick child so a long time ago I made the decision that I didn't want to be a parent. Ever.'

Kirby abruptly pulled her hand out of his, her face flushing bright red and her eyes sparking with glints of pure rage. 'So you just tossed away a precious gift?'

Her fury rolled over him in ever-increasing waves, instantly putting him on the defensive. He stood up and walked around the table until he stood next to her. Drawing on every ounce of control he had, he managed to grind out a reply. 'Look, this was *my* choice and it has nothing at all to do with you.'

Her chest pushed in and out quickly, her breathing suddenly ragged. 'How could you?' Her voice rose, tinged with a maniacal edge, and her body shook. 'How could you give away your fertility, just like that, as if it was a disposable item?'

The thump of her fists on his chest caught him by surprise. He grabbed her wrists in self-defence, planning to set her back from him, but he caught a glimpse of her eyes and his breath left his lungs. Her raw grief knifed him, harrowing in its candour. What the hell was going on?

Kirby felt his vice-like grip against her skin and a surge of anguish poured through her. How could he have terminated his fertility? How could he have willingly given up the gift that had been stolen from her? Searing pain burned her chest, silver spots flickered against inky darkness and she heard a wrenching, guttural cry.

A moment later she became aware of soft-spun cotton cushioning her cheek and the reassuring pressure of Nick's arms holding her gently yet securely against him. His hands stroked her hair and his voice, low and mellow, caressed her ear. 'Breathe deeply, sweetheart, breathe, it will be OK.'

His calming voice, the tenderness of his arms and the heat

of his body soothed her, and her anger ebbed away. A tiny part of her tried to hold onto it but the flames had been doused as fast as they had flared, and the only thing left inside her was exhaustion. Exhaustion and embarrassment. How could she have lost control like that? She valued her control—it protected her.

But today it had gone AWOL and left her totally exposed. She sucked down a deep breath and buried her barrenness back where it belonged—out of sight but rarely out of mind. With superhuman effort she dragged her head up from Nick's sheltering shoulder and stepped out of his arms. She pushed her facial muscles up into a wan smile and levelled her gaze at his left ear.

'Please accept my sincere apologies.' She splayed her hands out in supplication. 'Sleep deprivation has obviously taken its toll on me but I promise you such an outburst won't ever happen again.' She turned toward the door. 'We better get back to the children.'

His hand caught hers, the grip firm. 'Kirby, two minutes ago you were hysterical. You're not ready to go back to the kids and right now they don't need you. Judy and Phillipa have everything under control and we can take a bit more time.' His keen gaze held hers, swirling with care and questions as his finger trailed down her cheek.

She tried to steel herself against the blissful sensations that coursed through every part of her. 'I'm just overtired.'

'There's more to it than that. I saw complete desolation in your eyes and I heard it in your voice. Tell me what's going on, I want to help.'

The empathy in his eyes, combined with the warmth of his touch, eroded her fragile façade and she closed her eyes for a moment, knowing that when she opened them she would have to tell him the whole truth.

She opened her eyes and strode to the freezer, hauling out two much-needed creamy vanilla ice creams covered in dark chocolate. If she had to bare her soul she needed comfort food. 'Here, catch.'

'Thanks.' Nick caught the confectionary, ripped open the gold foil wrapper, saluted her with the ice cream and then raised it to his lips, his mouth caressing the chocolate.

The memory of their kiss thundered through her and she bit down hard on her own ice cream, marshalling her thoughts. 'You can't help me but you do deserve an explanation, especially as I hit you, and I have *never* done that before to anyone in my life.' She gave a snort of derision. 'Not even to Anthony.'

He winked. 'Now, he might have deserved it.'

She managed a smile. 'You don't have to be this nice.'

He grinned at her—a look of pure magnetism. 'It's what I do.' He moved in next to her, his back against the freezer, his arm barely touching hers, and yet it pinned her with his support.

She bit her lip. 'I guess I start at the beginning. I met Anthony at a charity fundraiser for underprivileged children. He was ten years older than me, witty and entertaining, and he came from a large family, just like I did. We shared in common growing up in a chaotic household of kids, pets and love. He talked about how much he wanted to re-create those special times for children of his own and I knew exactly what he meant.'

A shudder ran through her. 'At least, I thought I did. Looking back, he actively chased me—flowers at work, helicopter rides to dinner and a whirlwind romance that culminated in his proposal three months later. He wanted to start a family straight away.'

Nick frowned. 'What about your career? Wouldn't waiting two years have been better for you?'

She dragged in a steadying breath, hating it that he could see so clearly what she had allowed to happen. 'Yes, but Anthony was nothing if not persuasive. He told me he was financially secure, and that he'd be a hands-on father and he'd support me to return to work to finish my training. I'd always seen children in my future so although it was all a bit faster than I wanted, I agreed that we'd start our family as soon as the ink was dry on the wedding certificate.'

'An old-fashioned honeymoon baby?'

She winced. 'Yep, but plans have a funny way of not working out. A few months before the wedding, in the middle of working flat out and trying to appease Anthony's mother, who wanted her son to have the full-catastrophe extravaganza, I missed two periods. I assumed I was pregnant and we were over the moon but…' She faltered, and took a bite of her ice cream, bracing herself for the words she really didn't want to speak.

'It's not unusual to skip a couple of periods during high-stress times.'

Nick's understanding voice encased her and she pushed on. 'If it had been that easy I wouldn't be standing here. When the blood-test report came back there were no signs of hCG.' She cleared her throat against the tightening sensation. 'I wasn't pregnant, my FSH levels were enormously high and my oestrogen was below the floor.'

'Premature ovarian failure.' He softly spoke the words for her as his hand slowly curled around hers. 'Are you sure it wasn't just a hormonal aberration?'

She shook her head. 'I prayed for that but I had a series of tests and for some reason my ovaries packed in at twenty-seven.'

'That totally sucks.' He rubbed his free hand through his hair, the silver strands on his temples glinting. 'So you and Anthony discussed adoption, right?'

She stared at him, her heart breaking. How was it that this man in front of her, this man who didn't want children of his own, could see that there was another path available? Her breath shuddered out as she spoke the final indignity. 'Anthony refused to discuss egg donors or adoption. He blamed me for causing the POF, blamed my workload, my focus on my career—blamed me, full stop. I went into shock, unable to believe his reaction, but that's when I realised...' She fisted her hands, willing herself to stay strong and steady.

Nick's frown deepened but his voice was gentle. 'That's when you realised what?'

She bit her lip. 'That he didn't love me. That I was just the means to his end.'

'I don't understand.' Clear green eyes bored into her, searching for an explanation.

'POF exposed the truth about my relationship, which it turns out was a sham. I had invested all my love in something that didn't exist.' She rubbed her forehead with her forefinger, trying to marshal her thoughts into a coherent sequence. 'Anthony was older than me and from a large Italian family. I had no idea that he'd been promised a huge amount of family money when he produced a grandchild. Apparently, when I met him, his business was struggling and he needed a cash injection so he'd borrowed against this promise of money.'

Nick's sharp intake of breath sounded in her ears but she pushed on, just wanting to get the story over with. 'It turns out that he'd come to the fundraiser with the express purpose of meeting someone who loved kids and would fall for his charm and happily provide him with the child he needed. I was the bunny that fell but the moment he found out I was faulty goods, he replaced me with Lisa, who, it appears, is as fertile as a rabbit.' She blinked rapidly, hating her own weakness. 'Their first child is due in a few months.'

'He's a complete bastard.'

She gave a watery laugh. 'Yeah, he is.'

'So really POF saved you.'

Startled, she looked up at him, not believing he had said those words. 'Saved me? It stole everything from me.'

He tilted his head, his brows raised in question. 'It saved you from a loveless marriage, and that has to be a good thing.'

She rolled his words through her brain, thinking about everything she'd lost, and with sudden clarity she realised she didn't have a single regret about losing Anthony. But she had a suitcase of regrets about her future. She was damaged goods. Most men wanted their own biological child and POF had stolen her chance to give any man that.

Not Nick.

She immediately discarded the thought, not wanting to go there. That was just heartache on a stick. She wanted kids in her future and her infertility burned inside her, hot and painful every time she thought about it. But she didn't want to talk about her infertility with Nick. He didn't want children, he'd actively chosen infertility and he wouldn't understand. No, they were at opposite ends of that spectrum with an almighty and unbreachable chasm between them.

She tossed her head and gave him a tight smile. 'Anyway, that's the past, it's over and I'm in Port, working with kids and getting my fill that way.'

He squeezed her hand, his expression earnest. 'You could do foster-care when you've finished your GP training.'

He was trying so hard to help, trying to make her feel better, and it tore shreds off her heart. Yes, she could do foster-care and it probably would be great, but it would also emphasise what she'd lost. Like most women, she wanted a man who loved her and a family, and she couldn't ever have that.

Tears threatened, pricking the backs of her eyes, and she couldn't stand there one more minute or she'd burst into tears or, worse, she'd throw herself back into his arms. Neither was a good idea and crying wasn't a good look, especially after she'd already had one emotional melt-down tonight. 'It's something to think about but right now I need to think about the four a.m. round and so do you.' She dropped her wooden ice-cream stick into the bin and regretfully but crucially pulled her hand out from under his. 'See you out there.'

Nick watched her walk through the door—head erect, shoulders straight and hips swaying. The sexiest walk he'd ever seen, and she didn't have a clue. *Faulty goods, my eye.* That lousy ex-fiancé had stolen her belief that she was a gorgeous and desirable woman and after all she'd been through the least she deserved was to get that back.

She needed to know that she was all woman, one hundred per cent deliciously hot, and he was just the man to show her. He smiled as anticipation shot through his veins. Planning this was going to be fun—executing it even better.

CHAPTER EIGHT

KIRBY checked her watch, stretched and smiled. Five to six on a Friday evening and time to head home. After the drama of the salmonella outbreak, the rest of the week had been blissfully tame medically speaking, with straightforward consultations and only one tourist coming to grief. He now had a white cast on his leg—a souvenir to remember Port by and a reminder of the night he'd over-indulged at the pub.

Somehow over the last few days she'd managed to regain her equilibrium and had done a reasonable job of faking an 'Aren't we good colleagues?' persona with Nick. She hated it that she'd completely broken down in front of him and she knew that because of that one emotional outburst he now thought of her differently. She'd caught him in the act of a sideways glance a few times—he was probably panicking she'd break down again and was counting the days until the summer was over and he could get back to Melbourne and more sane company.

He'd never mentioned their conversation again but she kept revisiting the pain on his face when he spoke about his sister. She chewed her lip and sighed. Everyone had their own share of heartache.

Just keep moving forward one step at a time.

She quickly scribbled down a list of jobs for Monday, including a phone call to Melinda's oncologist in Melbourne to get a treatment update. Then, gathering up her case histories and her bag, she headed out to Reception.

'Here you go, Vicki, all signed, notated and ready for you.' She dumped the folders onto the laminate counter.

'Thanks, dear.' Vicki's brown eyes bored into her from behind purple-framed glasses. 'So what have you got planned this evening?'

Kirby swallowed a sigh. Vicki asked her this question every Friday and never seemed satisfied with the answer. 'I'm picking up a new book from the newsagent's, grabbing a huge plate of seafood from the festival and then I'm going to sit on the deck, open a bottle of Barago merlot and watch the sunset over the ocean.'

And try not to think about Nick. Not think about how wonderful it had felt to be nestled against him, her head in the crook of his neck, his firm chest against hers... She pulled her attention back to Vicki, who had pursed her lips.

'Drinking alone, dear, that's not very wise.'

'But it's merlot so I can put the cork back in.' Kirby plastered on a smile and scooted to a safer topic. 'What are you doing this weekend?'

'My nephew, the lawyer from Melbourne—the one I was telling you about—arrived yesterday and is staying for a few days.' Vicki efficiently slotted the histories in the floor-to-ceiling filing cupboard.

'That will be fun for you, having a bit of company.' She knew how much Vicki missed her children.

The older woman nodded. 'Yes, but he won't want to

spend all his time with his old aunt.' A cunning smile twitched the corners of her mouth upward. 'I'm a bit weary tonight and I'd really appreciate it if you took him to the jazz-and-seafood festival.'

Kirby tried not to groan audibly. Vicki had been very good to her and she didn't want to hurt her feelings, but on the other hand she really didn't want to spend her Friday evening entertaining her nephew, no matter how rich and gorgeous he was purported to be. Her mind trawled for the right combination of words to gently reject the suggestion but the creak of the front door opening interrupted her. Nick strode in, radiating vibrant good health with a broad smile on his handsome face to match.

An increasingly familiar surge of undisguised need immediately flared deep inside her and her buttocks tightened instinctively. He looked good. More than good—bronzed, toned and holding a toolkit, he looked liked her fantasy.

A well-known surfing-brand T-shirt caressed his broad chest and crisply ironed stone-coloured shorts clad his muscular legs, but her eyes zeroed in on his wet hair, which she noticed now had enough length to curl at the nape of his neck. He looked fresh, clean and sun-kissed and she realised he must have recently stepped out of a shower. A vision of Nick naked slammed into her, drying her mouth.

Nick raised the red metal box in his hand. 'Vicki, I was on my way past and had my toolkit in the truck so I've fixed the wire door. It now closes properly and keeps the flies out, instead of inviting them into the waiting room.'

Vicki gave a cry of delight. 'Nick, you're wonderful. Talented *and* handy, and if I was thirty years younger, look out.'

Nick gave a deep rolling laugh, his eyes crinkling up with

the ease of a man comfortable in his own skin. 'You would have been far too much woman for me, Vicki.'

She chuckled. 'Well, that's right, I probably would have—I wore out Roger, bless him.' She started pressing the buttons on the security pad. 'So, Kirby, if you come with me now, I'll introduce you to Andrew.'

Kirby thought she saw a ripple of tension cross Nick's shoulders but she didn't have time to wonder about that and it was probably just his muscles countering the weight of the toolbox. She *so* didn't want to spend the evening with Andrew and desperate situations meant desperate measures.

Ignoring every lesson she'd learned at her mother's knee, she prepared herself to lie. She'd make something up about a clinic problem and she fervently hoped Nick would just roll with it and not question her in front of Vicki. She'd apologise and explain it all to him later, after Vicki had left and she was off the hook from dating Andrew. 'I'm really sorry, Vicki, but Nick didn't just come to fix the wire door. I asked him to come in because—'

'The fact is, Vicki, she wants me, not Andrew.' Nick winked, his eyes sparkling with pure devilment. 'She's taking *me* to the festival.'

Kirby almost choked on the spot. His audacity was unbelievable and a barrage of indignant words poured into her mouth, preparing to unleash her wrath. But they immediately clagged against her tongue as she realised none of them could be spoken without giving her away. Her lie neatly corralled every word, leaving her completely exposed and at its mercy. At Nick's mercy. What was he playing at?

Vicki's grin almost split her face and she gave Kirby a knowing look, one that said, *You're a sly one but he's as sexy as hell, so of course you want him.* 'Why didn't you just say that you and Nick are an item instead of hiding behind that silly story about drinking alone?'

Oh, great, now she looked like a desperate alcoholic. 'I—'

Nick slipped his free arm through Kirby's, his fingers firmly entwining with hers. He tilted his head, giving Vicki a serious look. 'We wanted to keep it quiet. You know what Port's like.'

Kirby could feel his body vibrating with suppressed laughter and it took every ounce of control not to kick him. Although Vicki could keep patient confidentiality, when it came to relationships, she was Port's biggest gossip. The moment her foot hit the outside step, this bit of news would roar through the town faster than a cyclone.

'Absolutely, Nick, I understand completely.' Vicki crossed the waiting room with a firm and decisive step and turned just as she reached the door. Tapping her nose with her forefinger, she beamed at them. 'You two have a lovely time. Your secret is safe with me.'

The moment the door banged shut Nick's hand tightened on Kirby's. 'Come on, we better get to this festival.' A wolfish grin moved across his face. 'After all, the entire town will be expecting us.'

She stared up at him, drawn by the look in his eye— laughter mixed with a simmering charisma. She should be furious with him, she should be vibrating with indignation at his highhandedness and she should be saying, *No, I'm not coming to the festival with you.* Instead, she followed him out the door, her brain stuck fast on the fact that the entire town would be assuming she was having sex with Nick Dennison while her body ached on the fact that she wasn't.

* * *

The mellow sound of a saxophone drifted across the air and Kirby fell back on the picnic rug. 'I couldn't eat another thing.'

'I'm surprised you managed that last plate of calamari.' Nick grinned as he leaned over her, sipping his wine. 'It's wonderful to see a woman with a healthy appetite, although more of my veggies wouldn't hurt.'

She gazed up him, taking in the way his thick chocolate-brown lashes brushed his cheeks, how his stubble creased along deep smile lines that converged into dimples, and how much younger he looked than he had a few weeks ago when she'd first met him. The last vestiges of his treatment had completely faded, leaving him more handsome than any man deserved to be.

He'd been attentive all evening in a casual way—slinging his arm across her shoulders as they'd wandered from stall to stall, feeding her samples of everything from prawns to oysters, and choosing the perfect local sauvignon blanc to match the delicious food. He'd made a point of holding her hand when they'd met the self-obsessed Andrew, and he'd teased her on and off all evening that she owed him big time for saving her from an evening of boredom.

Now he put his glass down and grabbed her hand. 'Come on, you'll feel better if you move.'

'I don't believe you.' She groaned as she let him pull her to her feet, enjoying the way his other arm snaked around her waist, holding her close.

'I wouldn't lie to you.' His eyes danced as he lowered his head and his voice rumbled against her ear. 'And I promise you, I'll make it worthwhile.'

Shimmering tingles raced from her head to her toes, streaking through her like wildfire and igniting everything in its wake until she quivered and she felt sure he would feel it.

'Hello, Doctors, lovely evening for it.'

She looked up through dazed eyes to see Doug Reardon tipping his hat as he walked past arm in arm with his wife.

Nick laughed and waved. 'A perfect evening for it.' He turned back to face her, shooting her a deadpan look. 'It's a funny thing but the whole town has been giving us indulgent looks all night.'

She rolled her eyes. 'I can't imagine why.' She broke away from him and started to walk, needing to move, driven by a need to leave the crowded foreshore park and get away from those knowing looks—looks that inferred something that didn't exist and never would. She headed out along the pier road, suddenly desperate to be home.

Nick fell easily into step with her. 'They like to see a couple in love.'

She increased her pace. 'We're not in love.'

'No, we're not.'

His words relaxed her. They weren't in love and the fact they both wanted totally different things out of life made them almost incompatible, but they laughed together and they were friends. *Think friendship.* A crazy laugh bounced around her head.

He stepped in closer so his arm touched hers and his heat soared through her. 'But we are in lust.'

His husky voice filled with desire brought her to an abrupt halt. She swung around to face him, her hands gripping her hips as she desperately tried to keep some distance. 'Speak for yourself.'

'I am.' His eyes, shaded by the fading light, flared with unconcealed desire. 'You're the sexiest woman I've met in a long time.'

Her heart hammered hard and fast as his sweet words rolled over her like honey. But she couldn't listen to them—she'd learned that words counted for little and these ones had heartache written all over them. 'You don't get out very often, do you?'

'I get out plenty.' He trailed his finger down her cheek. 'You're gorgeous, you're sexy and you're driving me crazy.'

She wanted to slam her hands against her ears to drown out his beguiling voice. 'This is crazy. We're colleagues, we want different things.' She started walking again with no clear direction, just letting her feet take her as her body buzzed with need and her brain raced with incoherent thoughts that tumbled chaotically over each other.

He quickly caught up with her, his voice insistent. 'Pretending we're just colleagues and friends is the crazy part. You want me as much as I want you.'

She strode along the road, hating it that she did want him so badly. Hating that he knew. Folding her arms across her chest, she forced herself to be the sensible one. 'I didn't know conceit was a tool of seduction. Is that how you've always got women to jump into bed with you?'

His hand touched her sleeve, his expression suddenly serious and his mouth curving into a wry smile. 'I've never had to try this hard with any woman. You've reduced me to begging.'

She stared at him in amazement. Raw need rolled off him, almost toppling her with its intensity. Deep inside her something cracked and she steeled herself against a crumbling sensation. 'It won't work.' But her voice sounded unconvincing.

Surprise streaked across his handsome face as if the thought had never occurred to him. 'Of course it will.'

'No, it won't.' She shook her head, trying to hold onto the

last shreds of her resistance and common sense. 'You have your carefree childless life all mapped out, and that's the opposite of what I want.'

'You're over-thinking this.' He ran his hands down her arms, a touch gentle yet packing a seismic punch. 'This isn't for ever, this is all about now. It doesn't have to be complicated—in fact, it's pretty simple. I want you, you want me. It's summer, the season of being carefree, and we're both here for the summer so let's use this time we have together, use it for fun.'

His hand cupped her jaw, his expression suddenly earnest. 'Hell, both of us deserve some carefree fun after what we've been through. Let's wind the clock back to real carefree times and pretend we're sixteen.'

This is all about now. Tempting images bombarded her, collapsing all her worries about her future into a locked box. 'I was a very organised and responsible sixteen.'

His mouth curved up into a long, slow, seductive smile and his eyes twinkled. 'Then this is your chance to reinvent yourself.'

Reinvent herself? The thought tumbled through her, over and over, gathering massive appeal. She'd always been thoughtful, conscientious, a planner, and where had that left her? Shattered and alone. She was tired of worrying about what came next in her life so perhaps it was time to try something new, something just for her, just for a short time. Real life would intrude soon enough and knowing that they wanted such different things would protect her. Yes, this would be fun.

Bad idea. Very bad idea.

She instantly argued—no, it wasn't. Hell, the whole town thought they'd been at it like rabbits so why not do what was already considered a done deal? Standing strong against the constant barrage of need that burned inside her had worn her to a frazzle. Nick was right, she did want him. She wanted him so badly she throbbed with emptiness. This was her chance to reinvent herself, take something for herself. 'No plans, no future, just the summer?'

'No plans, no future, just the summer.' Nick held his breath, watching the war of emotions on Kirby's face. From the moment he'd capitalised on her lie earlier and set her up in the clinic, the entire evening had been a gamble—exciting, enjoyable and totally unpredictable. He'd loved every minute of it and now it all came down to this moment.

Silently, Kirby stepped forward, looped her arms around his neck, tilted her head up and seared his lips with a kiss of pure hunger, devoid of any restraint.

Yes! Hot, firm and fast, the kiss thundered through him, and he instantly hardened while his head spun. His arms moved to pull her tightly against him but as abruptly as she'd kissed him she stepped away, turned and ran down the empty pier.

'Hey! That's not playing fair.'

Her laughter came back to him on the evening breeze. With sheer strength of will he managed to force enough blood back to his limbs so he could walk down the pier. As he got closer, the yellow light of the rising moon illuminated her hair, giving her a golden halo. An angel with a body for sin.

She threw him a crooked smile. 'What kept you?' Grabbing his hand, she quickly started jogging down the pier steps toward the moored boats.

A moment ago with the smugness of experience he'd thought he had her, but now he wasn't quite so sure. Somehow he'd lost control of the situation and now his planned seduction was unravelling in front of him. Nothing about Kirby was predictable. 'Where are you going?'

She didn't reply but kept walking, her feet slapping against the boards of the lower pier. Dropping his hand, she hauled hard on a rope and then jumped down onto the deck of a yacht, its sleek white bow glowing against the dark water. She shot him a smile loaded with the promise of all good things. 'You said you wanted sixteen, so that's what I'm giving you.'

The fantasy hit him so hard he nearly lost his balance and pitched into the water. Staring down at her, he concentrated hard and managed to force out the words. 'I said carefree, not breaking the law. Are you allowed on this boat?'

She stared straight back at him, blue eyes swirling with a wildness he'd never seen before. Keeping her gaze fixed with his, she crossed her arms across her chest and hooked her fingers around the base of her T-shirt. Very slowly, she drew the clingy Lycra over her head and let it trail through her fingers until it fell to the deck.

The sonorous sound of a double bass and clarinet combo, carried by the breeze, and the steady slap of the water against the boat instantly faded as his brain emptied and every sense zeroed in on creamy white breasts nestled against a black lace bra. His pants felt tight.

She tossed her head back, the action full of sass as a curtain of hair swirled around her face and brushed her shoulders. 'So, are you coming?'

Probably. Letting go of every cautious thought, every shred of common sense, he jumped down onto the deck as Kirby disappeared through the hatch and into the cabin.

He found her skirt on the third step as he stumbled into the

tiny space. 'Don't you dare go any further without me.' The
words came out on a growl loaded with sexual frustration.

Laughing, she lay down on the tiny bed, a vixen smile on
her face as she bent her knees and crossed her long legs,
twirling one ankle at him. 'Well, hurry up, then.'

Somehow he managed to shuck his pants in the tiny space
without banging his head. He lowered himself onto the
mattress, supporting himself on his left elbow, his right hand
trailing through her hair. 'A good lover is never rushed.'

'Is that so?' She raised her hand to his cheek. 'I've never
met a good sixteen-year-old lover—they tend to be fumbling
fingers, expired condoms, all talk, and mighty quick on the
main event.'

He stilled, realising he wasn't as prepared as he'd thought.
He'd planned to seduce her at his house. 'I don't have a condom.'

She bit her lip, the fun in her eyes instantly dimming.
'Neither of us really needs one, do we?'

Her bleak look pierced him—it didn't belong in their
fantasy and the need to banish it consumed him. He traced the
line of her jaw with his finger, savouring her softness and
breathing in her jumbled scent of wildflowers and salt. 'Then
we have the perfect fantasy, don't we? A stolen space and no
contraception, but there is going to be one very big difference.'

'What's that?' Huge blue eyes absorbed him.

'The main event is going to take all night.'

The moment his mouth touched hers, Kirby gave herself
up to him. Nothing existed except Nick—the pressure of his
mouth, the graze of his stubble, his taste of salt and wine, and
the scorching touch of his body against hers.

His deep kiss penetrated way beyond her mouth, his tongue
eliciting a surge of response from every cell between her lips

and her toes. And when he'd kissed her to the point where her mind had completely melted, he trailed kisses along her jaw, across the hollow of her throat and down to the lace of her bra. She was vaguely aware of his right hand under her back and a moment later her bra fastening was released, the cups falling away and her breasts spilling out.

She gazed into emerald eyes. 'You've done that before.'

A sheepish look crossed his face. 'I learned that technique at sixteen.'

But her quip morphed into a moan of bliss as his mouth closed over her breast, his tongue tracing her nipple, drawing it up into a hot, hard peak and sending spirals of white light thudding through her.

He lifted his head and grinned. 'I learned this technique a bit later.'

She caught her breath. 'I think you've refined it.'

He lowered his head again, this time paying close attention to her other breast. Exquisite shafts of tingling sensation—half pleasure, half pain—shot from her breast to a single point deep inside her. Gripping his back, she gasped in delight as her hips rose instinctively up toward him, needing to feel him hard against her.

His wicked laugh rained down on her. 'If you like that, then you might enjoy this.' His lips started to press hot kisses down her belly.

Every part of her craved to lie back and let him give her what she knew would be beyond wonderful, but instead she grabbed his head to stop him, sinking her hands into his hair.

'Problem?' He raised his head, a questioning expression clinging to his cheeks.

'Big problem.' She'd fantasised about running her hands

through his hair, pressing her palms against his smooth chest and exploring him in the same way he was exploring her, but if she let him continue, she'd miss her chance. Somehow she managed to get her liquid muscles to function and she wriggled out from under him, pushing at his right shoulder and laughing at the confused look on his face.

He rolled over onto his back, bringing her with him. 'I thought you would have enjoyed that.'

Straddling him, she leaned forward, her hair caressing his face. 'I would have adored it and I'm only taking a short rain-check.' She leaned back, her fingers flicking up the base of his T-shirt, pushing it up his chest, before pulling it over his head. Golden skin, taut abdominal muscles and a trail of dark hair that knifed downward from his navel assaulted her gaze and she sighed. 'You once told me I'd enjoy this sight. I hate it when you're right.'

The rich green of his eyes darkened. 'Gaze all you want, I'm yours for the night.'

Yours for the night. She hugged the words close. 'I'm done gazing.' She reached out, splaying her fingers over his heart and feeling the fast beat vibrating underneath her hands. A heart beating wildly and matching her own erratic rhythm— one of blissful anticipation mixed with unfulfilled need. 'I've wanted to touch you like this from the moment I met you.' Tracing his pectoral muscles, her fingers roved over the small patch of thickened skin—scar tissue from his treatment and the only flaw on a perfect landscape. Then she dipped and curved until she circled his nipple, tweaking it gently between her fingers.

His pupils dilated and his thighs stiffened underneath her. She laughed, loving it that she could get such a response from him.

With a feather-light touch she continued downward, outlining the sinew and tendon of the solid pack of muscles and then trailing down to outline and cup the straining fabric of his jocks.

He bucked underneath her as a low growl left his throat. 'It's been a long time, Kirby, so if you don't want real sixteen…'

Her fingers caressed as she hooked his gaze. 'Can't you handle the heat?'

Challenge flared in his eyes and he immediately slid his hand down between them, sliding a finger firmly along the crotch of her panties.

Sensation exploded and her breath came hard and fast. She lost all focus on him, her body pushing hard against his hand, needing to rise on the surge of ecstasy that fireballed through her, leaving every part of her begging for more. 'Don't stop.'

'Sweetheart, I've hardly started.'

He flipped her over onto her back and using his mouth and hands he fuelled her already ragged need until every muscle deep inside her quivered, desperate to tense against hard flesh. She was past flirting, past banter, past pretence. She didn't care about anything except the driving need to have him deep inside her. 'Nick.' She almost sobbed his name. 'Now.'

Nick stared down at Kirby, her hair spread out on the bed, her eyes large and wide in her flushed face, and he didn't think he'd ever seen anything so beautiful. It had been so long since he'd been with a woman and she was driving him past control, but he wanted to give her this, she deserved it. 'Just enjoy, this one's for you.'

Her fingers sank into his shoulders with an iron grip and her eyes, wild with hunger, fixed with his. 'No, this one's for us.'

He'd dreamed about this moment for weeks. He slid into

her with ease, as if he belonged there. She rose up to meet him, capturing him deeply, stroking him as he stroked her and they rose together as one, flinging themselves out to the stars, beyond the pull of reality.

CHAPTER NINE

NICK stood in waist-deep water, his back fiery hot from the sun, in total contrast to his belly where occasional trickles of icy Southern Ocean water chilled his skin, having penetrated his thick, black wetsuit. White, briny foam buffeted him and the sand under his feet moved as the tail end of each wave raced past him to the shore.

'Now!' Nick cupped his hands around his mouth like a megaphone, trying to make himself heard over the surf. 'Stand up now, Cameron.'

The determined twelve-year-old gripped the side of his board and launched himself from his knees for the fourteenth time in a row, his feet swinging forward to stand against the lumps of wax that roughened the surfboard. He stood, he wobbled, and he fell as the board soared skywards before slamming back down onto the waves, brought to earth by the black cord attached to the ankle strap. A moment later Cameron's head appeared above the waves, water streaming across his face.

'Do you want to take a break?' Nick motioned to the boy who'd been at it for half an hour.

'No.' Cameron shook his head and doggedly clambered back on the surfboard and paddled back out to try again.

Splashes of cold water unexpectedly hit Nick's back and he turned to find a laughing Kirby, body board hooked under one arm, scooping water and tossing it at him with the other. Her eyes sparkled vivid blue, matching the ocean, her face glowed with vitality and her full-length wetsuit clung skin-tight, outlining every sensual curve. Despite the icy water, his body instantly responded. Like it did every time he saw her.

Still splashing him, she continued moving forward until she stood next to him, her cinnamon-apple scent circling him, taking him instantly back to last night when he'd buried his face in her hair. *Buried yourself deep inside her.*

He splashed her back, laughter rocking through him at her joyful shrieks. A week had passed since the festival, a week of fun, hard work and the most amazing sex of his life. He felt alive in a way he'd never known before, different even from his life prior to getting sick. Colours were brighter, sounds more complex and his energy for work and his energy for Kirby bounded out of him.

She wrapped the body board's Velcro strap around her wrist, her expression filled with curiosity. 'I didn't expect to see you down here—I thought you said you had capsicums to pick.'

He gave a wry smile. 'I do, but when I called by KC the unit C boys cornered me and asked if I'd teach them how to surf.' He swung his arm in an arc. 'Today's conditions are perfect.'

'You called by KC?' Incredulity clung to the words, matching the surprised expression on her face.

He nodded stiffly. 'Judy asked me to talk to one of the boys.'

Her eyes widened. 'And you said yes?'

'Judy can be very persuasive.' A ripple of irritation mixed with discomfiture wove through him. He didn't want to examine too closely why he'd deliberately not mentioned

Judy's call to Kirby, but the disbelief on her face that he'd got involved at KC unexpectedly morphed his irritation into a jag of indignation.

He tried to shrug it off because, if the truth be known, he'd been just as surprised as Kirby at the 'yes' that had slipped out of his mouth when Cameron had asked him to stay and help with surfing.

Two boys shot passed them, riding their boards expertly into the shallows.

'Great going, guys.' Nick raised his arms to shoulder height and held out both his thumbs above two closed fists.

Grinning widely, the two boys waved back before running back out toward the breakers, ready to try again.

'They're going really well. Perhaps I should ask you to teach me because I can never manage to get up off my stomach.'

'Ben and Steven are naturals.'

She threw him an arch look. 'And you're saying I'm not?'

He wasn't falling for that one. He moved his head close to her and whispered, 'You're amazing, beautiful and you have skills and talents in other areas.'

Her face flushed and he laughed at her blush. 'After last night I didn't think anything would embarrass you.'

She tossed her head, her plump lips forming into a pout. 'You're totally wicked, mentioning *that* in daylight.' She turned away but a smile lingered on her lips as she stared out toward the horizon.

Nick longed to pull her into his arms and kiss her until her breath was ragged and she collapsed hard against him. But he was on duty and he could already predict the reaction he'd get from the group of pubescent boys if he kissed her, which would range from 'Oh, yuck' through to jeering sniggers.

'How's Cam doing?' Kirby pointed to the red-headed boy in the group of other wannabe surfers from KC.

'He's determined, I'll give him that, and he's almost got there a few times. He just has to find his centre and go with the movement rather than fighting it.' He cupped his hands again and yelled, 'Try this one, mate.'

She elbowed him gently in the ribs. 'You've got a bit of a soft spot for him, haven't you? That's why you're here.'

He bristled against her words. 'No, I'm here because seven boys tackled me to the ground and refused to get off me until I said yes.'

She rolled her eyes. 'Yeah, right. Come on, why not just admit it? You like the kid.'

He felt a muscle in his jaw twitch. 'No more than any of the other kids.'

'Yes, more than any of the other kids. During the salmonella outbreak and in the post-recovery check-ups I saw you taking a special interest in Cameron.'

He should have known nothing got past Sherlock, she noticed everything. In the last two weeks he'd recognised a lot of his twelve-year-old self in Cameron, but he didn't want to talk about it. Avoiding her gaze, he tried to sound offhand. 'He's had a tough year with his diagnosis of diabetes.'

Kirby tilted her head, as her eyebrows rose. '*And* his younger brother is severely autistic. I saw him in full flight the day Cameron arrived and it was pretty distressing for everyone.'

He let her words hang on the salt-tinged breeze, not wanting to acknowledge that he understood some of the stuff Cam was facing. Not wanting to risk getting close to the guilt that hovered around his heart whenever he thought of Sarah and how he'd lost her just when he'd been old enough to really understand.

Her free hand touched his shoulder. 'I think it's wonderful that you can help each other.'

Her words rained down on him, exacerbating the already swirling emotions that pulled at his gut, but it was anger that emerged from the melee. Hell, he didn't need any help! 'It's a surfing lesson, Kirby, that's all. It's a way of spending time before I return to Melbourne Central.' He shrugged off her hand, shrugged off her inference and waded out a bit further, shouting to Cameron. 'You can do this. Hands forward, knees in the middle of the board, paddle, paddle, now up!'

The boy planted his left leg forward and with a very wobbly stance rose up with his arms outstretched. The board nudged forward on the crest of the wave and scooted down the curve with Cam standing tall and proud.

Thirty seconds later the wave collapsed completely and Cam fell off, victorious. 'I did it, Nick, I did it!'

Nick slapped his palm against the boy's, an overwhelming sense of triumph fizzing in his veins. 'That was awesome. I'm really proud of you.'

Cam flicked water from his eyes, his achievement suddenly dimming on his face. 'I wish Dad could have seen me.'

The wistful words kicked Nick hard in the gut. He remembered those moments when his own father had been caught up with the care of Sarah and had missed out on seeing his successes. As an adult he knew his father must have hated the choices he'd had to make but as a kid Nick had never understood. It was yet another reason why he was never going to be a father.

He clapped his hand onto Cam's shoulder. 'I know, mate, but by Parents' Day next week you'll be a pro and you can show your dad then.' He hoped the weather co-operated and that Cam's dad could actually make it.

* * *

'Can you lift it a bit higher?' Kirby called to Nick, who stood high on a ladder.

'Like this?' His strong arms swung the large rope around one of KC's imposing brick gateposts.

Kirby clapped her approval, childlike excitement flicking through her. 'Perfect.'

Leaning sideways, his tanned legs locked in a solid stance and his muscular back taut with tension, he tied the KC banner in place so it hung high over the entrance.

With his back to her, Kirby took the chance to openly stare at him. It didn't matter that she knew every part of his body in intimate detail, she never tired of gazing at him, watching and loving the way his work-hardened body moved—poetry in motion.

The light morning sea breeze fluttered the red, blue and white bunting as a flock of fifteen pelicans flew overhead, their enormous wings slicing through the air with stately grace, as if giving their approval to the events below. Nick moved quickly down the ladder and walked over to Kirby, his face creased in a wide and mischievous grin. 'I now declare the annual Kids' Cottage fete open.'

She laughed. 'I think perhaps the celebrity patron does that in a couple of hours.'

'That'd be right. I do all the hard work and that other bloke gets the glory.' His grumbling tone was at odds with his twinkling eyes.

She stepped up to him, wrapping her arms around his waist. 'Are you feeling under-appreciated?'

He dropped his forehead down to touch hers. 'Well, I did risk life and limb at the top of that ladder.'

'So you did.' She brushed away a curl of his hair that had

fallen across his eyes, loving that it was now long enough that she could do that. Leaning in, she pressed her lips to his, her mouth so familiar against his that it zeroed straight to the place that always made him shudder against her. She looked up and grinned. 'Feeling more valued?'

His eyes, sparkling in myriad hues of green, glinted back at her. 'Almost, but I'm sure I can take some more thanking tonight after this shindig is over.'

She loved teasing him. 'It's going to be a huge day and I'm sure you'll be way too exhausted.'

'Never.'

The word rolled out low and guttural, loaded with energy that swirled around her, pulling her in.

'Well, I might be. By the time I've done my time on the face-painting stall, read two books in the story-time tent and staffed the first-aid tent, I'll be ready for a long soak in the spa and a foot rub.'

A long, lazy smile moved into his cheeks, carving out swirling dimples. 'I'm sure that can be arranged. But meanwhile to keep your strength up and to make sure you actually stop for lunch, how about we meet at twelve o'clock at the barbeque tent? We'll both be ready for a hamburger by then.'

Warmth flowed through her at the suggestion. 'I'll be there. But what are you up to for the next few hours?'

He winked at her. 'It's a top-secret mission and I'd have to kill you if I told you so don't ask.' He then kissed her on the bridge of her nose and with a backwards wave walked off with his ladder.

She stood watching his retreating back, unable to keep a huge smile from her face despite the fact she was completely confounded by his caginess about what he was doing with his morning. He had moments of being deliberately vague and she suddenly realised it always happened when it involved the kids.

Just like with Cam and the surfing. He'd been great with Cam but whenever she tried to talk to him about it he sent up a towering brick wall between them and clammed up completely or changed the subject. She didn't get it. He obviously enjoyed the things he was doing at KC and was becoming increasingly involved with the children—he'd even arranged for someone else to man his Saturday market stall today and offered his help to Judy to be part of the biggest fundraising event on the KC calendar.

The annual fete was huge. All the favourite drawcards were in place—the giant jumpy castle and a calliope playing carousel for the pre-schoolers, the stomach-churning Rota and dodgem cars for the teenagers, the enormously high and long slide and a petting zoo for kids of all ages. Then there were the rows of white marquees, starting with the white elephant stall where one person's trash was immediately converted to another person's treasure. The handicraft stall was the domain of the Ladies' Auxiliary, where a year's worth of production was on display from lovingly knitted football teddies to layers of brightly coloured tulle used to create dolls, the ardent wish of every little girl's heart.

Kirby was never certain which stall was her favourite—the cake stall, with its fluffy cream-filled sponge cakes with passionfruit icing, home-made buttery shortbread in clear cellophane bags tied with gold curling ribbon, and deep-red raspberry preserves, or the quiet retreat of the Devonshire Tea tent, with hot tea, hot scones and lashings of Port Bathurst cream straight from the farm.

She quickly walked past a clown who was surrounded by

a circle of fascinated children intently watching his hands quickly sculpt long thin balloons into animal shapes, and she took her place at the face-painting table. The crowd was building as every good fete attendee knew the tip was to get in early to get top pick of all the stock and be back at the beach by the time the sun got really hot.

Kirby angled the large market umbrella so it cast a large circle of shade over her and her customers, tied an apron over herself to protect her clothes from the paint and displayed her designs.

'I'd like to be a tiger, please.' An eight-year old girl with a helium balloon tied to her wrist held out her coin.

'One tiger coming up.' Kirby dipped her brush into the yellow and set to work, loving the delight on the kids' faces when she showed them their new look in the mirror.

The morning streaked past in a blur of faces, conversations and storytelling and by eleven-thirty Kirby had finished her morning's duties and was starving. With half an hour before she had to meet Nick she jammed her sunhat onto her head, bought a fruit smoothie and took the chance of exploring the fete before her afternoon duty in the first-aid centre started. Teenagers congregated around the stage, enjoying the Battle of the Bands, which was in full swing, and further over children cuddled in their parents' laps, squealing with delight as they raced down the bumpy slides.

That should have been me. Kirby sipped her drink against the lump that formed in her throat, trying to push the hollow feeling that pervaded her every time she saw families together. Looking for distraction, she headed toward the noisiest queue of shrieking and laughing children and as she got closer she realised most of the kids were KC campers who got to enjoy the fete too.

A form of scaffolding with a swing seat had been erected in the centre of a pool of water with a large painted target fixed behind it. The banner above declared, 'Dunk the Doctor' and Nick, wearing boardies, a rash top and a lifesaving cap, sat high in the chair.

Kirby blinked, unable to believe her eyes. The doctor who'd been so adamant a few weeks ago that he was not working with children had put himself up as a sideshow attraction. By the look on his face, he was loving every minute of it.

First there had been his work with Cameron and now this. Her heart soared. They were having the best summer and he no longer held himself back from children. Perhaps what they both wanted had drawn closer together. Suddenly a daydream floated through her mind of Nick and herself surrounded by children. Adopted children.

Be careful, no plans—remember.

But she ignored the voice. Nick was nothing like Anthony. She and Nick shared a million things in common, including great sex and laughter.

She returned Nick's big wave to her and the huge teasing smile on his face, watching him as he leaned forward and called to the kid at the front of the line. 'I'm getting hot up here.'

'Do your best, Cameron,' Kirby called out. 'Take him out.'

Cameron grinned, straightened his shoulders and hefted the basketball he was holding above his head, aiming for the big black circle.

The crowd chanted, 'One, two, three.'

Cam threw the ball, putting his entire twelve-year-old

effort behind it. It hit the target with accuracy, the chair tipped backwards and Nick somersaulted into the water with a satisfying splash.

The crowd roared, Cameron stood taller and Kirby laughed so hard her ribs ached.

A sopping wet Nick surfaced, water streaming off his handsome face, and he climbed out of the pool, immediately clapping Cam on the shoulder. 'Great throw, mate. Now go and get yourself a prize from Mrs Dalton.'

A glow of success emanated from the boy. 'Thanks, Doc. That was awesome!'

Cameron ran off and Kirby handed Nick a towel. 'I wish I'd known. I would have been here earlier with my camera.'

He slung the towel around his neck and gave her a wicked grin loaded with mischief. 'The local paper beat you to it. I'm next week's centrefold.'

Kirby shook her head in smiling bemusement. 'Is there any room next to that giant ego for me to walk beside you?'

'For you—' he put on a fake Italian accent '—always. But so you can walk close I'll just get changed out of this wet gear.'

'Meet me in the food line.' Kirby followed the aroma of barbecued onions and joined the meandering line, enjoying chatting to Jake, Gaz and Meryl while she waited, still stunned that Nick had got so involved in the fete. *He's got involved with the children.*

She'd just paid for the burgers when he arrived by her side, all tousled hair and glowing good health. She held out the ubiquitous white bag with the two twisted ears. 'Yours has the lot, including pineapple and beetroot.'

'Sweet.' He ripped open the bag and took a big bite from the burger.

'Hungry, are you?' Smiling, Kirby pulled some stray onion out of her bun and nibbled on it.

He pretended to be affronted. 'You try being knocked into the water fifteen times. It generates an appetite.'

They sat at a table in the shade of a grove of gnarled tea trees and Kirby neatly pulled open her white bag, dividing it down the seam line to make a mat for her hamburger. Nick had almost finished his and was eyeing hers when the music on the loudspeaker stopped and Judy's voice came on instead.

'Could Dr Atherton or Dr Dennison please come to the sick bay *now*.'

'Must be something more than a cold pack or a plaster can fix or Phillipa would have dealt with it.' Kirby stood up and started walking.

Nick picked up her burger and handed it to her. 'Eat and run. We don't need you getting sick too.'

They jogged to the sick bay. Jordan, one of the unit C boys, sat in the chair, his face alabaster white underneath a large trickling bloodstain. Phillipa had a gauze-covered ice pack on his head and looked up with relief as they walked in.

Kirby stepped up to the boy who looked so little and immediately felt for him, knowing he probably wanted his mother. 'Jordan, you poor—'

But he looked past her, straight to Nick.

'Mate, what have you done to yourself?' Nick immediately pulled on a pair of gloves and lifted up the ice pack.

'I ran into a pole.'

'Jumped out at you, did it?' Kirby opened up some saline, feeling slightly ignored. 'I think unit C is going to win the camp award for most admissions to the sick bay.'

'You wouldn't have let Ben run off with your prize, would

you, Dr Nick?' Jordan shot Nick a conspiratorial look that clearly said, *A girl wouldn't understand.*

'No way. I would have chased him down as well.' He bobbed down in front of the boy and shone a torch into Jordan's black hair. 'But you hit that pole so hard you've split the skin.'

'Skin glue?' Phillipa opened the medical kit, her fingers hovering over the tray.

Nick shook his head. 'It starts on his forehead but extends into his hairline so it's going to have to be stitches.'

'No way.' Jordan's eyes welled up.

Nick squeezed his shoulder. 'You'll have a manly scar and a good story to match it. I've got a few of those.'

'Have you?' Watery curiosity shone in Jordan's eyes.

'Yep. See this one?' He pointed to a faint line on his forearm. 'I fell off the top of the brick fence when I was trying to be Superman. I also broke my leg.'

'Did you have crutches and a cast?'

'I did.'

'Cool!' Admiration shone in the boy's eyes before dimming slightly. 'But I won't need crutches.'

'No, but you'll have a bit of a pirate scar, which is mysterious.'

Needing something to do now she'd finished her hamburger, Kirby drew up the local anaesthetic and handed it to Nick, who chatted away to Jordan about the current test cricket match, as if they were walking down to the beach for a surf instead of injecting lignocaine into his scalp in preparation for suturing. She watched him bring the skin edges together with tiny stitches, his brow furrowed in serious concentration, yet all the time trading sporting statistics to keep Jordan relaxed.

Deep inside her something ached—this was the man who so unalterably believed he didn't want to be a father. Couldn't he see he'd be great?

He snipped the black nylon, separating it from the final stitch, and dropped the needle into the suture tray. 'Phillipa will put a dressing on that and you won't be able to wash your hair for five days, which probably won't be too much of a hardship given your allergy to shower water.' Humour played through his words while the sound of latex snapped sharply as he stripped off his gloves and dropped them in the bin. 'You have to stay in sick bay for the rest of the day due to the bump on your head.'

Jordan slumped. 'But I'll miss the rest of the fete.'

'Yes, but you'll get ice cream and jelly and a personal visit from the celebrity patron.' Nick helped Jordan up onto the bed. 'He's a pretty famous runner and he might just autograph your camp book if you ask him politely.'

The boy settled back into the pillows slightly more happy. 'That would be great but can *you* come see me again later?'

Kirby caught the longing in the boy's voice. First Cameron and now Jordan. Nick had an easy way with these boys that generated respect and admiration.

Nick nodded. 'No problem. I'll drop by before I go home and I'll ring your mum and tell her what happened and that you're OK. Catch you later.' He gave the lad a playful punch before crossing the room.

'Here you go, Jordan.' Phillipa bustled about with gauze and tape.

Nick caught Kirby's arm and propelled her through the door. 'Come on, I'll buy you some tea and scones, I know they're your favourite.'

'Bye, Jordan.' She gave the boy a wave, before savouring the warm touch of Nick's arm through hers, and stepped out through the external doors. 'I felt a bit superfluous in there.'

'It was a simple suturing job and either one of us could have done it.'

'True, but I wasn't thinking about medical skills. You wanted to do the stitching and Jordan obviously wanted you to treat him.'

'Did he?' Nick looked surprised. 'I guess I've done a bit with that unit and he knows me.'

A bit? 'That would be the understatement of the day. You've done heaps with those boys in the last couple of weeks.'

The surprise on his face rolled into pleasure. 'I suppose I have but it's been fun and…' He shrugged his shoulders as if he couldn't find the right words.

'Gratifying?'

He nodded. 'Yeah, I guess it has been.'

She gave him a sideways glance, stunned that he hadn't made the connection between how he felt and the work he'd been doing at KC. 'You're really great with the boys. The way you talk to them and respect their growing independence, you're a natural.'

He cleared his throat. 'I don't know about that.'

'I do.' She spoke emphatically, the culmination of all her thoughts about him and the children unexpectedly forming into words. 'You genuinely like kids.'

He gave a wry grin. 'I guess I do.'

She smiled and hugged her secret daydream to her heart. 'Yes, you really do. I've seen you in action and you'd make a wonderful father.'

He immediately stiffened against her, his arm taut with

tension. 'There's more to being a father than being able to chat to kids.'

'Obviously.' She stopped walking and turned to face him because this time she wasn't going to back away from the topic. 'But the thing is, you seem to really love being with them.'

'I love cats too but I don't have one.' His voice developed a chilly edge. 'My parents never recovered from the blow parenthood dealt them—spending so much time caring for Sarah and then losing her so young—and my life isn't suited to fatherhood. I don't want to be a father and I don't for one minute regret the choice I made.'

She stared into his eyes long and hard, looking for a sign that belied his words. 'Really?'

A flinty hardness she hadn't seen before glinted back at her. 'Really.'

A chill spread through her at odds with the heat of the day, spiking her like jagged shards of ice. Her daydream imploded, the faces of imagined children instantly vanishing.

Nick's hands suddenly cupped her face and he brought his mouth down onto hers in a kiss that rocked her all the way down to the soles of her feet.

He pulled back, his eyes loaded with the haze of desire. 'Summer fun, remember? This isn't for ever, it's all about now.'

She dug deep, burying her pain that he had no vision of her in his future, and she unearthed her sixteen-year-old self. 'In that case, you need to win me a doll on a stick.' She ran her finger down his shirt. 'And if you do, you might just get lucky.'

He gazed down at her, his voice huskily deep. 'How lucky?'

'Shelter-shed lucky.'

He grabbed her hand and marched her toward the shooting gallery.

CHAPTER TEN

KIRBY switched on the clinic's security and slammed the door behind her, pleased the long day had finally come to a close. The heat wave meant too many sunburned tourists suffering from heatstroke and dehydration, and the evening clinic had been full. She dumped her laptop and green enviro-friendly shopping bag that held her dinner—a can of chicken korma— onto the front seat of the four-wheel drive and then slid her key into the ignition.

The engine roared into life and she pushed the gear stick into first, preparing to turn right. *Home time.* But every part of her wanted to turn left and head out to Riversleigh, head out to see Nick and spend some time lying on the cool, mossy grass surrounded by ferns. Spend time making love with him.

She gripped the wheel harder and tugged right. She would *not* be needy. It was possible to go eighteen hours without seeing him, without inhaling that complex scent of soap, fresh pine and masculinity, and without feeling his strong arms around her, cradling her close.

Possible, yes. Enjoyable, no. Her mouth curved up into a private smile as she recalled his earlier goodbye kiss when he'd left the clinic at two p.m. He'd found her in the supply room, kicked the door closed and pinned her to the wall with the gentle caress of his entire body. His heat-filled gaze, filled with raw hunger, had shot through her so hard and fast that she'd almost orgasmed on the spot. She'd never experienced such powerful emotions from a man or for a man. It was wondrous, incredible and terrifying.

But it was also make-believe and she must remember that. This was summer frivolity, a summer fling. Nothing else, and she needed to focus on that. The summer would end, Nick would return to Melbourne City to his life in A and E and the lecture circuit, and she would finish her rotation in Port and get on with her single life that involved kids in some way.

But that was the future. For now, nothing serious was allowed to dent this time with Nick and she'd learned that at the fete. She'd pushed him to acknowledge how good he was with kids and he'd frozen on her. Knowing that, she now avoided all talk of children and as a result the last three weeks had been wonderful. Who would have guessed there were so many clandestine places for a couple to make love?

That would be sex. The realistic and grounding voice instantly reminded her that love was not part of this summer pact and it never could be. This time with Nick couldn't be anything but fun because ultimately, somehow and some way, she wanted children in her life and Nick didn't. That one thing was a huge gulf between them, impossible to bridge.

She bit her lip against the tug of concern and rounded the final corner, catching sight of her tiny fisherman's cottage with its bright display of petunias, their purple and white heads waving welcomingly in the salt-laden evening sea breeze. Her stomach rolled over in pleasure. Nick's muddy truck stood parked out front.

She jumped out of the truck, grabbed her bags and opened the gate. Turbo's stocky form charged around from the side of the house, a stick in his mouth, a hopeful look in his brown eyes.

'Hey, mate, great to see you.' *Because if you're here, so is your master.* Kirby scratched the dog hard behind the ears. 'Sorry, there's not much room in my tiny garden for sticks.' She left the doleful dog and opened the front door, stepping into the blissful coolness that only a solid stone house could offer in midsummer. The pungent aroma of fresh basil immediately permeated her nostrils and her stomach growled hungrily. 'Nick?'

'I'm in the laundry.' His deep voice sounded muffled and far away.

'I don't have a laundry.' Confused and intrigued, she walked along the long central hall to the very back of the house where a lean-to had been added, probably over seventy years ago. She used it to hold her body board, bike and as a place to dry her wetsuit. Other than that it contained an old copper and a hand-turned mangle, and going by the cobwebs neither had been used to wash clothes in a very long time. Kirby, like previous tenants, spent Sundays at the laundrette.

She walked through the kitchen, passing her island bench, which groaned with fresh produce from Nick's garden. Pausing only to pop one of his plump and luscious strawberries into her mouth, she stepped down into the lean-to. 'What are you do—?' Heat roared through her.

A shirtless Nick, all golden skin and rippling muscles, with a tool belt strapped low on his hips, leaned over a shiny metal laundry trough, tightening a set of taps. Her heart hammered erratically as her breath came hard and fast. This was her fantasy, except he was real flesh and blood.

'Hey, Sherlock.' He put down his wrench and pulled her into his arms. 'You're later than I thought. Busy evening clinic?' His lips caressed her forehead as his tool belt pressed into her.

'Huge evening clinic.' She didn't care that a hammer pressed into her hip and a spanner imprinted itself on her belly. She leaned in, looping her arms around his neck, and breathed deeply. Kissing him long and lingeringly, she absorbed his taste, his touch and his boundless energy. A flash of white caught her eye and she reluctantly drew back, curiosity pushing her as she peered over his shoulder.

The old mangle and copper had vanished. Instead, a small white washing machine nestled snugly between the trough and a laminate bench, which had a power point fixed to its back board and two cupboards fitted underneath. High above the bench was an old-fashioned but very functional clothes airer suspended from the ceiling with a rope and pulley system so clothes could be aired and retrieved. Total surprise swirled through her, absorbing most coherent thought. 'What's all this?'

He turned, keeping one arm slung around her waist, his face creasing in a wide grin. 'You needed a laundry so I traded vegetables for the reconditioned machine and bartered time in Jason's joinery to make the bench against keeping Jase supplied with tomatoes so he can make his famous Port chutney.'

He stepped forward and slipped open the top drawer under the bench and a small ironing board appeared. 'What do you think?'

'I…I'm speechless. I didn't expect… I…' Words failed her as her throat tightened. No man had ever done anything so thoughtful for her in her life.

A hint of a worried frown hovered on his brow. 'You do like it?'

Words couldn't come close to describing how she really felt so she kissed him hard and fast, hoping she wouldn't cry on the spot. She pulled back, breathless. 'I love it. Thank you. I can't believe you did this.'

He undid the tool belt, laying it on the bench, and then pulled on his shirt, which had been hanging behind the door. 'It's crazy for you to not have a laundry. I had a chat to the hospital board and they said if I wanted to do the work they had no objections, and you know how I enjoy working with my hands.'

She stepped in close, remembering exactly what his hands could do when they touched her body. She trailed her finger down the front of his shirt. 'I do know that and you're extremely good at it.' She couldn't keep the husky tone of desire out of her voice.

A flare of heat surged in his eyes but instead of pulling her hard against him, as she expected, he kissed her quickly on the cheek and grabbed her hand. 'Come on, that can wait. It's eight o'clock and I know you won't have eaten. I've got organic chicken with pesto and a home-grown salad all ready and waiting.'

She pulled against his hand, glancing over at the bench. 'What happened to being carefree, irresponsible and sixteen?'

His lips curved into a crooked smile. 'We've been sixteen a lot lately and right now I'm hankering for some long, lazy loving in a bed after a healthy meal.'

She stepped up against him. 'A bed? You're sounding like an old fuddy-duddy.'

His brown brows rose as his hands gently gripped her shoulders to keep a slight distance between them. 'No dessert for you until you've eaten all your veggies.'

'Is that a promise?'

'Absolutely.' The word sounded strangled as he moved toward the door, tugging her behind him in the direction of the kitchen.

She followed, surprised he hadn't wanted to christen the laundry but happy in the knowledge he wanted to have long, leisurely sex. She was totally up for a new experience.

Nick pulled the can of chicken korma out of the shopping bag and held it by the tips of his fingers as if it were poison. 'Seriously, though, you really don't take very good care of yourself, Kirby. When did you actually cook something decent to eat?'

'Hey, that has vegetables. Besides, I've been busy.' His words rankled but she appreciated where he was coming from. He'd faced a life-threatening illness and as a result treated his body with more respect than she treated hers. The horrible hot flushes that scorched her body twice a day might improve if she made sure she ate more soy and ate less processed food. 'I promise to try harder.'

'Good.' But his expression clearly showed he didn't believe her.

She poured their drinks and set the table while Nick plated up the chicken salad, enjoying the camaraderie of being in the kitchen with another person. The truth was she hated cooking for one. Hated that no matter how hard she tried she always ended up with enough food for two, hated that she had to cook *and* clean up, but most of all she hated the silence that came with the meal for one. So she ate on the hop, standing up, or with a plate balanced on her knee, watching a movie, any way that didn't scream, *You're all alone*.

But she couldn't tell Nick any of that. She refused to admit her loneliness to him—after all, he hadn't signed up for anything more than sex and fun.

He's feeding you. He built you a laundry.
Don't go there, don't read more into this than there is.

But she disregarded the warning and let the words circle her heart, sending out fine connecting threads as she sat down opposite him. 'This looks sensational, thank you.'

His eyes sparkled with warmth as he raised his freshly squeezed glass of orange juice toward her and clinked it against hers. 'It's my absolute pleasure.'

She lost herself in his gaze as she forked some of the moist chicken into her mouth, letting the flavours of garlic and basil explode against her tongue. 'This is divine. I've never tasted chicken like this before.'

He nodded slowly. 'This is one reason why I grow my own food but I won't get back on my soapbox about it again tonight.' He drizzled virgin olive oil and balsamic vinegar over his endive and smiled at her as he ate his meal.

She basked in his gaze and asked him about his plans for the farm. With his fork waving, he enthusiastically outlined his success with some of the home-made anti-insect remedies given to him by the old Italian gardeners in the nursing home.

He asked about her day, laughed with her over her story about Meryl reducing the antagonistic, skull-and-crossbones-wearing, tough motorcycle rider into a compliant, polite and slightly scared patient with the flourish of a large glass syringe. From that point their conversation roamed wide and free, taking in the politics of health, the value of popular fiction and why it generated such rancour amongst the literati, and finishing with the importance of quality coffee on a Sunday morning. Kirby adored and savoured every single moment.

Nick drained his glass, scrunched his napkin into a ball and tossed it onto his now empty plate. 'Seeing as I've taken over your kitchen tonight, how about you take over mine on Friday? I'll have been harvesting all afternoon, ready for Saturday's market, so I won't be in the mood to cook.'

Something akin to pure happiness streaked through her as she pictured herself in his warm cosy home, sitting down with him at his huge farmhouse table and sharing eclectic conversation.

Be very careful—you're not playing for keeps. 'You'd let me loose in your kitchen to play with the Aga?'

He grinned. 'I think you'd be a perfect match for my kitchen.'

Perfect match. Recipes spun through her head as miniature castles rose slowly in the background of her mind. 'I'll ask Gaz to get me some prawns, mussels and calamari so I can make us paella. How does that sound?'

He stood up, walked around the table and pulled her to her feet. Gazing straight at her, a smouldering look in his eye, he spoke softly, his breath stroking her cheek. 'It sounds fine but I'm really more interested in what you have planned for tonight's dessert.'

'Let me think.' She leaned forward, nonchalantly trailing her forefinger along her bottom lip in a provocative gesture. 'Strawberries, cream and me.'

He shuddered against her and cleared his throat. 'I'll take it now but in reverse order.'

'Come with me.' Smiling, she took his hand and led him down the hall to her bedroom, glorying in the fact he wanted her so badly. She walked through the doorway, dropped his hand and slipped her dress from her shoulders. It cascaded down across her belly and pooled at her feet. She stepped out of it and turned to find him standing with his back against the closed door, his simmering gaze fixed on her.

A flush of need raced through her and instantly her breasts

tightened as her body readied itself for him. She held out her arms. 'What are you doing over there?'

'Watching you. You're totally gorgeous, do you know that?' He walked toward her and pulled the clip from her hair, sending it tumbling down around her face. 'I've wanted to do that all day.'

She tilted her head back looking up at him. 'I've dreamed of this all day.'

He buried his face in her hair and she closed her eyes, wanting to block out everything except his wondrous touch.

The next moment her feet left the floor. He lifted her into his arms and swung her around before lowering her onto the bed as if she weighed nothing more than a child. The mattress moved as he lay down next to her and she opened her eyes to find him straddling her.

He gazed down at her, his expression a mixture of desire and decisions. 'Being sixteen has been fun but I want to show you what an experienced lover with all the time in the world can do.'

She grinned up at him. 'That sounds very smug.'

A dangerous glint shimmered in his eyes. 'I doubt you'll be disappointed.'

He lowered his mouth to hers as his hands travelled to places he knew made her heart race and her body lush with wanton hunger. She lost herself in his touch, craving it like a drowning man craved air and giving in to the most exquisite sensations she'd ever experienced in her life. Opening her body and her heart, she gave herself up to him completely and utterly, letting herself freefall into the glorious abyss of wonder in a way she'd never allowed herself to do before.

Much later Kirby lay in Nick's arms, the moonlight streaming in through the uncovered window, illuminating the white sheet that covered their naked bodies. His soft breathing sounded reassuringly behind her, and his exhaled breath tickled her neck. His promise of expert loving had hit every target. Her limbs now felt like hot treacle—thick and runny and deliciously unable to support her. She couldn't keep the smile off her face.

Before tonight their coupling had been hot, frantic and edgy as if they'd both feared they might never have another chance of being in each other's arms. And the moment the sex had been over they'd gone back to their respective homes or jobs, depending on the time of day. But tonight had been totally different.

What had Nick promised? Long, lazy loving, and he'd more than delivered. Her body, so overloaded with pleasure, now relaxed into his embrace, feeling like it had come home.

It's just sex.

It's way past sex. It's a new sparkly laundry, it's delicious food and conversation, it's companionship, it's having things in common, it's… Clarity sucked the breath from her lungs as she came face to face with reality. *It's love.*

Oh, God, she loved him.

Her hands gripped her temples, as if squeezing hard would change things. Loving Nick was dumb, stupid, senseless and a one-way ticket to heartache. They wanted totally different things from their lives so how had she let this happen? How had the protective barricades around her heart melted away, leaving her vulnerable?

But how it happened wasn't really important. The fact was it *had* happened and this was her new reality.

Nick moved in his sleep, his legs entwining with hers so his body wrapped around her, cocooning her completely. What would it be like to lie like this every night?

It wouldn't work.

The memory of the night on the pier flitted across her mind, complete with audio. *We're both here for the summer so let's use this time we have together, use it for fun.* Nick had his plans. *I don't want to be a father.* She wanted somehow to create a family so this summer together was all they could have, and then it was over.

Stop it now before you get in too deep. But she knew that depth was just semantics and she was already in way over her head. So she would do the only thing she could do and that was take and enjoy every last minute of the time they had left together, banking every experience to last her a lifetime.

The clock showed five p.m. and Nick switched off his computer ready to head home. It was the first afternoon he'd ever worked at the clinic but Kirby had looked so exhausted at lunchtime he'd sent her home to the quiet of his place for a restorative afternoon nap. Initially objecting to the idea, she'd finally compromised by insisting on cooking them dinner in his kitchen. It had turned out that, given the time, the recipe and the ingredients, Kirby could actually cook. He smiled in anticipation of the meal and the evening ahead—lazing on the couch with a full-bodied red wine and a full-bodied woman.

'Just before you leave, Nick, your mother is on line two.' Meryl's voice crackled down the clinic's intercom.

Son guilt immediately snagged him. Over the last few days his mother had left three messages on his mobile and two on his home answering-machine and he hadn't rung her back. He wasn't deliberately avoiding her, it was just he'd been really busy.

Busy having fun. Between the farm, the clinic, KC and Kirby his days raced past with lightning speed, as was his summer.

He pressed the button under the red flashing light. 'Hi, Mum, how's it going?'

'It's going very well, darling. You sound bright and happy.'

An image of Kirby, her golden hair spread all over his pillow and her face flushed with the joy of sex, thundered through him. 'You sound surprised.'

'Well, your father and I were a bit worried when we hadn't heard from you so that's why I'm calling you at work.'

'Sorry, Mum, I have no real excuse except things have been busy, but I should have called.'

'As long as you're well, Nick.'

He heard the strain in her voice and swallowed a sigh. He hadn't been fair to her, not returning the calls. She'd lost one child and had faced down the possibility of losing another. 'I'm great, Mum. Really, you don't have to worry about a thing.' He heard a sniff and a rustling of paper and something that sounded like the laugh of a kookaburra. That had to be wrong—kookaburras didn't hang out in inner Melbourne. 'What's up?'

'A couple of things. Melbourne City telephoned. They've sent you a letter and are waiting to hear as they're expecting you back on the first.' She hesitated for a moment and the silence strained down the line. 'Are you going back, Nick, or do you love the work in the country?'

He leaned back and gazed out the window, glimpsing the sweet curve of a wave before it broke over the reef. He leaned forward, tugging at his hair. 'I wrote them a letter last week confirming I'd be going back.' He just hadn't quite got around to posting it.

'As long as you're sure it's what you want, darling. You *do* seem to have embraced country life.'

You've embraced Kirby. He stood up abruptly, completely forgetting he wasn't on his mobile. The phone slid sideways, teetering on the edge of the desk, and he grabbed it just before it fell. 'Of course I'm sure it's what I want, Mum. It's my career, everything I've worked for.' The words sounded overly firm as they ricocheted back to him off the bookcase-lined walls.

'That's great then. So, seeing as you don't have too much time left down there, your father and I thought we'd come down to the farm for a couple of days and visit, if that fits in with you. Dad wants to fish and I'll take you up on the offer of berry picking.' Her smile radiated down the line. 'I quite like the idea of making my own raspberry jam.'

He ignored the selfish part of him that railed at the thought that a visit from his parents meant less time with Kirby. *They'd enjoy spending time with Kirby.*

He immediately pushed the thought aside as being completely untenable. He'd never actively sought to introduce the women he dated to his parents as he'd always moved on to dating someone else by the time he caught up with them again.

His gaze caught the date on the calendar—he only had a couple of weeks before he returned to Melbourne and Kirby had to stay in Port so there was no point introducing Kirby to his folks. Nothing about his time with Kirby was any different from his time with other women. *It's been all summer.*

He shrugged the voice away. Summer had a finite endpoint so despite this fling being longer than the norm, just like every other relationship, it would end. They wanted different things out of life so it had to end. He turned the desk calendar face down. 'It would be great if you and Dad came to visit. When are you coming so I can make sure you can actually get into the spare room?'

'Actually, darling, we're already here.'

A ripple of unease tightened every muscle in his body. 'In Port?'

The taunting laugh of a kookaburra vibrated down the phone line, followed by a familiar bark.

Turbo. All his blood drained to his feet. 'You're at Riversleigh?' His usually deep voice had developed a squeak.

'That's right. Your father has cleared out the spare room and Kirby and I have dinner cooking so we'll see you soon.' The click on the line sounded with precise finality as the line went dead, but not before he'd heard the delight in his mother's voice.

He groaned and sank his head into his hands. Since Sarah's death his mother had turned her full parenting attention on him and despite his dodging and weaving, and straight-up statements of 'It's not going to happen', she never wearied of her own position on the subject of him settling down. Meeting Kirby in *his* house would only have fuelled that desire and ramped up her expectations.

His plans for a long lazy evening vaporised. His carefree and easy summer had just got complicated.

CHAPTER ELEVEN

KIRBY sat outside on Riversleigh's veranda in the large and comfy rattan chair with her feet up on the wood box, watching Turbo round up the last of the chooks for the night and deny the foxes their dinner. Exhaustion clung to every muscle, making her body feel like it was made of metal and pinning her to the chair. She should be inside washing the dinner dishes, but Nancy and Michael, Nick's parents, had shooed her out of the kitchen and the thought of having to move from the chair was just too much.

Besides, Nick needed some time alone with his parents. His mother had been nothing but polite and friendly but Kirby could tell she had a thousand questions to ask Nick, starting with, *Who is this woman I found in your house?* Poor Nick—when he'd come home he'd looked more like he thought he was facing a firing squad than his loving mother.

If she'd felt less tired she would have stayed in the kitchen as a protective device, but the aroma of cooling lamb had made her feel queasy and she'd taken up the offer to watch the sun set.

Nancy and Michael were completely different from what she'd expected. Nick had painted her a picture of a couple worn down by trauma, a shell of their former selves. Instead, she'd met a vibrant and positive couple in their early sixties with a very close and loving relationship. When she'd taken the clean bed linen into the spare room, she'd found them with their arms around each other, and she'd noticed how Michael always seemed to touch Nancy with a caress or a pat when she passed him.

The squeak and bang of the wire door made her look up.

Nick strode down the veranda, waves of energy rolling off him, pervading the surrounding air. She swallowed—half moan, half groan. How could he be so gorgeously sexy and full of get-up-and-go when she just wanted to sleep for ever?

He walked straight over to her and bobbed down beside her, his hands resting on the arm of the chair. 'You OK?'

She gave a wan smile. 'I've been better. For some reason I'm really, really tired. I think the frantic pace of summer medicine has finally caught up with me.'

He plunged his fingers through his hair, leaving behind a trail of spikes. 'But you've just had two nights when you haven't been out on call so you should be jumping out of your skin.'

She stifled a yawn. 'I know, and up until yesterday I've been feeling really great, better than I have for a long time.'

No hot flushes. The thought popped unexpectedly into her head and she realised with a shock that it had been a while since she'd had one. Perhaps her body had finally adapted to menopause.

'You didn't eat much.' Faint disapproval hovered in his eyes before he leaned forward and kissed her on the forehead. 'You probably just need a good night's sleep and a hearty breakfast of free-range eggs.'

Her stomach heaved and acid burned the back of her throat.

She swallowed against the bitter taste and thought of how much she wanted to be tucked up in her bed. She moved forward, preparing to stand. 'I'd better go home.'

Nick instantly shook his head. 'No way are you driving down that winding road when you can hardly keep your eyes open.'

The clink of crockery and the murmur of voices drifted out through the open front door. 'What about your parents?'

'We're adults, Kirby, and so are they.' A determined expression matched the set of his shoulders. 'How I live my life is up to me and I've told my mother she's not to read more into this than there is.'

Kirby chewed her lip. 'You told her we were a summer fling?'

His eyes crinkled up as a wolfish smile loaded with pure, unadulterated lust crossed his face. 'Something like that.'

A sharp jagged pain exploded out of the centre of her heart and she caught her breath, hating it that she'd let herself be this vulnerable. What had she expected him to tell his mother? That they were a couple who belonged together for ever? She blew out a long breath, blaming fatigue. No one was rational when they were exhausted and tomorrow after a long sleep she would be back to normal and able to enjoy their last couple of weeks.

'Come on, Sherlock, bedtime.'

She let him haul her to her feet and take her to his bed, savouring the warmth of his arms, as she gave in to much-needed sleep.

Nick had slipped out of bed an hour earlier, leaving a sleeping Kirby, and had gone for a run with his father up the fern-lined gully and along the creek. Swirls of morning mist lingered, trapped between granite rock faces, keeping the temperature lower than on other parts of the farm. Nick loved this time of day, when the air was slightly damp and cool before the sun blasted its summer heat into every nook and cranny. Turbo had joined them, beside himself with delight at having Michael running with them, and he'd bounded between them, not knowing who to run alongside.

Now showered, shaved and ready for breakfast, Nick had been surprised to find Kirby still in bed, the sheet pulled up over her head.

'Hey, Sherlock.' He gently shook the outline of her shoulder, the sheet warm to his touch. 'Time to get up.'

A muffled groan and a barely audible 'OK' came from under the covers.

He kissed the top of her head and breathed in deeply, never tiring of her familiar scent and savouring it while he could. 'I'll have hot tea waiting.' He left the room whistling and headed to the kitchen.

'Good morning, Nick.' His mother stood at the stove, poaching eggs. 'I've made a bowl of fruit salad and the bread is just out of the oven so help yourself.'

'Thanks, Mum.' He plugged the kettle in and took the tea-caddy out of the cupboard. 'How did you sleep?'

'With all this country air I slept like a log until Turbo padded in, gave us his hangdog look and your father got up.' She removed the eggs from the stove. 'Seems like Kirby slept well, too.'

'Mum.' The word came out as a warning.

'I know, it's none of my business.' She scooped the eggs from their hot cocoons and transferred them onto a warmed plate but her shoulders had squared as if she wanted to say a lot more.

He let the silence sit, thankful that the kettle boiled quickly. Pouring the bubbling water into a fine china mug, he watched the way the fragrant tea leaves floated in the captivity of an infuser, every leaf a different shape. No wonder people thought they had a message. He glanced at the hall doorway. Still no Kirby.

He picked up the mug and walked into his bedroom. Kirby lay with her golden hair spread lankly all over his pillow, her face the same alabaster white as the pillowslip. A trickle of concern ran through him.

Putting her tea down on the bedside table, he instinctively placed his hand on her forehead, expecting to feel the burning heat of a fever. 'You look like you've come down with the summer virus that has laid low a fair percentage of Port. Is your throat dry and scratchy?'

Her voice, usually so lyrical, came out soft and flat. 'No, I just feel listless and blah.'

'Gotta love that technical medical jargon.' He smiled as he sat down beside her. 'Yesterday's tiredness was obviously your body fighting something. Do you have any neck stiffness?' Meningitis was always a possibility that needed to be considered and hopefully ruled out.

She moved her head from side to side against the pillow. 'No, but I've got a dragging pain down here that woke me up and bites me when I move.' She pointed to her right iliac fossa.

He blew on his hands to warm them up. 'I'm guessing you still have your appendix?' His fingertips pressed down gently.

'I do but— Ouch!' She bit her lip and stiffened in pain as he pressed a bit more firmly.

'Sorry.' He stroked her hair as a potential diagnosis came together. 'Dr Atherton, I don't think you have a virus.' He grabbed her shorts and T-shirt and handed them to her. 'Time to get dressed.'

'I just want to sleep.' The words came out on a wail.

Any other time he would have kissed away her pout but right now he needed to be the doctor. 'Kirby, I'm driving you to hospital for a full blood examination and an ultrasound. I think you might be taking a trip to Barago Hospital later in the morning to part company with your appendix.'

Kirby's foot hit the bottom step of the footstool as she struggled to wrap the hospital gown around herself, regretting that she hadn't grabbed a second one to wear as a coat. Not that Nick hadn't seen every part of her body naked, but that didn't mean she wanted to expose her behind as she hopped up onto the examination couch.

'Are you feeling dizzy?'

Nick's palm cupped her elbow, steadying her as she positioned herself on the narrow couch.

'Not really.'

He fixed her with a disbelieving stare.

'OK, sometimes, but that road into town from your place would make anyone motion sick. Mostly I feel tired with occasional jabbing pain when I move too quickly.' She pulled the modesty sheet over her legs and up under the gown.

When they'd arrived at the hospital, the staff had clucked around her while Nick had taken the blood sample, but now it was thankfully just the two of them in the treatment room.

'I've warmed up the transducer gel.' Nick grinned at her as he squirted the clear gel onto her abdomen.

'Thanks, but at 33 degrees in the shade it would probably have been OK cold.' She tried to joke but she just wanted to lie back and close her eyes.

He switched off the light so the images on the ultrasound

screen could be seen more clearly. He tilted it so Kirby could see part of it. 'Let's see if this appendix has a reason to grumble.' His large hands flexed over the transducer and zeroed in on the appendix. The image slowly came into blurry focus.

'Hmm.'

'Hmm, what?' She couldn't really make anything out.

'Well, your appendix looks fine and healthy.'

Kirby shifted slightly, trying for a better look at the screen, and a sharp, hot pain caught her as she moved. She immediately stiffened against it. 'Oh, but something really hurts.'

Nick's forehead furrowed and he gave her a wry smile. 'I guess I need to be Sherlock this time. You lie back and relax while I go hunting for the culprit.' He moved the transducer across her lower abdomen.

She tangled her fingers, turning them over themselves. 'You can rule out an ovarian cyst because that is *never* going to happen.' She lay back on the pillow, feeling sad and sorry for herself and hating it that she did.

Closing her eyes, she let Nick take over and be the doctor, and instead of second-guessing what was wrong she concentrated on feeling the smoothness of the transducer move across her skin, listening to the click and burr of the machine and trying to relax. *Hah!*

The transducer suddenly pressed down hard. She opened her eyes with a start. 'That hurt!'

Nick didn't reply. Instead, he leaned forward, staring intently at the screen, his knuckles gleaming white against the transducer. He moved it a fraction and pressed again.

A shaft of alarm sliced through her. 'What is it?' She struggled to see the screen.

Nick's face was in profile, his strong nose silhouetted by

the light of the screen, his cheeks hollow. He didn't answer her, he just kept staring.

Real fear tore through her. 'Nick, what is it? What can you see?'

He captured the image. 'Two heartbeats.'

'What?' She struggled to her elbow, bewilderment compounding dread and confusing her even more. 'You're nowhere near my heart.'

His Adam's apple moved convulsively in his throat as he turned the screen to face her. 'Here.' His shaking finger pointed to the fuzzy image. 'You're pregnant with twins.'

'I'm pregnant?' Disbelief rocked her and she stared so long at the screen that her eyes burned, but her brain had seized and wouldn't compute the image. Pregnant? That wasn't possible—she had the bloodwork and the letter from a Melbourne specialist to prove it to be impossible. She blinked three times but still the image stayed the same. Two tiny embryonic sacs could be clearly seen on the screen.

'I'm pregnant!' Sheer joy exploded inside her, making the New Year's Eve's fireworks display look like a dim light show. She sat up quickly, ignoring the jab of uterine ligament pain in her side, and threw her arms around Nick. 'I'm pregnant.' She heard herself babbling as euphoria bubbled inside her. 'I can't believe it…I never thought it could happen to me, it's a miracle…' She pulled back slightly, cupping his cheeks in her hands, gazing into his eyes as wonder and elation filled her to overflowing. 'We're pregnant! I love you and we're pregnant.'

'Against all odds, so it would appear.' Impassive emerald eyes stared down at her and his voice sounded hoarse as he removed her hands from his face and sat her back on the couch.

She grabbed his hands. 'Oh, Nick, I never thought I could be this happy.'

A muscle twitched in his jaw. 'It's hard to take in because, technically, we're both infertile.'

She nodded, her mind whirling. 'I know, and that just makes it even more of a miracle. For some reason I've ovulated and with twins perhaps both of my ovaries fired off at once.' Words poured out of her as her brain skipped from thought to thought as she tried to make sense of the most wonderful situation. 'And your sperm count, which should be zero, has obviously changed, and your body has somehow been able to produce at least two healthy swimmers.'

She laughed and kissed his hands. 'No one should ever underestimate the power of the human body to heal and reproduce. It must have been all that healthy organic food you've been feeding us.'

'Right.' A faint wry smile hovered for a moment on his lips as he tugged his hands from hers and crossed the room to switch on the light. 'We need to plan what we're doing.'

'Yes, there's so much to plan.' She couldn't stop grinning as an image of her future rolled out in her mind. Two bassinets in the front room at Riversleigh, a double all-terrain pram that could bump along the track down to the creek, with Turbo running close beside it, a baby snuggled against her chest in a sling, and Nick with his broad hand gently pressed against a baby's back, holding him nestled against his shoulder, fast asleep.

'Who's the obstetrician in Barago?' Nick started flipping through a health department folder, his fingers working so fast that the pages scrunched as they turned. A moment later he unexpectedly tossed it back onto the desk, the spine of the folder splitting as it landed with a loud crack.

A tiny stab of unease pierced her euphoria.

'Forget it.' Nick pulled his mobile out of pocket. 'I'll ring Jasper at the Melbourne City and pull in a favour so you can have chorionic villi sampling tomorrow.'

A sensation of cold jetted up inside her, quickly spreading into every cell and chilling her to the bone. 'I don't need to have chorionic villi sampling.'

His gaze, always wide and full of fun, now hooked hers, shuttered and resolute. '*Yes*, you do.'

She didn't recognise him. Nothing about his stance, expression or tone of voice was familiar. Sliding off the couch, she crossed the room, driven by the need to touch him and reconnect with the man she loved. The father of her babies.

Her hand rested on his forearm. 'Nick, I'm almost twenty-eight, not thirty-five. The risk of the procedure causing a spontaneous abortion is higher than the risk of a problem with the twins.'

'*No*, it isn't.' His hands rested on her shoulders, his cheek-bones stark and stern. 'Kirby, I had heavy-duty chemotherapy and my ability to make sperm ended with that.'

Tension coiled off his body, threatening to knock her over, and as he blew out a long slow breath, the temperature of it almost scorched her cheek. She smiled up at him like she would smile at a child who didn't understand something pretty simple. 'But that doesn't matter because obviously your body recovered.'

He spoke through gritted teeth. 'The chance that the sperm was damaged is very high.'

She felt the muscles of her face move, felt her brows pull down, and heard her quick intake of breath as his words penetrated her brain. She spoke as if in a fog. 'So you're saying the twins *might* have something wrong with them?'

His hands gripped her shoulders. 'That's exactly what I'm saying.' His tone softened slightly as his hands relaxed. 'Have the test, Kirby, and then we'll know. Our lives are going to be turned upside down by twins—we don't need them to be disabled as well.'

Her insides turned to ice as the room seemed to tilt. 'We don't need…' She heard the rising inflection of her voice, heard herself stop speaking, not prepared to voice what he inferred.

He pulled her close. 'Kirby, you have to listen to me. I've lived through this with Sarah and I watched my parents struggle for seventeen years with a grief that never healed. Hell, my mother still does grieve. Neither of us deserves that.'

His arms crushed her against him and she struggled to move air in and out of her lungs. For the first time ever she wanted to be—needed to be—out and away from his touch. She pushed against him and stepped back, wrapping her arms around herself to stop from shaking. 'Nick, these babies are a gift and I won't do anything that could put their lives in jeopardy.'

He threw his hand up in the air. 'Technically, with all the odds stacked against them, these embryos shouldn't even exist.'

Every part of her shivered. 'But they do.'

'Yes, they do.' He touched her arm, his fingers gently pressing into her skin. 'The least you can do is make sure they have a chance at a good life. Kirby, take the test.'

His words pummelled her hard and sharp like hail, unrelenting and shockingly painful. If he loved her how could he be asking her to do this? Asking her to risk her one and only chance at being a mother?

I don't want to be a father and I don't for one minute regret the choice I made.

All the air swooped out of her lungs as bile soared up, burning her throat, but she welcomed the physical pain because it hurt a hell of a lot less than the truth.

He didn't love her.

She'd been nothing more than a summer diversion now gone belly up.

He didn't want her or their children in his life, which was why he was asking her to risk everything and have this test. If the test showed there was a problem with the babies, he would ask her to do something that she couldn't do.

Her castles in the air shattered like crystal, falling down into a black abyss. There was no future as a loving couple and a family. But the children bound her and Nick together inextricably and his sense of duty would keep him in their lives, making him resentful and bitter.

She and the twins deserved more than reluctant duty. Tears pricked her eyes but she refused to let them fall. Taking in a steadying breath, she stood tall and made the hardest decision of her life. 'I release you.'

'What?' Nick ran both his hands through his hair, his fingers digging into his skull against the pounding in his head. How had summer fun turned into this nightmare? Kirby wasn't supposed to love him. She shouldn't be pregnant—how the hell had that happened?

Wild sex with abandon. Pretending you were sixteen.

He wanted to roar and silence the voice in his head. Every logical part of him railed at the unfairness of the situation.

Damn it, he hadn't taken a risk with pregnancy when there had been no risk to take. He raised his head to look at Kirby, trying to centre his thoughts. 'What are you talking about?'

Her jaw tilted up, the action full of purpose. 'I'm really sorry that *my* pregnancy has ruined your plans never to be a father so I release you from all paternal responsibilities.'

The pity and hurt in her eyes ripped into him and anger surged at her wilful misinterpretation of his request. He knew his obligations and he wouldn't walk away from them. 'That is *not* what I'm asking.'

'Isn't it?' Her brows rose into a perfect arch. 'It's nothing to be ashamed about—I mean, you've been more than upfront and honest about it. You never wanted children and you've never deviated from that line. This thing between us was supposed to be a summer fling, carefree and fun.' Her voice wavered for the briefest of moments. 'It was me who broke the rules by falling in love with you.'

He hated it that she was hurting. 'Kirby, you know that I resp—'

She shook her head and held up her hand to silence him. 'It's me who's always wanted children although I never expected them, so now we're at this impasse and there's no compromise. You don't want kids. I do. End of story.'

The image of Sarah's tiny contracted body, held upright by the head brace on her wheelchair, thundered through him. 'No, it isn't the end of the story, hell, Kirby, it's just the start.'

She tucked her hair behind her ears, the action decisive. 'I'm pregnant. Given my history, this might never happen again so no way am I risking the lives of these babies by having an unnecessary test. Come what may, I'm in it for the long haul.'

Memories of a parade of allied health professionals who'd visited his childhood home and yet hadn't been able to change a thing, assailed him. 'You have no idea what you're in for.'

She folded her arms. 'Yes, I do. I'm in for sleepless nights, heartache and worry, but I'm also in for joy, laughter and a journey into the unknown.' She raised her vivid blue eyes to his. 'It's called parenthood, Nick, and it's what I want. If it was a perfect world then you'd want it too.'

'Then have the test so we can have a chance as a family.' He heard the begging tone in his voice.

He saw the shudder race across her face, down her neck and shoulder, vibrating all the way down to her feet.

Her head came up, her jaw tight. 'We have a chance but you don't want to take it. Love doesn't come with conditions, Nick. If the world was perfect you'd love me and be prepared to take this journey with all its inherent risks.' Her eyes flashed with betrayal. 'And you would never have asked me to take the test.'

Her look seared him. He needed her to understand, needed her to realise what she might end up dealing with. 'My parents took that journey.'

'And I don't see any regret on their faces. They're incredible people, so full of life.' Her hands extended toward him, palms upward, full of entreaty.

'You don't know anything about it, how it changed them. Their life, my childhood, it was no walk in the park.'

'But it wasn't all bad, was it Nick?'

Her quiet words drilled into him, winding back the years, taking him down into the black hole of grief and despair that he never wanted to visit again. 'Yes, yes, it was and I can't risk doing it again.'

She stared at him, a long look that started at his hair and

finished at his feet, as if she was memorising every detail about him. Then she silently picked her clothes and bag off the chair, and hugging them close, walked to the door. 'In that case, we don't have anything left to discuss. Goodbye, Nick.'

The door closed with a loud but controlled and final click.

The roar of pain, frustration and anger he'd held in for half an hour exploded out of him as he thumped the wall with his fist, welcoming the bruising pain that radiated from his knuckles to his shoulder. How could she have just walked out on him? How could she say she loved him and then just leave?

A trail of guilt tried to carve a path through him but he refused to let it make a mark. They'd had an agreement and love hadn't featured in it. He pulled open the treatment-room fridge door and wrapped an ice pack around his fist.

Kirby had absolutely no idea what she was saying or doing, not a clue in the world. But he knew. He was the one with the first-hand experience and she should be the one listening to him. Damn it to hell, he should be the one making the decisions.

Running footsteps sounded in the corridor and the door swung open. 'Is everything alright, Nick?' Concern was on Meryl's face as she took in the ice pack around his hand.

'Everything's fine.' He picked up his keys with his other hand and stormed past her toward the clinic where at least his patients would listen to him.

CHAPTER TWELVE

SWEAT poured from Nick's forehead as he brought the axe down hard against the red gum, watching the splinters of wood fly high before spiralling down to the ground. The wood pile had grown over the afternoon and the kindling pile even more so as he'd taken refuge in hard physical work. Chopping wood was a lot easier than thinking.

When he chopped, his concentration centred entirely on the act of raising the axe and slicing it cleanly through the air, driving it down hard into the waiting wood. Creating kindling demanded precision cutting and was even better at keeping every single errant thought at bay. Keeping thoughts of Kirby at bay.

He hadn't seen her since she'd walked out on him yesterday morning. On autopilot, he'd gone on to work a full day in the clinic, but today Meryl had said she'd be back at work this afternoon so he'd only worked his usual morning, leaving before Kirby arrived. An hour ago a box containing some of his clothes, his tool belt and the shelf he'd planned to erect in her laundry had been delivered by courier to Riversleigh.

The sharp crack of splitting wood rent the air. Sending back the shelf was just crazy. She needed that shelf to store her iron and laundry liquids. She worked too hard to be wasting time hunting through cupboards looking for things, she needed to be able to easily reach up and grab.

She'll be washing baby clothes.

Thwack! The axe landed hard in the chopping block.

Fatherhood had never enticed him but for the last thirty hours he hadn't been able to think of anything else. His dreams had been filled with chasing kids along the beach, teaching them to surf, and he could almost feel the touch of his hand over theirs, holding the string of a kite.

Two children permanently incapacitated like Sarah. A dull ache throbbed near his liver.

She had to see things his way. He'd give Kirby a few days and then he'd go and install the shelf and try to talk to her again. Make her see reason.

Goodbye, Nick.

The finality of her tone hammered nails into his heart. He brought the axe down harder than ever.

'Planning for a long, cold winter, are you?'

He turned at his father's voice, wiping his forehead on the sleeve of his T-shirt. 'Technically it's autumn in a couple of weeks and the evenings can be chilly.'

Michael's brows rose questioningly. 'True, but I thought you were planning on being back in Melbourne then.'

He ignored his father's logic and kept chopping.

Michael's hand came down onto the axe handle. 'How about you give it a break, son, and come up to the house? It's far too hot to be out here and, besides, your mother's serving scones topped with her just-made raspberry jam.'

No, I don't want to. The petulant version of his childhood self stamped his foot in his head, but the unusual paternal expression in his father's eye, one he hadn't seen since he'd been eighteen, brooked no argument. 'Good idea, Dad. Come on, Turbo,' he called to the dog, and strode back to the house.

His mother had everything set out under the shade of the veranda, which caught the faint wisps of any passing breeze.

They sat down, drank tea, discussed the lightness of the scones—soda water apparently being the key—and the flavour and texture of the jam, which had set well.

He let the conversation wash over him, letting it drown out the constant argument in his head. He'd had every right to ask Kirby to have the test for genetic abnormalities, given the medical treatment he'd been through. He was the one being sensible. She was sticking her head in the sand and—

'…today, Nick?'

He heard his mother's voice. 'Sorry, Mum, I didn't hear what you were saying, I was too busy savouring your jam.'

She rolled her eyes and smiled. 'Of course you were, dear. I was asking if Kirby was feeling better today.'

'She's working this afternoon.' He spoke briskly as he sliced open another scone, not wanting to think about how she really was.

'Yes, but is she feeling better?' His mother's green eyes speared him with their intent.

His eye caught sight of the large transport box at the end of the veranda. 'She's well enough to organise a courier.' The resentful words came out before he thought to stop them.

His father refilled his mug with steaming tea and dropped a slice of lemon into the pale brown liquid. 'Why would she have sent you a shelf? It's not your everyday gift but, then, again, Kirby isn't your everyday woman.'

'What's that supposed to mean?' Nick snapped, wanting

the conversation to just stop. If there was any sort of justice to the world he should be home alone, dealing with the mess that was his life, without his parents offering commentary.

His father smiled a knowing smile. 'Nick, for years you've dated a parade of women and none of them have come close to Kirby.'

'How would you know? You only spent one day with her!'

Michael leaned back in his chair, his body slack with relaxation as he sipped his tea. 'I don't entirely know, although first impressions are a strong indicator. But I do know you built her a laundry.'

'So?' *You're sounding very sixteen.*

Shut up.

His father shot him a smile full of superior understanding. 'So, that tells me that she's very special to you. I built your mother a kitchen once, remember?'

He did remember. Flashes of a summer long past flickered in his mind—a black-and-white chequered floor, the scent of freshly shaved wood and drying paint, his mother's arms wrapped tightly around his father's neck, the immense pride on his father's face, and Sarah's wide smile.

Tumbling in on the picture came his summer with Kirby— cooking together, laughing together and sleeping with her cuddled in close, and a sense of peace he'd never really known before.

Was that love?

Hey, you left out the sex. How could you forget the sex? His sixteen-year-old self sounded very bewildered as the images of shared times other than sex kept reeling on.

The ground seemed to tremble under his feet as a seismic realisation hit him. God, it was love. He loved Kirby. How had he been so stupid? He'd been so focussed on the glorious sex he'd missed the significance of the important stuff.

His mother leaned forward. 'And we're worried that our arrival yesterday, completely out of the blue, might have caused a problem between the two of you.'

I wish it was that simple. He sighed. 'It's nothing to do with your arrival.'

His mother touched his knee, care and concern clear in her gaze. 'Then what's the problem?'

He'd held it in for a day and a half, letting it eat away at him, and he couldn't do it any more. 'She's pregnant.'

Utter confusion swam across Nancy's face. 'But I thought you weren't able to…' Disappointment chased the confusion away, leaving only sadness. 'Oh, I see, it's someone else's child.'

Every part of him raced indignantly to Kirby's defence. 'No, Mum, you've got it wrong. The twins are mine.'

Ignoring his parent's collective gasp, he ran his hands through his hair. 'I came to Port for wellness, remember, to get my health back. Ironically, it appears it came back with a vengeance and that's the problem.'

His father put down his mug, every part of his body alert. 'But you do love Kirby, don't you, so exactly where is the problem?'

How had his father worked out that he loved her when he'd only just realised it himself? A sigh shuddered out of him. 'There's a chance, due to the chemo, that my sperm may be damaged, but Kirby and I have very different views on how to deal with this risk.'

He dragged in a breath and raised his gaze to his parents, knowing they would understand. 'She's not like us, she has no idea what it's like, living with a child like Sarah, how shattering it is, and how you never recover from something like that.'

His mother sat stock still, her fingers clasped in her lap. 'Is that what you think? That my life is shattered and I've never recovered?' Unreadable emotions raced across her face. 'Yes, Sarah's arrival changed me from the naïve young woman I was, but life would have made that happen anyway. Sarah made me a stronger person, Nick, she made me a fighter and she made me…' She caught Michael's hand. 'Made us realise what was important in our lives. I miss her every day but I don't regret a moment.'

His mother's words, so unexpected, fell like lead weights, stunning him. 'But I remember you crying. I remember you getting so angry sometimes…' He tried to align his feelings with his mother's but nothing matched and he was left feeling as if he'd been hit.

Nancy gesticulated as she spoke. 'I was angry at the system, Nick. At how hard we had to fight for everything so Sarah and other children like her could have the best life they could. But I was never angry at her being in our lives.'

His father nodded. 'We know things were tough for you, Nick, and we're sorry, but that's why we were so keen for you to go to those camps so you could be a normal kid for a few weeks every year without any constraints.'

Or were you given the opportunity to have some freedom from your family? Kirby's soft voice sounded loud in his head. His gut twisted, being pulled in different directions. How had Kirby been so wise and how the hell had he misinterpreted things so badly?

Michael continued, 'For some reason you've only remembered the difficult times with your sister and you've forgotten the love she so freely gave us in the years she was with us. You used to play with her and I'd hear you both laughing.'

But it wasn't all bad, was it, Nick? Kirby's voice lanced him, making him hurt everywhere. When he thought of Sarah the first image that came to mind was her contracted and wasted legs peeking out from under the tray of her wheelchair, followed by the familiar surge of pain.

He closed his eyes and tried again. He saw Sarah smiling in the kitchen and then a faint and muffled sound bite of her squeals of delight as he raced her down the driveway in her wheelchair slowly pushed aside the sadder thoughts.

Memories stirred in Nancy's eyes. 'Nick, do you remember, whenever we danced, Sarah would try and sing?'

Nick gave a wry smile. 'Half the time she sounded better than your singing attempts.'

'Hey, I can do a wonderful rendition of "Hey Big Spender".'

'Nick's right. I love you but you're tone deaf.' Michael laughed and dodged his wife's playful hit.

His mother's laughing face suddenly became serious. 'Nick, no one puts their hand up for challenging events but you've fought cancer and won. You've been a loving brother to a girl who loved us dearly and gave us so much for the short time we had her—both those things have made you the strong person you are.'

Michael cleared his throat, his grey eyes filled with empathy. 'No one can give you a crystal ball but avoiding experiences in case they're not perfect is not a way to live your life. You've fought too hard for your own life to do that.'

We have a chance but you don't want to take it. If you loved me you'd be prepared to take this journey with all its inherent risks.

His head pounded so hard he thought it would explode. He'd faced cancer head on but he'd hidden from the most important thing in his life. He'd been so blinkered, so stupid. He'd convinced himself he didn't want to be a father but this summer that conviction had taken a pounding.

He pictured Kirby's face and pressed his fingers hard against his temples. He'd hurt her more than anyone deserved and in the process had risked losing the love of his life and his future family. He'd risked *everything* that could make him happy.

He had to talk to her. He had to tell her he loved her, had to. *Move!* He stood up abruptly, the plate on his lap falling with a dull crash onto the wooden boards. 'I have to go.'

'Of course you do, son. Good luck.'

Michael's heartfelt words underpinned his fear—that he'd realised everything too late and Kirby would refuse to forgive him.

Kirby reluctantly shut the clinic door, needing to pull it hard against a sudden gust of wind. She glanced up at the lead-grey sky where dark clouds streaked past, full of threatening intent—the sunny day had suddenly come to an end. As she pocketed her key, she caught sight of the ocean now dark and menacing with whitecaps that collided against each other, sending spray high into the air. Kirby could picture all the holidaying families quickly gathering their possessions, dismantling their sunshade beach tents and scurrying home to play board games and read books.

She started to walk home, her feet dragging against the pavement. Although her afternoon at work on almost no sleep had taxed her to the nth degree, and her fatigue made her feel like she was wading through mud, walking home was preferable to driving as it delayed her arrival by a good fifteen minutes. She'd wanted to stay at the clinic longer but Vicki had pointed out there were no patients, and had wanted to lock up a bit early.

Her stomach rolled and she decided to walk to the supermarket and buy more ginger tea and dry biscuits. Anywhere was better than being at home, where evidence of Nick's presence declared itself in every room from the repaired window sash to the immaculate laundry she couldn't bear to use.

He didn't love her.

She swallowed hard and fast against the pain. For five or six glorious minutes yesterday she'd thought she'd been given the world. She'd thought she'd been blessed with a man who loved her and a long-desired family to share with him.

But she'd got it all horribly wrong. Nick didn't love her and without a cast-iron guarantee that the children would be perfect, he didn't want them either.

She bit her lip. *Focus on the babies.*

She had two children to plan for and that was what would get her up every morning and keep her going through every day. She had to finish her time in Port and then decide what to do next.

A rumble of thunder vibrated in the distance, interrupting her thoughts, and on the spur of the moment she changed direction and walked along the pier. She'd always enjoyed watching the way a storm blasted across the ocean, Mother Nature unleashing her fury and reducing humans to pawns in her path. Today she wanted the wind to buffet and whip her, she wanted the salt to sting her cheeks and make her eyes water, but most of all she hoped against hope that the gale would blow all her pain away.

The fishing fleet hadn't sailed in the late afternoon as

usual. Instead, the boats bobbed crazily at their moorings, safely away from being tossed against the pier. Only Gaz's boat remained and she waved to him as he prepared to sail out to his buoy.

'Crazy weather, Doc. You should head home.'

Waves crashed against the white wooden pylons, the vibrations racing through her body. Her stomach lurched and her nausea surged almost as strongly as the waves, but she'd rather be out here that inside her cottage. 'I've always enjoyed a good storm.'

But the wind caught her words, carrying them up and away, and Gaz just gave her a grin and a salute as he concentrated on his vessel.

A few large drops of rain started to fall, but were immediately whipped sideways by the wind, denied the right to land. Kirby stared out to sea, her eyes seeking the flat line of the horizon, but the waves prevented her from seeing it. Something caught her eye. She squinted but could see nothing but waves.

She peered again and caught a flash of yellow. Her stomach dropped as adrenaline poured through her, making her shake. She'd recognise that distinctive striped colouring anywhere. One of KC's inflatable dinghies was being blown out toward the reef. She sprinted across the pier yelling, 'Gaz! Wait!'

The fisherman didn't respond.

With every ounce of effort in her she screamed again. 'Help!' He turned.

Waving her arms, she ran toward him. 'There are kids out there in a boat.'

He didn't hesitate. 'Hop on.' Throwing her a lifejacket and the satellite phone, he swung the boat away from the pier. 'Ring the police and let them know.'

A seed of panic sprouted inside her. 'Is this the best boat for a rescue so close to the reef?'

He tilted his head, his face sobering. 'I guess we'll find that out, won't we?'

Nick breathed a sigh of relief as he pulled up outside the clinic. The drive down from Sheep-wash corner had been horrendous, with rain lashing the ute so hard that the windscreen wipers on full tilt had scarcely made an impact. He killed the ignition, jumped out of the car and ran to the front door, rehearsing for the thirty-sixth time what he was going to say, which started with, 'I've been the biggest jerk' followed by, 'Please forgive me' and finished with—

His hand failed to move the handle. He looked up and read the after-hours sign directing people to the hospital. Damn! Five o'clock was early for Kirby and Vicki to have gone home. Perhaps they'd been caught up at the hospital.

He strode through the rain, rethinking how he would talk to her now she was in a more public place. The automatic doors slid open and he came face to face with Meryl and Constable Masterton, worry lines etched on their faces.

Meryl hurried toward him. 'Thank goodness you're here, Nick. I've got the air ambulance on standby and Theo's just left for the pier with the road ambulance so you must go now with the constable.'

Nick tried to keep up as she shoved the bright orange emergency worker's overalls and protective jacket into his arms.

Meryl gave his arm a squeeze. 'Gaz is a very experienced seaman. I'm sure they'll be fine.'

His confusion immediately transformed to anxiety. 'You're sure who will be fine? What's going on?'

Two deep lines made a V at the bridge of the nurse's nose. 'Didn't you get our message?'

He immediately patted his body, feeling for the distinctive rectangular shape of his phone and realising he'd not picked it up again after changing out of his work clothes. He'd been too distracted after finding the box with the laundry shelf in it.

The young constable put his hand on Nick's shoulder, gently pushing him back toward the doors. 'We just got an emergency call from Dr Atherton. She and Gaz are attempting a rescue of a KC dinghy with kids caught in the storm.'

'In Gaz's boat?' Incredulity became fear. The fishing boat could negotiate the narrow reef entrance in calm to medium rough weather, but in a storm like this it just didn't have the manoeuvrability. An image of the boat floundering against the rocks, its wooden beams splintering, slugged him so hard he lost his breath.

Kirby.

The twins.

He couldn't lose them, not now when he'd just worked everything out. Not now when they didn't know he loved them all as much as life itself.

You drove her to this. If you hadn't been such a jerk she would be tucked up in your bed, safe. Like a geyser, guilt shot through him, ramping up his fear into a hot and terrifying beast. He spun around, catching the police officer by the jacket. 'What the hell were you thinking, letting a pregnant woman out in weather like this when it's your job?'

The constable staggered back as Meryl grabbed Nick's arm. 'Nick, stop it. We have no idea how it happened, but it has.' Sympathy filled her eyes. 'We love her too and she's in good hands.'

He dropped his hand and muttered an apology as he hauled on his coat. 'I don't care what the policy is, I'm going out with you on the police boat and *nothing* is going to stop me.'

Kirby could barely keep her balance as the boat rocked violently, every weathered board creaking terrifyingly loudly. The binoculars' lenses fogged as rain poured over her, trickling down the too-big sleeves of the anorak, but she didn't care. All she could think about was finding the dinghy.

The storm had darkened the sky to the levels of dusk, making visibility tough, and Gaz had turned on the bright fluorescent night-fishing lights, but so far she hadn't been able to sight it again.

Gaz's hand's gripped the wheel, his knuckles white as he scanned the sea. Kirby knew he was as worried about the threat of the reef as much as he was about the children. She couldn't think about the reef and how boats always came off second best. She couldn't think about the risk she was taking, the risk she was putting the twins into… She stifled a hysterical laugh—she'd wanted Mother Nature to drive all thoughts of Nick away but she hadn't quite envisaged this.

Yellow caught the edge of her eye. She looked again. 'There!' She waved her arms and pointed as the dinghy rose on a wave, disappearing almost as quickly into a deep trough.

Gaz steered the boat according to her directions as waves washed over the bow, completely drenching her. Kirby pulled the life preserver off its holder, checking the knot that secured it to the boat.

As they got closer she recognised two terrified boys from Unit C huddled in the bottom of the dinghy. *Thank goodness.*

She waved her arms out wide, hoping Lochie and Matthew would understand that it meant she could see them as all her words were captured by the wind.

Gaz yelled out instructions. 'Kirby, I need to keep the engines running so we can avoid the reef so we'll have to go past twice, getting one boy at a time.'

She nodded her understanding, hating it that one boy would have to wait longer than the other before he was safe but knowing it had to be that way or all lives would be at risk.

The waves pounded the boat, pushing it inexorably toward the reef, while the engine throbbed hard against them, desperately attempting to counter the relentless pressure. The dinghy was only three metres away but it could have been have been three hundred.

'One at a time.' She yelled the words as she hurled the life preserver out like a Frisbee to the waiting boys. As it arced in the air an almighty wave cascaded over the dinghy, picking it up as if it was a feather before upending it and tipping the boys into the foaming sea.

Kirby's scream was trapped in her throat as her brain went into automatic and time seemed to slow down. She scanned the water for bobbing boys but she couldn't see a thing.

'I have to bring her round,' Gaz yelled from the wheelhouse.

The rope in her hands tugged. 'Wait.' Using everything she had in her, she pulled.

Lochie's terrified face appeared in the trough of a wave, the life preserver around his middle.

'Kick, mate, kick.' Leaning over the side, being hammered by the waves, Kirby managed to haul him on board.

Almost dropping him onto the deck, she checked the bare basics—that he was conscious and breathing. Broken bones or anything else would have to wait. 'Get into the wheel-house. I have to find Matthew.'

Gaz had brought the boat round to avoid the reef and for a moment she was completely disoriented. Where the hell was Matthew? She stared at the dinghy, hoping he was clinging to its upturned form, but all she could see was yellow and black plastic.

'Look!' Gaz's arm pointed and she swung around.

The distinctive blue and white police boat was rapidly getting closer. *Thank God, more eyes.* But would they arrive fast enough? It took three minutes to drown and two minutes had already passed.

The white lights from the fishing boat lit up a small area but with salt-stung eyes and driving rain it was hard to see anything at all.

And then she saw it. A boy, face down in the water. Not moving.

She snapped her neck left and saw the jagged outlines of the reef. She swung back the other way and saw the police boat with its reinforcements had almost reached them.

At that moment she knew exactly what she had to do. Grabbing the life preserver, she dived into the roiling water and swam toward Matthew.

CHAPTER THIRTEEN

'No!' NICK's heart stalled in his chest. He was unable to believe his eyes as Kirby dived over the side of the boat. The love of his life and the mother of his unborn children had just disappeared into a raging sea before he could fix everything between them.

'Aidan, over there!' He pointed with an extended arm, his eyes never leaving the water, willing her to appear above the waves.

The smaller police boat moved quickly, able to change direction more easily than the larger fishing boat. White foam swirled around them, decreasing visibility, but adrenaline and raw fear had acutely honed Nick's eyes.

Bright orange bobbed up ten metres away and then disappeared behind a wave. 'Throttle back, she's over there.'

The constable skilfully brought the boat in close and Nick saw Kirby, her arm around a boy's neck, tilting his head up using the pistol grip and maintaining him in rescue position. Then her other arm shot straight up in the air—the international sign for rescue.

Thank you. Thank you.

'I see her, Nick. You get them on board.'

'Kirby, over here.' He leaned over the side, holding out a long pole.

She kicked hard and her free hand gripped the pole. A wave covered her and she came up spluttering. 'Take Matt. He's not breathing.'

Nick wanted to pull Kirby into the boat, feel her heavy in his arms to really know she was safe and unhurt, but triage left no room for feelings. Matthew was his first priority. 'I'll take him, you use the ladder.' He reached down and with Kirby's help heaved the lifeless boy out of the water.

He laid him down on the bench, clearing his airway and checking his carotid pulse. Nothing. Tilting Matt's head back and closing his nostrils with this fingers and thumb, he covered the boy's mouth and blew in two rescue breaths.

Behind him he heard the emergency radio and Aidan instructing Gaz to return to Port, heard the request for the air ambulance and confirmation that Lochie was uninjured, just cold.

The boat rocked, jolting him sideways, and he deliberately fell to his knees. Placing the heel of his left hand on the boy's breastbone and interlacing the fingers of his right hand, he immediately started cardiac compressions. 'Come on, mate, come back to me, you can do this.'

A sopping Kirby knelt down beside him. 'I'll breathe.'

He wanted to say no, he wanted to say, *Wrap yourself up in a blanket and just keep warm, look after yourself and the babies, you're a patient too*, but Matthew needed both of them.

They settled into the pattern of thirty compressions to two breaths. He remembered the first day they'd met and how she'd been doing mouth to mouth then as well. He caught her gaze and right then his own heart wanted to stop.

Kirby's clear blue eyes, usually so full of warmth and what he now realised was love, were harrowingly empty. Although she was so physically close to him that their hair almost touched, he knew without a shadow of a doubt that she'd left him emotionally.

'We're five minutes out of Port.'

Aidan's firm, controlled voice reassured Nick about extra help for Matt but not help for himself. He'd hurt Kirby too much, asked her to do the unthinkable, and had pushed her past the point of no return.

Matthew vomited.

Kirby immediately turned him on his side and cleared his airway and checked his air entry. 'He's breathing.' Sheer relief permeated her words.

'Matt, can you hear me? Matt?' Nick shook the boy, whose eyes fluttered open for a moment. 'I'll get the oxygen.' He managed to secure the small tank so it didn't roll and he carefully placed the mask over Matt's face.

'And Gaz, is he OK?' Kirby moved to stand.

'He's coming in behind us, Doc. Don't you think you should have a blanket around you? You're shaking.' Aidan reached up with his spare hand, grabbing the space blanket from the storage cupboard. Ripping the package open with his teeth, he shook it out and by using his knee to control the boat he wrapped it around her shoulders.

'Thanks.' Kirby smiled at up the young constable, gratitude shining on her face.

That's my job. Nick, halfway through checking Matt's pupil reactions, wanted to knock Aidan Masterton sideways. Damn it, he should be taking care of Kirby but absolutely nothing about the last few hours was going the way he'd planned and he had an aching suspicion that no matter how hard he wanted it, the situation wasn't going to change.

* * *

Kirby sat wrapped up in flannel pyjamas and a dressing gown, which seemed ludicrous in summer but she just couldn't get warm. Meryl had supervised her having a warm bath, had fed her hot chicken broth and now had tucked her up under a doona with a heated wheat pack at her feet.

'Kirby, I rang the hospital and Matthew's doing well at Barago. He's conscious and alert, which is wonderful, and Lochie is fine with a few cuts and bruises which will heal in no time. Considering what could have happened, it's a wonderful result.' Meryl clucked around, adjusting her pillows. 'You're sure to get a bravery medal for today.'

'I just did what anyone else would have done.' *Saving Matthew had been the easy part of the afternoon.* Working with Nick on the police boat had been the hardest thing she'd ever done.

Nick. The clock struck seven and she swallowed a painful sigh. Nick would have returned by now from escorting Matthew to Barago. Would have returned to Riversleigh. She took a big slug of her chai tea, welcoming the scalding liquid in her mouth. She really had to stop thinking about Nick and what he might or might not be doing because he'd made it clear he didn't want to do anything with her and the twins.

Meryl stood back with her arms crossed. 'So are you sure you'll be OK? I can stay longer.'

Kirby smiled. 'Thanks, Meryl, but I'm fine. Nothing that a good sleep won't fix.' But she felt the lie clean down to her toes.

The caring nurse hesitated as if she was going to say something else but then thought better of it. Instead, she picked up her bag and tucked it under her arm. 'In that case, ring me if you need anything and I'll see you tomorrow. Sleep well.'

Kirby listened to her retreating footsteps against the floorboards, heard the familiar squeak of her front door opening and waited for the banging thud of it closing. Instead, she heard voices—Meryl's strident accent along with a deep rumbling baritone she'd know anywhere.

Nick.

She simultaneously went hot and cold but before she had time to put down her tea and move from the couch he was standing in the doorway of her living room, sucking the air from the space and filling it completely with unusually re-strained energy. 'Hello, Kirby.'

Hey, Sherlock. He used to greet her with dancing eyes. This serious greeting rammed home how much she'd lost and she wanted to dive under her doona and ignore him and the whole horrible situation. Instead, she held her head high. 'Hello, Nick.'

He rocked back on his worn boots, his hands jammed into the pockets of his jeans. 'How are you feeling?'

'I'm fine.'

He nodded slowly. 'That's good.'

She hated this. Hated the chilly air of politeness that now sat between them, suffocating all the passion and fun that had once connected them with every look and word.

He swallowed, hard, his Adam's apple moving quickly. 'And the twins? No problems there?'

A spark of anger surged up through her paralysing grief. 'No. Swimming generally doesn't disturb a pregnancy if that's what you were hoping to hear.'

He swayed as if he'd been punched. 'God, Kirby, is that what you think of me? That I'd wish for a miscarriage?'

His ragged words shocked her and she sought clarity. 'Yesterday you said—'

'Yesterday I was an insensitive fool.' In two strides he stood before her, staring down at her, his eyes filled with contrition and regret. He knelt down next to her. 'I'm so very sorry.'

Her hand tingled to touch his hair, to pull him close and soothe the devastated look from his face, but too much was unresolved and too much hung in the balance. 'What are you sorry for?'

His eyes flared with scorn for himself. 'For hurting you, for only telling you I respected you. God, what a pompous idiot I was.' He ran his hand through his hair, tugging at the curls at the nape of his neck, his expression begging her to understand. 'Until I met you I'd never been in love and even when it was banging me hard over the head I didn't get it. I didn't recognise it.'

He put his hand over hers, his touch gentle and warm in sharp contrast to the desolation in his eyes. 'But, Kirby Atherton, I love you. I was on my way to tell you when I heard you'd gone out in that storm and when I saw you dive into that water I knew right then that if you died, then part of me would have died too.'

I love you. She wanted to laugh, she wanted to cry as his words caressed her, stark in their truth, calling to her to believe. But after yesterday some doubt lingered. 'You love me? Why do you think you love me?'

His lips twitched up into a knowing smile. 'Because I built you a laundry.'

Her heart sang—he really did love her. She wanted to throw her arms around his neck, bury her face in the crook of his neck and feel his comforting arms around her, but still she held steady because too much was at stake and loving her might not be enough. 'But the laundry isn't finished.'

A sombre expression captured his face. 'No, it isn't. I have to enlarge the ceiling airer and it's missing a shelf and two nappy buckets.'

She held her breath. 'Two nappy buckets?'

He nodded, his smile now wry. 'I'm told that twins generate a lot of washing.'

Her heart hammered wildly in her chest. 'Are you saying you want to come on the journey with me no matter what might happen?'

'No matter what, with all its inherent risks.' He gripped her hands tightly. 'You were so right and I was so ridiculously wrong. Growing up, things were not as black as I remembered them and I now know that my parents survived and grew closer. So, come what may, we can and we will survive and grow old together. I love you with all my heart, Kirby. Will you have me along for the ride of our lives?'

She looked down into green eyes filled with uncertainty but backlit with a love so strong it almost took her breath away. Her palms cupped his cheeks and she lowered her mouth to his, claiming her man and giving her answer in her kiss.

'I'm taking that as a yes.' He grinned up at her. 'I know we have a lot to discuss, like where we're going to live, how you're going to finish your GP training and how you feel about me returning to Melbourne Central. Not to mention which hospital is the best one to have these babies, and most importantly how to restrain my mother from taking out a paid advertisement in the Melbourne papers announcing she is going to be a grandmother.' His smile changed to a more serious expression. 'But while I'm down here on my knees I need to ask you one more thing. Will you marry me?'

Her squeal of delight said it all.

EPILOGUE

Turbo bounded out of the four-wheel drive, his bark one of pure pleasure as his feet hit the gravel drive of Riversleigh.

The Dennison family was back for the summer.

A blond-headed boy ran straight to the back of the vehicle, opening the rear door and clambering onto the bumper bar. 'Dad, where did you pack the fishing rod? I'm going straight down to the creek.'

'No, we're going swimming first.' A girl with vivid green eyes and a determined expression pulled at her brother's legs. 'Aren't we, Daddy?'

Nick raised his brows at his eight-year-old twins, both of whom had spent most of the last two hours of the drive asking, 'Are we there yet?'

He gave them a teasing grin. 'Actually, I thought we might spread the manure first and get things ready to plant the lettuces.'

'Oh, Dad!' The wail of dissension was deafening.

'Let's get the car emptied first.' Kirby lifted an eager William out of his car seat. At four, unlike his older siblings, he loved to carry things in from the car.

Leaving Nick to organise the ferrying of gear, she walked up the straight path, the box hedges now at hip height. Sliding the heavy, flat key into the lock, she turned both the key and the handle and the door swung open.

The scent of fresh flowers and beeswax polish wafted out to meet her and she smiled. As much as she adored her Victorian home with its spacious extension in a leafy suburb of Melbourne, she loved the simplicity of the cottage and the way over a summer it deconstructed their city lives.

Sunlight filtered in through the windows, lighting up the old house, and the grandfather clock struck four. At the end of the hall she spied a ginger fluff sponge and a plate of sandwiches, sitting next to a vase of white and pink sweet peas on the wide Baltic pine table.

She called back over her shoulder. 'Hey, guys, work fast. Meryl and Vicki have made us cake.'

'Yes!' Like a whirlwind, Carter grabbed a box of food and ran up the steps.

'I love this place!' Melissa tore past her slightly older brother, crossing the threshold first.

Twenty minutes later the twins, with traces of cream still clinging to their lips, took it in turns to throw a ball to Turbo, who was starting to look longingly at the shade of his favourite tree. At ten, he'd slowed down some but he could always find some extra energy to round up the chooks.

Dark-haired William, trowel in hand and bright yellow gumboots on his feet, busily dug over the herb patch, holding up worms and slaters for inspection before dropping them back into the fragrant soil.

Kirby sat on the veranda with her feet resting on the worn bluestone step and her back against Nick's chest, feeling the regular and soothing rise and fall of his breathing, her hands in her lap resting over his. She still marvelled at how the touch of his hands made her knees buckle and her heart race.

She turned in his arms, slinging her own around his neck. 'It's great to be back.'

He smiled, his eyes sparkling with wicked intent. 'You're so right, Sherlock. We've got two months of long, lazy summer days and glorious nights.'

She laughed. 'With three kids?'

He winked and dimples carved into his cheeks. 'The fresh air exhausts them and they'll be in bed early and sleep like logs.' Tilting his forehead, he rested it on hers. 'Even so, I've made some plans that involve my parents visiting for a few days so they can get their grandparent fix and I've booked the same few days for us at an isolated beachside shack just down the road at Dolphin Bay. Complete beach frontage and no one else around for miles.' He grinned. 'I haven't visited that beach since I was sixteen.'

'Really?' Her fingers trailed down his cheek and toyed with the buttons on his shirt. 'Do you plan on reliving your youth?'

His teasing gaze faded. 'Hell, no. I plan on living my present, with you.' The heartfelt words spun around her. 'The last nine years have been brilliant and I wouldn't change a second, but I'm looking forward to the future.' He lowered his head, his lips grazing hers, full of love and simmering desire.

She answered his kiss, reaffirming her commitment to him and promising a summer of fun and sensual delight.

Tumbling arms and legs suddenly slammed into them as children wriggled and squished between them.

'Do you *have* to do that mushy stuff?'

'Yeah, you said we would go fishing.'

'Look at this big worm!'

Laughing, Kirby avoided the dangling worm and caught Nick's gaze. 'You wouldn't change any of this for a second?'

'Not one thing.' He swung William up onto his shoulders, grabbed her hand and slung his free arm around both twins, capturing them against him. 'Come on, you lot, hurry up. The Dennisons are going fishing and swimming down at the creek.'

Turbo barked his approval.

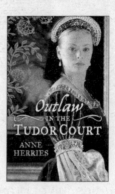
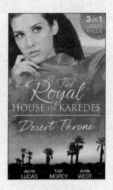

 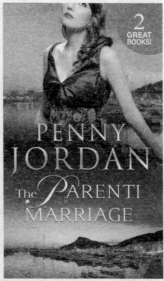

The World of Mills & Boon®

There's a Mills & Boon® series that's perfect for you. We publish ten series and, with new titles every month, you never have to wait long for your favourite to come along.

By Request
Relive the romance with the best of the best
12 stories every month

Cherish
Experience the ultimate rush of falling in love
12 new stories every month

Desire
Passionate and dramatic love stories
6 new stories every month

n o c t u r n e
An exhilarating underworld of dark desires
Up to 3 new stories every month

For exclusive member offers go to
millsandboon.co.uk/subscribe

M&B/WORLD4a